IT WAS AS IF THE[...] CONNECTION BETWEEN THE TWO OF THEM, A SILVER THREAD THAT WOUND TIGHT – TIGHTER, DRAWING THEM TOGETHER . . .

'If it is too soon . . .' he murmured, as if suddenly unsure of his ground.

And her heart trembled for this man who was a warrior and medicus, and God alone knew what, and was yet made uncertain by this attraction between them. Their need was a tangible force in the chamber.

She shook her head and whispered, 'No. I . . . I want this too.'

She felt the desire for him spreading through her veins. Even the tips of her fingers tingled. She was all eagerness, a map of melting curves and moist flesh. How shameless, how wanton she had become and she gloried in the fact. Her lip curving in a smile as old as time, she spread her arms in welcome . . .

Cleo Cordell is the author of nine erotic novels, a number of short stories and a forthcoming anthology. The bestselling *Captive Flesh*, published in 1993, was followed by *Senses Bejewelled* and *Velvet Claws*, and Cleo was established as 'the new queen of suburban erotica' in *Today* and 'queen of the undieworld' in the *Woman's Journal*. Her subsequent titles, *Juliet Rising*, *Path of the Tiger*, *Crimson Buccaneer* and *Opal Darkness*, confirmed her position as first lady of historical-fantasy erotica. Writing as Susan Swann, Cleo's alter ego explored contemporary erotica in *The Discipline of Pearls* and *The Ritual of Pearls*.

Cleo began working for Northamptonshire Libraries at the age of sixteen. This gave her ample opportunity to explore the world of dark fantasy fiction, her first love. When not reading or researching, she enjoys the cinema, her cats, wildlife and cooking gourmet vegetarian food. At present she is working on the sequel to *The Flesh Endures*, continuing the fortunes of the enigmatic alchemist Lord Karolan Rakka.

CLEO CORDELL

THE FLESH ENDURES

A SIGNET BOOK

SIGNET BOOKS

Published by the Penguin Group
Penguin Books Ltd, 27 Wrights Lane, London w8 5tz, England
Penguin Books USA Inc., 375 Hudson Street, New York, New York 10014, USA
Penguin Books Australia Ltd, Ringwood, Victoria, Australia
Penguin Books Canada Ltd, 10 Alcorn Avenue, Toronto, Ontario, Canada m4v 3b2
Penguin Books (NZ) Ltd, 182–190 Wairau Road, Auckland 10, New Zealand

Penguin Books Ltd, Registered Offices: Harmondsworth, Middlesex, England

First published 1996
1 3 5 7 9 10 8 6 4 2

Set in 10/12pt Monotype Plantin
Typeset by Datix International Limited, Bungay, Suffolk
Printed in England by Clays Ltd, St Ives plc

This book is dedicated to Shirley Russell, who believed in me and was there at the beginning.

ACKNOWLEDGEMENTS

Thanks to Jo, Chris, and Cheryl for friendship, support and laughs. Also to Caroline Montgomery and all at Rupert Crew for being on my side. Unreserved and overdue thanks to the girls at NK. Most of all, thanks to Graham – for always.

CHAPTER ONE

It was gloomy inside the low room, the air thick with the oily smoke from rush tapers. The lavender and sweet woodruff that strewed the beaten earth floor had long since wilted and failed to mask the smells of stale sweat and unwashed clothes.

At the back of the room, in an area of deepest shadow, Lord Karolan Rakka lay on a pile of tawdry cushions. He watched his companion caressing the two young women, his perceptions blurred by the poppy drug coursing through his veins. The three naked bodies were shiny with sweat and the smells of sex and exertion clotted his nostrils. He wondered, for a moment, why he had stayed. There had been no reason to linger after Jack had given him the things he required, but he had felt a desire for human company. And so he had poured a measure of the opiate into a tankard of ale and settled back to watch Jack indulge his sexual appetites.

For a while the two women worked on his companion, taking it in turns to kiss Jack's mouth and caress his body. Then they put on a show for the two men, moaning loudly as they kissed each other, rubbing their breasts together until the nipples stood out like ripe cherries. Inflamed by the display, Jack reached for Isabeau, preferring her rich womanly curves to Adeliz's more girlish form.

'Come and join us, why don't you?' Jack mumbled, surfacing from between Isabeau's spread legs and wiping her moisture from his chin. 'There's enough here for two. You don't mind sharing your honey pot, do you my pretty?'

Isabeau giggled and surged against him, her slug-white thighs rubbing against his ears.

Karolan shook his head. 'Need my help, do you? You must be losing your touch.'

Jack gave a roar of laughter and moved up to lie on top of Isabeau. She slid her arms around him and pulled him between her legs, groaning loudly when he thrust into her.

'That's it my lusty. I'll take you,' she murmured.

Adeliz, the younger and prettier of the women, propped herself up on one elbow and watched Jack pounding into Isabeau. Her face wore a bored expression. She threw Karolan an expectant glance. He shrugged his shoulders, then raised his tankard to his lips, before looking away towards the window where the icy river breeze pushed inwards against the greased membrane, sending draughts to rustle the carpet of herbs.

Adeliz pushed out her bottom lip. Proud of her fairness and her high, round breasts, she was popular with the customers and was not used to being ignored. Just who did his lordship think he was to look at her as if she was something that had crawled past him in the dirt? She knew what the other women said about him. Lord Rakka never touched any of them. He came here only to watch, and paid well for the privilege.

Perhaps he thought he was too good to sully himself with the touch of a whore. Or perhaps, as Isabeau said laughingly, he'd had his privy parts mutilated while fighting the French and lost the urge to pleasure a woman. Pity. He was beautiful, quite upsettingly so. And intriguing with the rushlight gleaming on the sharp planes of his cheekbones and softening his chiselled mouth. His neck and throat were slim, but muscular. The skin looked white and firm and had none of the usual coarse weathering of a knight or a working man. Then he glanced at her again and the chill of his beauty was softened by a smile.

Emboldened to approach him, she slid off the straw mattress. Neither Jack nor Isabeau noticed that she had gone. Their moans were rising in pitch, conjoined as were their bodies. Adeliz straightened her shoulders so that her breasts stood out and her slender body was shown to advantage. Sliding over to Karolan, she stood with her hips level with his head, giving him time to focus on the soft fuzz of dark blonde hair on her mound of Venus.

Her hands planted on her hips, she parted her legs, giving him a view of the pouting folds of her coynte. When he gave no sign of interest, she sat down next to him on the stained silk cushions.

'It's a sin to sit alone, when there's company for the asking,' she said.

It was the first time that she had been this close to him. Strange, but she had gained the impression that he was much older. Perhaps it was his air of melancholy or the depth of emotion she glimpsed in his deep-set dark eyes. It seemed to her that here was a man who had done many things in his life, perhaps questionable things, and who considered that he owed no one an explanation. He was self-contained, as few men were who visited the bawdy house by the river.

She studied him closely, under the pretence of making herself comfortable and pumping up the cushions. Karolan's face was pale and fine-boned and had a hard, hawk-like beauty. Once, when she had been small, she had been taken to the monastery of Holy Penitence and there had seen the newly installed window. The face of the saint had looked like Karolan. He too had been beautiful and fierce, but somehow tragic too.

3

Moved by some emotion she could not fathom, Adeliz raised her hand and brushed her fingers against the hood that lay in deep folds on Karolan's broad shoulders. As he turned towards her, his long black hair swung forward, framing his cheeks like dark wings.

'Don't,' he said tightly. 'Don't dare to pity me.'

Adeliz managed not to flinch, but it took all of her courage to stay seated. For a moment his face had been twisted by a murderous rage. She thought he was going to strike her and she almost hoped that he would. It would at least prove that he noticed her and was not looking through her. But he only slumped a little and took a deep swallow from his tankard.

She laid a tentative hand on his sleeve, feeling the softness of the costly black velvet under her fingers. 'Forgive me. I meant no offence, my lord.'

He covered her fingers with his own, removing them with a gentle but firm gesture. She had time only to register how cool his hand felt, before he stood up and gave her an oddly formal little bow.

'There is nothing to forgive. The fault is mine. I should not have come here. I must go. My work awaits me.'

Suddenly she was desperate to keep him there. 'Wait. I beg you. There must be somethin' I can do for you. Somethin' I can get you . . . I'll do whatever you want and I won't charge you.'

This time the smile enlivened his whole face, so that her breath caught in her throat. If he said the word she would go with him, now, naked as she was, and never regret it. Something about him drew her, even though she was repelled by the hunger inside herself. When he looked full into her eyes, like that, it was impossible to look away.

'I would demand something you would not wish to

surrender,' he said, his eyes glittering like chips of mica. 'Leave it be, wench. And save your charity for those more worthy of it.'

Turning on his heel, he strode towards the door. Only then did she feel able to move. It was as if his going had set her free. She watched him go out into the night, before she looked back towards the entwined figures on the straw mattress. Lord Rakka was a strange one indeed. She did not understand his final words, but only a fool would have missed the menace in his voice. It occurred to her belatedly that she had had a lucky escape, but from what she could not imagine. A shiver snaked down her spine and she was surprised to find that she was trembling.

'Adeliz? You finished makin' sheep's eyes?' Isabeau said acidly. 'Then come over here and attend to Jack. He's paid fer two and he's fair wore me out already.'

Glancing at Jack's heavy body, the damp mat of hair across his broad chest and his heavily muscled limbs, Adeliz felt a surge of relief. Jack was stolid, crude, and possessed of a rough-edged charm. He smelt sour and could be brutish at times, lashing out when he was in his cups, but he did not scare the life out of her like the tall, elegantly attired and saint-like Lord Rakka.

The moment Karolan left the ramshackle building he forgot all about Adeliz. But the sexual tension that her nearness and the freshness of her young body had fostered in him remained as a dull pressure in his belly.

He had long ago trained himself to subdue the clamourings of his flesh, but that did not mean that he was unaware of the movement of the tides within him. He observed himself with a sort of amused detachment, gaining a perverse pleasure from testing his self-control in the same way that one worried at an aching tooth.

5

As he walked down the narrow, cobbled alley, careful to avoid the piles of nightsoil and food scraps, he felt the subtle difference in the atmosphere that heralded the approach of the spirit being which was his constant companion. What had taken it so long? he mused. Normally it would have been attracted by Jack's labours.

There came the familiar folding and pleating of the air directly in front of him.

An observer would have seen nothing untoward, but Karolan, with his preternatural senses, perceived the Fetch as a ragged shadow; an amorphous, reed-thin, almost human shape that wove in and out of focus, its constant movement deceiving to the eye. The Fetch's voice was shrill and high-pitched, resembling bird song or the sound of water trickling over a rock.

It whispered to him now, eager for whatever experiences the night might hold.

Karolan smiled grimly. 'You're too late for the bawdy house, but there'll be something later. There always is,' he said, amused by its measureless hunger for sensation.

Unlike humankind the spirit never seemed to tire in its quest. Its whole existence was focused on indulging its every whim. Misery was its food, violence its delight and if there was a sexual element involved, then so much the better. It was totally amoral, but then, he was little different. It was just a question of degree.

'Now. Want it now. Want to bathe,' it whispered, allowing Karolan to feel the heat of its breath and the faint touch of lips at his ear. 'As do you, Master.'

Karolan shivered. It could feel how he burned for sexual release and was offering its services. Images crowded his mind. Over the long years the Fetch had become expert at attending to his needs. The pictures it placed in his head were irresistible, obscene, tantalizing. It was everything he wanted it to be. A beautiful virgin, a lush, full-bodied woman, an adolescent boy. Twisting and turning it presented itself for him. Moist, willing. Soft curled petals of flesh, folded inwards over a centre of deepest-rose. Damp curling hair around a tight shadowed orifice. Perfume clouded his senses, amber, lilies, the spice of sexual exertion, the heady musk of a woman's sex . . .

He clenched his hands into fists as the heat throbbed in his loins.

'Stop that!'

The Fetch laughed wantonly, a sound like wind in the reeds. And obeyed him at once. The images faded, but the sweat broke out on Karolan's forehead. It knew that he would not hold out against its potent lure for long. He never did; the alternative was too painful to bear. Too many years, too many deaths. The loneliness of his existence was like acid, eating into him until he thought he would go mad. And the only companion in his personal purgatory inhabited the spirit world.

A single word of assent and it would be at him, on him, or in him – whatever was his choice – drawing energy from his pleasure, bathing in the emanations given out by the restrained violence of his arousal.

He would resist for as long as possible. Ah, but it was torture to deny himself the solace of pleasure. And why did he still try? Only for the hollow victory that self-control brought him and because it angered the Fetch to be kept waiting. It was one way of punishing it for its be-trayal all those long, long years ago.

He quickened his step until he broke free of the maze of alleys that clotted the area around the docks. Only the dissolute and those hardened by circumstance to a life of crime would be abroad at this hour, yet he felt no fear of walking alone and unarmed. He knew himself to be more a creature of the shadows than anyone he might meet.

The smell of the river was strong. At low tide the mud banks were exposed, their dark-green breath casting a pall over everything in the vicinity. In the thick, grainy light of early morn he could see the white shapes of oyster catchers dotting the banks. The bigger brownish humps were the bent backs of those who skimmed a living from digging in the mud, vying with the birds for their catch and as likely to turn up a bloated corpse as anything of value.

Along the waterfront the dark shapes of warehouses and small dwellings loomed up at him out of the gloom. There was a cog moored in the harbour, her sales furled and the web of her rigging imprinted on the brightening sky. He could smell the salt-sourness of her wooden hull and see the barnacles that clung to the slimed planks below the water line. At full tide she would be sailing to Flanders with her cargo of English wool.

Beyond the cog was another vessel, her elegant shape proclaiming her Venetian origins. It was from this ship that Jack had alighted the previous night, bringing with him the spices, opiates, chunks of perfumed resin, and other rare substances for which Karolan paid handsomely. The best thing about Jack was that he asked no questions. Anything could be had for the right price and there was no fear that he would go running for the authorities.

From the open doorways of the taverns, light spilled out onto the muddy path. Karolan could hear the voices of sailors and dock workers raised in song, but he felt no urge to join them. He was known in this area and would be tolerated, if not welcomed, but he felt the need to get back to his workroom. The furnace needed tending and there were things he needed to bury or burn. They were starting to smell.

As he walked past a dark and shuttered house, there was a stirring from a pile of filthy rags alongside the door. With his honed senses Karolan heard the rattling of diseased lungs and the sound of bare limbs scraping across the patch of dry path under the overhanging eaves.

The Fetch gave a pleased chirrup and rushed forward, leaving a faint trembling in the air in its wake. In that same instant, Karolan caught the stench of sickness and decay. The pile of rags resolved itself into a man. A begging bowl was thrust under his nose and a whining voice intoned, 'Will ye give alms, Master? For the love of God.'

Aware of the Fetch's antics as it flowed back and forth through the beggar, rapturously imbibing the miasma of human misery, Karolan averted his eyes from the ruined face. He was not unmoved by the ravaged pain-filled features and the suppurating hole where once there had been a nose, but the spirit's enjoyment in such bleak fare prompted him to smile bitterly. If the beggar had known about the fiend who was bathing in the sickly energy emitting from his every pore, he would have been paralysed by horror.

No, Karolan decided, looking more closely at the man and noting the wooden cross hanging on a piece of flax string about his scrawny neck, it was more likely that he would start babbling for forgiveness, imploring God and all his saints to come to his aid. It always amazed him that such suffering wretches held on to their faith, when he – with so many dubious advantages – had lost his. He saw with a faint stirring of pity that the threadbare rags were no protection against the sharp wind and did nothing to conceal the running sores which covered the skinny, cold-mottled limbs.

9

Taking full advantage of the fact that Karolan had not walked straight past him, the beggar spoke again, his voice sounding rusty and unused.

'Have pity, Master. The Lord will surely reward yer charity.'

'I doubt that,' Karolan said dryly and dug into the leather purse which hung at his waist. 'But you can say a prayer for my immortal soul if it so pleases you.'

'I will, Master. To be sure. God bless you.'

The beggar had missed the irony in his voice. At the thought of someone praying for him, Karolan threw back his head and laughed. What a fine joke that was. If God existed then he would have been struck down long ago. And as for Hell, there could be nothing worse than the life he was forced to endure. He moved forward and placed a hand on the beggar's shoulder.

'Surely you, my friend, can see that God is vengeful and capricious. At best He is totally indifferent to the suffering of men.'

The beggar flinched away, alarmed both by the unexpected contact and Karolan's words. Groping for the cross at his neck, he brought the wood to his lips.

'Leave me in peace, Master. I ain't done nothing.' Backing away he lowered his bowl.

Karolan had not meant to terrify the poor soul. He shrugged and tossed a coin into the air. It fell onto the path with a chinking noise. The beggar deliberated for a moment as if considering leaving the money untouched, then thought better of it. Stretching out a grimy paw, he scooped it up.

'God is not mocked,' he said stoutly as he loped off towards the open door of a tavern. 'Those that stray from the path are welcomed back into the fold. I will pray for thee, Master.'

Karolan grinned at this homespun philosophy. It was

a fine irony indeed that the humblest beggar should feel himself capable of doing him a service. The man had even felt superior for a few moments. Chuckling to himself, Karolan moved on, aware of the Fetch following in his wake. It had been invigorated by its ingestion of pain and misery and there was a dull glow in the centre of its shadowy form. Having bathed it was eager for a more rewarding exchange of energies.

Karolan felt its touch on his skin, probing, measuring the threads of desire within him, which had subsided but not disappeared. Its touch was a parody of a human caress, but welcome for all that. He felt the brush of lips against his mouth, warm and compelling, and a surge of renewed hunger blossomed in his belly.

'I give you good solace, Master,' it whispered. 'Shall it be now?'

Karolan closed his eyes briefly, tempted to slip into the alley between two houses and give himself up to the spirit's ministrations. Clenching his teeth he said, 'No. Later. Wait until we get back to the manor.'

The Fetch chittered angrily and tugged at his hair before disappearing, its passing causing the air to shudder and fold in on itself. Karolan walked on alone, glad to be free of the demanding spirit for a time, but certain that it would reappear when he required its services.

In a while he came to the inn where he had left his horse. The ostler led Darkus from his stall. Karolan paid the man and took hold of the reins, running his palm over the horse's velvet nose and stroking the elegant head.

'Fine animal,' the ostler said, his glance sweeping over the palfrey's glossy black coat and the high curve of his neck. Darkus's mane hung down like a curtain of black threads. 'Breed him yourself?'

Karolan nodded as he swung himself into the saddle,

thinking of the horse he had brought back with him from Arabia, another lifetime and more ago. That stallion had been the sire of a number of fine horses, culminating many equine generations later in the splendour of Darkus.

'If ever you think of selling him . . .'

'I'll marvel at my own folly.' Karolan lifted a hand in a wave as he exerted a slight pressure on the reins. Darkus wheeled and with smooth economy of movement navigated the small cobbled yard.

As Karolan approached the outskirts of his land, the morning sun appeared behind the banked clouds as a band of russet light. Coppiced hazel bushes threw deep shadows across his path.

He ran an eye over the fields with their ripe crops. It gave him a sense of satisfaction to see how much there would be to harvest. After five years of successive crop failure and animal murrains the price of bread and meat was well beyond the reach of most common men. There had been reports of starving people being reduced to eating cats and dogs.

But his vassals had fared better than their neighbours. Karolan had instructed his steward to oversee the planting of oats, beans, and peas and to set aside only a moderate amount of land for wheat. A careful watch was set for the first signs of disease in sheep and cows and the afflicted animals were destroyed.

So it was that when the wheat rotted in the field because of the high rainfall and high humidity, the oat crop thrived. And although there was a shortage of meat, enough cows remained to give milk.

He urged Darkus to a canter and they passed along the edge of the strip fields and headed in the direction of the village. The squat shapes of the thatched crofts were in view, when a movement in the hedgerow caught Karolan's eye and he drew the horse to a halt.

A small boy, his fist screwed into one eye, peered up at Karolan.

'Why abroad so early, Selwyn?' Karolan said, smiling encouragingly.

The lad looked scared out of his wits and was shivering in the early morning chill. His tunic and hosen of rough, home-spun wool were damp with dew. Bits of grass and twig were sticking out of his thatch of fair hair.

'Steward says . . . as how I'm to hide here and watch the fields. And . . . and run for help if anyone comes thievin'. Harvest's nigh on ready fer the gatherin'.'

Karolan nodded. 'Aye. Good lad,' he said. 'Have you been here all night?' Selwyn nodded, his arms hugging his thin body against the cold.

'Well then. Climb up behind me and I'll take you to the manor house kitchen for a bowl of hot porridge and a sup of milk. I'll tell Steward to send along another boy to watch the fields. You've done your duty, right enough.'

The look of eagerness on Selwyn's face was chased away by an expression of alarm as he looked up at the great horse. His eyes slid sideways to Karolan's face and the colour rushed into his thin cheeks. Karolan understood the boy's dilemma. While he longed for food to fill his empty belly and a fire to warm his bones, he was loath to sit on the horse. Besides, he would have to press himself against his lord's body and everyone knew that that was a more dangerous act by far. Karolan's peasant vassals respected and trusted him, but they remained wary of him as if instinctively aware of his strangeness.

'Do I look as if I'm going to eat you?' Karolan said, grinning down at the boy. 'Believe me, Selwyn, I'd pick a fatter morsel to dine on if I had a taste for such flesh!'

Selwyn's mouth twitched nervously then widened into a smile, showing uneven, yellowish teeth. Karolan leaned down and extended his arm. Selwyn gripped it with both hands.

'Up with you, lad,' he said and swung the boy up behind him.

As Darkus started forward, Selwyn gave a gasp of terror and clung on tight to Karolan's cloak. 'Be not afraid. Darkus is gentle. You feel near frozen, lad. Pull a fold of my cloak around you if you wish.'

Selwyn mumbled his thanks, but made no move to obey. Karolan did not insist, although the boy's shivers vibrated through him. The sensation of the frail body pressed against his own was delightful, tempting him to indulge his passions. But this feeling was devoid of all baseness. Selwyn's proximity, the sweetish smell of his unwashed body, the sound of his pulses, and the heat of his breath, awoke only tenderness in him. But for the fact that the boy would be terrified out of his wits, he would have pulled him into his embrace and warmed him against his chest.

He felt a wave of sadness. The simplest things, like embracing his own child, would always be denied him. Thinking of the destruction he had wrought to past lovers, albeit unwittingly, he fell silent. Oh God, the eyes were what haunted him the most; eyes opened wide in agony, confusion, and horror.

And the blood. So much blood, pouring from torn flesh deep inside, running thick and poppy-bright down white thighs, clumps of stinking, scorched tissue mixed with the flow. His lips tightened as he thrust away the images, forcing himself to become absorbed by the rolling movements of the horse.

Selwyn, perhaps absorbing some of his lord's melancholia, did not speak until they reached the manor

14

house. As soon as the horse halted, he slid from Darkus's back and with a hurried word of thanks scuttled off to the kitchen.

Karolan took Darkus to the stable and ordered the lad there to rub him down with a handful of straw before putting him in his stall and giving him some oats. He decided against following Selwyn to the kitchen. The old memories had fostered a depression in him. He felt only an eagerness to go and check that things were progressing to his satisfaction in his laboratorium.

His personal living quarters were situated in the stone tower which could be reached either by going through the main hall or by entering directly through an outside door. As soon as he reached his bedchamber, he locked the door, then swept aside the thick, woollen carpet which hid the trap-door in the floor. Feeling for the key which he kept hanging from his belt, he opened the wooden flap and descended a flight of stone steps. The stairwell was dark, but the air smelt clean and dry. He needed no light, being able to see in the dark as well as a cat.

Karolan pushed open the heavy wooden door at the bottom of the steps and stepped into the laboratorium. The vaulted ceiling and walls were built of stone and were many feet thick. A complicated network of stone-lined ducts and metal pipes, all buried deep underground, led out from the tower to emerge beneath heavy metal grilles set into the floor of the forest. The tales of hauntings and unquiet spirits, fostered by the villagers and having some base in fact, were a useful deterrent to anyone who showed undue curiosity.

A chemical smell greeted him as he walked across the laboratorium. It was dark inside, lit only by the faint glow from the furnace. Karolan lit a taper and then moved around the room lighting candles. Before he went over to look at the alembic vessel, set in its bath of boiling water, he went to his workbench to consult his notes. The waist-high table was neat and ordered; metal scales stood next to a wooden rack which held many vials of coloured liquids. Beside the open ledger there was a globe of the world and a detailed astrological chart.

Karolan sat on a stool and ran his finger down the row of neat figures, checking the detailed grid of times, dates, ingredients. He knew the contents by heart, but it was his habit to check and double-check each entry. Contained in this and the other ledgers was a note of every experiment, every failure, every success – great or small. The huge, leather-bound volumes were piled high now. They littered the wooden shelves that covered the workroom walls, many of them encrusted with the dust of ages and flecked with powdery mould.

He sat for a moment composing himself and performing the mental exercises which would put him into the state of higher consciousness he needed for the task in hand. Nothing of the outside world must be allowed to intrude. It was a simple matter to put himself into a light trance. The familiar feeling came over him almost at once. It felt as if a breeze was blowing through his skull. He felt insubstantial, his veins brittle – like glass.

Totally absorbed now, he skimmed down the long columns of entries. He began reading aloud, his voice echoing around the silent room.

'Primal matter for purposes of possible transmutation acquired on the feast day of St Eusabius.

Item. One, healthy, day-old male child – purchased at the cost of two shillings from Jack Spicer.

Said child dispatched forthwith on the day following the feast and known henceforth as prima materia.

Prima materia put into alembic vessel and covered with

aqua fortis – previously prepared by a process of distillation, using nitrate, alum, and ferrous sulphate.'

There followed a detailed account of all the complicated and arcane processes to which the prima materia had been subjected. As he read them he ticked them off mentally. Calcination. Solution. Separation. Conjunction. Putrefaction. Congelation . . .

Now the alembic vessel resided in the double-walled bath of metal. The lower part of the vessel, the curcubit, was surrounded by water, which was kept at a constant heat until all the stages of distillation were completed. It would be many months before Karolan knew whether he had succeeded this time. The end result of his experiment would hopefully be the Philosopher's Stone or 'seed' – a red, waxy substance which held within it the pure, spiritual essence of renewal.

Walking across the room he looked into the alembic vessel, peering intently at the thick, greenish glass. The process of putrefaction was advanced and there was a dark, slimy mass in the bottom of the vessel. The glass walls were coated with a sooty residue.

'Ah, the blackening. The nigredo,' Karolan murmured, well satisfied that things were progressing in the correct manner.

Now was the time to add the next ingredient. He assembled everything he would need, smoothing the piece of vellum until it lay flat on his workbench and then laying out a knife and a metal dish. Calling on the names of Hermes and Mercurius, he began to read aloud from the tract in front of him. After a moment's pause, he reached for the knife and brought the wickedly sharp blade up to his neck.

Holding the skin taut between two fingertips, he sliced into his skin then inserted the tips of his fingers into the cut to widen the wound. It hurt like the devil, but he gritted his teeth and probed, keeping very still. Blood made his fingers slippery and it was difficult to push aside the strap-like muscle and reach around the throbbing artery. The sensation of reaching into his own body made his stomach churn, but he fought down the revulsion. It was a few moments before he found the tiny, thread-like vessel he sought. Using the very tip of the knife, he pierced the vessel. At once he was aware of a subtle altering of his body's rhythms. A trickle of thin, straw-coloured fluid seeped out, mixing with the blood flowing freely from the wound.

Swiftly, before his flesh began to heal around his fingers, he collected the two liquids in the bowl. The wound stung for a while longer, but the flow had stopped and the edges were already knitting together. In a few minutes there would be no sign of a cut. Carrying the bowl over to the furnace, he tipped the liquid into the alembic vessel.

Placing his hands around the curved glass sides, he closed his eyes and concentrated hard, mouthing the words of power. When he finally opened his eyes again, there were bubbles of sweat on his forehead. He peered into the slimy mess of the prima materia and felt a surge of exultation. The blackness seethed and churned. It began to glow, taking on a pearly tinge, the glass side of the vessel reflecting the iridescent colours.

'The starry sky,' Karolan breathed with awe.

With regular additions of his own essential fluid over the next few weeks he would expect to see a further change in colour, signifying that the next stage – the albedo – had been reached. Then the resultant 'seed' must be allowed to come to term. Forty days was the required period, a time corresponding to the forty week gestation period. After extinguishing all the candles he went back up the steps to his bedchamber, locking the trap-door behind him. Now that he had finished he felt exhausted. The rituals and the effort of concentration always weakened him for a short time. He threw himself down onto his bed, pausing only to kick off his high, leather boots before relaxing against the silken pillows.

On the borders of sleep he became aware of a presence close by. Opening one eye he saw that the air beside him was trembling as if with a silvery heat haze. A jagged tear appeared and the silver fabric peeled back to admit entry to a woman. The Fetch was back and this time it would not be gainsaid.

'Now, Master,' it purred, confidently. 'Solace you, shall I?'

Karolan did not try to resist. The Fetch chuckled with throaty eagerness. The form with which it had clothed itself was soft, rounded, lushly curved. Perfume rose from the valley between deep breasts. The 'woman' smiled invitingly, running her palms down over her pouting belly and rubbing them across her thighs. She reached for Karolan, her soft lips trailing down his neck. He felt the lacings of his tunic being pulled free, the flaps of black velvet peeling open to lay his chest bare. A hot mouth closed over one nipple, suckling, drawing out the sweet sensations from his body. As teeth grazed his skin, his flesh rose up strongly. He arched his back in readiness for what was to come.

Yes. Oh, yes. Why deny himself this pleasure? He no longer cared that the Fetch would exact a price for this service. A few moments' possession. That was all it wanted. To look out of his eyes, to feel blood coursing through its spirit veins, to experience the heavy beat of his heart, to imagine for that brief time that it was human. It seemed little enough to grant it.

Karolan moaned as the pleasure increased in intensity. Fingertips teased him, running up the insides of his thighs, smoothing and pinching his flesh by turns. A long nail scratched gently at the tight, creased rose of his anus. He was aware that a shadow passed across his face. The warm heaviness of a body settled over him. Thighs clamped the sides of his head. There were perfumed folds against his mouth. He stretched out his tongue, lapping eagerly at the rain-tasting flesh. He stabbed inwards and felt his tongue enclosed by warm, pulsing wetness.

The Fetch's laughter was soft, exultant as it used its artifice to seduce its master. Karolan was lost in sensation. The Fetch's flesh seethed, re-formed against him, offering pleasures that no mortal woman ever could. While Karolan's tongue was still deep inside the perfumed vulva, hands smoothed down his body, gripped his hips and drew him towards a second orifice. And then Karolan was inside her, thrusting his cock deeply into a cleated wet maw.

She was hot and tight. The muscular walls squeezed gently, milking him. He seemed possessed by a welter of aroused flesh. Bucking and thrashing, holding nothing back, he gave vent to all his pent-up frustration. While he toiled, fingers plucked at him, urging him on to greater efforts. He was soaked in sweat, enclosed by sensation, every orifice invaded, plundered. His lips, anus, cock, the whole surface of his skin, throbbed, ached, pulsed. He caged a scream behind his teeth, desperate to reach a climax. The Fetch crooned, its enjoyment as deep as his own. As the pleasure peaked, tipped over, Karolan ejaculated in great, tearing spurts.

Before the last sensations had died away, the Fetch was inside his skin. Karolan's mouth stretched open in a rictus of agony as the spirit occupied his body. He felt it rattling around inside his skull, pushing against his flesh from the inside. The skin on his arms and legs rippled and bulged as it explored him. His eyeballs burned and his vision clouded as the spirit claimed them for its own. He ground his teeth together. 'Enough!'

The Fetch left him instantly. Drunk with sensation it scurried over the surface of his skin, tasting his sweat, dabbing at the moist surface with hungry, mindless avidity.

'Go now,' Karolan said, tiredly. 'Leave me in peace. You've had what you wanted. Damn you!'

'As have you, Master,' it whispered exultantly, the moment before it faded into another dimension. 'As have you.'

Karolan groaned and turned over, pulling the sheets over his half-naked body. Seconds later he was asleep.

CHAPTER TWO

Garnetta hurried down the cobbled street towards Mercer's Yard.

The basket on her arm was heavy. Inside it, wrapped in a clean cloth, was the dough she had taken along earlier to the bakehouse, now transformed into two crusty loaves. As a treat she had also bought some of the savoury beef coffyns favoured by her father. Although she had looked wistfully at the curd tarts stuffed with dried fruits, she had decided against spending any more of their hard-earned money.

The weather was raw. She pulled the woollen muffler more closely around her head. Even so strands of fair hair whipped across her face stinging her chilled skin, blowing into her eyes. She tucked in her chin, leaning into the wind. Her heavy woollen skirts were forced against her legs, exposing her ankles. She was glad that she had thought to wrap bindings around her boot tops and up to her knees.

It was a moment before she became aware of the church bells. They tolled out a single, doleful, note. Another death then. She crossed herself, mouthing a *Miserere* for the departed souls. Death was not unusual, yet there was a difference this season. Winter had followed hard on the dismal summer. Many folk were already weakened by lack of food, their faces grey and lacking in vitality. There seemed a tension in the air, as if something was gathering, waiting.

The week before, Mistress Bowles and her new baby had died. Nothing unusual in that either, women died all the time; childbirth was fraught with danger. But the

Bowleses' eldest had followed a day later and Master Bowles himself had perished of the same morbidity. All of Mercer's Yard had paid their respects, standing in silence as the sad little parade made its way to the churchyard. A whole family gone, snuffed out like a candle, Garnetta thought as she passed the little thatched house which stood at the entrance to Mercer's Yard. Today there was no child playing five-stones in the dust outside, no sound of bustling activity as Mistress Bowles swept and cleaned. The door was boarded up, the unglazed windows bland and shuttered. The only sign of previous occupation was a pile of animal bones near the door and the dung heap at the end of the yard.

She sighed. It seemed only hours since she had taken the scrap of cambric across to the house. 'For the baby,' her father, Franklin Mercer, had said as he cut the length of fabric. 'Tell Mistress Bowles it's the end of a roll.'

Garnetta had kissed his cheek before she left on her errand. Her father was a kind man. He knew the Bowleses resented being shown charity and had taken care to make them think they were taking the cambric off his hands. It had come in useful after all. The poor babe had not needed a gown, but there had been enough cambric to make a winding sheet for both mother and child.

Garnetta turned into the yard, avoiding the open drain that ran down into the alley opposite. The drain stank strongly of urine and rotting meat. It was clotted with a variety of refuse. Rat turds floated on top of the scummy liquid. She made for the two-storey building, above the door of which hung a painted sign advertising the mercer's trade of the shop owner. The sound of bells was muted here.

She was proud to live in this place with its fine,

23

half-timbered buildings, many of them with their lower storeys whitened with quicklime. Opposite the shop was the Pen and Flower tavern and next to that the apothecary's shop, the window shutters spread wide to display neatly labelled boxes of medicaments. Coloured oils in glass jars glinted like jewels. Garnetta walked past a fenced area where a pig was nosing about amongst the mud and straw. At the back of the plot a few chickens were roosting in the open doorway of a coop.

'God give you good day, Mistress Mercer,' called out a smiling woman who had come out to scatter grain for the chickens. A ruddy-cheeked babe sat astride her hip, its hand curled around a cracked and chewed marrow bone. Garnetta returned the greeting as she passed by, then waved to a small, round woman who was drawing up water from the central well which served all the buildings in the yard.

Mistress Wood had her hair tied up in a red scarf. She had a small-featured, pointed face which seemed incongruous against her plumpness. Her eyes were bright and alert, like a robin's. Around her shoulders she wore a brightly patterned shawl. Garnetta liked Mistress Wood who made her living by giving music lessons. She had a room on the top floor of the Pen and Flower and was often to be seen on her balcony in summer tutoring her students. 'What's to do, Mistress Mercer?' Mistress Wood called out, cocking her head. 'Is it St Bertrina that's ringing?'

Garnetta nodded. 'Aye. Three dead, according to the baker.'

Mistress Wood tutted. 'It's four now,' she said. 'Apothecary was called to the Pen early this morn. Old Dickon the tap-man's gone to his maker. God rest his soul.'

Garnetta made the holy sign on her breast, the odd

24

feeling gathering pace within her. 'Dickon was a good age,' she said. 'God grant him rest. I'd best get on. The Blessed Virgin keep you, Mistress Wood.'

'Indeed, my dear,' Mistress Wood replied. 'As she keeps all we womenfolk.' Garnetta quickened her step, feeling a sudden urge to get inside the shop and check that all was well. The bell over the door clanged as she entered. A charcoal brazier in one corner of the shop gave out a fitful heat. The familiar smell of fabric dressing filled her nostrils. Clean rushes rustled against her boots as she went across the room. Deep wooden shelves lined the walls, each of them crammed with rolls of cloth, bundles of ribbon, and lace in every shade from wheat to ivory.

Everything looked normal. No reason for her to have the jitters. Her father was using a yardstick to measure lengths from a bolt of cloth. He wore his usual indoor winter attire of a soft velvet hat, thick knitted doublet over a long gown, and woollen gloves with the fingers cut out. Franklin Mercer paused, looked up and smiled. The wooden counter where he worked was transformed into a king's dais by the shot silks, murry velvets, and embroidered brocades which were unrolled across it.

'Ah, love, you're back quickly. Good. I have to get this order filled. Her ladyship's sending her maid to collect it within the hour.'

Garnetta returned his smile, rubbing her palms together. It was warm inside the shop, but she still had cold shivers running down her back. 'I'll just hang up my cloak, then I'll lend you a hand,' she said.

Her father's once handsome face was thin, worn by the worry of keeping up the shop and feeding three unmarried daughters. As he bent over the counter, he pushed his hat back from his forehead. She saw that his grey hair was thinning and felt an almost painful pang of love for him. 'I bought the pastries you like, father,' she said, uncovering the basket. 'Shall you have one at once?'

He nodded. 'Aye, lass. Jessica has made some mulled wine. Have a cup yourself, then bring me one with the pastry.'

It was dark in the narrow passageway which led into the living quarters. The kitchen was a small separate building at the back. Washing was boiling in a vat of soapy water set over the fire. The room smelt of strong lye soap and was full of steam. From the open door she glimpsed the wet sheets which snapped and danced in the wind. They were lucky to have the large plot, bordered by elderflower trees. Rows of leeks and cabbages, brown-edged with frost burn, covered the soil. Their six hens scratched at the ridged earth between the rows, pecking in vain for worms and insects.

Garnetta smiled with the pride of ownership. Everyone else must beg a space from a neighbour if they wished to plant vegetables. Most women strung washing lines between the overhanging upper storeys, above the filth of the street below. Her father, a gleam in his eye, had once commented that Mistress Wood's washing was as decorative as bunting. She smiled at the recollection. Who would have thought that the plain little woman wore shifts trimmed with green ribbons?

Garnetta began to relax as she helped herself to a cup of the mulled wine, then replaced the wooden cover on the pitcher. Everything was as it should be. The rhythms and patterns of her ordered life were comforting. In Mercer's Yard, the spectre of famine and hardship had less power to harm her family. She took another sip of wine. The hippocras with its flavours of lemon and cinnamon warmed her through to her bones. It was quiet in the kitchen, with Jessica and Sellice nowhere to be seen, the only sound the vat of washing bubbling away merrily. Lifting her cup to take another sip, she froze as a sound reached her ears.

The sound came again, louder. A strangled scream. In a trice she was out of the door and into the garden, pushing aside the sheets which flapped wetly against her, impeding her progress. Against the far wall, crouching beside a bundle on the ground was Sellice. 'Garnetta!' she called, her voice tight with fear. 'Come quickly.'

'What's happened?' Garnetta bunched up her skirts and raced across the vegetable patch. 'By our Lady, Jessica!'

She knelt down and cradled Jessica's head in her lap. Smoothing back the hair from her eldest sister's face, Garnetta examined her. There was a bruise on the side of her face and a graze on her forehead, the blood welling from it in tiny beads. Neither injury was serious. She was more concerned with Jessica's skin which was burning to the touch. Her forehead was clammy. There was a pinched look about her mouth. Jessica moaned faintly, her eyelids flickering.

'She . . . just fainted,' Sellice said, her voice rising on a note of panic. 'Keeled right over, she did. Banged her head on the ground. What's wrong with her?'

Garnetta shook her head, her earlier worries surfacing again. 'I don't know.' Looking into Sellice's drawn face, she saw her own fear reflected there. She forced herself to stay calm. 'It's probably just a fever. Run and tell father what's happened, then go across and fetch the apothecary. Hurry now.'

Sellice went at once, glad to be told what to do. As soon as her sister disappeared inside the house the worried look returned to Garnetta's face. Hands shaking she unfastened the hooks on Jessica's woollen basque. She peeled open the neckline and pulled down the loose

27

neck of her shift. 'Oh, dear Lady. Oh, no . . . I had feared this, but I hoped I was wrong.'

Eyes widening with horror, she looked down at the red spots on the white skin, some of them with yellow heads standing proud of the swellings. A few of the eruptions had gathered together into rings. The tell-tale tokens of the pestilence. Not Jessica, she's the strongest of us all, she thought Oh, not Jessy. She began rocking back and forth, unaware that she was stroking her eldest sister's hair.

'We'll make you well,' she murmured. 'Don't you worry, love. We'll look after you.'

Garnetta sat beside her sister throughout the rest of that day, watching her grow worse with each passing hour. The apothecary was not to be found. When he arrived finally it was far into the night. A tall, robust man normally, he was pale with exhaustion.

Garnetta stood with her arm around the sobbing Sellice's waist as the apothecary examined Jessica. By now Jessica was raving. They had to tie her wrists and ankles to the bedposts to stop her hurting herself, but there were deep gouges on her face where she had raked herself with her nails.

The apothecary lifted his head and said tiredly, 'It's the pestilence right enough. There's little I can do. I've called on twenty similar cases since noon.' Fumbling in his pack he took out a bottle of ridged green glass. 'Give her three drops of this electuary in wine, four times a day. It might help. Jessica's in God's hands now.'

'But is there nothing more we can do?' Garnetta asked. 'There must be something.'

The man shook his head, his face blank with weariness. 'You might try praying to St Pernel. He's patron over fevers.'

Franklin Mercer showed the apothecary out, his face set in lines of sorrow. Garnetta knew what her father was thinking. First my wife and now this. Although their mother had been dead five years, he had never become resigned to the loss. She saw how he averted his eyes from Jessica. He seemed stupefied by grief. It was as if he had given up without a fight and was mourning her before she had gone. Sellice gave a strangled sob and wrapped her arms around herself, rocking back and forth. Garnetta glanced at her elder sister. All day Sellice had been alternating between abject terror and blank acceptance.

'We'll all die,' Sellice whispered. 'The pestilence spares no one. We must have sinned somehow. God is punishing us. What've we done wrong Garnetta?'

Garnetta had no answer. She sighed deeply. It was obvious that neither her father nor Sellice were going to be much help. It seemed that she must take charge. 'We'll move Jessy's bed downstairs,' she said. 'Is the laundry dry? We're going to need plenty of clean linen.'

At that moment Jessica gave a groan. There was a bubbling, liquid sound as she voided her bowels where she lay. A vile, throat-catching smell filled the room.

'Oh, dear Lord,' Sellice said, pressing her fist against her mouth.

Garnetta clamped down the revulsion which made her gorge rise and began gathering up the fouled sheets. Doing something, anything, made her feel better, less afraid. The mess that stained Jessica's shift was thick and as black as tar. The stench was indescribable. 'Well don't just stand there with your mouth hanging open!' she said sharply to Sellice. 'Fetch hot water to wash her. I'll need a clean shift and sheets, then fill the vat and set it to boil. If we don't launder this bedding at once it'll stink the house out.'

'Oh, Garnetta . . .' Sellice whispered. 'How shall we bear it?'

'We'll do it because we must.' Garnetta made her voice hard. Sellice was lost without Jessica to lead her. The two of them had always been inseparable. 'We have to be strong for Jessy. For father too. You just go and fetch hot water and soap, there's a good lass.'

Not until Sellice had left the room, moving slowly as if she had just wakened from a nightmare, did Garnetta give way to the terror that dried her throat and made her ears buzz. She could feel the tears pricking behind her eyes, but she had no time for them. Sorrow was an indulgence she could ill afford while there was work to be done. While she was bundling the linen into a pile and struggling to remove Jessica's encrusted shift, her father came back into the room. He could see that she was having difficulty undressing Jessica but made no move to help her. He looked ghastly. She forgot her own fear for a moment.

'Father? What is it? Has the apothecary thought of something more we can do for Jessica?'

Franklin shook his head, his eyes not meeting hers. 'Nay, lass. It's not that. We're to be boarded up. The watch are hammering boards over the windows and doors of the Pen and Flower even now.'

Garnetta rocked back on her heels. 'The tavern? But Dickon died of old age. Mistress Wood said nought of anyone else when I saw her at the well but a few hours ago . . .' An awful presentiment twisted her guts. For a moment she was dizzy. The room spun around her. 'No. Oh, no . . . It cannot be.'

Franklin turned his back, throwing the words bleakly over his shoulder as he left the room. 'I'm sorry, lass. Mistress Wood died an hour since.'

★

Jessica battled for her life for eight days, while Franklin Mercer took himself off to bed and refused to get up.

Garnetta and Sellice took it in turns to sit with their sister. It hurt Garnetta to see what Jessica endured. There had been little enough love lost between them, but Jessy did not deserve this. No one did. The pestilence seemed to delight in stripping the humanity from a person, making them into a babbling tortured wreck. There was no dignity in the way that skin erupted into pus-filled blaines. Every orifice poured forth a stinking black fluid. The house reeked of the sickness. The stench of it clung to Garnetta's skin, no matter how hard she scrubbed at herself. She thought she would never get the stink out of her hair.

The apothecary's electuary did no good. Although she shouted for help from the upper storey of the shop, he did not visit again. She knew that he must be taken up with visits to other victims of the illness, but that did not help her feeling of isolation. Dear God, what good did it do to shut up the healthy with the sick? She had heard that the pestilence was a miasma, a noxious cloud that came drifting in from the sea, carrying with it all the rot and foulness from the ocean floor. If that was so, the very air they breathed was poisoned. What chance did any of them have? She felt helpless in the face of such an implacable enemy.

'Please God, deliver Jessica from this torment,' she prayed. 'Forgive her sins, whatever they are. Merciful Father, I beg you, forgive us all.'

Time after time she repeated the words, kneeling with her hands clasped so tightly together that her knuckles showed white under the skin. She implored St Pernel to take away Jessica's fever, read aloud from a psalter and prayed, head bowed, with Sellice, both of them confessing to imaginary sins and the smallest of shortcomings in the faint hope of placating the Almighty. But God did not listen. As Jessica grew steadily worse, Garnetta's heart hardened against a deity who could visit such anguish upon his subjects, whose ears were deaf to her cries for mercy.

Jessica could keep nothing down save plain water. The flesh had fallen from her bones. She was barely nineteen, but she had the hollowed cheeks, dull hair, and shadowed eyes of an old woman. Her skin was like paper. Her lips and eyelids had a greyish-purple cast. As Garnetta sponged water over her sister's ravaged limbs, washing away the thin black fluids that trickled from her, Jessica screamed in agony and rose up against her bonds. The swelling in her groin was as big as an apple, the skin covering it blackened, stretched, and shiny. When it began to suppurate, an evil-smelling pus leaked into the dressing they had bound over it.

However they tried, they could not keep her clean. Garnetta decided that they would no longer cover her with a shift. They could not wash and dry them fast enough. 'But it's sinful to display her body,' Sellice protested.

'Who's to see?' Garnetta said wearily. 'It will save on the washing. Jessica no longer knows what is happening to her.'

The world had gone mad. There was nothing left of beauty or charity. Their existence had narrowed to a single room where the air was so foul you could cut it. They were probably all going to die. What did it matter if they went naked or clothed to stand before God? Her eyes felt gritty from lack of sleep. She had worn the same gown for days. It was crumpled and stale smelling. Dampness prickled at her armpits. Her skin felt itchy. She could not remember when she last washed. They could hardly provide enough hot water for cooking and for Jessica's needs.

The days ran into each other. The boards at the widows and doors made it gloomy inside the shop. The supply of candles was fast dwindling. They lit one only when strictly necessary. Luckily there was a good supply of charcoal. The brazier served for both heat and light. Garnetta's nerves were strained to breaking point. Her fear that she would fall ill before Sellice or her father made her edgy and short tempered. She insisted on them examining each other for pustules. To her relief none of them yet had the signs. The occasional views of the yard through cracks in the planks were a reminder that life still existed outside. Goodly souls from St Bertrina's church had arranged a round for delivering water and food for those entombed with their sick relatives. Twice a day she leaned out from an upstairs window and let down a length of cloth with a pail tied to it. Such visits broke the monotony of the bleak dark days. Even the rumble of the death carts was a sign of life. She saw how the bearers used long-handled hooks to drag the shrouded bodies across the cobblestones. Now and then the watch appeared, checking to make sure that people remained boarded up the required time and keeping looters at bay.

Garnetta hung on to her sanity only by a great effort of will. She forced herself to believe that the pestilence would pass without scything down everyone in its path. But it was hard to believe that anyone would survive. Perhaps this truly was the end, as prophesied by the white monks. She had seen them in the town square, the brothers of the monastery of the Holy Penitence, wearing boards tied over their white breech clouts. On the wood were painted graphic scenes depicting horrifying images of suffering humanity. Demons tore at human skin with white-hot pincers or turned them on spits over fires in hell's kitchen.

She shuddered. The white monks were fanatics, but perhaps they had been right. If only there was someone to talk to, someone to share her thoughts with, who would makes sense of what was happening. But Sellice could only cope by following orders, dwelling on mundane tasks. Father was locked away in his own world where everything was beautiful and no pain or ugliness intruded.

Daily the death toll mounted. The bells of all the churches in the surrounding parishes rang by night and day. She recognized the tones of St Ralphite's, St Kate's-in-the-Meadow, the great mournful bass note of Holy Penitence. In the silence of the shop, where Jessica's dry rasping breaths and whimpers of pain filled her ears, the bells were a blessed comfort.

'Selly?' Garnetta said, as she came back from the kitchen late the next afternoon. 'Selly? You must have dozed off. Go and get some rest. I'll sit with Jessy for a while. But first will you go upstairs and shout across to the Pen and Flower? Ask them how many dead today.'

Sellice nodded, rubbing her fists into her eyes and yawning. In a short while she reported back. Fully awake now and white-faced, she said, 'Five more today. Josh, the cellar-man. Mistress Stokes, her eldest and two travelling men.'

'Mother of God bless them,' Garnetta murmured. If the deaths at the Pen and Flower were representative, then the whole town was now in the grip of the disaster.

When, two days later, Sellice complained that there was no more meat left to make stew, Garnetta's fragile control finally snapped. 'Mercy, but I'm sick of your whining! I have to think of everything. Father's no good at all and you're next to useless. If only you'd use your wits. There's a sack of dried beans and two strings of onions. Use them and shave down the last of the chicken bones to make soup.'

Sellice stuck out her lower lip, her face crumpling. One fat tear ran down her cheek. 'It's not my fault that I'm not brave and strong like you. I know I'm older than you and I ought to be helping more, but I'm doing the best I can.'

Garnetta's shoulders sagged. She did not feel strong. She felt very young and afraid. Her nerves were brittle threads which would shatter like glass at any moment. She clenched her hands into fists, fighting for control. She wanted to weep, to have someone put their arms around her, tell her that everything would be as it was. It did not matter if that was a lie. 'Oh, Selly. I'm just so exhausted. You know that I don't mean it. Come and give me a hug. That's better. Where's father?'

'In bed,' Sellice said sulkily, wiping her face on her skirt. 'Same as he was yesterday and the day before.' Her voice took on a waspish note. 'Why should we have to fetch and carry for him? Tell him to come and help with Jessy.'

'It wouldn't do any good. I've tried,' Garnetta said resignedly. 'Just take him up some soup when you've made some.' She hadn't the strength left to bully him into facing up to what was happening. There was enough to do with keeping Jessica washed, coping with the laundry, and trying to keep her spirits from flagging. If she saw his tragic face she might give way to her own panic and despair.

Franklin had always been a weak man – loving but lacking in moral courage. The mainstay of the marriage had been his wife. Yet, once he had come to terms with her death of childbed fever he had worked hard at building up the business, somehow still finding the time to teach Garnetta her letters and explain the complexities of keeping the shop's ledgers. She recollected how Jessica had complained at the favouritism.

35

'I'm the eldest. It should be me as does the learning,' she had said, her voice rising on a whine.

Sellice had agreed. She always followed where Jessica led. Garnetta had held her breath, waiting for her father to sigh and give in as he usually did. One look from Jessica, who was the image of her mother, and he was lost. But on this occasion he stood firm.

'Garnetta has the brain for bookwork. I need someone to help me keep accounts, make a tally of what is sold. You and Sellice are best suited for keeping house. That's how it's to be.' When Jessica would have spoken up, he held up a warning hand. 'Enough now. You'll do as you're bid.'

Despite Jessica's sulks that was the way it had been. Consequently, unlike most other women of her acquaintance, Garnetta was able to read and write. She was conscious of the many disapproving looks from customers when they saw her entering the sales in the leatherbound book on the counter.

'No good'll come from book-learnin' that girl,' said Maud Flesher the butcher's wife, wagging her finger. 'It's just storin' up trouble for her. She'll get to thinking she's special. No man'll take a wife who be cleverer than he is.'

'Then it'll have to be a special man who takes Garnetta from me,' Franklin said, smiling mildly, proud of Garnetta's nimble brain and the fact that her writing was neater than his own.

Well, much good her learning and her enquiring mind would do her now. Garnetta sighed deeply, pushing back the heavy fair hair which was escaping from the band she had tied around her forehead. The pleasant hours spent at her studies, the rows of neat figures on the rolls of parchment, the illuminated book of hours – all those things seemed a hundred years away, part of a different lifetime. The only reality was the shut-up building, the all pervading stench of death, the back-breaking work of looking after Jessica, and Jessica herself who was beginning suddenly to scream away her life's strength. She writhed weakly on the fouled bed, the cords standing out on her scrawny neck, her mouth stretched wide as the terrible, ear-splitting sound rang around the room.

'Oh, dear God,' Garnetta groaned. 'I can't bear it any more. Shut up can't you! Just shut up! Shut up!'

She banged her bunched fists against her forehead, screwing her eyes shut in an access of grief and horror, her eyelids pricking with unshed tears. Jessica obliged at once, letting out one long sigh that ended on a strange little whistle. After days and days punctuated by the rasping sound of her sister's breathing, the ensuing silence was absolute. Slowly Garnetta lowered her hands and looked down at her sister. Jessica's eyes were open. A string of black vomit hung from her parted lips.

'Oh, Jessy. Oh, God help me. I didn't mean it. Forgive me.'

Reaching out a trembling hand, she closed Jessica's eyes. It was over. Her sister was at peace. Instead of the expected grief there was only a dreadful relief. She put her hands together and prayed.

A few moments later, Sellice came into the room, a steaming bowl of soup in her hands. 'I found pepper at the bottom of the spice chest and a few costmary leaves. Here you are. It tastes good.'

From force of habit Garnetta thought first of comforting Sellice. She took the bowl from her hands. 'I'll eat it in back by the hearth,' she said gently. 'There's no need to watch over Jessy any more. She's in God's keeping now.'

Together they knelt in prayer, Sellice white-faced and

37

trembling. Even though they had not expected Jessica to live, it was a shock to see her lying lifeless. 'Come with me now,' Garnetta said after a time. 'We're both exhausted. We'll eat and rest a little, then you shall help me dress Jessy and sew her in a sheet. I'll not have her go naked into her death sleep.' Sellice crossed herself, looking dumbly down at Jessica. We are both of us too worn out with grief to mourn decently, Garnetta thought. She did not realize that she was weeping until Sellice put up a hand and stroked her cheek.

They ate the soup in silence, Garnetta surprised to find that she was ravenous. Sellice ate little, skimming her spoon across the surface of the broth, chasing the floating circles of fat around the dish. She kept pressing her left hand to her breast, every now and then smoothing her hand across to her shoulder. Garnetta saw the tell-tale gesture, but did not want to believe what it signified. She put down her spoon and looked sharply at her sister. 'Sellice? What is it?'

Sellice avoided her eyes, her mouth pulling away at the corners. 'It is possible to have the swelling and get better is it not?' Her voice was brittle, the terror barely hidden below the surface. 'I . . . I feel so well. I have hardly any pain.' Her eyes pleaded with Garnetta to agree with her.

Somehow Garnetta managed to smile encouragingly, although her throat and chest hurt so much she could hardly draw breath. 'You'll get well again. Never fear. Why don't you go and lie down? After a rest you'll feel a lot better.'

Rufus jumped down from the cart, leaving Bunner to secure the reins, and swaggered across the cobbles of Mercer's Yard. 'Bring out yer dead!' he called cheerfully. It was more likely that he and Bunner would have to break down doors to collect any corpses that remained after a whole family had perished, but he kept calling out anyway. It made him feel important.

Lights burned in a few windows. He knocked respectfully on the doors of those houses. A sobbing and wailing accompanied the opening of one door as the occupants pushed two shrouded forms into the yard. One woman had to be restrained by her husband from rushing out into the yard as the bodies of her two children were carried out onto the cobbles.

Lowering the scrap of filthy cloth that covered his mouth, Rufus gave her what he imagined was a sympathetic smile. 'God will keep the little uns, Missus,' he said gravely. Sometimes kind words earned him a few pence. This time none were forthcoming. He made a sound of disgust. Digging the hooked pole into the tiny bundles he dragged the corpses over to the cart and left them in a heap.

Four today in the yard. Not bad. But it was the buildings where all was dark that interested him the most. He had had his eyes on the mercer's shop for a few days. The coming of the pestilence was a godsend for a man like himself. Ordinarily he would be travelling the country, seeking work wherever he could find it. Winter always brought hardship. He had often been reduced to begging. This was the best employment he had ever had. St Bertrina's kept the tally of the deaths in the area, paying four pence for each corpse brought to Christian burial. Then there were the 'extras' to be had as long as he and Bunner avoided the watch. He recalled the previous night's work, grinning with satisfaction.

The wench who opened the door to them in Coster's Alley had been too terrified by their threats to refuse them anything. She was a sweet piece, no mistake. Rufus scratched at his groin, his penis thickening as he remembered how she had looked spread out on the dirty straw of the stable.

Her body was lush, her skin soft and white. When he had pulled down the basque her fat breasts had lolled free. He had pushed her skirt up above her waist and looked down between her sturdy thighs. She had a lot of hair on her coynte. He liked that and straight away thrust his fingers into the fragrant furrow, searching for her opening and laughing when she brought her thighs together to trap his finger. She whimpered when he pushed his knee between her legs and leaned his weight onto her.

'Wench don't seem too eager,' Bunner had chuckled, as Rufus fumbled with his belt. 'You is losing your touch!'

Rufus ignored him, his senses inflamed by the musky scent that rose from between the woman's legs. Grasping the shaft of his cock he positioned himself, then pushed into her in a single stroke, feeling the heat of her flesh enclose him. She was tight and dry and moaned with pain, but he thrust away at her until she loosened up. The look of fear on her face quickened him. He licked at the tears which had slid from the corners of her eyes. Lovely. He was excited by the way she tried to hide her pleasure. She must be liking it. All women were whores. Did not the church preach that women were slaves to their ungovernable desires? And he had a fine thick staff of Adam to punish her for the sins of Eve. He jabbed at her entrance, making her wince and slid his tongue across his filmed teeth as he ploughed a fine furrow.

She pleaded and wept, still pretending not to like it. He was impressed. It proved that she was no cheap wanton, but a decent soul. It would never have been possible for him to tup such a woman in normal times. She would have twitched her skirts aside as she passed him in the street. The sweat stood out on his forehead as he laboured inside her. It was soon over. He grunted as he came. Withdrawing his dripping cock he grabbed a handful of the woman's skirts and wiped himself. As he turned to go, she had spoken directly to him for the first time.

'You've had what you want. Now take my poor master out to your cart.' Her voice was frosty, but a bleak smile hovered around her mouth. 'May you rot in hell.'

He knew what she was thinking, the sickness was already apparent in her over-bright eyes. Silly bitch. He was armoured against the pestilence, having ensured his protection at the earliest convenience by queuing up at the nearest whore-house along with all the town's worthies. He grinned as he recalled the sight of the Reverend Harris standing in line with Flesher, Tyler, and Simkin – Captain of the Watch. He left the woman without a backward glance, leaving Bunner to drag her master's corpse out behind him.

Glancing around Mercer's Yard now, Rufus took a swig from a bottle of geneva in his pocket, feeling the satisfying warmth hit his stomach. Alcohol kept away the infection, as did the pox. Pushing his dirty red hair back from his forehead, he pulled up the scrap of cloth to cover his mouth and nose. He hammered loudly on the door of the mercer's shop. No answer. Good.

'Here Bunner, bring a flambeau,' he called, taking the jemmy from his other pocket. ' 'Tis dark and quiet within. Good pickings 'ere to be sure.'

Bunner came around the cart, holding the light aloft. He was a stooped man with grey hair and watery blue eyes. Like Rufus his clothes were covered by a ragged apron which bore a hell's patchwork of stains. Together they levered off the boards, the sound of screeching nails and splintering wood loud in the silence of the yard.

'Well, well. Would you lookee here,' Rufus said with satisfaction.

41

CHAPTER THREE

Rufus shouldered aside the door, which hung on shattered hinges. Even in the gloom he could see the many bolts of cloth, bobbins of lace and silk ribbons.

'God's bones, but it's rank in 'ere,' Bunner said, stepping into the darkness.

Rufus sniffed laconically and pushed past him to light the way. 'Bound to be. Shop's been boarded up fer well on a month.'

Picking their way through the shop they went into the back room. Bunner saw the bodies at once. Three of them, lying side by side, covered with a stained sheet. He gave them only a cursory glance, his eye caught by a movement in the shadows. 'Mercy, I reckon we found a live un,' he said, going over to investigate.

Rufus followed, eyes widening with interest. 'A wench is it? Has she her wits?'

A number of pleasant possibilities presented themselves. Those who had not yet been touched by the sickness were often moved to offer money or goods, so that the bearers would leave them and their property untouched. Or like the night before he might be inclined to demand other services. The woman sat on a couch, her arms crossed over her breasts, her head down. She rocked slowly back and forth. Her loose hair tumbled over her shoulders. She wore only a shift. The whiteness of her skin shone through the fine fabric.

Rufus's belly tightened with lust. No red-necked country lass this, but near-on a fine lady. Young too. Hardly more than a girl. Even better than yester eve. His cock twitched and stirred against his groin. He reached out to touch her. 'How now, pippin? How about rattling my ballocks fer me?' he said in his most charming voice. 'And then we'll see what ole Rufe can do fer you, eh?'

The girl looked up as if she noticed them for the first time. Her face was gaunt, her eyes unfocused. Wits have left her for certain, thought Rufus. No matter, he did not want to make converse with her. She need do nothing but open her legs and lie still. Didn't need no reasoning to do that. As he closed a hand on her arm she recoiled. 'Life in yer yet then, eh,' he grunted, plucking at her shift and lingering a moment to feel the fine fabric with its lace trim. 'I'll give you a portion more.' As he dragged the garment from her shoulder, the shift tore open to reveal her breasts. They were high and round, pert-looking. He smacked his lips. Nice. She was as soft and white as a nun.

'Please . . . leave me alone . . .' the girl murmured, her voice toneless.

Rufus ran a filth-encrusted palm over her breasts, fondling the tender nipples. They were as soft as silk, cool against her hot skin. The girl flinched away, trying to cover herself. He grabbed at her, holding her still while he pinched and stroked her breasts until the nipples tightened into buds. She was just like the other one, pretending she was pure and didn't want it. Well old Rufe wasn't fooled.

Bunner, who had been watching with interest, sniggered. He spat a gob of phlegm on the floor. 'Can't leave any of 'em be, Rufe? You randy beggar. This one's got the tokens on her. Good as dead she is. Pity. Mun 'ave been a beauty once.'

'Ain't bad now.' Rufus decided to have her anyway. 'Want to share her?'

Bunner shook his head, pushing his lank grey hair

43

behind his ears. 'Don't like the live uns. Do what thee want. I'll take these three stinkers outside.'

His needs were well catered for. He took his pleasure with corpses. It had been difficult to indulge his particular lust in normal times. But the pestilence had changed all that. Many of the young died with hardly a mark on them. He could do as he liked; stroke their cold limbs, rub his engorged cock against their dead flesh and push into tight, cold orifices. Rufus was more picky, he'd tried it Bunner's way and pronounced that 'It an't no fun swyvin' a cold oven. I like mine to move and moan a bit. All the better if they fight.'

The girl let out a strangled scream as Rufus pushed her back on the bed and began forcing open her closed thighs. Bunner yawned and turned his back. He grabbed hold of the feet of one of the corpses and yanked it off the bed. The head banged onto the floor with a hollow sound. The rushes crackled as he dragged it towards the passage way. There was a sound like a sigh as the putrid gasses escaped from the bloated flesh. Bunner blew out his breath, avoiding breathing the stench. A dirty black smear trailed all the way down the passage to the back room. Trust Rufus to leave the hard work to him, he thought with disgust. Then he heard the sound of a slap and a cry of pain and chuckled to himself. Ah, well, a man had to have his fun. It did not sound as if Rufus would take long.

Rufus's voice rose in a curse as the woman cried out. She had some fight left in her then, Bunner thought. Rufus would enjoy subduing her. Maybe he would stay and watch after all. He left the corpse lying in the narrow passage way and went back to lean against the door frame.

In the back room Rufus knelt beside the struggling girl, his filthy trews around his knees, his buttocks bare.

44

The torn shift was rucked up around the girl's waist, showing her flat belly, the floss of pale hair at her groin. As Rufus covered her, the girl writhed under him, long pale legs flailing helplessly. Rufus hit her again. She lay still, her cries subsiding to a whimper. He grunted as he fell onto her, jabbing around until he found her entrance.

'Lord, but she's dry,' he said, drawing away momentarily and flashing Bunner a grin. Rufus appreciated an audience. 'Better'n a mummers' play at Eastertide, this, eh Bunner?'

Spitting onto his palm he rubbed the spittle around his glans, then tried again. After a few more attempts he managed to breach the closure of her flesh. With a great thrust forward he rammed into her, burying his cock to the hilt. The girl's scream of agony was high-pitched, an animal sound. 'Lovely. A virgin,' Rufus said, his buttocks pumping back and forth as he leaned on her upper arms.

Despite his earlier lack of interest, Bunner began to get aroused. He was used to Rufus's brutality, was unmoved by it, but the way the young woman lay there, so white and still, her pale limbs spread out in disorder, reminded him of a corpse.

Rufus gave a hoarse moan and lunged forward. Bending his head he bit down hard on one breast. His buttocks clenched a final time. Groaning, he spilt his seed. After a moment he pulled away. He laughed when he looked down and saw the maiden blood that smeared his cock.

The woman lay still, her legs open wide. All the fight had gone out of her. One side of her face was swollen and discoloured. Tears streaked her cheeks. The livid bite mark on one breast oozed dark blood. Bruises showed on her shoulders and upper arms. Bunner could not look away from the joining of her thighs, from her poor, abused coynte. How tender it had looked with that floss of pale hair, the neat, pinkish folds. Now the sex looked raw and puffy, streaked with blood and semen. Rufe had torn her up a bit as he took her maidenhead. Poor little lass. She had been pure. Now she was spoiled.

Something dark and formless rose up in Bunner. Suddenly his cock was heavy against his thigh. Desire pulsed and twitched inside him. It was as if all of his vitality was centred in his groin. He felt faint with the pleasure of it and pressed his hand to his cock. Rarely these days did he feel young or energetic. Approaching the bed he leaned down and thrust his hand between the girl's thighs, staining his finger with her blood and Rufus's slick emission. Fumbling at his belt, he opened his trews. His erect penis sprang free. Rufus would be impressed. By God, *he* was impressed. Getting up onto the bed, he knelt between the spread thighs. Grasping her behind the knees, he eased her open, his breath coming fast and shallow. She parted beneath him like a bruised fruit.

'No . . . no more . . .' she murmured, struggling weakly. 'It hurts. Have pity.'

'Go on, Bunner. Give it to her,' Rufus chuckled, coming to stand beside the bed. 'Stoke a live un fer a change.'

Bunner pressed inwards, holding his breath as the bruised passage enfolded him as firmly as a fist. He shivered with the pleasure of it. God it felt good. He felt powerful, potent, effectual. The woman shuddered and sobbed.

'That's it,' Rufus laughed, shouting encouragement as Bunner bent the woman's legs into her chest. 'Tip her up. It's sweeter that way. Give her sommat to remember yer by!'

Bunner's breath came in short bursts as he laboured, pulling almost all the way out of the girl before plunging back in. 'Oh, Lord,' he grunted, sweating. 'Oh, Lord.'

Rufus felt himself growing hard again as he watched Bunner's skinny arse bobbing up and down. He hadn't realized that grizzled old Bunner had so much juice left in him. It was not long before Bunner shuddered and groaned, his fingers digging into the soft, white flesh of the girl's thighs as he came.

Rufus moved forward, licking his lips eagerly. 'Here Bunner, get off. Help me turn her over. Watchin' you has got me all hot. I'll have her again. Kick them other two corpses on the floor. The stink's puttin' me orf.'

Bunner put his clothes to rights, then obliged. The body of the old man thudded onto the rushes. He looked over his shoulder to see that Rufus was holding the girl down by sitting on the back of her thighs, his thick fingers probing between her buttocks. He grinned and shrugged. Dirty young beggar! Ah, well, might as well make a start on the corpses. Rufus looked like he would be no help for a while yet.

Rufus groaned, his eyes closed with pleasure, preparing to force himself into the girl a second time. Leaning forward he balanced himself on his hands. He bunched his muscles. Just then the girl twisted violently. A choking sound came from her. A stream of black vomit poured from her mouth, splashing onto one of Rufus's hands.

Bunner laughed hugely as Rufus cursed and scraped his fouled hand down the side of his apron, using the woman's hair to wipe the filth from his sleeve. 'Serve thee right thee randy bugger!' he said, wiping away tears of laughter.

Rufus gave a snort of disgust, his brutish young face flushing under the freckles. He thrust viciously between the woman's buttocks, but his cock had wilted. Angry that she had robbed him of his pleasure, he slapped her hard and shoved her off the bed. She rolled face down onto the frowsty rushes and lay still. Rufus got up and adjusted his clothing, looking down at the crumpled figure. The woman turned over, her body jerking in a convulsion. Her eyes had rolled back to show the whites. Rufus aimed a kick at her head, missed and kicked out again, his foot connecting with her ribs.

'Come on, Rufe. Lend a bleedin' hand will yer,' Bunner called out irritably, dragging a corpse up the narrow passageway. 'Ain't you finished yet? Leave orf playin' with er now.'

Gawd, but this one stank something awful. Black fluid was leaking through the sheet like steam off a boiled leek pudding. Good thing it was winter. Had it been hot weather there would have been swarms of flies. Rufus gave the woman a final nudge with his toe, then let her be. Cursing under his breath he went to help Bunner. Grunting and complaining the two men man-handled the sheet-wrapped bundles out of the front door.

Behind then Garnetta raised her head. Her whole body was a map of pain and soreness. She felt somehow removed from it. Everything was all mixed up. The fever raging in her blood warped her vision. She could see, far off down the passageway, a square of night sky. It was blue-black, pricked with stars. Beautiful. For a moment she was almost lucid. The clean night air blew into the shop, thinning the stench of sickness and death.

In a moment Rufus came back into the shop. He began pulling bolts of cloth from the shelves. 'Look'ee here,' he said to Bunner, smoothing a filthy hand over the silks, the embossed brocades, frosted laces and murry velvets. 'Should furnish us with a pretty penny, eh? There's too much to carry though. Cart'll be about full when we get this lot aboard.'

Bunner nodded sagely. 'We mun come back after we unload at the pit. Best nail up the door again, lest some others come lookin' fer pickings.'

Both men turned at the sound of rustling. Bunner's mouth dropped open in astonishment. Rufus slapped his thigh. 'Blast my lights! Would yer look at that. The wench's crawlin' t'wards the door. Where you think you're goin' then?' He bent down and grabbed a handful of her hair.

'Oh, do leave orf baitin' the wench, Rufe. Let's get on now. I got a supper of ale and oysters waitin' on me.'

Rufus let go of Garnetta. Together they went out into the yard, picked up the pile of corpses by their wrists and ankles and swung them up onto the cart. As they worked their breath fanned out on the cold air. The sound of their nailed boots was loud in the silent yard. Frost gleamed on the cobblestones. When the last body had been thrown onto the cart Rufus jumped aboard. He pushed and kicked the corpses into a more solid pile. Jumping down he rejoined Bunner who was blowing onto his fingers to warm them.

'What's to do about this un?' Rufus said, indicating Garnetta who lay sprawled across the threshold.

Bunner shrugged, his belly growling with hunger. All he could think about was the plate of oysters and the blazing fire he would sit by to eat them. 'She's near dead. Won't last long in this cold anyways. Throw her up with the others.'

As they swung her into the air, Garnetta revived enough to struggle weakly. She moaned once when she landed on the cold hard flesh, then was still.

★

The smell of freshly dug earth filled Garnetta's nostrils. There was a fainter smell underlying it, cloying, sickening, which she did not at first recognize.

Cold. Bone-freezing, all encompassing, it ate into her. She was shivering so badly that she could hear her teeth chattering. She lay flat on her back, unable to move. Everything hurt. For a while she drifted in and out of consciousness, her mind fuzzy and unfocused. Then all in a rush, she remembered everything; the pestilence, the weeks of enforced isolation, the men breaking into the shop and abusing her. Oh dear God. Jessy, Sellice, Father – gone. All of them dead. She was alone. But where?

Something hard pressed into her side. It was the jutting hip of the body beneath her. A cross-hatch of bleached limbs supported her lower body. Gradually she became aware that the back of her hand was pressed to the cheek of an old woman, her skin discoloured by purple-black blotches. A child's head, achingly small, was pressed into her shoulder. Turning her head she saw that all around her were piled corpses; hundreds of them, a uniform grey in colour, their eyes sightless. The old lay side by side with the young. A mother clasped her dead babe to her breast, her ravaged face peaceful in death. Others had been food for the crows. Through gaping wounds, teeth, shreds of entrails, and bone were visible.

Garnetta shrank from the dead faces. The expressions of purest agony echoed the visions of purgatory displayed on the placards of the brothers of the Holy Penitence. A rime of frost, like flour, lay over everything making the dead look as if they had been sugared for some ghastly celebration. *I'm in a death pit. But I'm alive. I don't belong here.* This was some dreadful macabre joke. She felt the urge to laugh and laugh, but knew that if she began she might never stop. *Have to get out*. The smell of corruption seemed to seep into her. Her gorge rose. With a groan of horror she wrenched her hand free, hardly feeling the skin tear away as it separated from the old woman's frozen face.

She tried to sit up and found that she had to tug at her shift to free it – it too had frozen to the bodies lying beneath her. Pushing and kicking at the corpses with her bare feet, she worked her fingers in underneath them, scrabbling to pull herself loose. The dead flesh was as hard as stone. The faces stared at her as if in reproach. Thank God she could see no sign of her father or sisters. They must have been thrown in first and other bodies tipped on top of them. Her lips moved in the words of a prayer as she scraped and dug, frantic to be free and away from this golgotha.

Her fingers were sore and bleeding by the time she had torn her shift free. Sobbing with reaction as well as from the pain and cold, she clambered over the piled bodies, elbows and knees jamming and sliding against the frozen flesh. She fell more than once. Finally she reached the edge of the pit. Above her head the sloping earth gave way to sky. The pit was almost full. It was easy enough to climb out of it. Lying on the grass, she gathered her strength.

Someone would surely find her. Grave-diggers would come along soon, bringing lime to sprinkle on the corpses, it being impossible to shovel the frozen earth over them. Weekly services were held for the dead, the priests saying prayers over mass graves. A priest would help her to a warm bed, soothe her burning throat with a hot posset, put a healing unguent on her wounds. *Please. Someone come. I can't bear this*. But no one came. In a while she raised her head and looked around.

The light was thick and grainy. Shapes of bushes and

trees loomed out at her. There were no flares of light in the gloom, no rumble of cartwheels, no sign of anything moving at all. Where was the shadowy bulk of the church tower, the sound of bells tolling? She was alone with the dead in some Godforsaken, unhallowed field. No one would help her. She had not the strength nor the will to help herself. How easy it would be to just close her eyes.

Then she remembered that there must be other corpses to dispose of, many of them. The bearers who had cast her into the death pit would be coming back. Fear of what they would do if they found her there gave her the impetus to move. On her hands and knees, her teeth clamped down on the pain in her lower belly, she began crawling forward. The frozen mud, rutted by cart tracks, made it difficult to make headway. The back of one hand hurt. She glanced at it, surprised to see that it was raw and bleeding. Ignoring the minor discomfort, she kept moving, dragging herself forward.

There were no landmarks by which she could get her bearings. She could be anywhere. A wave of dizziness came over her. She pressed her face to the grass. Why bother to go on? There was nothing left to live for. The pestilence raged in her body, only the heat of the fever stopped her freezing to death. Another failure by default for St Pernel, she thought. No one had helped her or her family, not God, not his saints. Had they all been so wicked? Had she?

She could not think. She was so tired. The temptation to stop moving and go to sleep was strong. Yet something impelled her to move. Someone should be told about what had happened to her family. The bearers must be brought to justice. She felt a surge of hatred for her abusers and would-be murderers. She would have revenge. *Oh, Jessy, Sellice, father – I'll make sure you're not forgotten.*

Her hands touched a wooden post. She used it as a support to pull herself upright, the breath rasping in her lungs. Her throat burned like fire. She retched weakly, spitting out a gob of stringy black vomit. Somehow she moved forward. It was easier now that she was on her feet. A slow, warm trickle snaked down her thighs. Blood, she thought with detachment. At least that proves I'm alive. Shakily at first, then with grim resolve, she began walking.

Karolan bent his head to navigate the low-hanging branches, urging Darkus along the forest path. Thickly carpeted frozen leaves rustled against the delicately placed hooves. The horse's breath blew out into a cloud in the crisp air. Karolan patted the high-arched neck affectionately as the palfrey champed at the bit. 'Impatient to be out in the open fields, Darkus? Don't you know that patience is a virtue?'

His sculpted mouth curved in self-mockery. Aye, a virtue he did not possess, it had been forced upon him by circumstance. There was a rustling in the trees away to his right. The Fetch was keeping pace with him. He deliberately ignored it, wanting nothing to spoil the pleasure of the early morning ride.

In a few moments he sensed that the spirit had fled into the forest, off seeking emanations of negative energy to replenish itself. From long practice, Karolan detected the subtle signs which had attracted the Fetch. Far off in the distance he caught a single flash of a reddish coat. Moments before he smelt the fox he picked up the hectic ticking of a vulpine heart. Slowing the rate of his breathing he emptied his mind, re-attuning it to the faster cycles of life inhabited by the animal world.

Sometimes he could gain an impression of an animal's thoughts – as with Darkus – but more often it was simply a sense of urgency, of survival. Animals lived short, intense, hot lives. Instinct was their caretaker. They had no need of reason. An enviable state.

Some way farther on he sensed the panicked, blood-heat of rabbits as they dived into their burrows. He caught the calmer essence of the older, experienced males who sat up on their hind legs, drumming a warning. The Fetch could never resist the chance to gorge on the violence as an animal moved in for its kill. How it would chitter and caper with the pleasure of blood-lust as the fox ripped into a still-warm underbelly, its blood-ied snout nosing into the steaming, pulsing entrails.

He felt no disgust any more, only acceptance. There was little difference between them. He and the Fetch were both predators, the spirit at least partly what he had made it. Useless to dwell on what could not be changed. Better by far to think of what waited in the laboratorium. As he urged Darkus along the path which led out of a clump of rowan, he felt the stirring of excitement and hope.

Another breakthrough had been reached. The 'seed' had come to term. Even if that was only the first step in a complicated chain of events, it was farther than he had come for a very long time. In his mind's eye he saw the ledger, spread open on his workbench.

Seventh day of Christ Mass. After many months of constant heat the prima materia is undergoing another change. Have added more of my own personal essence at regular intervals, corresponding with phases of the moon. The purpling is at hand!

Sennight after the Feast of St Valentine. It is done. This morning I discovered the colouring of the rubedo in the alembic vessel. The prima materia has transmuted. In the vessel is the 'seed': that which is a microcosm of the majestic process of creation.

A few lines only – hardly enough to express his feeling of triumph and joy. Now he was ready to try the experiment again. He dismissed past failures. Then he had simply chosen unwisely. The human host had to be strong in mind and body as the process was rigorous, depleting. The need for secrecy meant that he could only conduct his experiments upon the poorest, weakest, most easily dispensable souls. What he needed was someone of singular strength and intelligence – someone who might eventually become a fitting companion.

But there was another element involved. It was not enough to simply procure a healthy man or woman and subject them to the process. Something within the very make-up of humankind refused to encompass the bodily changes. At the most basic level, human flesh and spirit shrank from embracing the invasive power of the alien substance, preferring death to ultimate deliverance.

How furious that had made him. And how full of despair. The terrified faces of the dead haunted him. None of them had understood what he offered them. All the deaths – so perverse and wasteful. Sometimes he had seen the glimmer of a way forward, but the white-hot power of the 'seed', the danger of the ritual, the involvement of the Fetch, all had combined to terrify the host or to burn out his or her humanity entirely, leaving behind only a mindless husk. Then came the messy and distressing process of consigning the ruin to the furnace.

It sickened him to play God. But then *he* had been given no choice either. God had allowed the thing to happen to him and now he lived on, inviolate, unpunished for his many sins – unless God thought that the form of his existence was in itself punishment enough. Karolan clenched his fist and struck the palm of his other hand. He *knew* with every fibre of his being that the changeover into a new existence could be reproduced. He was the living testament to that fact.

He sighed deeply, wondering if he would ever succeed. Generations had passed him by; still he had no answers. Was his punishment for cheating God and the Devil to be to walk the earth alone for ever? His mind rebelled against such a proscription. As an alchemist he had faith in science and natural order. Male energy in itself was a potent force, but he needed the deeper, darker power of a female counterpart before he could grow and develop further. Where his was the power of the sun, hers would be the power of the moon. Sol and Luna. Adam and Eve. The elemental fire and ice. The King and Queen – united in the mystic marriage of conjunctio. More simply – as a man he yearned for companionship.

Dragging his mind back to the beauty of the morning, he looked out across the frozen landscape. The palfrey's muscles moved under him. He felt the rhythm of its blood, the strong, noble pulse of its heart. Scenting the frozen river and flats of the water meadow, Darkus snorted with pleasure. Karolan gave the horse his head, leaning forward, taking deep breaths so that the freezing air stung his nostrils. One of his greatest pleasures was to ride. He loved to feel the horse's powerful muscles bunching and releasing. As he stood up in the stirrups, matching his movements to Darkus's, his long black hair streamed out behind him. His face, set in lines of concentration resembled that of a bird of prey.

The countryside sped by, a bleak landscape of half tones and grey shadows, stitched at intervals with the skeletal shapes of trees and bushes. Despite the fact that it was so cold that the birds had frozen upon the branches in the night, he wore only an open-necked, linen shirt beneath his doublet of padded black leather. Breeches of fine, figured velvet clothed his long legs. Black riding boots reached to his knees. No weapon hung at his waist – he had no need of one. Clods of frozen soil flew up under Darkus's hooves. The horse's sides heaved with exertion as he tore at full gallop across the open fields. They rode for some time, man in union with his mount, the clarity of the morning pure and elemental. Karolan felt his spirits rise as his soul flew free. At such moments he could almost imagine that he was as other men.

In a while they reached the tall hedge of pleached limes which marked the limits of the Rakka estate. Karolan drew Darkus to a halt and eased back in the saddle. While the horse stamped and puffed he rested one arm on the pommel, looking out beyond the patchwork of fields to Chatesbrook. Within the town walls were the three spires of St Ralphit's, St Bertrina's, and St Kate's-in-the-Meadow. Off to one side he could see the great square tower, topped with the ruby heart of humility, which marked out the monastery of Holy Penitence. His lip curled. He detested the fanaticism of the white monks.

Clicking his tongue to Darkus, he turned the horse around and cantered back along the boundary. He intended to ride back through the forest and approach the house by way of the ornamental garden. Even in the grip of winter he found pleasure in the sculptural shapes of the walnut and mulberry trees, the trained roses, the box hedges. The wicker hen-coops and the beehives of woven straw, which were kept free of snow, were reminders that not all life was subject to the cold.

Karolan's sharp eyes caught a movement through the trees. He heard the shriek before a sparrow hawk rose with its prey struggling weakly in its pitiless claws. No doubt the Fetch was again nearby, guzzling down sensual nourishment. He was so engrossed in his thoughts that he was taken by surprise when Darkus shied at an obstacle on the path. Only his unusually sharp reflexes saved him from being unseated. He sawed at the reins. 'Steady on, boy. What's amiss?'

As the horse danced sideways, nostrils flaring with alarm, Karolan saw the crumpled form on the path. It was the half-clothed body of a woman. She lay still, so thin and pale that she seemed to be dead. He detected the faint glimmer of her life-force. It was as fitful as a candle flame in the wind, but strong for all that. Dismounting swiftly, he knelt beside her, already running a practised eye over her for injuries.

Her limbs were blue with cold, the tips of her toes and fingers turning black. He cursed under his breath. She must have lain there for hours. There was blood on her feet and her hands. He saw how her nails were torn. How far had she crawled? The stained and ragged shift clung to her body, outlining the angle of a hip bone, the rack of her ribcage. He could see that she was no peasant woman. Her hands were slender and shapely; there were no calluses across the palms. Her feet too were soft, the soles unmarked by thickened skin. She had worn shoes all her life. Under the stains of blood and vomit, her shift was trimmed with lace. Her skin had the greyish cast of those who were near to death. Only her hair seemed vital, spilling like a golden shawl over the rusty bracken beside the path. Lying across her cheek, it masked her face from view.

Gently he reached out, slipped his fingers behind the delicate neck, lifted her head. She was as lovely as an angel, her bruised features small and clear-cut. He wondered what colour her eyes were. The side of her face was swollen, her lip split. The smell emanating from her was heavy with decay, dried blood, and the flatter scent of stale semen. Someone had beaten and raped her. He felt a surge of murderous anger against her assailant. What coward would treat a sick woman like that?

With gentle fingers he examined her wounds. They were not severe, but her breath was ragged. The pulse at her throat was shallow, thready beneath his fingers. He need examine her no further to know that she had the pestilence. It would be a kindness to put her out of her misery. He had only to tighten his powerful fingers and give a sharp twist. She had but a little neck. He had carried out such killings before, and others besides that were less merciful, but he felt an odd reluctance to snuff out her life.

Perhaps it was her beauty or the sense of tragedy that he perceived hanging over her – or perhaps he felt only curiosity. Whatever it was, he came to a decision. He needed a host. Surely the fates had lain her in his path? She would die anyway if he left her there. The hope of success was slim indeed, but still he felt compelled to try. Everything was ready in the laboratorium. The Fetch added the one component he could not supply. Silently he called out to the spirit. Instantly it was beside him, eager to serve. The ragged shadow shape of it thrummed and pulsated as it hovered over the sick woman. Its licorice smell was strong.

'Is she for us, Master?' it whispered excitedly. 'Ah, much pain. Lovely pain.'

Karolan's mind ranged over the complexities of the coming ritual. The necessary elements must be assembled at once. He must not allow himself to even think of failure. 'Hades,' he murmured aloud, 'let me be in time.' Shrugging off his leather doublet, he covered the woman with it. Lifting her in his arms, he stood up.

She weighed very little. He could feel the chill of her skin through his tunic. Darkus whickered nervously, lifting his head as Karolan approached with his burden. The horse smelt death on her.

'Hush,' Karolan said, making a calming gesture. 'You need not fear our guest. Stand easy now.'

Darkus stood still obediently, a tremor passing over his glossy black hide as Karolan mounted. There was a shifting movement near his shoulder, an infolding of the air. He knew that the Fetch was trying to flow through the woman, attracted by the dark streaks of suffering in her aura. The smell of sickness, coupled with the trace residues of violence and sex that hung about her, was a potent lure to the spirit. In her weakened state, any further draining of her life source would be enough to snuff out her spark completely.

'Leave her!' he thundered, gesturing towards the Fetch.

With a terrified squawk it leapt backwards, its reedy treble floating into the air. 'Forgive, Master. Forgive.'

The ragged shadow of its form flickered briefly over horse and rider. Karolan felt the hot, harmless tingling which meant that the Fetch had passed through him. He sensed the appetite beneath its desire to please. There was a faint glow around it, giving it a wispy form like silver smoke. 'Pretty, pretty. Is she for us?' it twittered next to his ear. 'Like her I do. Want her. Shall we make her ours?'

'Be silent,' Karolan said, irritated by its single-mindedness. The Fetch thought only of its own gratification, but he knew that it did no good to get angry.

As he urged Darkus forward with his knees, he looked down into the woman's gaunt face. It was difficult to tell her age, but he guessed her years to be less than a score. At that moment her eyes fluttered open, fastened on his face. Involuntarily he drew back, expecting her to show fear or recoil in horror. She did neither. Instead she looked at him calmly.

'Are you death?' the woman whispered, her voice sounding rusty, unused.

He smiled wryly. 'Not for you.' At least, he hoped not.

Her eyes were a clear blue. Beautiful. He watched the spark of awareness in them fade, before they rolled back in her head. Suddenly she stiffened, began to shake with convulsions. Her jaw clenched. Blood welled at the corner of her mouth. She had bitten through her tongue. Blood trickled down her chin and dripped onto Karolan's hand. It looked as bright as a holly berry against his white skin.

He cursed softly, holding her close against his strong warm body. It seemed impossible that she could survive. He tried to catch a hold on her thoughts, to compel her to live by his will alone, but she slipped away from him into a dark place where there are no boundaries beyond pain and grief and he could not follow. At his urging Darkus galloped like the wind, Karolan gripping the horse's sides with his powerful thighs, using both hands to balance his burden. His whole concentration was centred on getting the woman back to his house. It had suddenly become vitally important to save *this* woman.

'Hold on,' he murmured, blocking out the sound of the Fetch's incessant questioning. 'Just hold on a bit longer. Live damn you. Do you hear me? You *must* live.'

CHAPTER FOUR

Darkus slewed to a halt in front of the stables, Karolan leaping down the moment the horse stopped. At this hour of the day the stable lad was exercising the other horses. Karolan was able to lead the palfrey into a stall and leave the building without being seen.

If anyone realized that he had brought the pestilence amongst them it would start a panic. Also, should the woman die, he would need to dispose of the body discreetly. Just then she stirred against him, moaning weakly. Placing a gentle hand on her head he cupped the back of her skull. Her life signs were faint. He had to search for traces of them. The seizure had sapped her strength. It was obvious that she was dying. 'No,' he said through gritted teeth as he quickened his step. 'I refuse to give you up.'

Holding her close he hurried across the cobbled courtyard and through the wooden gate which gave onto the garden. As he passed the squat kitchen building, the noise of clanging pots and pans and the raised voice of the cook reached him through an open window. There was no one outside in the yard. He went past the main hall, entering his tower directly by the outside door. Despite taking the stairs two at a time, he was not even breathing fast when he reached the topmost room.

Once inside, he laid her gently on his bed. She looked so fragile against the silken pillows. Her face had the young-old look of those on the brink of death. The Fetch hovered over the bed, its spirit form fainter now. It was losing interest in the emanations of her suffering and, seeing that, Karolan experienced a jolt of alarm.

'Too late, Master,' the Fetch said peevishly. 'No pain left. No pleasure. Empty she will be soon. Lost to us.'

'It's not too late,' Karolan snapped, using his trained voice almost unconsciously. 'Do as I say, now.' Averting his eyes from the girl's thin chest which hardly moved as each painful breath was forced into her lungs, he said to the spirit, 'When I give you the word, you will obey me on the instant.'

Reluctantly the Fetch complied. Grey and purple streaks swirled in the shadows of its form. If he had not been so fearful for the girl's life, he might have laughed. The spirit was so obviously sulking. When he spoke to it in the voice of power it had no choice but to do his bidding. That was one positive aspect of their unholy alliance. Joined on a level beyond the physical they might be, but in Karolan's dimension the Fetch's strength and influence were limited.

Bending close, Karolan searched for the signs of life in the girl. There was the faintest movement of a pulse in the side of her neck. Lifting the thin arm he exposed the hard black swelling of the blaine which bulged from her armpit. The blaine was an ugly thing, like the back of some submerged beetle. The skin covering it was stretched and shiny. This was the site of the infection. Without hesitation he bent down, covering the swelling with his mouth. Biting hard, he pierced the skin. A rush of tainted matter flowed onto his tongue. His gorge rose at the thick, gamey taste of it, but he sucked hard, draining the pus and swallowing it.

The woman writhed, churning under him, too weak to scream, but still fighting. A thin noise, like the sound of a terrified rabbit, bubbled up in her throat. Karolan felt a flicker of hope. She had a strong will to live. Good. She was going to need every last measure of that tenacity. Handling her as gently as possible he stripped off

63

her ruined shift. Then he held her down easily, while he repeated the process of draining the other swellings at the armpit and groin. Choking on the foul taste he drew back to survey his work. A trickle of stinking black pus ran down one thigh. The bite marks in the blaines leaked sluggish dark blood.

As he bent to lick away the pus and to spread his caustic saliva on her raw wounds, his cheek brushed against the scant fleece of her pubic hair. Even through the stench of sickness, the staleness of dried blood and sperm, he caught the personal odour of her sex. Her own scent was fresh, sweetly musky, clean. He combed the soft fair curls with his fingertips, brushing away the flecks of filth that coated them, smoothing the hair back over her neat slit. Poor abused little wench.

The rush of tenderness and desire he felt was shocking in its intensity, all the more so for being inappropriate. He had never experienced anything like it. He felt aroused and excited, hopeful too, yet somehow guilty and full of compassion for her. It was guilt and compassion which was new to him. Trembling he pushed the emotions away, submerging them beneath his sense of purpose. Every shred of his concentration, all his acquired skills might not be enough to save her. He could not afford any distractions. There would be time enough to examine his own thoughts later.

The punctures he had made in the blaines, and then cauterized, were closing up. He had drained the main sites of infection and she was still alive – if only just. There was no more time for preparations. He must act on instinct alone. Scooping her up, he carried her towards the trapdoor. The Fetch was waiting in the laboratorium, no longer sulking but eager for the part it must play. Even as he worked, laying the girl on top of his work bench, assembling the vials and jars he would need, Karolan began emptying his mind, performing the mental rituals which would prepare him for the ordeal to come.

This work held danger for him. In the past he had almost been drawn down into the darkness along with his victim. The death force exerted a powerful pull on the unwary. Without the help of the Fetch, a creature who could cross the barriers between the material and astral worlds, there would be no hope of saving the woman. As soon as he had administered the potion containing the mixture of poisons, the Fetch must enter the woman's body, holding her together body and soul, until the 'seed' could do its work of transmutation.

The crucial matter now was to obtain the girl's permission for the possession. Without that, the Fetch would be unable to do more than skitter around outside her skin, weaving in and out through her aura. It was imperative for the success of the process for the Fetch to enter her completely, melding at the physical level of bone and blood, possessing her essential etheric body. The only way that might be accomplished was to trick the girl into agreeing to the unholy coupling. As I was tricked, Karolan thought wryly, all those long years ago.

He picked up a glass vial, swirling it around to mix up the contents. The potion contained henbane, belladonna, mandragora and a number of rare tropical poisons. Tipping up the girl's head, he poured the liquid between her lips. She gagged, choking, but swallowed a little. It was enough. He sensed the slowing down of her heartbeat, the deep, steady beating of her pulse. She was no longer trembling on the brink of death, but held somewhere between in a dimension that traversed the two states. For a brief time the poisons would regulate the tides of her body.

'Now,' Karolan said urgently to the Fetch. 'Do whatever you must.'

'As you wish, Master,' the Fetch purred, flecks of gold and silver dancing in the smoky realms of its form.

Karolan watched the spirit, sensing rather than seeing it transform itself into a column of light. Somehow it knew what shape to assume to appeal to a given individual. It always knew. Even in the beginning, with himself, it knew how to seduce him. Later, when jointly they performed the countless abortive rituals, it exhibited the knack of appearing as a pleasing image to each individual. Sometimes it made itself gentle, sometimes wise, sometimes beautiful and seductive. At other times it appeared as a fiery messenger. How wise it had become in the ways of humankind. Long association with himself had made it ever more wily, its hunger more sharp-edged.

Karolan felt a vague sense of alarm as the Fetch approached the girl, its softly glowing arms held wide. The benevolent features, formed of planes of light and shadow, shifted into a tender smile. How innocent, how saintly, were the deep-set eyes. 'Take care with this one,' he found himself saying. 'She is special. I sense it.'

'Yes, Master,' the Fetch said, its voice sibilant, fawning. 'When did I not do your bidding? Trust in me. Want her too do I.'

Karolan could hardly suppress a shudder. What did the Fetch know or care of trust? Even now he found it disquieting to see the love and fascination which the spirit felt for human flesh. Part of him was revolted by its hunger, its constant bargaining and offers of sexual favours. It had a dreadful, gnawing need to experience the world of matter. Its whole existence was centred on its desire to become corporeal. But Karolan did not judge it too harshly. He could never forget that he owed his life – whatever it had become – to the Fetch.

Now this girl must be wooed by trickery to give away part of what made her human. The bargain was that she gave something of her living flesh to the Fetch and it gave her part of its spirit back. That was the price of longevity, but she would not know that she had made the transaction until it was too late to change anything. Would she hate him, Karolan mused, once she knew what she had gained – and lost? For she would never be able to enjoy physical love with another human; not without taking a life. It was already too late for regrets or compassion. This way she had a chance to live. Later she would either thank him or curse him.

Karolan looked down at the pale, small-featured face with its look of shuttered pain. Her long fair hair was bunched under her, cushioning her fragile skull. Her deep eyelids were fretted with purple veins. He remembered that her eyes were blue. Saxon colouring. It was unusual to see it in its purest form. Long ago he had been fair of hair, blue eyed, his colouring causing much comment amongst his olive-skinned Norman kin. It was a pity that the girl must lose her yellow hair and blue eyes.

He watched her intently, concentrating on the play of emotions across her face. What pretty dreams and images was the Fetch imprinting on her mind? The girl's wasted features relaxed. Her lips moved. One of her hands twitched, as if she would reach out, but she had not the strength to lift her arm. Although she made no sound, she shaped the word. Yes.

It was enough. The Fetch entered her. She screamed and threw back her head, her throat stretching, the cords standing out on her neck. A golden flush spread over her skin as if she had been lit with candles from the inside. Karolan clenched his hands into fists. He hardly dared to breathe. The final process had begun. Picking up the alembic vessel, he tipped out the scrap of reddish waxy substance, kneading the 'seed' between finger and thumb. Grasping the girl's jaw he placed the 'seed' on her tongue.

'Do your work within this form Celestial Child,' he said aloud, while in his mind he repeated the words of power and protective mantras. 'Do your work and give this young woman the gift of longevity.' Then he gripped her hands, joining his mind with hers, careful to keep himself above the level of the dark chasm which was waiting, waiting, to drag them all down into oblivion.

Garnetta was aware only of heat and pain. Pain within her, burrowing into her vitals. It was unbearable, as if she was being disassembled. A long way off a woman was moaning. Her throat ached abominably. Sound rattled up through her dry lips. *It is me who screams*. Was this Purgatory then? She must be burning in the flames, consumed for her sins, whilst demons tore at her flesh with hot pincers. She saw her sisters stretched on the rack of the pestilence, their eyes wide open. Black filth caking their mouths. Her father writhed on fouled sheets, choking to death with a look of bewilderment on his mild, sad face. The white monks of Holy Penitence preached the truth then. Death was this endless torment, this reliving of pain and sorrow, over and over again for all eternity.

A light pierced the darkness; a tall column, beautiful and bringing with it a feeling of calm and deliverance. Within the light she saw a human form. An angel. She reached out towards the noble face, hands extended in supplication. In her head was a voice. It was soft, so soothing, but strong too. She could not resist the pull of it. *Do you repent? Will you let me in? Only let me in and I shall grant you forgiveness and bring peace to your troubled soul.*

Her lips moved. 'Yes. Oh, yes.' Tears started from her eyes. Peace was what she craved. Blessed peace. An end to suffering. Just to sleep for ever and forget. God, who had forsaken her, was pledging to deliver her from this torment. She opened herself, body and heart to His angelic messenger.

At once she felt a great pressure. There was a hot tingling over her entire body. More pain as something slipped over her tongue, burned a path down her throat. Her skull felt as if it would burst open. Something pressed against her skin from the inside. Her eyes bulged. There was a coiling in her veins, squirming threads spread down her throat, into her stomach. The same invasive touch entered her between the legs, seeking out her bowels and bladder. Her womb pulsed and bucked as it too was plundered. The horror of it was too much to bear. Everything turned black.

Some time later, a long time, she surfaced from the pit. There was a presence beside her. A tall shape, which brought with it a scent of something subtle and mysterious. She smelt spikenard and musk. Gentle hands wiped her hot face with cool, wet cloths that smelt of herbs. For a moment the nightmare vision of the death pit rushed in on her. The memory of agony pushed at the edges of her consciousness, but it all seemed so far away. The tall figure spoke. A deep, male voice soothed away her terrors. It was a beautiful voice, smooth and cultured with the barest trace of an accent. The tones of it fell on her like something tangible, bringing peace in its wake. She relaxed again, slept for long hours, surfacing into a sort of waking-dream, where the world had narrowed to the comfort of a warm chamber and a soft dry bed.

She was unaware of time passing while she tossed and turned in the grip of a fever. Days and nights slipped past in a fog of disorder. The whole surface of her skin ached, even the roots of her hair felt sensitive. If she was hurting, that meant that she was alive. Everything became clear. Pain and suffering were states of being. Death was the void – an icy blackness where all feeling, all vitality was leached away. From far away a bright light beckoned to her. In the heart of the light was a crimson glow. It pulsed and throbbed with vibrancy. She went slowly towards the light, half in fear, half in longing. The crimson glow grew brighter, surrounded her. She knew finally, that death had rejected her.

It was night when she first opened her eyes to find herself in a chamber. The darkness flickered, pricked by candle-light, warmed by a fire in the wall hearth. There was the sound of logs crackling, the scent of apple-wood burning. Rushes whispered as someone walked across the chamber. Too weak to do more than turn her head she saw a shadow pass before the hearth. The now familiar dark figure bent over her. She saw the man's face clearly for the first time. The firelight made the beautiful, angular face into a mummer's mask. His eyes were deep-set, strange looking, the irises grey and reflective like metal.

Garnetta coughed. Her throat felt as if someone had poured sand into it. 'Water. I beg you,' she croaked, her tongue cleaving to the roof of her mouth.

The figure bent close to lift her head and place the rim of a goblet against her lips. His doublet was of mulberry velvet. A tress of his long black hair fell forward, brushing against her hand. She gulped at the fluid as it trickled between her lips. The drink tasted of herbs and wine and left a bitter aftertaste. Her mind was still fuzzy. It seemed that the man had a halo of light around his dark head. She realized that it was the light from the fire in the background which had formed the illusion. He removed her hand from the goblet and began studying her wrist and forearm.

Garnetta's attention was drawn by the movement. She felt a sudden urge to laugh. Her mind was playing tricks. It could not be *her* hand he held. There were long strips of dead skin hanging from it, like streamers of the thinnest grey bark. Her wrist and hand looked thin, white as milk. The nails too were pale, mere slivers like blanched almonds. No, not her hand or arm. It was an illusion. When he laid her back down, she sank gratefully onto the pillows. Even that small exertion exhausted her. Then his eyes looked directly into hers. She gave a shiver of alarm. There was something unfathomable in that steady gaze.

'Who . . . who are you?' she murmured.

'Lord Rakka. You can call me Karolan. Rest now,' he said in the gentle persuasive way she had come to recognize. His voice had a deep brown timbre. In a strange way she thought that she felt the words as well as heard them.

'Where am I?' she whispered.

'Safe. You are safe,' Karolan said. 'Do not be afraid. You have been very ill, you need to rest.'

It seemed again that the voice moved inside her head. It was gentle and like warmed honey, but it would not be denied. *Sleep now*. Obediently, she slept.

Early morning. A week later. Garnetta opened her eyes and almost closed them again in surprise.

Colours, so bright they almost hurt, flooded her vision. A scene swam in and out of focus. She concentrated hard, feeling an odd shifting movement inside herself as if someone had twitched a curtain. Her vision settled. She realized that she was staring up at a painted ceiling. The scene was a depiction of the Creation, but there was something out of kilter about it.

The trees, plants, and animals were beautifully wrought, each of them richly gilded. In the centre of the painting was a tree, its golden boughs hung with strange fruits. On the end of each branch sat a raven. Under the tree a naked man and woman held hands. Garnetta blushed at the immodesty of the depiction. The woman's breasts were crowned with prominent, rosy nipples. There was a luxuriant thatch of hair between her legs. Likewise the man's genitals were depicted graphically. She had never seen such a painting. Even in the visions of hell, on the placards of the white monks, the naked bodies were pale, sexless, devoid of all body hair. But she could not find this painting obscene, it glowed with sensuality, with a generous love of all life.

Looking more closely she saw the serpent which was coiled around the woman's shoulders, but it was the man who held the snake's head and was kissing it on the mouth. Garnetta was fascinated. The more she studied each detail, the more shocking the painting became. She looked for the figure of the Creator, usually prominent in religious paintings. Ah, there. Surely that was the figure of the living God. The tall slim figure in the background looked as if he was part of the scene and yet not master of it. The God figure had a beautiful face and long, glossy black hair. He had both male and female attributes. His beauty was blinding, disquieting. There was a presence at his side, a shadow, something of smoke and coiling air.

Garnetta looked away, deeply shocked by the heresy contained within the painting. But she was also disturbed by the fact that she felt herself responding to the warped sensuality of the God figure. There was something so compelling about the forbidden images that she could not help but look back at them. Who could have been moved to adorn a dwelling place with such a disturbing and daring work? And by what arrogance had he ordered himself depicted as God?

When she dragged her attention back to herself, she found that she was in a richly appointed bedchamber. A diffuse light, along with a breeze scented with snow, poured in from the window opposite the bed. A fire of logs burnt in an enormous hearth which took up most of one wall. The walls themselves were curved and built of stone. Tapestries of silk, richly woven, sewn with jewels and circles of metal adorned the walls. Similar curtains hung around three sides of the bed.

Whatever this place was, it was no monastery. The tall dark man, her nurse and protector, must be a rich man indeed. As the daughter of a mercer, she had lived in relative comfort within the town, but she had never been inside a dwelling which had an imposing wall fireplace and a woollen carpet as well as floor rushes. Garnetta pushed herself into a sitting position. Immediately she became aware of something different about herself. Her head felt light and small. She put up her hands and felt the soft stubble where once there had been a mass of silky hair. It was common practice to crop the heads of those in the grip of fever, but for a moment she was dismayed. Father loved her hair. It was like her mother's. Then she remembered.

Her father was dead, along with Jessica and Sellice. Nothing would be the same again. She had nothing left. No one to cherish. There was a pain in her chest when she thought of those she loved lying in the death pit, crushed and forgotten under the piled bodies. They must have prayers said for them, candles lit in the church of St Bertrina. She would attend to that first thing when she left this place. Then she must go back to the shop in Mercer's Yard to salvage what was left of the business.

Pushing back the covers, she swung her legs over the side of the bed. A wave of dizziness seized her. She waited for a moment before standing up. As she yawned and stretched, the sleeves of her loose shift slipped back to reveal her forearms. How grey and flaky they looked. Her skin was shiny, as if it had been oiled or peeled. She stroked her arm, rubbing at it with her fingertips. Little curls of skin came away as she rubbed harder. Underneath her arm was white as milk, the healthy, honey-tone of her natural colouring had disappeared.

Was this an after-effect of the pestilence? A memory stirred uncomfortably within her – of strips of skin hanging in tatters from a hand – but that image belonged to the time of fever, pain, and nightmare. She thrust it aside. As she walked unsteadily across the chamber, the sound of her own footsteps echoed in her ears. Something seemed wrong with her sight and hearing. Everything was too bright, too loud. When she crushed the strewing herbs underfoot, their scent rose to clog her nostrils, acrid and sickly sweet. She almost gagged at the intensity of the odour.

Approaching the window, she saw that the folded-back shutters were glazed with panes of red, blue, and green. How beautiful the coloured glass looked, like jewels. She leaned on the deep stone sill, drew in a breath of the freezing air. It slipped down her throat like ice-cold wine, as tart and fresh-tasting as apples. She took another gulp, delighted by this new discovery. Every experience was a sensory delight. Was this the joy of finding herself alive? She had thought she wanted to die, but now knew that to have been a false wish. She felt humbly grateful to be breathing, to be standing looking out at this God-given beauty.

Far below she saw a formal garden with clipped trees, neat herb and vegetable beds, grass paths, all of it covered with a layer of powdery snow. To one side there were stables and outbuildings. In the distance she could see the strips of cultivated fields. Beyond them was the mist-shrouded forest. All of it seemed unnaturally bright and clear. She blinked, finding difficulty in focusing. The light dazzled her. When she opened her eyes wide, the horizon rushed towards her. Now she could see the shape of a hare in the farthest field. Every detail of it was clear; the faint fog of its breath, the deep, soft warmth of its brown eyes. She could even detect the sound of its claws as it moved across the frozen ground.

There was something else. A sort of heat, a rapid blood-beat, a quick light intelligence transforming itself to her. Impossible. But she seemed to be gaining a sense of the hare's very thoughts. She jumped back from the window in alarm. Screwing her eyes shut, she covered them with the heels of her hands. Had her illness left her blighted?

'It would be best if you came away from the window,' Karolan said behind her.

Garnetta whirled round in surprise, her heart missing a beat. For a second she thought that the man from the painting stood in the open doorway. Then she realized that her saviour stood before her. It truly was Lord Rakka then. He was not part of her waking-dreams.

'I'm glad to see that you feel well enough to get out of bed,' he said, smiling. 'Might I know your name?'

'Garnetta,' she said. 'Daughter of Franklin Mercer.'

'Garnetta,' he mused. 'Daughter of a cloth merchant. And named for the dark-red gemstone. How apt.'

She did not know how to reply, so she studied him in turn. He was tall, taller than she remembered, but then she had only seen him bending over her in the bed. The way he was spoken of in the town had led her to expect a much older man. Surely this could not be the veteran of so many campaigns; the ex-soldier whose prowess in the field was almost legendary? Long black hair, glossy as a raven's wing, framed his pale face. He was whipcord thin, but his shoulders were wide. His legs, in hosen of black wool, were strongly muscled. His doublet of soft, red leather was worn over a white linen shirt with a drawstring neck. Red felt boots with laced fronts reached to his knee. Garments of excellent quality, she thought, her mercer's training coming into play.

Behind the smile, she sensed a wariness, a watchfulness and something else. He is looking at me with the pride of ownership, she thought with sudden clarity. Something deep inside her rose up as if to a challenge. Again there came that subtle movement as if a curtain twitched in her mind. Karolan smiled again, this time with satisfaction. His long mouth parted to show even, white teeth. Garnetta had the feeling that he had caught hold of her thoughts, understood everything she was feeling. The reflection of light in his strange eyes was like the moon on glass. Something about Lord Rakka drew her, yet terrified her. She took a step backwards and missed her footing.

Instantly he was at her side, his arm under her elbow, steadying her and leading her across the room towards the hearth. His perfume of spikenard and musk was intoxicating, making her senses swim. Between her thighs an insistent throbbing began. Her cheeks burned with mortification. He made her feel like a wanton and she did not even like him. Why was she so attuned to him? His presence burned her. It was as if her blood called out to him.

'Forgive me,' he said gently, ignoring her mental disarray. 'I didn't mean to startle you, but I was quite lost in the delight of seeing you on your feet. For a time I thought you would not live. Come, sit near the fire. I'll bring you food.'

'I'm not at all cold . . .' she murmured, lowering herself onto a wooden settle. To her surprise that was true, despite the wide-open window, the single garment she wore. Which must be revealing every detail of her body. She crossed her arms protectively across her stomach and hunched over a little. Her body might be weak still, but her mind felt sharper than a blade and was teeming with questions. The stories about Lord Rakka were burned into her imagination. He was rarely seen in the town, his business being conducted by his steward. Some said that he was a mis-shapen monster, scarred from his many fights, who could not bear to be looked upon. That was patently untrue. How much were the other stories about him exaggerated, she wondered.

Karolan heated a poker in the fire, using it to warm a goblet of spiced wine for her. Then he put a hunk of manchet bread and some goat's cheese onto a gilded platter. She balanced the food on her lap, sipping delicately from the goblet, picking at the food. The wine and cheese were delicious, the flavours of fermented fruit, the salty creaminess of milk slid luxuriously on her tongue. The bread was the finest she had ever tasted.

She felt conscious of the distance of rank between Karolan and herself. In the house at Mercer's Yard food was eaten from a shared bowl or placed on a trencher of rough bread. Karolan seemed unconcerned by any such differences. He took a seat by her side. Reaching out for her free hand, he closed his fingers on her wrists.

'May I?' he said, pressing his fingertips to a place on the inside of her arm.

77

'What are you doing?' she said, as he studied her skin and stroked a finger along a vein.

'There are places on the body where it is possible to feel the movement of the tides within. I can tell whether your heart is strong, whether or not your blood flow is obstructed.'

Garnetta had never heard of such a thing. By tides, he must mean the humours of bile, phlegm, and blood which caused a body to become too hot or too cold. She knew something of those. It was common practice to let out the evil humours with a blood-letting when a body suffered from an ague or had too much heat. 'Are you going to bleed me?'

He shook his head. 'That won't be necessary. The efficacy of that practice is doubtful at best. I just want to look at you.'

It was disconcerting to be examined as if she was a prize animal. She sat in silence while Karolan looked into her eyes and pressed his fingers to the sides of her neck. It would not have surprised her if he had opened her mouth to count her teeth. At the thought her mouth twitched. She took another sip of hippocras to conceal her expression. There seemed no sense in feeling any shame at having his hands on her. She knew well enough what nursing a person through the pestilence entailed. Karolan was as detached and absorbed in his observations as any apothecary. Still it was disquieting to feel the touch of his cool skin against her own.

'Are you a medicus?' she said.

'I belong to no physicians' guild, but I have some knowledge of ailments and medicaments. I had a good teacher. An Arab nobleman.'

She was shocked. 'You used heathen practices to cure me?'

He flashed her a grin. 'The world of knowledge is

larger then Christendom. You have survived when so many have perished. Does it matter how you were cured?'

'It does if my immortal soul has been put in danger,' she said primly. 'I'm not sure I wish to hear about these Godless practices.'

His mouth curved in a dry smile. 'Then you must rest assured that your God wished you to live. You had best give your thanks to him, not to me. Now, I'm sorry that I had to cut your hair but it will grow back quickly.'

She nodded, noting the casual inclusion of 'your' before the word 'God'. Karolan made no secret of the fact that he was a dangerous heretic. She knew that already. Why else would he have the painting in his bedchamber? What other kind of man dared to discourse with pagans and revere their foul practices? She ought to be fearful for her life, and more importantly, for her immortal soul, but she was strangely calm, absorbed only in watching his changes of expression as he bent close. His face had a certain delicacy, yet it had no trace of weakness or indolence. It was a face that seemed schooled to hide his emotions.

'You did not feel cold, just now, at the window?' he said, looking up to catch her studying him.

For the second time she felt the heat rush into her face. Her skin felt sensitized from his touch. The short hairs at the back of her neck prickled. Her breasts seemed to swell and grow heavy. These feelings were new to her. There must still be traces of fever in her body, for never had she been so affected by any man's nearness.

'Not cold, but strange,' she said at length, controlling the trembling of her voice with an effort. 'I cannot see properly. My hearing is all wrong. Has the pestilence harmed me?' The fears which had been submerged until now burst forth. She clutched at his hand. 'You can tell me the truth. Am I blighted? Will I be able to work and make my way in the world?'

He did not meet her eyes, but his voice held conviction. 'You will be strong and well. Better than before, but . . . a little different. It's early yet to tell. The healing process takes time. Have patience. Your body is making adjustments. Have you pain or discomfort anywhere? Does it hurt to breathe? Lift your chin so that I might look into your eyes. Excellent.' And so it went on.

Garnetta answered all his questions, waiting for him to finish his examination. 'Why did you bring me here?' she said at length. 'You could have left me to die.'

He shrugged. 'Call it a whim. Perhaps I wanted to test my healing skills.'

Rising from the settle, he walked across the room to a wooden chest which stood against one wall. She watched him closely as he dug into the open chest and emerged with an armful of garments. He did not look like a man who acted on impulse. She sipped her drink, looking over the top of the goblet as he came back towards the hearth, his movements were economical and graceful – like a dancer or a hunter. She had never seen anyone move like that, as if he was entirely at one with himself and his surroundings.

Handing her the garments, he said, 'Everything in the chest is yours. I hope that you will consent to be my guest for the present.'

She took the clothes, feeling the quality of the fine wool gown and the embroidered silk of the shift. 'I owe you my life,' she said, her eyelids lowered. 'You brought me to your home, knowing that I was sick with the pestilence. I am grateful. Thank you.'

He gave a wry grin, his expression unfathomable. 'Sometimes it is best to reserve one's thanks.'

CHAPTER FIVE

Karolan locked the door of the tower behind him and went swiftly down the steps. *I am no longer alone* – the words resounded in his head. There was a spark between them already, like calling to like. She might not know it yet, but already she was his. It was incredible. After all this time there was another like himself, a possible companion.

But he must go slowly. There was everything to teach Garnetta. He must be prepared for reaction; disbelief, horror, even revulsion at first. She would come to accept what she was, as he had done, for the simple reason that she had no other choice. He regretted the need for trickery, but she would surely forgive him for that once she understood. Until she had been told the truth he would allow nothing to alarm her. To this end, he had ordered the Fetch to keep away from her.

'Want to see, want to feel,' the spirit whined. 'Why not? Won't harm. Hunger for her, do I. She is mine too now!'

'As I am yours?' Karolan said bitterly. 'Never forget who brought you into existence! You will obey me!'

He sensed the spirit's agitation, knew that it was eager to deepen the bond with its new host. It wanted to establish an intimacy at every level, exploring, examining in the way peculiar to its kind until it knew the taste of Garnetta's breath, the scent of her skin, the texture of every secretion, was master of her deepest secrets – physical and mental. No wonder it was eager to test the parameters of the new bonding. For centuries the spirit had yearned to be joined with a human female. Now it had its wish.

Karolan's voice deepened, ringing with power. 'I charge you not to reveal yourself to her. You may watch only. Seek only to penetrate her aura. I must prepare her for your presence. The last thing she needs is to cope with your incessant demands.'

Although the Fetch mumbled and complained, pulsing with dingy colour, it could do nothing without his permission. After a few moments a glow appeared in the depths of its form. It glided close, rubbing seductively against Karolan's cheek. He felt the warmth of fingers on his skin, a waft of rose-musk filled his nostrils. Protuberences broke out on its surface, forming mounds of flesh that resolved themselves into palpating genitals. The effect of human organs seen against its spirit form was disquieting, obscene, but oddly tantalizing.

'Then you, Master. You desire pleasure?'

Karolan swatted the air with the back of his hand. 'I have no stomach for your wiles. The woman has survived the transmutation. The first person to do so in over two hundred years! I must record all that has transpired. Do you think I am interested in the clamourings of your base flesh?'

'Not mine, yours,' the Fetch whispered, a note of triumph in its voice. 'You want her, I sense it. Your need burns. It draws me.'

'You dare mock me!' Karolan gave a cry of rage, the power rising into his throat and leaving a taste like metal on his tongue.

Heeding the warning signs, the spirit flickered. It gleamed with sullen lights, the genitals reabsorbing back into its form with a sucking sound. As it blinked out, he heard its reedy laughter. It sped into the astral plane, off to find some foul entertainment.

Karolan clamped his lips together. God rot the spirit. It was too observant by far. He could keep the Fetch at a distance for a time, but he knew that he could not expect to control its actions for ever. Once Garnetta tested her strength she would become aware of her ever-present familiar. It was possible that she would be beguiled by its offers of sexual favours. It would be disastrous if she became addicted to the potent and perverted pleasures the Fetch pressed on her before she knew how to protect herself from it. The more the spirit experienced of the physical dimension the greater was its hunger to obtain a lasting human form. If ever it became adept at controlling a human host, then its capacity for destruction would be formidable. It was doubtful whether even *he* could control it.

For the first time since bringing Garnetta to his house, Karolan allowed his doubts to surface. He could not help but question the wisdom of allowing the Fetch to grow in strength. But there had been no choice. Without the spirit's intervention, Garnetta would be dead. Now he had a companion. With Garnetta beside him he could advance his studies. The mystic marriage of the alchemical king and queen was a real possibility. In his mind an image arose.

Sol and Luna, fused into a double-sexed unity. Balance, equilibrium, was represented by the hermaphrodite form. When male and female energy were utilized, great things could be accomplished. Garnetta would be the light to his dark, the silver to his gold. And their physical joining would be an ecstasy of the spirit as well as the flesh. The reality of that fact rushed in on him. By Hermes they could become lovers. His caustic sperm would not burn away her sexual parts. She would accept his seed deep within her body and no destruction would result. No more need he kill to satisfy his lust, torture himself with fruitless longings, or give in to the Fetch's sexual bargaining. The exultation he felt was like a hot

83

wound in his chest. *Oh Garnetta, such things I have to tell you!* First there were practicalities to consider. Garnetta's presence must be explained. It was not possible or practical to keep her a prisoner in his tower.

'Your . . . niece, my lord?' The steward's long face was set in an expression of utter disbelief.

'That is what I wish you to tell the servants, Romane,' Karolan said, putting his arm around the old man's narrow shoulders. Her name is Garnetta. She's to be given the freedom of the house and grounds and treated with the same courtesy and respect you accord me.'

'I will tell the servants whatever you wish,' Romane said gravely, 'But surely you do not expect me to believe this fabrication?'

'Ah, no,' Karolan laughed and rubbed his jaw. 'I owe you, at least, the truth. It's a delicate matter. I smuggled the wench into the house a sennight since –'

'When you sent word that you did not wish to be disturbed at your studies?' Romane cut in. 'Yes. I remember. It had to be a woman, I suppose.'

'Just so. Forgive me for not confiding in you, old friend, but I knew you'd disapprove. It was easier to say nothing. The woman was near death and might not have lived. I could not risk anyone knowing that I had a corpse in the tower. There's been trouble enough in the past.'

Romane rolled his eyes. 'It was fortunate that the charcoal burner was hanged for that peasant woman's murder. I can see why you would not want a repetition of previous disasters. So you've a new mistress? A charity case by the sound of it. What's amiss? Have you carried her off from a jealous husband?'

Karolan tapped Romane's hollow chest with the back

of his hand in a conspiratorial gesture. 'Should have known I couldn't fool you, eh? Truth is the bastard found out about us and beat her within an inch of her life. I brought her here for her own protection. If she goes back to him he'll surely kill her.'

Romane gave him a withering look. 'Can you not take a gadling wench when you feel the need of fleshly easement? Pay her and forget her. No good can come of this. The husband's bound to bring a petition against you. He'll want compensation if not your blood.'

Karolan hid a smile, wondering what Romane would have said if he had told him the truth. 'You sound more and more like an ageing mother hen,' he said with affection. 'I'll pay the fellow to keep his silence. Nothing's earned without risk, as well you know. What's done's done. Don't lecture me on my moral failings.'

'I would not presume to do so, my lord,' Romane said stiffly.

'That's a mercy – you usually do,' Karolan said, grinning. 'You'll do as I ask?'

'When have I ever failed you?'

'Very well. There are a few things you should know about Garnetta. She's been very ill and is not looking at her best. I want strict orders given that no one is to comment on her appearance. She's very thin. I had to cut off her hair when wound-fever raged through her. The temporary loss of her looks would be a great shock to her, so I have removed all mirrors from the tower. I want you to make sure that there is nothing reflective in the house. Nothing. Is that clear?'

Romane nodded, his lined face grave. His master must be sorely taken with the wench to be going to so much trouble. He only hoped she was worth it. It had been many years since Karolan had brought a woman to his tower. He sighed, picturing a blowsy trull with yellow hair and a pert bosom. Thank all the saints that his loins no longer troubled him. It was a blessing to be free of the snare of womankind.

Garnetta paced around the tower room, the woollen skirt of her over-tunic swishing through the rushes. She had found a linen wimple and padded circlet in the wooden chest and covered her shorn head with them. She knew that she must appear pale and drawn, so had pinched her cheeks and bitten her lips to put some colour into them. In the chest were many gowns, tunics, and scarves, some of them of fine cloth, trimmed with frosted braid or strips of fur. The sumptuary laws forbade anyone of her class wearing silks and bright colours. She expressed her misgivings about wearing the clothes to Karolan.

He laughed away her fears saying, 'On my land I am the only law. You may do as you will. Dress to please yourself.' His eyes glinted as he added. 'But you might endeavour to delight my eyes also, if you've a mind to.'

Garnetta wondered who the clothes had belonged to. Then she coloured. Of course, a man like Karolan must have had many mistresses. Perhaps he kept a woman in the main house. If he did, he could not be spending much time with her. She found herself pleased at the thought, then was angry for caring. Before long she would be leaving. With each passing day, she felt better. Although it was the season of Lent, Karolan insisted that she eat well, dismissing her qualms about falling into a state of sin with a mere wave of his hand. Despite his reassurances, she felt guilty for not observing the rules about fasting.

The food he brought her was the best she had ever eaten. It amazed her that it was so plentiful when the years of famine had brought food shortages to everyone. She ate ravenously of leek and pea pottage, salt meat with parsnips, boiled pudding containing scraps of pork fat. With every meal there was bread – sometimes stuffed with dried fruit. There was always spiced wine, sweetened with honey, rich with the flavours of cinnamon and nutmeg.

Her weakness had disappeared and she felt full of vitality. She was restless, eager to be up and doing. There was so much time in the day, her only task to enjoy herself. It had never been her habit to lie overlong in bed or sit idly staring into the fire. There had always been work to do in Mercer's Yard. She was accustomed to rising at first light to fetch water, then see to the charcoal brazier. By the time her father left his bed the shop would be warm, the boards swept, and a dish of bread sops in hot wine placed ready for him to break his fast.

Karolan had been surprised to find that she could read. He took great pleasure in selecting books for her from his extensive collection. She, in turn, was amazed to discover that he was a man of such learning. Together they discussed the merits of Virgil, Plato, Homer, and Aristotle. All her life Garnetta had been encouraged to put her education to use, the main aim of her endeavours to make sure that the shop showed a profit. There had been time only to read a few verses from the Bible before going to bed and rarely a spare moment to study the beautiful illuminations in her book of hours. Now that she had time to read for the simple love of it, she could not get enough of books.

In particular she loved the romance of the *Châtelain de Coucy*, which told the tale of Renault who loved the Dame de Fayel. She wept when Renault was wounded by a poisoned arrow while on crusade. His farewell letter to his love was dispatched in a box along with his embalmed heart and a lock of his hair. The jealous husband intercepted the box, serving up the cooked heart to his wife, whereupon she swore never to eat again and expired for love. It was a pretty conceit and she was delighted to find such a fanciful book in Karolan's collection. When she commented on it, he smiled thinly and gave one of his characteristic dismissive gestures.

'The book was a gift. I forget who gave it to me. Courtly love is an illusion. I have no stomach for melancholy and amorous foolery. How can it ennoble a man to make sheep's eyes at another's wife, but not to look for love within his own marriage? Such works foster dangerous illusions. Has not a knight the right to kill both his unfaithful wife and her lover? Why fill women's heads with such nonsense?'

'True enough,' she countered swiftly. 'But it is refreshing to read of a woman who inspires male glory. In the real world we are simply chattels, objects for the breeding of children and free to be ill-used by any man if it so pleases him.'

He looked at her in amazement. She smiled, seeing that he had never given this matter much thought. And why should he? He inhabited a world where men held the right of property and ordered women's lives. Women lived in a different world. In truth, she was a little amazed at her own reasoning. She had never spoken out so boldly before and was at a loss to discover where her bravery had come from. She looked sideways at Karolan to see if he would rebuke her for her presumption. Instead he chuckled as if her asperity was something entirely expected. She saw that he was regarding her with new respect and something else – something she could not comprehend. Reaching out he took her hand. Conveying it to his mouth, he brushed it with his lips.

'Forgive me. My words were churlish. You are right to

remind me of the world's cruelty. You have been sorely used. The wounds on your body told their own tale.' His strange grey eyes gleamed with secret triumph. 'But no more, Garnetta. No one can hurt you, ever again. No one.'

She was too astounded to ask him what he meant. His touch on her skin stirred her senses, confusing her. When he dropped her hand, she could still feel the place where his lips had touched.

'Let there be honesty between us at all times,' he said. 'You may speak freely before me as an equal. I am not bound by conventions as are other men. I want you to be yourself. Say whatever is in your heart. But outside these walls it would be best to guard your tongue.'

The strange concept took some time to encompass. Women never spoke freely, but deferred to men in all things. All her life she had been taught not to look a man in the eyes, never to speak first when a man was present. Karolan was urging her to act in a way that was unnatural. And what a glimpse of freedom that was. What could he mean by, 'no one can hurt you ever again'? Was he offering to become her protector? Surely he was not speaking of marriage. She had no dowry, nothing to give her any status at all. It probably amused him to pay chaste court to her, practising love for its own sake, while he kept a mistress near at hand for the relief of his more base passions. And yet, she did not think him so shallow. The other explanation, that he meant what he said, was just too unlikely. For that would make Karolan a strange breed of man indeed.

After only a few days, the pleasures of learning to play dice and backgammon began to pall. She felt eager to be outside. The snow was beginning to melt and the scent of spring was in the air. Soon it would be Easter and the beginning of a new year. Her restlessness increased hourly, her thoughts bounding ahead of her, seeking new stimulation. The strange acuteness of all her senses had not diminished. She became used to her clarity of sight and hearing. Gradually she learned that she could control the alarming impressions of sight and sound. It was possible to shut them off, draw upon her new ability at will. The same applied to her sense of smell. The pungent odour of the floor rushes no longer sickened her.

She told Karolan about the tingling of her skin, the itching of her scalp. He examined her, as he had done that first time, explaining that after such a grave illness she must expect to feel different. 'Do not be alarmed,' he told her. 'Any feeling of strangeness is your body settling.'

She lowered her eyelids against his penetrating gaze, hardly daring to admit to the feelings that his nearness brought out in her. There was a growing tension between them, a promise of things to come, which both drew and terrified her. Karolan continued to treat her with unfailing courtesy. He was a considerate and entertaining companion. If not for the fact that she was still grieving for all that she had lost she would have been completely happy. She found him fascinating to watch. He was graceful without being in the least effeminate. He had a knack of appearing soundlessly in a room. Sometimes, from the tail of her eye, she caught a subtle movement. Turning she would find that he had traversed some distance across the floor without seeming to have actually moved.

Karolan left the tower most mornings to go riding on Darkus, returning well after midday. She knew that there must be many tasks for him to oversee on such a large estate. An army of servants was needed to run the house and tend the flocks. She felt nervous at having to meet them all. She said as much to Karolan that evening.

'The only person you need to impress is Romane,' he said with a grin. 'The others go in fear of his sharp tongue. Just remember that you are my niece.'

'But will anyone believe that? Ought there not to be some kind of resemblance between us?'

'It matters not whether they believe it, as long as they appear to and act accordingly,' he said. 'My vassals do as I bid them.'

'As I am expected to?' Garnetta said, before she could stop herself. She had noticed before that this unthinking arrogance was natural to him. He had been bred to order the lives of others, while she was part of the newly emergent merchant classes – free, but without the trappings of nobility which conferred the protection of rank and wealth.

Karolan grinned, not in the least offended. 'Of course not. You are my guest. Have I given you any cause to think otherwise?'

Garnetta held his gaze with difficulty. This candour between them was hard to get used to. 'No cause at all. Forgive me. You have done so much for me. I do not mean to be uncharitable. It is just that there is no way of repaying you.'

There was a pause before he answered. 'I need nothing. Your presence is payment enough. Do you not yet realize how much I value every moment I spend in your company?'

The tone of his voice was like silk. She could feel the timbre of it, throbbing within her as acutely as a note of music. Her mouth dried. The silence stretched between them. This was dangerous. A feeling like thirst rose up inside her. And he was the well from which she would drink. She felt her natural reserve melting, slipping away like butter down hot meat. 'Karolan . . .'

He smiled and his eyes were soft, dark pools. 'That is the first time you have called me by name.' His slanting black brows drew together. 'There is no need of payment. I . . . I want something of you. But I wish it to be freely given.' His voice was intense.

Under the onslaught of his regard, she lifted her chin. Had he saved her only to demand that she warm his bed now? She felt a surge of righteous anger. He was just like any other man, treating her like his chattel. The church warned against a woman surrendering her virtue to anyone but her husband. She was about to answer primly that he asked far too much, when something sparked between them. There was a burning pressure in her temples. She heard him without surprise.

'You must know that I mean to lie with you,' he said huskily.

'I do know it, my lord,' she said.

In that moment everything changed. His glamour seemed to blind her. Her response was immediate and shattering. This feeling had nothing to do with courtly love, everything to do with condensed animal attraction. She gasped at the sensation between her legs. A hot throbbing spread outwards from her centre, curling over her belly, running down the inside of her thighs. Karolan had not touched her and she was on fire. Had he cast a spell over her? Her breasts swelled, the nipples standing out as berries. Little shocks of sensation stabbed at her as the sensitized tips brushed against her silken tunic.

Her new determined self seemed to be struggling for precedence. *This is wrong. I do not care.* The old Garnetta was being subsumed beneath a stronger, more determined persona. It was as if there was some connection between this new person and Karolan, a silver thread that wound tight – tighter, drawing them together. She wanted him as much as he wanted her. It was a glory to acknowledge that fact.

'If it is too soon . . .' he murmured.

Her heart trembled for this man who was a warrior, medicus, and God alone knew what else – yet was made uncertain by the blinding attraction between them. Their joint need was a tangible force in the chamber. She was blind and deaf to anything other than him. She shook her head, whispering, 'No I . . . I want this too.'

The desire for him spread through her veins. Even the tips of her fingers tingled. She was all eagerness, a map of melting curves and moist flesh. How shameless, how wanton she had become. Her lips curving in a smile as old as time, she spread her arms in welcome.

Karolan took a step closer, his eyes glittering like jewels. 'If you knew how long I have waited for you,' he groaned as his mouth covered hers.

She wanted to ask what he meant, but found herself straining against his hard body, opening her lips to accept his tongue. Then there was nothing in the world but sensation. His taste thrilled her. It was unique – fresh and heady, strong like spiced wine. His hands pressed against the small of her back. The evidence of his arousal was firm and potent between her thighs. She knew what he would do to her. He would push his hard maleness into her, hurting and possessing her as all men did to women. She ought to have been terrified; it had been agony when the bearers violated her. She was afraid, but she wanted this – badly. Besides, even if she had wanted to stop, her body and instincts were running on ahead of her. She had become a stranger to herself.

Her breath came in short gasps as Karolan's long fingers stroked her face, cupped the back of her head. His lips burned her mouth, her chin, her neck – his kisses a cautery iron that burned away the morbus of her fear. Somehow they moved across the chamber. She felt the bed against the back of her knees. Laughing with sudden self-consciousness they fell backwards. She turned to face him as he plucked at her shift, desperate in his eagerness to have her naked. The fabric was trapped beneath them. He gave a sound of impatience and gripped the low neck in his two hands. The linen parted with a tearing sound. She gasped as the velvet of his tunic prickled against her naked breasts.

She helped him to disrobe, fumbling at strings and laces, pressing kisses to his bare white skin when shirt and hosen were snagged at elbow and knee. Then they lay close, flesh cleaved to flesh, too awed by what was unsaid between them to move at all.

'Do you know how beautiful you are?' Karolan murmured.

So was he. Merciful God, so was he. If his beauty was of the Devil, and this an enchantment, she did not care. Gradually, slowly, his lips pressed a burning path down the side of her neck and came to rest in the hollow of her throat. She knew that he was pressing the tip of his tongue to her pulse. Something hot and primeval exploded in her head. His tongue moved and his breath fired her damp skin. It felt as if he was reading her soul. 'Ah, no. It is too much,' she whispered in an agony of need and confusion.

How could something be this sweet, the feelings so welcome yet so desperate? Was this what love was? Feeling like this made her afraid. Karolan moved against her. She meshed her fingers in his long black hair as he bent and began to suckle at her breast. Then the pleasure was all of the body and less of the mind. It was bearable, but only just. For a long time they simply lay naked on his bed, twisted in a tangle of silken sheets. Her shift was crumpled under her where Karolan had thrown it aside after tearing it from her body. She sensed a subtle shift between them. It seemed that they obeyed a sub-conscious signal as they strained to get closer, ever closer. Her fear changed then, to something deeper and darker.

Karolan's caresses became more intimate. She twisted in his arms, her head thrown back to expose her throat. The violence of his passion excited her beyond measure. She arched against him as he bit at her nipple, grazing it gently with his teeth. He pressed his long, naked body against her as his hands stroked her skin, exploring the dip of her waist, the curve of her hip, then moving inwards to her hot, pulsing cleft. The smell of his arousal was mingled with the scented oils he always wore – spikenard and musk. She parted her thighs to allow him access, moaning softly when his slender fingers parted the lips of her coynte.

Tensing a little she waited for him to push his fingers into her, anticipating resistance and soreness. But he only used the pad of his thumb to press against the place that throbbed and burned. She felt it as a small swelling, a sensitive bump under his touch. As he rubbed gently she grew wetter and more swollen. The most exquisite feelings radiated outwards. She tossed her head from side to side, moaning wantonly. Lifting his head Karolan looked down at her and smiled tenderly. She sensed that he was holding himself back, wanting her to enjoy the experience in full measure.

'What . . . is that you're doing to me?' she asked.

'Something I learned from a woman who was prac-tised in the art of giving pleasure. It was very long ago.'

She felt a surge of jealousy, hating the unknown woman who had taught him about women's bodies. Then she forgot to think as he changed position so that he was lying half on top of her, his cock hard and heavy against her inner thigh. The swollen tip of his glans rubbed bluntly against her wet folds. In a single stroke he was inside her. She felt a crimson gash of sensation. There was no time to feel pain, if pain there was. She could no longer tell where pleasure ended or began. As he moved inside her, she drew up her legs, drawing him in deeper, ever deeper.

He filled her completely, utterly. Why did it feel so right? She held him tenderly when his whole frame began to shudder and she knew that he was weeping. She felt the tenderness of a mother towards him then. It was something beautiful that such a man could weep for need of her. His tears fell onto her lips. She tasted the spiced salt of them as he thrust into her, pulling almost all the way out of her before slamming back in.

Digging her fingers into his lean, hard buttocks, she urged him to move faster and deeper. Tipping up her hips, she matched him stroke for stroke, never wondering where she had gained the knowledge to do more than lie quiescent beneath him. No one had prepared her for this. No one had ever told her that it was such a glory, such gorgeous sport to give in to the bewitchments of the flesh. She would gladly do penance for the sin of it later.

It ought not to be like this. Mating was but a duty, something painful and abhorrent which women endured. This was something else. This was hunger, beauty, the joining of more than the body. She felt swamped by pleasure. Karolan held her tight, his mouth clamped to hers as he spilt himself into her. His seed was hot, bathing her womb, drawing down an answering response. She cried out as she crested a wave and was held for a second on the brink before it broke. As he rocked within her, she spasmed strongly, milking him of the final drops.

For a long time they lay entwined, too exhausted to move, then Karolan stroked her shorn head and traced her small features with a gentle hand. 'You have no discomfort?' he asked, his brow furrowed by concern.

Garnetta stretched voluptuously, feeling the warm slipperiness of their mixed fluids between her thighs. The smell of him was all over her. She could smell her own warm musk too. 'You were not gentle,' she said with a grin. 'But I did not wish you to be.' He smiled tenderly. She had the feeling that he had meant something else. 'The cart bearers took my virgin blood,' she said. 'Do you not care that I have been dishonoured?'

'The sin was not yours. Forget dishonour, forget everything but this moment. Nothing went before it. Did you not feel it, Garnetta? Something happened. We have been forged anew. We belong together, you and I. For always.'

She felt the truth of it, but marvelled that he could give voice to what was in her heart. What kind of man was he who was not afraid to speak of such things? 'And you scoffed so at courtly love, my lord!'

Karolan flashed her a wicked smile. 'There is nothing courtly about this love of ours.' Moving down the bed, he parted her thighs gently, separated the folds with his fingertips and put his mouth to her coynte.

'What are you doing? Oh no . . . do not! I am not clean . . .' She tried to move away, to close her thighs, but he held them in place. When he tasted her, she pressed the back of her hand against her mouth, tears sliding from the corners of her eyes. Her breathing became ragged as he sucked and licked. The evidence of her pleasure oozed into his mouth. After she had crested for the second time, he came up to lay beside her, putting his mouth over hers and bringing her taste to her. Seed and sap clung to his lips like pollen. Their mingled musk slid on her tongue.

'We belong together. Never forget it,' he whispered.

Holding him close to her chest as they finally slept, Garnetta fancied that in the aftermath of their joining she could recall the moment of her own birth.

CHAPTER SIX

The days passed in a welter of pleasure and sexual indulgence. Karolan felt renewed, made whole, humbled by love. Feelings he had thought long buried surfaced to plague him. It was an uncomfortable experience to feel himself responsible for another person. And yet, it cost him no effort to make Garnetta happy. Her delight was its own reward.

Two mornings after their first joining, he lay on his side, his chin propped on the heel of his hand, looking down at Garnetta as she slept. The curve of her cheek was clear-cut against the silken pillows, her mouth soft, as relaxed as a child's. The short, spiked hair, now dark at the roots, revealed the exquisite shape of her skull, the delicacy of her neck and shoulders. She had been lovely with her fair hair tumbling around her shoulders, but now, with the glamour of transmutation suffusing her every fibre, she was something finer and rarer.

Conflicting emotions roiled within him. There were truths of which she must be made aware for her own protection, but he was reluctant to break the spell of their happiness. Surely it would not matter if they spent a few more days indulging their senses, getting to know each other. They had been lovers for such a short time. This fabulous intimacy of the flesh and spirit was a wonder to him. He felt consumed by the power of attraction, a humble worshipper before the altar of her flesh. It was clear now that his body fluids could not harm her. During the process of change, her internal chemistry had become the same as his. Might they not found a dynasty of their own? It was something he hardly dared to consider.

Almost hourly, it seemed, Garnetta grew more confident, more poised. He could sense her mind expanding, questioning. Each tiny detail of her persona was enchanting. How fascinating it was to observe the changes in her. She now had a measure of control over the enhancement of all her senses. Her capacity for sexual pleasure was remarkable. Before long she would be moved to test her burgeoning intellect. Then what might she discover?

He had heard her praying, giving thanks to the Virgin and St Catherine, the patron saint of unmarried women, for her deliverance. Her belief in God and all His saints was the matrix of her life. Hardly an hour passed when she did not say a *Miserere* for the souls of her dead family. No doubt now she would recite countless *Ave Marias* as penance for her imagined human frailty in lying with him.

He grinned wryly and with a trace of sadness. Soon enough she would question her religious beliefs, as he had done, for her – his – very existence was an affront to God. But he could not bear to wound her with that knowledge at present, she was still so new to his world. He thought of her as a fledgling who was not yet equipped to leave the nest. A surge of fierce protectiveness swept through him. She was more than a lover, she was his salvation, his child. In his arrogance he had never imagined that he could be fearful. His powers set him apart, armoured him against the travails of common men. But no more. Love had made him afraid – for Garnetta and for himself.

Garnetta awoke, but concealed the fact from Karolan. She smiled inwardly, watching him through half-closed lashes. His face was luminous in the light streaming in through the open shutters, his expression soft and unguarded. Her heart turned over with emotion. What an impossible, wonderful situation this was. Out of pain and suffering had come this joy of the body, this lightness of the spirit. Surely this splendour could not be damned as lust, this desire to appear beautiful in Karolan's eyes could not be vainglory.

There seemed to be a wavering, a trembling in the air to one side of Karolan. She focused on the disturbance, unconsciously utilizing her newly acute sight. The movement in the air became more pronounced. Fascinated she watched as a pattern of striations formed a rib-like web behind Karolan's shoulder, then melted into nothing. Had she imagined it? No. There was a ripple behind his other shoulder now. This time it was barely a flicker, a silver line that shifted in and out of focus. She followed the movements with her half-closed eyes, keeping her head still. It was like watching the swirling eddies on fast-running water.

As she was about to speak Karolan stiffened and muttered something under his breath. The disturbance in the air ceased at once.

'What was that?' she asked sleepily, pushing herself up on her elbows.

Karolan grinned. 'So you *are* awake. I thought as much. It was nothing. Some trickery I have been practising in the hope that it will amuse you.'

His long black hair spilled over his broad shoulders. The neck of his linen tunic was wide and the muscles showed under his pale skin as he moved. She reached up and took hold of a lock of his hair, pulling him down and fitting her mouth to his. 'God give you good day, my lord,' she murmured against his lips. She loved the taste of him, so sweet and fresh – like rain. Never had she imagined that a man could smell so good, that his skin would feel like silk against her own.

The desire bloomed swiftly within her. It seemed that she could not get a surfeit of this pleasure. It was as if, having discovered that her senses could thrum to the dark, heady notes, they continued to resonate like harp strings, needing only the touch of his hands to give out more of their sweet music. Just being in the same room with him was enough to make her hungry for his touch. Her blood seemed to cry out for him. She found that she wanted to touch him in lewd ways, to engage in forbidden, devilish pleasures. Elation bubbled up in her, for nothing was forbidden between them.

Pushing him backwards laughingly, she straddled him, her thighs pressing against his hard-muscled legs. Swooping down, she bit at his tight male nipples, lashing them with her tongue until he winced in pleasure-pain.

'Witch-woman,' he grunted through bared teeth. 'You are a natural wanton!'

She giggled huskily, revelling in her power to arouse him. He stirred under her, his hands moving bonelessly over her back and buttocks. She avoided his embrace and slid down to lie between his thighs. There was the object of so much pleasure. How potent it looked just now, standing up rigidly, the darkly flushed skin soft as velvet over the engorged centre. And yet how foolish and amusing it was too, with the two stones in their hairy sac, the flaring tip that crested the shaft looking just like a moist, ripe plum.

Reverently she bent close and took the cock in her mouth, feeling the hot beating of his flesh against her tongue. Karolan swore softly and arched his back, surging against her. His response urged her on to greater experimentation. As she sucked and licked at him, she slipped her hand between his legs, stroking gently at the firm pad behind his ballocks. She tasted the salty dew of his pre-emission and exulted in the fact that she could give him such forbidden delights.

When he whispered hoarsely for her to stop, she lifted her head to grin at him before resuming her ministrations. Using her lips to collar the swollen glans she worked up and down the shaft, one hand pressed to his flat belly to hold him down. Karolan uttered a series of sharp cries as she drew him more deeply into the wet cavern of her throat and spilled his seed into her mouth. Amazed at her own capacity for shamelessness she swallowed the hot, slippery fluid, then moved to cover Karolan's lips with her own. The kiss tasted of salt and heat and something earthy, faintly metallic. When Karolan broke from her embrace, he looked at her with wonder in his eyes.

'By Hermes, woman, but you learn fast!'

She preened and said playfully. 'I have the best teacher, do I not, my lord? I can see by your face that you are glad of my skill. And who is this Hermes you are always calling on? Is he a saint?'

Settling her into the crook of his arm, he drew her close. 'Nay, love, no saint. I was introduced to Greek texts attributed to him whilst in the Holy Land. In time I shall show you these works and many other things besides. Hermes is the mythic patron of the art which has been my life's work.'

'What art is that? Already you have told me that you possess the priestly skills of a physician, taught to you by an Arab – for which I have cause to be grateful. Now you admit to being familiar with many teachings of infidels? Should I not fear for your immortal soul?'

There was a hesitation before Karolan replied. Then he said teasingly, 'You fear *for* me? I would rather that, than you had fear *of* me.'

'Should I fear you, my lord?'

He kissed her lightly. 'Many have and will again, with good cause. But, you? Never. Remember that, whatever happens. Mark this well. You and I are one.'

She would have asked him to explain, but he began speaking and the moment passed.

'You know of astronomy – the study of the heavens?'

She nodded, pleased to be able to answer with conviction. 'I have read of it. The monk engaged by my father to teach me my letters had a great love of learning. He spoke of many things. He said that the study of the heavens is the noblest science.'

'Ah, then you know also of astrology?'

She nodded again. 'After God it is the power of the stars and planets which governs the affairs of men. Does not our king, the third Edward, have such an adviser at his court?'

'Just so. No doubt he consulted him before he set out to do battle with France. You are well informed, Garnetta. It will be a pleasure to tell you of all that I have studied. I have long been a seeker of the truth, fascinated by science, both natural and occult.' His brow furrowed. 'Listen to me, Garnetta. You might come to believe that I am a warrior who has stepped into a forbidden country. When you know all you may think badly of me.'

Garnetta kissed his cheek, amused by the seriousness of his expression. She would not allow the curling of unease in her belly to colour her sense of well-being. 'I know all I need to know of you. You looked into the stars and saw my fate written there. You petitioned God for His help in saving me, asking for His divine mercy and intervention. For how else except with His grace would your skills have had the desired result? I have so much to thank you for, my lord. And I give thanks daily in prayer.' Her brow wrinkled. 'One thing puzzles me still.

You have not told me why you decided to save me. I am no one special. I have not position or lands.'

That was true, she knew. Karolan had told her that he had made enquiries about the shop in Mercer's Yard. The bearers had stripped the shelves clear of every roll of cloth before setting a torch to the place. Briefly she mourned for splendour lost. There had been thick worsted and fustians, percale cambrics, maroon samites and raw silks and rare, light shalloon for cloak linings. Latterly her father had invested the last of their money in bolts of dowlas linen from Britanny. She had nothing now, not even the means to buy her way into a nunnery.

Karolan touched her cheek. His smile held pride and tenderness. 'But you *are* special, Garnetta. The will to survive was strong within you. Even on the brink of death, you fought so hard to live. Now you are whole, stronger, better than before. Soon you will know just how different you are. You are precious to me, do you realize that? Together we shall achieve such wonders as are only dreamt of.'

His passionate words stole her breath. The doubts which had surfaced briefly evaporated. She would forever give thanks to the Mother of the Lord for bringing her to the attention of this man. Perhaps it was tempting the Devil to think herself so blessed, but she could not help it.

Karolan sat up and pulled her to her feet. 'Now, no more talk. The morn is advanced. It is time you left this tower and came down to meet the house staff. I've told Romane to expect us and to choose a horse for you. I shall teach you to ride. A lady must be on horseback to look over her lord's demesne.'

She gave a cry of delight, imagining how wonderful it would be to ride beside him. 'Will you help me dress?' she asked, indicating the fine woollen tunic which fastened with lacing all the way down the back.

Karolan tightened the laces deftly, then held up a fur-lined super-tunic for her to slip on. Garnetta raised her hand to her head and smiled ruefully. 'I must look so ugly. Wait. I will cover my head with a veil.'

He gripped her shoulders and bent to kiss the exposed nape of her neck. 'You look beautiful as you are. If it were summer I would weave you a chaplet of meadow flowers. Since it is but the fifth week of Lent I will search out some greenery. With a circlet of ivy leaves you'll look as grand as any May queen!'

The laughter bubbled up inside Garnetta as she laid her hand on Karolan's arm. Even the ache of losing those she loved had lessened somewhat. The terrible experiences of the sickness and her violation might have been but a bad dream – now was the only reality. Inside the tower, with Karolan at her side, she could forget that people were still dying in the town, that the dead must be piled in the streets. The spectre of the pestilence held no power to harm her here. Oh, but it was a mortal sin to enjoy being closeted in luxury while the world suffered. She was possessed of uncontrollable lusts, dishonoured, damned for catching the guilty thread of pleasure and weaving it into a golden tapestry.

What was the word for the soulless hunger of the flesh? Ah, yes. *Concupiscence*. There ought to be a better word for the dream-flush brought on by Karolan's touch. If she was so bad, why was it that she felt such elation – such a bone-deep sense of rightness and well-being? She did not recognize herself as the girl who had been dutiful, self-effacing, obedient to her male betters. Suffering had given her the courage to lay claim to happiness. When the time came to pay, as she knew it surely would, she would face it gladly.

'Come then, Madam,' Karolan said. 'Remember, you are my niece. I've been tending your fever in my tower to contain any spread of infection.'

'That part is true enough,' she said, swaying gracefully so that her body brushed against him as they descended the stone steps. 'You've been tending to my body's needs rather well, my lord.'

She sensed rather than heard his withdrawn breath. His long fingers closed over hers, squeezing them gently, managing to convey reassurance and intimacy combined. A flush warmed her skin. It seemed not to matter how often they lay together, the hunger burned deeply and abidingly within them both.

At the bottom of the twisting staircase, they emerged into a small room. Garnetta hardly had time to take in the richness of the wood carving on the wainscotting before she was shown into a vaulted hall. Servants stood in line, shifting from foot to foot with impatience. She hid a smile at the thought of why they had been kept waiting. Did her shamelessness show on her face?

The steward, Romane, stood a little to one side. Garnetta saw a tall, silver-haired man with a slight stoop. He was dressed in a flared black gown, covered with a fur-lined, quilted surcoat. A huge bunch of keys hung from a belt at his waist. The steward took a step forward, only the slightest hesitation betraying the fact that he was lame. He bowed, his face impassive, but Garnetta saw the flicker of pleased surprise in his faded blue eyes. She wondered what Karolan had told him and glanced to one side to find that Karolan was grinning in a conspiratorial manner. Lifting her chin she prepared to act like a lady.

'Welcome, my lady,' Romane said. 'Allow me to introduce the servants.' Garnetta smiled as each person was presented. According to their rank, they either nodded or bobbed a curtsy.

'Pleased to meet 'ee, Ladyship.'

'God give thee good day, mum.'

After the introductions, Romane offered to accompany Garnetta on a tour of the house before she and Karolan left to go riding. Karolan nodded his assent. 'I'll away to the stables and see that the horses are ready. There's a sweet brown mare I have picked out. Now remember, Romane, you are not to tire Garnetta.'

Romane inclined his head. 'I understand, my lord. I am pleased to see that your . . . niece is making such a rapid and splendid recovery.'

Garnetta saw the look which passed between them and heard their complicity of tone. The steward knew that she was Karolan's mistress, but there was nothing in his demeanour to give away the fact. As Karolan turned on his heel, Romane clapped his hands, dispersing the servants. 'If you will come this way,' he said pleasantly, standing aside for her to precede him.

'The original building was a single hall with a solar at the far end,' he informed her as they passed rooms with lime-washed walls and exposed oak beams. 'Lord Rakka had an upper floor and staircase built and partitions put in to make a number of small chambers.'

Besides the usual sparse furniture of trunks, tables, and high-backed settles, there were shelves on which were set carvings inlaid with mother of pearl and lamps of stamped and incised brass. The walls were hung with armour of strange and archaic design. Garnetta looked with wonder at a cabinet of red lacquer decorated with toothed creatures breathing fire. There were low couches of intricately carved wood, piled with silken cushions, rows of metal plates set with gleaming cabochon jewels.

'Lord Rakka is much travelled,' Romane explained, when Garnetta commented on the diversity of all she saw. 'He brought back some of these things from Cathay and others from the Holy Land. My lord is a collector of the arts as well as of knowledge. He is an extraordinary man.'

'That fact had not escaped me,' Garnetta murmured. 'Is it not . . . unwise to leave so much on display?'

Romane emitted a creaky noise, which she realized was a laugh. 'No one would dare to steal anything. They know better than to risk Lord Rakka's anger. He is a hard master, but fair. Every vassal has enough to eat and is allowed to bring any grievance before the justice. Of course,' he smiled thinly, 'Few would wish to make such a petition.'

The chambers on the upper floor were meticulously clean but with the musty smell of rooms unused. It surprised her that the house should be so spacious, so richly furnished, yet devoid of family members. She looked questioningly at the steward.

'We have few visitors,' he said with regret. 'My lord guards his solitude.'

She gained the impression that he was avoiding broaching the weightier question. So be it. She would ask Karolan about his wife. The poor woman had probably died in childbed. But it was curious that a man such as he had not remarried. How he must wish for a son, an heir. The rambling house was too quiet. It ought to be ringing with the cries of children. 'Is the lack of visitors because of the things people say about Lord Rakka?'

Romane did not look surprised. 'Of course you have heard the folk tales. Is it the nature of men to fear that which they do not understand. Tell me, what do they say? Since the pestilence gained a hold, I've heard no news of the outside.'

Garnetta shuddered. 'They say that the forest around the manor is cursed, that the intervention of Pope Clement himself – bless the Vicar of Christ – could not make the place holy again. I've heard tales of mad women running through the forest, clutching murdered children to their breasts. A demon is said to live in a cave. He pounces on the sinful and strips the flesh from their bones before hanging them from a tree, where they sway in the black wind like monstrous fruit.'

'And what has my lord to do with all this . . . this fabrication?'

Garnetta hesitated, unwilling to repeat the tales. Now that she knew and loved Karolan they seemed too ridiculous to repeat. Romane prompted her to speak, by a quizzical lifting of one eyebrow. 'Some years ago a charcoal burner was hanged for the killing of a mother and her child. The child, poor mite, was monstrously deformed. And the woman had been greatly torn . . . about the privy parts. The man was found scraping a shallow grave for the bodies, so there was no doubt of his guilt. But he accused Lord Rakka of having a hand in the sorry mess. Nothing was proved of course – how could it be? – but many people thought Lord Rakka was not entirely without knowledge of the events. It was known that he engaged in doubtful practices. But alchemy is a noble Christian art, practised by kings and monks.'

Romane nodded and murmured, 'It is indeed.'

Garnetta paused before continuing. 'The charcoal burner's corpse was tarred and suspended in a gibbet from a tree. Some misguided souls, who reckoned the man to be innocent of the murders, took gifts of flowers and goods to lay at his feet. Even now, anyone who wishes to harm a neighbour will sneak into the forest at night and make a blood offering to the tree of woe.' Garnetta took a deep breath. 'Lord Rakka saved my life. Why would he do that if he was such a monster?'

'My lord's ways were ever his own,' Romane said enigmatically.

With her heightened senses she became aware of the increase in his heartbeat. There was the slightest tang of nervous sweat rising from his clothes. She knew with certainty that he was hiding something from her.

Romane gave her a searching look. 'If I may make so bold, may I offer you some advice?' When she nodded he went on. 'Experience has taught me that truth is a slippery thing indeed and not at all easy to gain a hold on. It's best to reserve one's judgement until you are sure of a thing.'

He seemed to be talking in riddles. She smiled placatingly. He was an old man and old men's minds were apt to wander. 'Shall we move on?' she said, with an authority with which she was only just becoming familiar. 'I have yet to see the kitchens before I join your master in the stables.'

Taking her comment as natural to her assumed station, Romane shook out the folds of his long back gown and afforded her a shallow bow. 'Of course. Forgive me for presuming on your time. Cook is eager to meet you. She wishes to ask whether you have a special way of preparing lenten cakes.' His eyes twinkling he said, 'I, for one, would be heartily glad if you would furnish her with such a receipt. 'Twould be a blessing to us all. I understand that your illness has made you exempt from the rigours of fasting, but I confess that I'm hardly able to stomach any more stockfish and black bread! They're mortal hard on an old man's teeth. Won't you have pity?'

Laughingly, Garnetta accompanied the steward. She liked this old man who was trusted with the running of the household and lands. He obviously had his lord's interest at heart, but she also perceived that he was fond of Karolan and held him in high esteem. There had been genuine liking between the two men earlier in the hall. Romane must have been with Karolan for many years. Was he privy to all Karolan's secrets, she wondered?

She felt again the thrill of her lover's glamour and charisma, but there was still that underlying – something. It was nothing tangible, rather it was a subtle impression, another of the strange, unwanted messages given out to her by her newly sensitized mind.

CHAPTER SEVEN

Garnetta awoke with a shock and sat upright. The threads of the dream were woven around her still. The spell of it, the dark eroticism, held her in thrall.

Reaching out she felt the empty space beside her and remembered that Karolan had told her he would not be coming to bed for many hours yet. No doubt he was in his workroom – that secret place to which she was denied entry. He had explained that there was an unusual configuration of the planets he wished to study. When she expressed an interest in accompanying him, he had kissed her cheek and told her firmly that she still needed to rest.

Closing her eyes, Garnetta allowed herself to drift back into the dream. Almost instantly she found herself looking down on an open-air courtyard, where the sun cast a pall of heat over a terrace of blue-patterned, mosaic tiles. Slim, white archways, intricately carved and gilded, curved overhead, reflecting in the still water of a pool. On a low couch, shaded by the fronds of delicate trees, lay two naked men, both sleeping.

One of them was dark-skinned, a colour like burnished copper. His body was mature, well-formed, heavily muscled. A cap of curly black hair fitted closely to his skull and his features, which were half in shadow, were strong and angular. The other man was young and fair-skinned. He lay face-down, his long yellow hair spread over the silken pillows, his slender, muscled limbs spread in a way that suggested total surrender to the pleasures of sleep.

Beside the low couch, there was a metal table holding

a bowl of fruit, glass bottles of coloured oils, and something which Garnetta did not recognize. Long sticks of
burning wood protruded from a slim-necked flask and
sent blue-grey smoke spiralling upwards, spreading a
heavy, soporific perfume into the air. As Garnetta's
dream-self watched, the blond man stirred, turning to
face the older man, presenting her with a view of his
broad shoulders, narrow hips, and taut buttocks. His
limbs were long and finely made. There was not a single
trace of spare flesh on his body.

The blond man's lips moved and she heard him
murmur a name, 'Harun? Harun, my friend. Are you
awake?'

With a low growl Harun gathered the young man into
his arms, one hand meshing in the tangled flaxen hair.
They pressed closely together, lips meeting in a joyous,
passionate kiss. Harun uttered some words in a strange
language as his hands slipped down the other man's
body until they came to rest on his buttocks. Moving
delicately he caressed the tight globes, trailing his fingertips down the damp crease, dipping into the furrow
where thighs and buttocks joined.

As Harun cupped his firm scrotal sac, the flaxen-
haired man sighed with pleasure and worked his hips,
rubbing his engorged shaft against the other's dark belly.
Their tongues lashed at each other between wide-open
lips. In a while the blond man pushed the other to lie on
his back, all the time running his palms over the planes
and hollows of the hard, polished muscles.

Harun relaxed against the embroidered silk, his dark
curls gleaming with droplets of sweat. Now fully revealed, his face was seen to be handsome although running to flesh at the jaw-line. His most striking features
were his piercing black eyes and wide, sensual mouth.
Deep grooves led down from the sides of his nose to the

corners of his mouth. He was strongly erect, the thick phallus jutting up from a mat of dark curls at his groin. The purplish glans was smooth and uncovered by a hood of skin.

The younger man sat up, his long hair swinging forward to mask his face. Reaching out he encircled the cock with one hand. Harun arched as the other man worked on him, then he grinned, his white teeth flashing against the mauve-brown colour of his lips. 'Ah, no. This is not the caress I crave,' he said in a deep accented voice. 'Onto your belly, for this day the infidel shall lay siege to and conquer a Western portal!'

With a husky laugh, the other man did as he was bid, murmuring, 'As it shall please you to pleasure me. I bow willingly to your onslaught.' Sweeping his long, fair hair to one side, so that it lay over his shoulder, he pressed his belly to the couch. His revealed profile was pure and clear-cut, the light, honey-coloured skin without a blemish.

Garnetta's dream-self registered shock. She moaned in her sleep, twisting so that the sheets wrapped around her body. Her lips parted and she uttered a sound of denial.

Harun looked down at the body spread before him, his face bound by desire and fascination. His brown fingers slid over the lightly tanned skin. 'Ah, but you are passing fair, Karolan,' he murmured, softly, then his voice deepening with humour added, 'For an accursed Christian!'

Karolan chuckled and looked over his shoulder. 'I imagine you wish to do more than just look.'

Reaching for what looked like a brass lamp, entwined by a snake, Harun closed his lips over the brass mouthpiece and took a deep pull of the water pipe. The fragrant blue smoke seeped out of his mouth and nostrils and he closed his eyes as the drug spread through his veins. 'Here,' he said, passing the pipe to Karolan. 'Draw deeply of the *nargileh*. The mixture is of my own blending. It will make your pleasure more acute.'

As Karolan sucked at the pipe, Harun dipped his fingers into a bottle of oil and with slow sensuous movements stroked his cock, squeezing the bulbous tip until a drop of clear fluid trembled at the slitted mouth. The oil gleamed on his dark phallus. Easing the younger man's buttocks apart he lubricated the shadowed rift and slipped his fingers into the tight entrance. Karolan closed his eyes, murmuring with pleasure. Harun laughed huskily as he stroked and probed, urging the muscled thighs to open to him. Soon Karolan's hips began to work. His breath quickened. 'Now. Let it be now,' he grunted.

Kneeling between the widely spread thighs, Harun pressed his oiled glans against the anus and dug his fingers into parted buttocks. Karolan jerked under him, crying out. Harun shuddered as the ring of hot flesh closed around his rigid shaft. 'By the One God,' he murmured, as he probed the depths of the other man's vitals. 'You are a sweeter drug than any elixir ever made by Jabir the Persian.'

Karolan spoke in a breathless voice. 'Elixirs? You speak of *al kimiya*? All these things and more, you will teach me as you have promised?'

'When the time is right, impatient one,' Harun said, his face screwing into a rictus of ecstasy. He thrust powerfully between the parted buttocks, the sweat pouring down his face. 'I shall teach you more things than you have dreamed possible. Oh, yes. Just that way. Tighten around me. Ah, you are becoming very skilled, matchless one.'

Karolan bucked and ground his hips against Harun's

pubis. His damp blond hair whipping out as he threw back his head with total abandonment. 'Then . . . when shall you reward . . . me with my . . . heart's desire?'

'Soon. There . . . are so many secrets I shall impart . . .' Harun whispered, the breath hissing through his stretched lips. Then his whole body went rigid as he emptied himself. 'Ah, the *samum* possesses my body!'

After their frenzied coupling the men lay intertwined on the couch, now and then drawing on the water pipe. In the dream, the day grew long. The heat went out of the sun. Spreading leaves cast a map of shadows over the interlocked bodies.

Garnetta woke for a second time. This time she was fully awake, her heart beating fast. Thoughts crowded into her head. She was both revolted and aroused by the forbidden images. Why had she dreamt of Karolan and that other . . . Harun? Nothing in her own experience could furnish her with such lewd imaginings. Shuddering, she pulled the bedcovers over her. The dream had been so vivid, so detailed. Then her preternatural senses came into play and she understood.

Instinctively she knew that she had experienced a vision of something which had actually taken place, but she was unwilling to believe that Karolan had ever lain in the arms of the handsome dark-skinned man. He frequently expressed views which bordered on heresy, but he could not be a sodomite. Sodomy was a grievous sin, denounced by the Church as worse than murder. The punishment for such foul practices was death by burning.

Then she laughed with relief. Of course. The young blond man had only resembled Karolan. It was not truly him. Karolan was white-skinned, his hair as black as ebony. Somehow her reasoning gave her no comfort. She found herself staring into the darkness, unable to rest, and searched back through past conversations with Karolan. Had he not told her that he had gained his knowledge of medicine in the Holy Land? The darkly handsome man in the dream was surely an infidel. The tiled courtyard, the pool – these things belonged to someone of wealth and culture, like a knight or a doctor. And he had called Karolan by name.

Eventually she threw back the bedcovers and padded across the chamber. She had to speak with him. From force of habit she threw a cloak over her shift even though she did not feel cold. As she passed by the open window, a movement caught her eye. She stopped and looked out beyond the fields to the edge of the forest. Moonlight shone on newly sown crops and silvered the tops of trees.

There came the subtle shifting, like the twitching of a curtain inside her. She knew at once that the tall, slim figure standing under the canopy of trees was Karolan. Even with her eyes closed she would have known it was him. She caught the subtle traces of his thoughts, touched the complexity of his persona. She focused expertly, hardly registering her body's adjustment now, and saw in the darkness that Karolan was looking skywards, a metal instrument against one eye. For a second she caught a glimmer of colour, a trembling amongst the newly emergent leaves on the branches of one of the trees. There came the blurring of a shadowy movement, then it was gone. She shrugged. Some trick of the moonlight.

Deciding to risk Karolan's displeasure, she pushed aside the carpet which masked the trapdoor and uncovered the staircase leading down to the workroom. She had discovered the opening for herself by accident when she renewed the stale rushes which covered the rest of the floor. There must be another entrance to the laboratorium, perhaps underground, leading directly out into the forest. For Karolan had not come back into the bedchamber before he left the tower.

The stone steps did not feel cold to her feet as she descended. The staircase was steep and she realized that she was going down deep into the earth. The sturdy door at the bottom of the stairs was unlocked. She pushed it open to reveal a vaulted room which blazed with candlelight. Immediately her nostrils were assaulted by a mixture of smells. She almost gagged. Overlaying the scent of herbs, unguents, the stink of sulphur, was something foul – bitter and meaty but with an odd sweetness. Garnetta recognized it at once as the stench of decay. She would never forget the pungent breath of the death-smell. The spectre of the death pit loomed out at her, leaving her shaking and nauseous. The feeling passed almost instantly and she took a few halting steps across the room. At first she could see nothing from which that smell might come.

This was not at all as she had imagined it would be. She had expected to find book shelves, but so many of them? There were books enough here to have been collected in ten lifetimes. Covering part of one wall was a chart depicting the earth and heavens, ringed around with astrological figures. Jars of dried herbs and coloured oils were ranged along the tops of chests of drawers. On the surface of a wooden table were a set of scales, a globe, and a ledger.

To one side of the room there was a furnace, the red glow of a charcoal fire seeping out around the edges of its door. A collection of strange apparatus was ranged around the furnace. There were metal tubes and glass containers, some of them bubbling and hissing. She walked to the back of the room, to the part in deepest shadow. Here the vaulted ceiling dipped low, spreading like the ribs of some great monster over the covered table in front of her. The smell was stronger here, coming from something under the sheet. She wrinkled her nose against the heavy odour of stale faeces. Whatever was on the table had been dead some time. It was a large animal, a wolf perhaps.

Reaching out she took a corner of the sheet and pulled. It slid to the floor, revealing the mess of blood, bone, and ragged tissue. The noxious smell rose in a wave, choking her and making her eyes water. 'Oh, dear God!' she cried, pressing her hand to her mouth and staggering backwards, at the same time overturning a rack of instruments. Sharp metal knives clattered on the stone.

The thing on the table had once been a man, but was now hardly recognizable as such. The skin was missing from the skull. The features, covered by raw muscle, glistened wetly. The eye sockets were empty and weeping a thin fluid. The teeth showed through the place where the lips had been. Garnetta gave a strangled sob and took a step backwards. She screwed her eyes shut, but could not rid herself of the image of the stripped limbs, the gaping ribcage, which was empty of all viscera, the glint of bone showing at spine and hip. Curls of skin were scattered on the table, which was stained with dried blood and scraps of blackened tissue.

As she staggered backwards, her stomach lurching, she swept out her arm, seeking blindly for a hand-hold on reality. This could not be real. If she accepted the evidence of her eyes then Karolan was a depraved monster, possibly a murderer. There must be some other explanation. Her heel connected with the base of some shelves which had been fitted into an alcove. Slamming to a halt, she drew in deep breaths, struggling to collect her thoughts. Turning her head, she froze. There was a glass jar at eye-level on the shelf she was leaning against. Something inside the jar was moving.

Whirling around she peered into the gloom. The thing that bobbed against the greenish glass, suspended in murky liquid was not alive; any movement was only in reaction to the fact that she had jarred the shelf. That did not help the horror or the ball of sickness in her stomach. She found herself staring into the lifeless face of an unborn child. Its skin was grey and bloated. Its eyelids bulged grotesquely out of its misshapen skull and its jaws jutted forward into a reptilian point. A long tongue, the end bitten and ragged, lolled out of its mouth.

Garnetta gagged. Bending forward she vomited onto the floor. The acrid smell clogged her nostrils, but it was better than that other smell. After a moment or two she recovered enough to straighten up. The thing in the bottle stared dispassionately at her. Moving slowly, bound by a morbid curiosity, she looked at the other shelves. There were many jars of all sizes, each of them filled with cloudy fluid and each holding a deformed child in all stages from embryo to full-term. Some of the bottled contents were so old that they had partly disintegrated into a pale spongy mass. Bits of tissue floated in the jars, suspended like pig meat in brawn jelly. At this thought her stomach heaved again. She swallowed hard, pushing down the nausea. One of the sad little corpses looked as if it had only just been put into the preserving fluid.

Garnetta's heart moved with pity. She was stunned by what she had seen and was hardly able to encompass the enormity of it. How? Why? Had Karolan collected all these things? What purpose could there be in desecrating the dead? She knew now that he was much more than a heretic, but she was not yet ready to condemn him. Had he not saved her life? There must be some explanation, however unlikely. She wanted so much to believe well of him. The future, which had stretched ahead full of hope and possibilities, could not just evaporate.

In a daze and shaking with reaction she walked back towards the wooden table and sat down in front of the open ledger. She intended to wait until Karolan returned and then challenge him. Trying not to think of the horror that lay on the table at the back of the room, she looked down at the open ledger. She began to read, slowly at first, then with mounting disbelief.

'It cannot be true . . .' she murmured as she flipped back the pages and read the entries concerning herself.

She felt chilled to the bone. Something terrible had been done to her. She did not understand the rows of calculations, the chemical symbols, but she could read the list of items used in Karolan's Godless experiments. He had bought and killed a child, then subjected the corpse to all manner of indignities. From the text she learned that she had undergone some kind of a process. There was mention of a spirit, a being, which had played some part in a ritual called – transmutation. Karolan wrote that this 'being' had tricked her into agreeing to some kind of unholy union with it. It appeared that this 'thing' had turned itself into an angel. She remembered the vision of a shining being. How joyful she had felt that God had sent his messenger to forgive her sins and to save her. But that had been an illusion, a device to gain her compliance.

Dear Lord, what had she agreed to? What had she become? She began to sob as she read the reports on her progress. The tears stung her eyes. Her throat ached with the force of her distress. Here was the evidence which she could not deny. Karolan wrote that he had great hopes for them both. He intended to tell her the things she needed to know before much more time had elapsed.

Garnetta pushed the book away violently. 'No!' she screamed. 'No!' She did not want to know anything more. She was terrified, filled with self-loathing. Karolan had damned her immortal soul to Hell! The thought of all the sweetness they had shared crumbled to dust. He had saved her for his own ends and had only been using her, observing her like that poor wretch lying on the table. She was trembling badly now, sick inside at the thought of his hands on her, his mouth on hers. Those same hands which had, mere hours ago, stripped the skin and removed the inner organs from a corpse.

'I even thought I loved him,' she whispered brokenly. Oh, what a fool she had been. The signs had been there, but she had refused to recognize them. His devilish glamour had blinded her, the force of his personality had seduced her. Her whole body felt hot with shame. He had woven a spell over her senses, made her a wanton and gloried in his triumph as her body wept for love of sensual pleasure. Well no more. She had to get away, now, before he returned. She had no idea where she would go and she did not care. Her only thought was to get as far away from Karolan as possible.

Outside the tower Garnetta moved swiftly, silently through the garden, passing the neatly trimmed box hedges and patches of vegetables. Karolan might return at any time and she wanted to be long gone by then. The garden was dark under the spreading branches of mulberry and apple trees, but her night-sight was as keen as that of a cat. The hens in a wicker coop, detecting her presence, set up an alarmed clucking. She silenced them with a thought, hardly registering the action.

At the far end of the garden there was a bower, planted with lilies, roses, and briars of sweet eglantine. The plants were only just bursting into leaf, but she had an image of how it would look. Karolan had told her how pleasant it was to sit here in the shade of high summer. Consumed by sadness, she allowed herself to linger for just a moment. It was likely she would never see this place again, never again set eyes on Karolan. Even knowing what he was, she felt torn by mixed emotions. Part of her wanted to go back and pretend that nothing had changed. She wanted so badly to recapture their intimacy, to feel again the first rapture of physical love. But everything was different, all of it tainted by the poison of the black arts he had used upon her.

She must fight the hunger for him which, even now, churned and roiled within her. It was part of the spell he had cast. She felt him as keenly as if he was part of her own body. Perhaps with distance her blood would no longer call out to him, her dreams would not be clouded with images of his past deeds. For now she knew that the 'dream' had indeed been a vision. Karolan was capable of anything. As she turned she caught sight of a movement. Instantly alert, she spun around, but it was only her reflection in the pool set beside a grass bank. She drew closer and stood staring down into the water. The moonlight pouring between the trees turned the water's surface into a mirror. The face of a stranger looked out at her.

Slowly Garnetta raised her hands and touched her shorn head. She stared at herself in utter astonishment. Instead of a blonde fuzz, the hair re-growth was black as pitch, clinging to her skull like a velvet cap. Her skin, which had been cream-toned, touched with pink at the cheekbones, was dead-white. It glowed softly against the darkness. She bent close to the water, hardly able to believe the other physical changes. Her eyes were no longer blue, but a reflective grey – like metal. There were specks of silvery light in their depths. They looked strange, disquieting – like Karolan's eyes. Exactly like Karolan's eyes. And her lips were full and red, she had the mouth of a wanton, or a fallen angel.

How was it possible that he had changed her so much? Small wonder that his household had accepted that she might be his niece. The dream made perfect sense. It had been Harun who taught Karolan the dark arts. Like herself Karolan had once been blond and blue-eyed. The process, whatever it entailed, had stolen his golden beauty and made him into night's creature. Harun had tricked Karolan into taking part in some filthy heathen ritual.

He has made me like him. I am his creature. But what manner of thing had she become? What was Karolan? The only way to find out was to go back and ask him, but everything within her recoiled at the thought of facing him. She stroked her white face with awful fascination. No one who had known her previously would recognize her. Garnetta Mercer no longer existed. *He saved my life. Perhaps this was the only way he could do that.* She thrust the thought away. If she was to weaken and feel gratitude, she would go back. Already she had wasted enough time. What might he do if he caught her? Kill her? Cut up her body? For he could not wish to draw attention to himself. She realized that her very existence put him in danger. He was not the sort of man to let a threat go unchallenged. Having once preserved her life, he might now seek to destroy it.

Moving away from the bower she left the garden by the wicker gate and made her way towards the hedge of pleached limes which gave onto the open fields. From there her view was unobstructed. In the far distance, she could just see the dark smudge that was Chatesbrook and the three spires of St Ralphite's, St Bertrina's and St Kate's-in-the-Meadow. Some distance from the town walls was the greater mass of Holy Penitence monastery, a regular configuration of dark shapes against the night sky.

She thought of going into the town, but knew that the gates had been locked against travellers since the pestilence gained a hold. It seemed that she must set her foot on the open road and rely, like so many others, on charity for her food and clothing.

She could detect traces of Karolan still. The vaporous mind-trail of his intellect was all around her, spreading a mist inside her head and throbbing in her blood like the fading echo of a great bell. It was going to be difficult to hide from him, for they were linked in some way. And if she, so newly made and ignorant of what had happened to her, was aware of him, then he, with all his honed and masterly talents, must be able to follow her every movement. Perhaps he knew already that she had left the tower. She turned her sights inwards, examining that place which had not been there before, and felt something like a shutter close in her mind. Karolan's presence receded. Ah, there was a way to shield herself from him. But the severing of that special connection brought with it a sense of loss. She felt a coldness within her as if an icy seed had taken root in her belly. This, then, was something else she must learn to live with.

Keeping to the shelter of the hedgerows she struck out for the forest. She felt a pang of regret at the thought that she must forgo the task of lighting a candle in St Bertrina's for her family, but shrugged off the feeling at once. The fact that she could do so with only a flicker of conscience was a mark of how far from grace she had fallen. Once her faith had been her strength, her belief in the mercy of God all encompassing. But God had not listened to her pleas for help. He had not come to her aid when Karolan and the unclean spirit had done their worst.

Now she was an abomination in the eyes of the church, unshriven, denied the comfort of her lost faith – set apart from others by the malady which had been visited upon her. What had Karolan said? *We are one. We belong together.* The words seemed sinister now. Her eyes glittered with tears, but she blinked them away. This was the last time she would allow herself to feel weakness. She was alone now and must make a way for herself.

It was very dark within the forest, the moonlight blocked by the dense canopy of trees. There were deer trails winding through the undergrowth of bracken which, so early in the year had reached knee-height. The new green growth, like bishops' crosiers, brushed against her bare feet as she passed them.

After a number of hours at a steady, running pace Garnetta still felt fresh and was hardly breathing fast. As she pushed more deeply into the forest, brambles tore at her clothes and skin. She hardly noticed them and did not feel the chill of the wet grass. The sky had lightened and the moon was low in the sky before she began to tire. Stopping for a moment she looked around. On all sides trees and undergrowth pressed in on her. She was completely lost. There was no sign of a path or a clearing, no smell of a dung heap or noise of animals, which would have indicated that habitation was near by. She concentrated hard, but could detect no life signs of any predators. If wolves were there, they were hunting elsewhere.

Weariness overcame her. She sank down beneath the spreading branches of an elm. Leaf litter formed a deep drift. She snuggled into it, scooping the dried leaves to cover her body. She slept immediately and did not dream.

All the next day she travelled at speed, stopping only to drink water from a stream. She found edible leaves and dug into the soft forest floor for pignuts. If she was to spend long in the forest she would have to hunt, but she had not even a knife or twine to set a snare. She could sell the cloak, it was made of good cloth, the clasp of silver set with precious stones. With the money she would buy food, a pack to hold the few things she needed, a tunic of homespun wool to cover her shift. The rest of the coins she would sew into the hem of the tunic. For the present, roots and leaves kept hunger pains at bay. She concentrated on keeping moving. The day passed swiftly. Except for birdsong and the rustling of small creatures in the undergrowth it was quiet. Sunlight filtered through the leaves, speckling the forest floor with coins of gold.

Despite her efforts to avoid thinking of Karolan, his face haunted her thoughts. She would never forget his arrogant beauty, neither would she forget the pleasure she had experienced in his arms. Even now her body awoke, burning and tingling at the memory of his flesh within hers, then she saw again the image of the flayed corpse. Her desire died as quickly as it was born.

As dusk fell she looked for a safe place to sleep. She was debating whether to climb a tree for safety, when she saw the glow of a fire through the trees. Her spirits rose at the prospect of food and company. Probably she had stumbled upon a company of charcoal burners or botchers. Such men lived deep within the forest, with their families, spending the warmer months accumulating wares which they sold at the glove and goose fairs of Michaelmas. They would have little enough to spare, living as they did from hand to mouth, but she might be allowed to spend the night by the fire in return for collecting firewood or helping the women with the children.

She began moving through the trees, the glow of the fire becoming brighter as she focused her attention upon it. Her mouth watered in anticipation of food. The smell of roasting meat wafted towards her on the breeze.

It was then that she heard the screams.

CHAPTER EIGHT

Karolan paced the floor of the laboratorium, his thoughts churning. A search of the house and immediate vicinity had yielded no sign of Garnetta. Romane had organized a group of men to search the forest, but they had returned when the light failed. This was the second night she had been missing.

'Tell the household that my ward has sunk again into the morbidity of the body which brought her to me for protection and healing,' he told Romane. 'Let them think she's wandering in the forest, out of her wits with a fever.'

'Very well, my lord,' Romane said, pursing his thin lips. 'Might I be permitted to know the real reason for her disappearance?'

'A man does not wish to speak of how he has been cuckolded by a wronged husband!' Karolan said, wishing that he did not need to lie to his steward. 'Suffice it to say that she has gone back to the brute. And after I gave her sanctuary!'

Romane shook his head. 'Aye, well. Who can understand the ways of women? She seemed like a fine wench too.' He looked sideways at Karolan. 'My lord? Nothing . . . untoward has happened to her, has it?' He did not add, *like the others*, but the question was there in his eyes.

'It has not,' Karolan said, his voice deliberately sharp. 'Was it not plain that I valued her highly? She came to no harm at my hands.' At least, he thought, what she has gained is more than equal to what she has lost.

'Forgive me,' Romane said. 'I know you held Garnetta in high regard. I'll set the men to looking again at first light.'

Karolan nodded absently. He wished now that he had told Garnetta everything and risked having her hate him. He imagined how she must have felt when she looked around the laboratorium and read the ledger. Seen through her innocent eyes, he was damned. He could not deny that many of his actions appeared to be indefensible. Useless to hope she would ever understand. She had not given him the chance to explain, but had fled from him in fear and disgust. He doubted whether she would want to set eyes on him again. He wondered what had shocked her the most, the revelations in the book, the jars with their testaments to his failure to reproduce, or the partially dissected corpse.

He cursed his failure to consign the cadaver to the furnace, but he had been reluctant to destroy it when there were still things to learn from it. What a marvel it was that the world of inner man reflected the greater world of the cosmos. As above, so below. He had hoped that Garnetta would share his fascination. But how could she while she still clung to the remnants of her Christian faith? She believed in a Church which reserved the power of healing for itself, denying physicians their craft, proscribing desecration of the human body – held sacred as the image of Christ. Prayer and fasting were the remedies for illness. Burning or cutting of the living flesh was not permitted. How much more sinful was he, who examined the conformation of the human body for his own ends?

He felt certain that Garnetta would, in time, be capable of radical new thought. To believe, like himself, that the progress of science was hindered by ignorance. But first she had to throw off the baggage of preconceived ideas. The signs that her intellect was sharpening, broadening, were there already. She had coped with the changes brought on by transmutation better than he had himself, but then, he had had no one to watch over him, no one to make the transition easier.

He ran his fingers agitatedly through his hair. Such thoughts were futile now. The fates had conspired against him. Garnetta was wandering the countryside, frightened and alone. In the midst of his fear for her there was a note of anger. Her rejection, understandable though it was, wounded him deeply. He had shown her nothing but kindness, but she had chosen to discard him. Just a little more time and she would have understood that the gift he had given her was priceless.

His straight black brows drew together in a frown. If he could find her, she might yet be persuaded to listen. But how was he to bring her back to the tower when she knew him to be a murderer and believed him to be a myriad of other vile things?

There *was* one way. As he gathered the things he would need to perform a finding ritual, he smiled bitterly to himself. One might detect the hand of God in the immediate events, except that he did not believe in the God of the Christians. Picking up a bowl formed from a single piece of obsidian he thought about how he had, in the past, cheated the fates, laughing in the face of the deity, whether God was called Jehovah, Yahweh, or any one of the ninety-nine names of Allah.

From a wooden box he took a number of candles, dyed black and scented with a pungent sweet oil. With a piece of chalk he drew a circle on the floor of the laboratorium. He assembled the elements of earth, fire, air, and water within the circle – a set of wind-chimes, the lighted candle, a piece of crystal, and the bowl filled with water. Checking carefully that the five-pointed star he now drew was perfect in every detail, he nodded with satisfaction.

The heavy, sweet scent of the burning candle rose into the air as Karolan stripped off his clothes and washed his body meticulously. When he was satisfied that he had purified his body, he stepped naked into the circle, settling himself in the centre of the star. He sat with a straight back, legs crossed, his hands clasped loosely in his lap. After speaking aloud the words which afforded him protection while travelling in the shadow realms, Karolan emptied his mind of all distractions and put himself into a light trance.

His body felt weightless, his senses drugged by the sickly sweetness of the burning oil, but his mind was knife-edge sharp. The scene around him began to change. The air trembled and the light failed. Within the circle the candle flickered. A cold breeze stirred the long tresses of his black hair. It seemed that the walls of the laboratorium moved outwards, receding farther away until he was sitting in a pool of darkness. The inky blackness of the space-between was without confines. It pressed against his skin like warm wool, muffling his ears against all sound. Only the circle held back the abyss from swallowing him whole. He banished from his mind the thought that he was alone in the Nothing, an insubstantial human form seated on a circle of light.

Gradually the black faded to grey. Dappled light licked at the edges of his vision. He was sitting under a canopy of trees. The sound of birdsong was sweet in his ears. The sharp odour of green things filled his nostrils. There were no landmarks. He could not tell how deep he was in the forest. Karolan looked around, using all his preternatural senses to try and detect a trace of Garnetta's life signs. There was nothing. He frowned, his concentration wavering for a moment. Instantly the forest grew dim. The blackness began flowing towards him like an ink stain on the grass. With a great effort of will he locked himself more firmly into the trance, beads of sweat breaking out on his brow. The forest scene wavered, grew sharp again. Still he could detect nothing.

Impossible. He had not developed masking skills for many months after his change, needing them rarely in any case. Only those of unusually keen intellect perceived his unnatural glamour and those were easily charmed or confused. It amazed him that Garnetta had become so adept. Refusing to admit defeat, he focused every last measure of concentration on probing for her mind-trail. There ought to be a scent left on the ether, like a slick of thin oil on water.

Back in the laboratorium Karolan's face took on a greenish tinge. Lines of strain appeared around his mouth. Sweat snaked down his face in rivulets, trickling from the point of his chin, dropping onto his clasped hands. His black hair was plastered to his skull, but still he held the trance.

It was no use. He could not feel her. She was completely closed to him. The dismay he felt was almost his undoing. Emotion was a distraction he could not afford while engaged in a ritual. He began to shake. His body sagged, hunching protectively over his solar plexus. His clasped hands tightened until the knuckles showed through the skin. The energy began to flow out of him in ripples of light. The waiting darkness absorbed it greedily. A bone-deep coldness crept over him. In the mortal world he was not troubled by cold, but this was a coldness of the ether, a draining of all life-force. This had never happened to him before. He had travelled the shadow realm many times, breaking through to other planes at will, but he had never been fearful in any way – until now.

Facing up to the fear, pushing it down and out through the soles of his feet, he gathered his will. With almost his last measure of strength he straightened his back and felt a flicker of the inner fire within him. He concentrated on that one point of heat until it grew stronger, spreading upwards until it centred in the space between his eyebrows. The cold began to recede. The ripples of light reversed, beginning to flow back into him. Seven points on his body began to glow with a pale-rose light. He visualized himself as a white form, seven jewels – each a different colour – set at the convergence of energy channels. The area between his eyes felt hot, solid.

It was tempting to end the ritual at once, but he knew that the formalities must be observed. There would be a heavy price to pay if a ritual was abandoned. Even he might not survive the damage to mind and body. Somehow he found the energy to retrace his steps and face the Nothing. The darkness was like a great maw, waiting to destroy him. In its suffocating embrace it would have been easy to lose his way. He had the sensation of spinning, then tumbling over and over, although he knew that he had not changed position. Grimly he held on, ignoring the illusion, willing himself to pass through the space-between, to enter the light.

The place in the centre of his forehead pulsed, radiating a life-giving heat, but he was barely conscious by the time the laboratorium resolved itself into matter around him. With a cry of agony he fell sideways and lay curled into a ball. After a while the pain receded to a bearable ache. He flexed his limbs, wincing at the tingling, but found that he could move his arms and legs. Coughing and retching, his lungs working like bellows, he raised his head to see the form of the Fetch at the edge of the circle. Unable to enter, it was flitting back and forth, its ragged shadow form undulating with colours of distress. The spirit's attenuated limbs stuck out at angles. Its movements were disjointed, unarticulated.

It was a moment before Karolan had himself completely under control. Slowly he stood up, said the words of completion, and left the chalk circle. Instantly, with horrible glee, the Fetch loomed close, unable to resist the opportunity to bathe in the emanations of his distress. Yet, as if it sensed that there was something different about him, it held off from actually coming into contact with his aura.

Shivering Karolan pulled on tunic and hosen, then sat on the stool next to his workbench. He ran his fingers through his drenched hair, smoothing it back from his pale forehead. His hands were still trembling. The Fetch hovered nearby, whispering and bleating in consternation.

'I fear, Master. You taste weak,' it said. 'Bitter is your scent to me. Why so?'

'You may well feel fear,' Karolan said dryly. 'I almost destroyed us both. I was nearly lost in the space-between.'

'Must not risk yourself, Master,' the spirit whimpered, the violet-brown streaks within its form fading to a more subdued rose. 'Precious you are to me.'

Karolan managed a grin at this declaration. The Fetch cared only for its own survival, but this was the nearest it had ever come to showing him true affection. Despite the fact that its words were redolent with self-absorption he felt an unwilling surge of warmth for it. It could not help its nature, any more than he could help being what he was.

'We've lost Garnetta,' Karolan said tiredly. 'I can feel no trace of her. She could be anywhere by now. I have no fear for her safety. Indeed I pity anyone who tries to do her ill, but it might be weeks before I find her.'

'Lost? Cannot be! I have not tasted, smelt, enjoyed her.' The spirit made a sound between a sob and a groan. 'Oh, too, too bad. I yearn. Hunger do I.'

Karolan raised his head, ignoring the Fetch's distracted mutterings. At least Garnetta was spared its incessant attentions. He had done right to keep the spirit from manifesting itself to her. 'The fault is mine,' he said. 'I ought to have foreseen something like this, but I was seduced by her innocence and beauty.'

Having once lain with her, he had become a prisoner of his own senses. Ah, that at least, he could never regret. A thought came to him. Of course. It was the only way. He would have seen the solution at once if he had not been so exhausted by the ritual.

'*You* must find her,' he said to the hovering spirit. 'I release you from the binding spell. Go after her. She does not know of your existence, so is not armed against you. Keep your distance then she may not detect your presence. Find her, establish where she is going, and report back to me. But I charge you to hold off with your tricks. If you terrify her out of her wits with your promises and demands you may tip her over the edge of sanity. And then! . . . I don't know if even I could bring her back.'

A soft golden light began to glow within the stretchy fibres of the Fetch's form. The momentary terror of sensing its master's weakness faded. It pulsed with eagerness, consumed by the desire to seek and find the female which it desired with a rampant lust. The infusion of womanly energy which it had taken from Garnetta during the transmutation had given it a new focus for its greed and certain strengths. Strengths which Karolan had so far underestimated.

Where before it had been bound solely by its master's demands, now it had a limited capacity for independent action. It stretched out its thin limbs as if luxuriating in the sulphur-tainted air of the laboratorium. The fabric of its spirit-form oozed, spreading on the air. For a moment only it formed itself into the remembered shape of the female.

Garnetta. How beautiful, how desirable, was she. In contrast to his handsome master, she was soft and rounded of limb. Her perfume was sublime – her skin like milk-of-almonds, her hair like warm hay. The shadowed recesses of her body were rich with a world of tastes and scents – musk, blood, the meat-rich smell of her body's wastes. It wanted to bathe in them all. Nothing was abhorrent to it. Its greed for sensation, for a fleeting experience of consciousness inside a female form, was all-encompassing.

The memory of being inside Garnetta's body was exquisite. Squeezed and confined inside the envelope of skin, subsumed beneath the pulsing life of her tissue, it had known the ecstasy of the living flesh. For an instant it had looked out through the eyes and seen another world. A world of depth, colour, possibilities. And it wanted more, more. It ached to become human – even for a few minutes. For that, it would dare anything, even the wrath of its master. The vague shadow-form undulated, seething with excitement. The representation of Garnetta's face and slender body hovered in the air before dissolving back into the amorphous mass of shadows and light, which was the spirit's shape in the physical world.

'It shall be as you order, Master,' the Fetch said. 'Find her will I.' And its voice was sibilant with hidden promise and self-serving need.

Clem struggled against the men who held him, but he was no match for them. He was barely ten years old and they were hardened fighting men, mercenaries who, like so many others, had turned to brigandage when the war-lord who had engaged them could no longer pay them for their services.

Tears pricked his eyes. Snot ran down into his mouth. Iron hard fingers dug into his thin limbs. Clem screamed again, weeping with fear and pain as they dragged him through the trees towards the blazing fire. His screams sounded small, lost in the great forest. That frightened him most of all. No one could hear him. No one would know when he died. The smell of his soiled hosen rose up pungently around him. The shame curdled in his belly. But the shame was not for the fact that his bowels had loosened with his terror, it was because he knew that he would tell them what they wanted to know.

The bigger of the two men gave his arm a vicious twist. Clem's scream dissolved into a kind of yelp. Bile rushed into his throat. He thought he might faint. He prayed that he would do so, hoping for a mercifully painless end, but he remained stubbornly conscious.

'Bring the scrap here. The iron, she is ready,' said Gille de Peyrac, his speech accented by his Norman roots.

He was the acknowledged leader of the band. A man of middle height, he wore a rusty iron breast-plate over a tunic so encrusted with dirt that no trace of the original colour remained. His face was small featured, pleasant, except for his eyes which were as expressionless as light-green stones.

The man holding Clem's arm chuckled. 'Won't need more'n a touch of heat to this tender young porker before he'll squeal, eh, Edwin?'

His companion nodded, concentrating on keeping their wriggling captive on his feet. A rugged-featured man, Edwin had been a farmer who had become a

139

mercenary when his farm was razed by bandits and his wife and children killed. He took no pleasure in killing, merely doing whatever was necessary to get a job done. It seemed to Edwin that it would not be necessary to torture the boy who looked half-dead from fright and willing to tell them everything they wanted to know. But he knew that Barnabas and Gille would not deny themselves the pleasure of a blood-letting; it had been too long since they fought in battle. Of all the ragged band, those two most missed the sport of killing.

The other men lay around the fire chatting companionably or cleaning weapons. Later, when the boy had told them where his village was, they would rouse themselves to the attack. Then there would be sport enough for everyone.

'Don't 'urt me, sires. I beg you!' Clem sobbed, his voice breaking on a high note.

'Oh, we won't hurt you, child,' Gille said, his sculpted lips curving in a smile that did not reach his eyes. 'Just tell us all that we wish to know. Then you will be free to go.' The tone of his voice belied his words.

'Oh, aye! Of a surety you will,' Barnabas sneered, giving the boy a shake and kicking out at the embers with a nailed boot so that a shower of sparks rose up into the air.

Clem, dumped on the ground, fell awkwardly onto his hipbone. The pain lanced through him, but he had no breath left to cry out. The one who was the leader, the pretty one wearing armour, knelt beside him.

Reaching out he ruffled Clem's dirty hair, took hold of his ear. 'So, what have we here? It looks like a dirty little animal, no? Might it taste good roasted? What say you brethren?'

Clem held his breath, not daring to look into the cold green eyes as Gille's fingers tightened like a vice, pinching the flesh of his earlobe until his eyes watered. Barnabas picked up the sword which had been resting in the flames. The big man advanced towards him, holding the sword outstretched. The white-hot tip glowed like a beacon, a deadly fire-fly against the background of the night. Clem watched it in horrified fascination, so enthralled by disbelief that he did not scream until the metal was held against his exposed calf. He heard the hiss, saw smoke rising, but at first it felt as if ice had been held to his leg. Then the pain swallowed his soul. His cry of agony rang out clear and true, wavering only as he choked on his vomit. The smell of scorched flesh tainted the air.

Gille de Peyrac watched the boy writhe, his blood drumming in his temples. There was a satisfying weight at his groin, the heat of excitement in his belly. Cries of pain were music to his ears. He smiled again, his handsome face as pleasant as if he was rubbing down his beloved *destrier* with a bunch of straw. Ah, poor Valoure. The war horse had taken a lance in the chest and died in agony. It had been an unlucky blow. A peasant – ignorant filth like this boy – had blocked his vision for valuable seconds and the lancer had slipped in beneath his guard.

Ah, well. The Lord giveth . . . Taking out his knife he cut off a piece of the boy's ear and popped it into his mouth. Clem convulsed with shock. A string of gluey spittle hung from his parted lips. His eyes were as wide and dark as a frightened hare's. Gille grinned. They had the whole night to play with the boy and they had only just begun.

'Put out his eyes, shall I?' Barnabas said helpfully. 'Send them boiling down his dirty cheeks?'

Gille made a sound of impatience, his gesture of dismissal almost effeminate in its delicacy. He had small hands, which were clean compared to the rest of his person. 'No, no, you buffoon. Later. I want to watch his fear. Begin by burning off his hair. It is riddled with lice and I do not favour adding to the number I foster.'

Clem gibbered, almost incoherent with mortal terror. Until that moment he had hoped against hope that they would free him. Now he knew that he was surely lost. Barnabas put a meaty hand on his throat to steady him, brought the hot iron close to his head. He felt the heat of it against his skull as his hair began to singe.

The other soldiers looked across with mounting interest. One or two of them rose to their feet. Clem closed his eyes tight shut and began to pray. A thin keening noise came from deep within his chest. He was powerless to stop it.

And then the woman burst from the trees, wailing like a harpy and laying about her with a wooden cudgel. For a few seconds the soldiers did not move.

'God save us it's a witch!' called out one.

'Nay, it's but a mad woman,' said another.

Some of them crossed themselves, others rushed for their weapons. To their eyes Garnetta moved so fast that she seemed to be everywhere at once. The flame-red cloak whipped out behind her as she swung the tree branch back and forth.

Barnabas cursed and clapped his hands to his arm, where a heavy blow from her club had numbed it. Taken by surprise Gille whirled to face his would-be assailant, a curse on his lips. Before he could draw his sword, he took a blow full in the face.

'Christ and all his saints!' he burbled through a split lip. His nose, which had taken the force of the cudgel, began to throb and swell. Blood poured down his chin. He ran his tongue over his front teeth. At least four of them had been loosened. Bloody hell and damnation, the wench had spoiled his looks.

'Run away,' Garnetta hissed through bared teeth to Clem. 'Go on. Run!'

Clem needed no second bidding. Despite having to drag his injured leg, he scuttled for the trees. Terror lent him wings. He wove back and forth, avoiding the hands which reached out to grab at his ragged tunic.

'Come then, you brave men who make war on children! Fight me!' Garnetta called out, spinning in a circle and brandishing the club. She was so fired up with anger that she felt as if she was St George facing the dragon. Even now she did not consider the rashness of her actions. There was a red mist before her eyes, a core of molten heat somewhere in the region of her solar plexus. She did not know where her strength came from, but it felt good. She was powerful, an avenging spirit. There was a point of pressure between her eyebrows. It felt as if light was pouring into her.

The soldiers held off, watching warily. The glow in her strange eyes, her abnormal strength, alarmed and disconcerted them. How could she, a mere woman, strike terror into their hearts? She must be accursed or perhaps she was an angel sent to punish them for their many sins. One of the men sank to his knees, his hands held out before him in supplication. Crossing his hands on his breast he murmured, 'Forgive me, Lady of the Rowan. For I have sinned grievously.'

Gille de Peyrac kicked the man in the side of the head. 'A pox on your pagan Goddess! There's your forgiveness! Get up you stupid bastard! Can't you see that she's naught but a skinny wench. She might be worth a ransom. That's no pauper's cloak she's sporting. She has probably been found swyving a priest and is fleeing from a nearby nunnery.'

The other men seemed to come to their senses. They tittered at the picture portrayed by his words. Ashamed of their superstitious fear they moved towards Garnetta. Two of them – small dark men, comrades of the man who had called on the ancient Goddess – held back, their hands held up before them, the middle fingers bent over their palms to form the ancient horned shape which would avert the evil eye.

'Sweet Jesu!' Gille roared. 'Take her! Or must I do every task myself?'

As the soldiers rushed towards her Garnetta felt the first flicker of fear. Instantly her belief in her own infallibility wavered, then died. In her belly the core of heat blinked out. The arm wielding the club suddenly began to ache. Her muscles protested and her arm fell to her side, but she kicked out anyway, screaming and struggling as they fell on her, their faces alight with the prospect of besting her. Garnetta scratched and bit at the grasping hands, but there were too many of them for her to make any impact. The man she had hit in the face barked out another order. A heavy blow landed on her temple. Stunned, only half conscious, she felt a nailed boot connect with the small of her back. The sharp ache pierced her through. Moaning with pain, she rolled onto her side, putting up her hands to protect her head. Fists rained down blows on her, punishing her for her arrogance in challenging the might of men. She bit back her screams, expecting at any moment to feel the cold metal of a knife or sword.

'Enough! I want the bawd alive! Get her up.'

Rough hands grabbed her, pulled her to her feet. She would have fallen but for the hands which held her upright. Her cloak lay at her feet, pulled off in the scuffle. The fine linen shift was torn and muddied, the neckline pulled down over one shoulder. Panting and spitting blood, she glared defiance at the man who came to look her over.

'Cursed, hell-cat,' Gille grated, sweeping her with a look that took in her slender form and ended at her bare feet and ankles. 'Where did you learn to fight like that, eh?'

She lifted her chin, biting back tears of pain, and saw with satisfaction that both of his eyes were fast blackening. The bridge of his nose was flattened and turning an ominous shade of purple. He grinned without humour, noting her appraisal. Deliberately he trod on her foot, mashing it into the carpet of leaves. The pain was sickening. She blanched, chewing at her bottom lip until she tasted blood. Her whole body ached and throbbed. There was a sharp pain in her back, another in her side. Every breath was an agony. She thought she might have cracked a rib.

Gille looked around at the other soldiers who wore various expressions of disbelief. 'Well? Why are you all standing there fly-catching?'

'There's just the one of 'er,' Barnabas, said stating the obvious. 'Who does she thinks she is, eh? You ought to be holding a distaff woman, not that bloody tooth-pick!'

'She was handy enough with that tooth-pick a few seconds hence,' Edwin said, smirking. He glanced at Gille's swollen face without the leader seeing. 'Mayhap we should ask her to join us!' The others laughed. Edwin clapped his big friend on the back. 'What's amiss, Barny? You ain't crackin' your face. You still favouring a sore arm?'

Barnabas sniggered nastily. 'It ain't my arm, I'm thinkin' of right now,' he said scratching at his groin. 'De Peyrac's thinkin' same as me, ain't you sire? Ain't much to go round though. She's lean as a skinned hare. A man could bruise himself on those hip bones.'

'There's enough for me and thee,' Gille said, attempting to smile and wincing instead. He dabbed at his ruined face with the hem of his filthy tunic. 'Christ's bones, she's given me a better wound than I've had in many a battle. For that she will pay. Strip her and bring her over here. I'll deal with this upstart wench first, then the rest of you can have her.'

'No!' Garnetta kicked and screamed, every nerve in her body jangling with terror. The spectre of Bunner and Rufus rose up before her. Karolan's touch had washed her clean of the bearers' foulness. Their joining in the tower had been a thing of wonder and sweetness. She tried desperately to hold on to that memory as a talisman against what was to happen. The soldiers would take it in turns to rape her.

At the thought of being violated for a second time, soiled and used like a privy pot, a cold hand gripped her heart. She could not bear it – but bear it she must. Would it help if she stopped struggling, offered to pleasure each of them in turn, begged for mercy? No. They would laugh in her face. Nothing would help her. The man called Gille took pleasure in torture. She had seen him cut off the boy's earlobe and put the bloody scrap of flesh into his mouth. There would be no mercy from him. Already he had unlaced the front of his hosen. His dangling penis was stiffening, standing up as he caught the acrid smell of her fear, saw the wildness of her eyes.

Her shift parted with a ripping sound. Willing hands dragged it from her, shoving and pulling her towards a fallen tree. Garnetta tried to focus her thoughts, to call up the strength which had come to her aid earlier, but she was made weak by her all consuming terror. Had she really fought all of them? Surely not. Her bladder relaxed and a stream of urine trickled down one leg. Seeing it, the soldiers laughed coarsely.

I won't cry out. I won't . . . She screwed her eyes shut as

146

they forced her to lie belly down over a fallen log. The rough bark scraped against her tender skin as she struggled. She could not see their avid, cruel faces, but she could hear their coarse voices and smell their unwashed bodies. Her gorge rose. Bile and water rose up from her empty stomach, bursting from her mouth and trickling down her chin. She moaned with pain as two men took hold of her arms, pulling them out to the sides. Another two took hold of her legs and pulled them apart. Her hip and shoulder joints protested. She thought she might be pulled into four quarters.

'You take her mouth, Barnabas. I'm for the tight nether portal,' Gille said, stepping between Garnetta's wide-spread thighs.

Garnetta was held fast, unable to do more than twitch a muscle, and forced to endure Gille's cruel, pinching fingers. He took pleasure in pushing his fingers into her dry passages, tugging on the sensitive lips of her sex. Tears ran down her cheeks as those holding her arms pulled and slapped at her breasts, but she did not cry out. Not until Gille spread her buttocks apart and rammed his cock hard into her anus. The pain was terrible. She sobbed and rose up against her captors, feeling delicate membranes tear and warm blood run down her thighs. Gille ripped into her, scoring her soft skin with his manicured nails, timing his thrusts to match her screams. Something gave in one of her arms, the hot ache of it almost lost in the torrent of other sensation. Despite her valiant efforts to hold herself apart from what was happening to her, Garnetta began to beg for mercy.

Then her mouth was stopped by Barnabas's onslaught. She gagged again at the smell of his unwashed parts. Stale urine warred with the cheesy smell of his member. Overlaying everything was the sour taint of his sweat. Holding the shaft of his cock, he stuffed it into her mouth, splitting and bruising her lips. He tasted like rotten meat. Gasping for breath, retching as the foul organ butted against the back of her throat, she writhed and twisted in an access of distress. The violation was both physical and mental. She strove to free her mind, to give it wings to fly, but the pain kept her earth-bound and she was spared nothing.

Gille made certain that she suffered as much as possible, using his maleness as a weapon. Each of his thrusts bruised something inside her. Her whole world narrowed to pain. It was raw-edged, gnawing at her vitals. Blackness hovered at the edge of her vision, but she remained conscious. It seemed an age before Gille mashed his belly against her buttocks one final time and spilt his seed into her bowels. At almost the same instant, Barnabas gave a great shout of triumph. His thick fluid filled her mouth. When he pulled away she choked out the semen on another gush of her blood and vomit.

Held in a space between agony and abject shame, Garnetta did not at first register the change in the men around her. Someone was screaming, a hoarse sound that held terror and surprise. Her ears still rang with the echoes of her own distress, so it was a moment before she realized that it was not herself but Gille and Barnabas who were making the sounds.

'God! Oh, God! Look at it! Look what the whore's done to me!' Gille screeched, his voice almost a falsetto. 'Help me someone. Oh, Christ! Oh, Sweet Jesu, it hurts!'

Barnabas bellowed and capered in front of her, his hands clasped to his groin. His lips were pulled back in a rictus of agony, showing dirty stained teeth. Garnetta lifted her head to see that thick, dark blood was trickling from between his fingers. Ropy trails of it were dropping to the forest floor. The men holding her limbs let go. She straightened slowly, painfully and looked at the two screeching men in confusion. Gille's eyes rolled back in agony. He fell to the ground, hunching over and jerking spasmodically. A litany of curses poured from between his lips.

Edwin hurried over to his friend and tried to prise Barnabas's hands away from his groin. His craggy face wore an expression of shock. A survivor of many campaigns, Edwin had seen men blown apart by culverins, men with torn and splintered limbs protruding from gashes in armour, but he had never seen anything like Barnabas's privy parts. 'Christ in Heaven, the fucking bawd's done for him!' He called out. 'Barny, lie still. I'll get the bag of sulphur powder from my pack.' Desperately he mouthed the invocation to stop the flow of blood. '*Sanguis Christi Maneat in te sicut Christus fecit in se! Sanguis Christi Maneat in te sicut Christus fecit in se!*' He had recited it a hundred times over men in battle, but had never thought to say it over a comrade slain by a wench. No one moved to help him. Edwin looked around at the others, taking in their looks of superstitious horror and confusion.

Gille still writhed in agony on the ground, his lower belly and hosen stained crimson. He lay in a spreading pool of blood. Edwin's lips thinned. He took charge. 'Someone get over here! You take Barny's hands. I can't see what's amiss for all the blood. Keep a hold on that bitch-witch. She'll pay for this pretty mess when I've tended to Barny and de Peyrac.'

Garnetta sagged against the fallen tree, feeling the weight of the branch against the small of her back. She felt light-headed, her senses dulled by pain and terror. It occurred to her that she could try to run away while they were all concentrating on the injured men, but her legs would not bear her weight. She hurt all over and could no longer distinguish what pained her the most. The stickiness of blood and semen cleaved her buttocks together. Her own blood slid on her tongue.

When two of the soldiers grasped her arms, half dragging, half carrying her to where Gille lay, she had no strength left to resist them. Moaning weakly, she sank onto her knees and found herself looking into the face of her tormentor. Gille's eyes were open and unfocused. He shuddered, his body arching into a final bow of agony. A dry rattle came from his wide-open mouth. He twitched once more and then lay still.

A moment later Edwin let out a great cry of rage and sorrow. He grabbed his friend's shoulders and shook him hard. 'No! Don't die on me, Barny! Ah, no. Oh, dear God!'

The silence was absolute. No one spoke. No one moved. Slowly Edwin leaned over and closed his comrade's eyes. He was pale under the weathering of his cheeks. After a moment he rose and walked over to Garnetta. Ignoring her he reached down to Gille, removing the hands which were still clutched to his groin. He held away the hands which seemed to be wearing wet, red gauntlets.

'See what the witch has done?' Edwin said through gritted teeth. 'Look well, all of you.'

There were gasps of horror as the damage was revealed. What had been Gille's penis was now a scrap of raw flesh. What skin was left on it was black and charred. There was a raw hole where his scrotal sac had been. His thighs and lower stomach looked as if they had been flayed. Strips of muscle glistened wetly in the wounds. He lay in so much blood that it was difficult to believe that there was a drop left in his body.

'But I did nothing . . .' Garnetta managed to choke, as

horrified by the sight as those around her. 'It was they who hurt me . . .'

'Aye, and they've paid dearly for it.' Edwin's face hardened. He grasped Garnetta's chin, forcing her to look at him. 'You're no fallen nun, nor yet are you as innocent as you look. It is unnatural for a woman to have the strength of three warriors. What in God's name are you?'

Garnetta whimpered, near to collapse. 'I don't know . . . Mother of Christ, help me.'

The soldiers closed in on her. Three small, dark men, their swarthy skins denoting their Celtic heritage, arranged their hands in the ancient sign of warding.

'Thou shalt not suffer a witch to live,' one of them muttered.

'What about the ransom? Someone will pay well to get her back,' another man said.

'Aye. The lass will bring in a pretty price. Edwin you lead us now. Gille and Barny would want that. What say you?'

'I say, fuck the ransom,' said Edwin. 'She's done for Barny. That's more'n enough for me.' So saying he unsheathed the skinning knife which hung at his waist. With swift economy of movement he slipped the blade in between Garnetta's ribs and angled it upwards to pierce her heart. Then, just to make certain, he forced her head upwards so that her throat was stretched taut and drew the blade in a wide sweep from ear to ear.

A torrent of blood frothed over his hand. Garnetta collapsed with hardly a sigh. 'Fashion some bunches of twigs into flambeaux, then kick some earth onto the embers,' he said flatly. 'We leave at once. This place is cursed.'

'Should we not give our brethren a Christian burial?' someone asked.

'Nay, leave the bodies for the crows,' Edwin said, his eyes flickering around the undergrowth. The hairs on the back of his neck stood up. He imagined that the shadows were moving towards him. 'You bury them if you feel the need. I'll not stay a minute longer in the witch's company.'

Stripping the weapons from Gille and Barnabas, Edwin stuck them into his pack. Without a backward glance, he strode towards Garnetta's discarded cloak. It was a fine garment. Edwin hated wastage. Settling it around his shoulders he fastened the clasp. He would find a priest when they next paused in a village and have him say a prayer to St Ninian – patron of those who performed the work of cleansing evil spirits.

Crossing themselves and muttering prayers for protection, the band of soldiers began picking their way through the trees.

Hidden deep within the tangle of undergrowth, Clem watched them go. He shivered with pain and reaction, having watched all that transpired. His teeth chattered so much that he was forced to clamp them down onto a fold of his dirty tunic, lest the noise attract the soldiers' attention.

He did not dare let out his breath until the last glimmer of flame faded in the distance, then he hunched over and began to rock back and forth, moaning softly in his distress. Tears made tracks down his grubby cheeks. His burnt leg and notched ear throbbed unmercifully. The deep scratches from wild briars bled into his clothes, but he did not dare move. He remained in his cramped position for the rest of the long night, his fitful sleep haunted by visions of the brave woman who had rescued him and who now lay dead next to the blood-soaked soldiers.

CHAPTER NINE

Garnetta opened her eyes and lay still, listening to the rasping sound of her own breath. The leaf mould where she lay was sticky with her blood. Beside her were sprawled the bodies of Gille and Barnabas, their faces twisted into expressions of the purest agony.

She tried to swallow and felt a soreness and obstruction in her throat. Even to move her head slightly was an agony. There was a terrible pain in her chest. Every time she drew breath, the soreness pierced her through. Raising her hand she felt the thick seam of raw scar tissue around her throat. In parts the skin had not knitted together and she could push her fingers under the wet flap of the cut. Her hand ought to have come away stained with blood, but the wound had been staunched.

Gingerly she slid her hand over her breast. Her fingers found the open leaves of flesh where the knife had entered. Like the wound on her neck, it was not bleeding. This was impossible. Edwin had killed her. She remembered the appalling sensation of the knife sliding into her flesh, burning an icy trail through her lungs, entering her heart. Something had given way inside her then. Black wings seemed to beat against her ears. She had been barely conscious when he cut her throat.

Either injury was a mortal wound. And yet she was breathing. It was unnatural. But unnatural or no, it appeared that she had survived. Every muscle, every nerve seethed with agony. She moved her hand further down over her ribs, and felt the rough edge of a bone protruding through the skin. Exquisite pain lanced through her as she pressed on the piece of bone, but it slipped inside her readily. She felt a sickening lurch as the bone re-aligned itself.

She snatched her hand away, revolted by her own flesh. 'Blessed Mary, mother of Christ, how can this be?' she whimpered.

After a moment she recovered enough to feel over the rest of her body. There did not seem to be a single area of her body that was not bruised and swollen. Edwin's words echoed in her head, *In God's name what are you?* and her own reply, *I don't know.* And God help her, truly she did not. What had Karolan done to her? No one could cheat death. She had seen each of those she loved die. They had been spared nothing. She had been powerless to help them. Yet, here she was, broken and suffering, but alive. Perhaps she had been dead since the pestilence raged through her. Now she was a husk, animated only by Karolan's foul magic.

She moved slowly, pushing herself into a sitting position. Her thoughts were clouded by the pain in her body. It sapped her will, making it difficult to concentrate. She stopped trying, centring all her efforts on moving. She had to get away, find someone who would help her. Someone who was close to God. A priest would know about evil spirits. She longed to be shriven, to be comforted in the bosom of the Church.

Gradually, stopping to take deep breaths when the pain was too much, she managed to get up onto her hands and knees and crawl over to her ruined shift. She propped herself against the fallen tree, overcome by weakness. For almost an hour she sat motionless, staring into space, thinking over all that had happened. The dead men mocked her with their silence. She averted her eyes from the terrible wounds at their groins. Somehow *she* had killed those men. Part of her was glad that the soldiers were dead. They had been wicked men, murderers, thieves, deserving of their fate, but God's commandments were clear. *Thou shalt not kill*. She had done so, indirectly perhaps, but she was culpable none the less.

The sin of it weighed heavily upon her. Her lips moved in the words of a *Miserere*. But the words of the prayer offered scant comfort. After a time she felt strong enough to pull the torn and muddied shift over her head. Biting her lip against the pain, she struggled to her feet. It was no use to stay where she was. She must walk until she came to a cart track and follow that to the nearest village. Hunched over, her hand pressed against her sore ribs, she started forward.

From the corner of her eye she thought she detected a movement. It was nothing tangible, more a disturbance in the air. There it was again, a sort of silvery whirlpool that blinked out of her vision if she looked at it directly. She had seen something like that before, but where? Then she remembered. It had been in the tower. She had woken from a deep sleep and lain looking through partly closed lashes at Karolan. For a moment only she allowed herself to think of him, her beautiful lover, her saviour. And her betrayer. She pushed away the emotions that thinking of Karolan stirred up.

The movements in the air changed. It seemed as if there was a pleating, an infolding. This is how it might look if the wind were visible, she thought. Those strange eddies and striations had been visible in the air above Karolan's shoulder. He had told her that this was a trick, something he was practising to entertain her. Now she knew that he had lied. He had conjured no gimcrackery to delight the eye, but something far more sinister. *It is his familiar. The unclean spirit I read about in the ledger. He has sent it after me*. Whatever the thing was, it was following her. She heard its voice, twittering and whispering in the overhead branches of a tree. Anyone else might have mistaken the sound for birdsong, but she knew better. Her preternatural senses told her that this was something entirely new, something of which she had no previous experience. There was a glimmer of soft light in the branches, a suggestion of a long shadowy form.

'What are you?' she called out, her damaged voice rusty-sounding. 'Are you a demon, a foul beast from the pit of hell? You tricked me once, but you won't do so again. Show yourself. What are you afraid of? Answer me!'

The only answer was a burst of trilling laughter. The tone of it chilled her blood. In that sound was a welter of experience. It was ageless, all-knowing – capricious and cruel – but there was something deeply sensual about it too. She sensed that the creature wanted her. Its fascination had an odour like licorice and almonds – a smell at once enticing and sickening. A wave of warm air swept over her and she felt soft tendrils brush against her face. Oh, God, surely they were fingertips that caressed her skin as if seeking to absorb the map of her features.

There was breath against her skin, hot and perfumed with spice. The trail of sensation moved down her chest. Her nipples rose in instant response, throbbing and burning, peaking under the ruined shift. The thing's scent was stronger, beguiling her senses. Her mouth watered. A whisper tickled her ear. 'Beautiful you are,' said a husky voice. 'Ah, lovely to me is your agony. Pleasure – much pleasure, we shall share.'

For a second longer she was consumed by the tactile quality of the spirit's presence. Tenderness radiated from it. She felt cherished, loved, desired. Against her better judgement she felt herself responding. Then, without warning, it was gone. Garnetta staggered and almost fell. The sense of loss was urgent within her. The forest seemed more silent than ever with the thing's passing. Only the breeze rustled the leaves. *Come back. I do not want to be alone. Help me.*

Now she knew that her wits had fled. Karolan's familiar would be devil-spawn, an ugly thing. She pictured a creature with a shiny black carapace, sharp, pointed teeth. Surely it crept on four legs and tore at its food with scythe-like claws. It could not be this sensuous being of light and shadow which promised fleshly delights. In her distress she was hearing and seeing things which could not exist. But even that was an illusion. She was living proof of the impossible. Nothing made sense any more. The only reality was the springiness of the forest floor beneath her feet and the pain radiating through her body with the clarity of plainsong. Then she thought she heard an echo of the spirit's laughter, far away.

'Leave me alone, can't you,' she called out, stumbling onwards, her voice breaking on a sob. 'Whatever you are, demon or dark angel, get away from me. Stop tormenting me. Have you not done enough? And damn you Karolan! Damn your black soul to Hell! I wish I had never set eyes on you!'

Clem rubbed the sleep from his eyes as he stood looking down at the bodies of the soldiers. They had died horribly and in agony. He was glad. He had seen them violate the woman and felt sick at his powerlessness to help her. At first he was at a loss to understand why they had been stricken with a blight to their privy parts. Then he had the answer. It was a miracle. The woman had come from a convent, he had heard the soldiers say as much. The Lord looked after his own. It was fitting that the soldiers had been stricken by the wrath of God and the Holy Virgin.

He pushed at one of the corpses with his bare foot.

This was the man who had notched his ear, the Norman. That other was Barny. But where was the woman? Looking around with a practised eye he saw the tracks leading through the trees. There was the trail made by the soldiers and, going in the opposite direction, he could detect the fainter marks made by the woman.

Clem scratched at his head, catching a louse and squashing it between his broken fingernails. He had felt sure that the woman was dead. True he had not seen every detail of what had been done to her – it was dark amidst the trees with only the firelight for illumination – but Edwin had stabbed her twice, he was certain of that.

Well he was right glad that she still lived. She must be injured and in need of help. Clem decided to follow her. There might be a reward for helping her. His injured leg, bound up now beneath a poultice of chewed grass, did not slow him down overmuch, but it was a while before he caught up with her. Even before he caught sight of her, he heard her call out and held back, fearful that the soldiers had come back. When he heard no other voices, he approached warily through the trees. Eyes widening as he took in her appearance, Clem hid himself behind a thicket of brambles. He knew himself to be a simple lad, never having had the benefit of a priest to teach him his letters, but even he could see that something was terribly wrong. How was it possible that the woman was on her feet? She looked like the painting of St Julitta which had been hung at the back of the mummers' wagon when it passed through his village. St Julitta had been stretched on a rack, beaten, then her sides were ripped apart with hooks. Clem had wept for the poor martyred saint, impressed by her terrible wounds.

This woman's body was almost as torn and bloody.

The ragged shift did nothing to conceal the marks of the knife. There was a livid wound at her throat, a deep cut under one rib. Almost the entire surface of her pale skin was disfigured with purple bruises and swellings. By the way she favoured her side, he thought that she had some broken bones. Any one of her wounds would have been enough to set a soldier on his back for a sennight. As he watched she began crying out, speaking to someone he could not see. Clem looked all around, but there was no one in sight. Standing still the woman raised her face to the sky. She closed her eyes. A look of rapture came over her face. Clem's eyes almost popped out as she lifted her hands and rubbed her palms against her breasts.

Cold shivers ran up his back as he heard her calling out. A woman should not curse like that. It was indecent. Surely a nun would not caress herself so wantonly. He crossed himself, muttering a prayer for protection. It was clear that the woman was possessed. But whether she was saint or demon, he could not tell. Filled with awe he followed her, keeping out of sight. As she stumbled and limped through the trees, the woman cocked her head as if listening to the voice of an invisible companion. Now and then she muttered something in a voice too low for Clem to hear. Doggedly he kept abreast of her, making sure that she did not detect his presence.

The sun was high overhead before the woman came upon a trackway. She did not set foot upon the dusty rutted surface, but hid herself in the long grass and brambles at the edge of the road. Clem settled himself down at a safe distance. He was tired and his feet ached. More than anything he wanted a drink of water. It was a marvel that the woman had made such steady progress. Despite her weakened state she had not faltered or stopped to rest. He remembered her unusual strength while fighting the soldiers and crossed himself again, just for good measure.

The shadows were beginning to lengthen before Clem heard hoof beats and the crunching roll of cartwheels in the distance. In his home village, half a day's journey away in the opposite direction, the men would be coming home from working their strip fields. Clem's stomach growled, reminding him that he ought to be eating the main meal of the day. His mother would be serving up a dinner of boiled leeks, bread, and ale. His mouth watered as he thought longingly of the food and of his brothers and sisters who would be quick to eat his share between them. He tightened the belt at his waist, resigned to a few more hours without food. When he returned to the village at last, he would have a few coins to show for his absence and a story to tell time and again when the cold weather kept them all inside the family croft. He grinned, showing strong yellow teeth. Many times he had been beaten for his laziness. 'Thee were born yawnin',' his father often said. 'Thee mun not be idle, lad. Devil maketh work for them that are.' Well, this time it was not Clem's fault that he was late back from market. This time his father would have to eat his words.

The cart trundled into view, preceded by two monks riding mules. Set up high in the drover's seat was a monk robed in the white habit of Holy Penitence. Clem recognized the man's heavy features, sunk within the folds of a cowl. Brother Amos, the kitchener from the monastery, was a frequent visitor to the markets and farms in his quest for the best food for the abbot's table. The kitchener wore a self-satisfied expression, as well he might, thought Clem. The main body of the cart was stacked high with barrels and covered over with a cloth of tarred canvas. By the smell wafting out, it was plain that the kitchener was replenishing his store of fish.

Clem's first thought had been to step into the road and wave the little cavalcade to a halt, but seeing the kitchener aloft, he hesitated. Brother Amos was not known for his good temper, and when returning to the monastery fully laden, was likely to brush aside any obstacle in his path. The two mules passed Clem by, then the cart's wheels rolled past, clattering and rumbling against the stones. A flap of the tarpaulin had pulled loose and was blowing open in the breeze. Clem saw the woman come out of the trees and lope after the cart. She was hunched over and grimacing with pain, but moving fast. He watched in amazement as she hoisted herself up and rolled inside the back, pulling the cloth to cover herself.

It had taken only seconds. Neither the kitchener nor the other monks had noticed anything amiss. Clem was impressed by the woman's resourcefulness. By the time anyone discovered her presence she would be inside Holy Penitence and decisions about her fate would be in the hands of the abbot. He decided that he too would go to Holy Penitence, but there was no need to hurry now. Although the skills of the infirmarer there, a certain Brother Stephanis, were of some repute, Clem thought that it would be some time before the woman was brought back to full health. He would make his way to the monastery in a day or two. By that time, from what he had already seen of her, the woman ought to be creating quite a stir.

He gave a sigh of contentment. His burned leg was throbbing fitfully, but the pain of it was bearable. His injured ear hurt him more. He would be marked for ever – a thief's mark when he was no thief. After all that he had suffered, reaction finally set in. He gave way to exhaustion. The sun was warm on his back and his eyelids felt heavy. Nestling down into the sweet scented grass, he pillowed his head on his bent arm and fell asleep.

*

Brother Stephanis de Mayne was preparing his own medicaments. Helping him in the still-house was young Thomas Wyatte, a layman of fifteen years, who had been his assistant for the past few months.

It was pleasant inside the airy stone room, kept warm by the charcoal burner placed under the still. Smells of fresh and dried herbs, betony, centaury, and elecampane rose in warm drifts. Stephanis found it satisfying indeed to make up recipes using the herbs from his own infirmarer's garden. For more complex medicines he was obliged, albeit grudgingly, to give his custom to the apothecary who served the monastery. An ambitious man and not unaware that he exhibited the sin of pride from time to time Stephanis tried, as far as was possible, to provide all of the medicinal waters, cordials, and lozenges that the monks might need.

'Take care now with that infusion of galingale root,' he said to Thomas. 'I want it strong enough to mask the bitter flavour of opium in this sleeping draft.'

Thomas grinned, well used to the infirmarer's meticulous eye for detail. He respected Stephanis and admired the man's dedication to his craft, but he could not say that he liked him. It had always seemed to Thomas that the infirmarer's calm exterior and even manner was a veil spread thinly over a cauldron of contained emotion. Sometimes he saw brief evidence of this underlying passion. When Stephanis treated one of the monks or a sick peasant he would lay his cool white hands on their diseased flesh with visible ardour. In part, this accounted for the infirmarer's reputation as a healer. Stephanis had the gift of inspiring trust and a sense of calmness in the sick. Thomas felt a little shame-faced at the uncharitable thought that the infirmarer gained much for himself in spiritual payment also.

Stephanis rolled up the sleeves of his habit, revealing

muscular forearms. Picking up a pestle and mortar he began grinding up the ingredients for the clyster which he would later administer to old Brother Marcus, who was afflicted with a morbus of the bowel. It was quiet in the still-house, save for the bubbling of the glass vessels. A faint sound of chanting came from the sacristy. Stephanis looked towards the open window with its view of the herb garden. Growing things, plunging his hands into God's good earth, these things soothed his restless soul. In the outside world of men there were many temptations to snare the unwary. Only here at Holy Penitence had Stephanis found some measure of peace.

'Should we not cleanse our hands, brother?' Thomas said. 'The day lacks but an hour to Vespers.'

Stephanis smiled, suspecting that Thomas's eagerness to leave his work had more to do with the fact that it was a minor feast day. The daily dishes, the generals, served to visitors in the misericord would be augmented by a number of extra pittances. 'When we hear the bell, it will be time enough to leave,' he said mildly.

Thomas pressed his lips together and continued with his work. He knew that the infirmarer's belly must be near cleaving to his backbone, as was his own. The single meal of the day throughout Lent was served after the singing of the early evening office, which meant that everyone, saving the sick, had been without food for many hours. Only an ascetic could remain unmoved by the prospect of filling his stomach and Thomas did not believe Stephanis to be immune to the solace of human comforts.

He sighed, having intended to sneak into the apple store and pocket some fruit on the way towards the well in the yard. For a while the two men worked on, Stephanis kneading together a sticky mixture of powdered hore-hound, pelesot, and honey, before pinching off tiny amounts and rolling it into pills. The sound of a commotion floated in through the window. Thomas lifted his head, glad of the diversion. Dusting off his hands and wiping them on the linen apron at his waist, he went to stand in the open doorway. Beyond the garden, the postern gate stood open. The kitchener's cart was being unloaded. Barrels of salted fish had been set on end in a line.

'What's amiss, Thomas?' Stephanis said, coming to stand beside the young man.

'I can't rightly say,' Thomas said. 'There is a deal of interest in Brother Amos's cart this day. Perhaps the brothers have got word that he brings fresh ling and haburdens with him for the morrow's pittances.'

Stephanis frowned. There was certainly something unusual happening. As he watched he saw an object being carried from the cart and laid gently on the ground. A figure detached itself from the group around the cart and began hurrying towards him. For no reason at all Stephanis felt a stirring of emotion. Afterwards he was to wonder whether he had been visited by a flash of intuition. Panting, the monk ran down the neatly clipped grass path, his habit brushing against the edging of lavender and sending the clean fragrance wafting towards Thomas and Stephanis.

'Come quickly, brother. Your skills are needed,' the monk said. 'A poor wench, sore misused, has been found hiding in Brother Amos's cart. Brother Amos is all for casting her out. He says that she will bring the pestilence among us.'

Pausing only to tell Thomas to lay out the things he might need, Stephanis lifted his habit to reveal bony sandalled feet and set off at a run. He reached the cart to find that the woman was surrounded by curious monks.

'Stand back,' he ordered, as he knelt beside her. 'Give the poor wench some air.' Dried blood encrusted most of her body, so that it was difficult to tell what her wounds were. Her limbs were swollen and discoloured by bruises. The torn and muddied shift concealed hardly anything of her slender form. What delicate hands and feet she had. And such a face. Even the violet shadows beneath her eyes and livid bruise that stained the whole side of one cheek, could not distract from the purity of her features.

Stephanis saw that a cursory glance would not be enough to establish what treatment was needed. 'Bring her to the infirmary,' he said.

The kitchener threw him a hostile glance. 'The infirmary? When the woman has the infection? Is this wise, brother? She's a felon. Crawled into my cart without so much as a by your leave!'

'I see signs of a fever, but no tokens on her skin. She's been attacked, violated, probably robbed. Look at the quality of her shift. This is no peasant wench, but a gentlewoman fallen on ill times. Should we deny her God's mercy?'

'I did not say that we should,' Brother Amos said sullenly. 'Only that it were wise not to act rashly.'

'And I've noted your comments. Two of you lift her, carefully now. And follow me. Thomas has all ready.' Not trusting himself to say more, Stephanis went on ahead to the infirmary. His mouth was suddenly as dry as bone. His head began to ache. He knew that he ought to have told the monks to take the woman away, but he could not. Seeing her lying there, so fragile and helpless, had awoken something long neglected within him. He winced as the pressure built up behind his eyes. Flashes of light distorted his vision. There was a darkness at the periphery of one eye. It had been years since he had been struck with a megrim. He tried to order his thoughts, to decide whether to go straight to his medicine closet and fetch his bottle of skull-cap and valerian tincture.

But the only thing that kept going around and around in his head was the certain knowledge that his days of peace and tranquillity were over.

CHAPTER TEN

Garnetta felt herself lifted gently and borne down a grass pathway. From all sides came the fresh scent of growing herbs. For a moment she was mindful of Karolan's garden. She opened her eyes and found herself passing along the open archways of the covered walk. The pattern of sunlight and shadow danced on honey-coloured stone. Cloisters. This must be Holy Penitence. She was safe in the House of the Lord. Mutely she sent up a prayer of thanks. Light streamed in through countless unshuttered windows. Those who carried her paused in a chamber, where hangings of red and green worsted divided the space into cubicles.

'Set her down there,' said a male voice. As he bent over her, his face floated in and out of focus. She saw a strong, well-made face, one which would have been better set on a soldier than on a monk. Coarse brownish hair, lightly streaked with grey, framed his big features. His gentle voice inspired her confidence. She tried not to cry out in pain as her attendants laid her down on a pallet. The chamber smelt of clean linen. The straw beneath the pallet rustled as she sank onto it.

'You may leave us now,' the monk said. 'Thomas, bring a bowl of vinegar water and soft cloths. I need to wash away this dried blood. Dear Lord, there is so much of it. It is a wonder that she lives.'

'I have everything here, Stephanis,' Thomas said, placing the objects on a low wooden chest which stood beside the pallet. 'Praise be, her eyes are open. Look, her lips are moving. She's trying to speak.'

Stephanis bent close. 'What is it, my child?'

'Garnetta . . . my name . . . Garnetta,' Garnetta whispered.

'Well, Garnetta,' he took her hand, cradling it against the rough fabric of his habit. 'You are safe now in God's keeping. I am Brother Stephanis, infirmarer here. This is Thomas, my assistant.'

As Stephanis's cool hands moved over her skin, gently washing away the blood and filth, Garnetta let herself go limp. For the first time in days she felt at peace. Her broken body would be healed, a soothing balm spread over her soul. 'My confession . . .' she murmured, recalling that this was somehow important. It was so difficult to order her thoughts.

'All in good time, my child,' Stephanis said. 'Rest easy now.'

The monks spoke quietly to each other as they examined her wounds. She heard the sharp intake of breath, the note of concern in the younger man's voice when he said, 'Someone wanted this woman dead. What could she have done to provoke such ire?'

'Little or nothing,' Stephanis said. 'There are brigands running loose who kill for the hank of bread in a beggar's bowl and find sport in stripping the habit from a nun.'

'For shame,' Thomas said shocked. 'It's a miracle that the knife did not cut her more deeply. A wound to the throat ought to bring death.'

Brother Stephanis murmured his assent. 'It ought to indeed,' he said, absorbed in examining the wounds on Garnetta's ribcage. 'See where the knife went in? And here where the edges of the flesh are torn? A broken bone came out of the skin. She must have fallen and knocked the bone back into place. How extraordinary that it did not puncture a vital organ.'

'This woman must be under the protection of the saints,' Thomas said.

'Hmmm. Then they were remiss in their attentions,' Stephanis said dryly. 'Look at the stains on this shift, the pattern of bruising on her buttocks. She was forced into carnal sin before being beaten and stabbed.'

Dimly, Garnetta sensed the younger man's discomfort. He reddened, averting his eyes as Stephanis examined her body more intimately. His touch was deferential and she did not resist as he parted her legs and examined her privy parts. They washed her clean of caked blood and semen with more of the vinegar and water. Their voices seemed to come from very far away. Garnetta lay listening to them, while the quiet of the monastery seeped over her. Between them the two men managed to roll her onto her side, strip off her soiled shift, and cover her with a clean sheet.

'Give this to the washer woman. Have them launder and mend it,' Stephanis said, his tone brisk and business-like. He passed the bunched up shift to Thomas. 'Well? What are you staring at, lad?'

'It . . . it is nothing . . .' he stammered. 'Just that she is passing fair. Such white skin and slender limbs, like the statue of Our Lady in the chapel. See her feet? They have a blush at the toes. Surely angels have such feet.'

Stephanis cleared his throat. 'Fair? I suppose she is by some account. Beware, lad. A comely woman is a lure to tempt the faithful into sin. Fleshly beauty is corrupt and belongs to the devil, God sees within. Now stop mooning over her. Save your sheep's eyes for a village lass. This here's a lady of breeding.'

'Yes, Stephanis,' Thomas said, chastened. 'I just thought that . . . well, do you not think it remarkable that she found her way to us, all broken and bleeding as she is? It is almost as if God sent her to us.'

'Hold your tongue!' Stephanis said. 'Do you dare to profess a knowledge of the ways of the Almighty?'

'No,' Thomas, muttered. 'I leave that to those who are nearer to God than I. But all the same. Does it not say in the Bible that common men have been visited by angels?' At Stephanis's hostile glare he dropped his gaze. 'Forgive me. My tongue has a will of its own. Will I get you a needle and twine to bring together the edges of the knife wounds?'

'Not yet. I'll spread some clean linen with healing salve and cover the cuts for the present.' Stephanis paused and stroked his chin, a habit of his when thinking. 'Have a boy run to the house of Mr Geoffrey Wenlock, the medicus who serves as adviser to Holy Penitence. I am in need of his expert opinion.'

Thomas looked sharply at the infirmarer. It was unusual for Stephanis to seek help with diagnosing an ailment. The last time the physician had been called to the monastery had been on the occasion when a knight had fallen from his horse outside the main gate, smashing his hip-bone. Stephanis had no liking for Mr Wenlock who would sweep haughtily into the infirmary, his face alight with self-importance and his robe – with the three fine furs of budge attached to the hem – swirling out and scattering the rushes thence and hence.

'But do you not remember? Mr Wenlock has left his office in the town and departed for his country manse, there to wait until the pestilence has run its course.'

'Ah, yes. I had forgotten. We shall have to manage as best we can,' Stephanis said, a frown creasing his face.

The two men were silent. Unanswered questions hung in the air. Garnetta felt the tension of the older monk and the curiosity of the younger. In the distance, muffled by the thickness of the stone walls, she could hear the bell tolling for Vespers. A feeling of relief seemed to flow towards her from Stephanis. She could tell that the infirmarer wished to be alone with her.

'Go you now to the misericord and eat your meal, Thomas,' Stephanis said. 'You have earned your corrody this day. There is nought more you can do at present. The wounds are clean, quite remarkably so. There is no sign of morbidity. I'll give the woman a sleeping draught and wait here a space until I'm certain that she is sleeping.'

When Thomas had left the cubicle, Stephanis dragged the wooden chest closer to the settle and lowered himself onto it. Pouring a measure of liquid into a goblet he lifted Garnetta's head so that he could dribble the potion between her lips. She swallowed painfully, feeling the liquid catch against the raw flesh of her unhealed throat. Stephanis waited patiently until she had drunk all of the draught, then he laid her back on the pallet. Garnetta closed her eyes. Already the soporific fumes were making her feel light-headed, stealing her thoughts.

She expected Stephanis to leave her to sleep, but after a few moments while he waited for the drug to take effect, she felt him lean close. He folded back the sheet, drawing it down until it lay around her hips. The clean air of the chamber was cool on her exposed skin. Stephanis sat looking at her for a long time, his hands pressed together as if in prayer propped under his chin. Her extended senses enabled her to catch the edge of his thoughts. So, Brother Stephanis was not as detached from worldly desires as he would have his young assistant believe. She watched him through the net of her eyelashes.

Stephanis's lips moved in the words of a prayer. He was trembling slightly. On his face was a strange expression. After another pause, he bent over her. His hands, slender for such a large man, passed over her skin as he examined her wounds again, this time minutely. 'Remarkable. Quite remarkable,' he murmured.

Although she longed to sink into the oblivion of sleep, Garnetta fought to stay awake. The fingers that brushed gently against her breast, swooped down to skim along the edge of her jutting hip-bone, were practised in the art of diagnosing and treating ailments, but she knew that this was more, far more, than a medical examination. Opening her eyes a little, she watched him. At first, he kept his head bent, revealing the paleness of the tonsure on his crown. When he looked up, she saw that his face was tight as if he was in pain, his fleshy mouth twisted by an inner distress.

'Can it be?' he said softly. 'An angel, Thomas said. Out of the mouths of simpletons . . .' Glancing up almost furtively at her face, he found her looking at him. Jumping back as if burnt, he jerked the sheet back up to her chin. Patting her arm awkwardly, he murmured, 'Sleep now, child. I shall watch over you. On the morrow I'll decide what is to be done with you.'

Garnetta nodded, amused by the guilt on his face. He had done nothing that his office as infirmarer did not merit, yet his broad face was flushed and sweating, his mouth folded in tightly over his teeth. What a burden is carried by the monks of Holy Penitence, she thought drowsily. It is hard on them to serve a lifetime's penance for the sins of the world, when it is heavy enough to carry the weight of one's own sin.

Stephanis went directly from the infirmary to the tiny chapel of Our Lady, deserted at this hour when the monks were having their supper in the refectory. Holy Penitence was a wealthy house, with a number of rich and influential patrons, one of whom had given the money to build the chapel after his safe return from the Holy Land. The walls were of polished shale, as shiny and black as obsidian. Long pointed windows, set with squares of red and white glass, threw lozenges of jewel-coloured light onto the white marble floor.

Stephanis approached the altar, where stood the reliquary holding the fingernail of the Mother of Christ. The statue of the Virgin above it looked down on him with mournful, blue doe-eyes. For a moment he had thought they were grey, dark and with shifting motes of light in their depths. Her face was a white oval, surrounded by a coif and veil. There was no hair visible and, if there were, it would not be close-cropped and as black as sin. Her lips were pale, like the inside of a mussel shell – not red as poppies.

Stephanis shook his head to clear it and shrank before the purity of the icon's expression. The Virgin was beauty and chastity. Ideal woman, with nothing of skin and bone to put damning thoughts into his head, to make his flesh rise up strongly from his loins and throb in the maddening way it was now. Dropping to his knees, Stephanis gave a groan. Lowering his chin until it brushed against the cold white marble, he crawled forwards. Muttering an *Ave* through his slitted lips, he stopped directly below the statue and lay face-down, his arms extended outwards in the shape of the cross.

Tears pricked his eyes. All these years he had been safe. No one knew about the perverted desires which raged within him. He had battled manfully, despising himself for his failure to attain the purity of spirit which he sought, resisting the temptation to take one of the child-oblates into his bed, as many a monk did. But he was cursed with a flawed nature. His dreams were filled with images of seething flesh. High round breasts, soft bellies, and that most devilish of temptations the female vulva. Ah, soft and fragrant it was, offering up all manner of earthly delights, tempting him with all its sinful artistry, confounding him with its tainted promise of comfort.

He had hidden his shame well, submerging everything of self beneath his vows of Holy Orders. But now, now, he was discovered, made naked, peeled bare until his very bones glistened with his lewdness. The eyes of the woman in the infirmary were all-wise, all-knowing; young-old in her exquisite face. She was the arbiter of his retribution, he felt it in his blood. She had looked into him and seen the awful taint of desire upon his immortal soul.

No. No. She could not have seen. She was near out of her mind with suffering. And he was her healer, appointed by God to relieve the travail of her sinful body.

His lips moved in the words of the Holy Office, reciting three psalms, a paternoster, meditative verses. Even while he prayed, his flesh grew stiffer, throbbing and pulsing. He pressed himself more closely to the marble, forcing the engorged organ down with the weight of his body. It was no use. The cold did nothing to relieve him. His senses swam, the blood drubbed in his ears.

He looked up at the Virgin, imploring her for help. It seemed to his fevered gaze that the statue moved. Her hands opened her robes to reveal a slender, white body. High breasts, tipped by wanton, cherry teats pointed at him. Her waist dipped down to a rounded belly. Her navel was a cup to drink from. And there, Oh, God in his Heaven, there was the fount of woman's wickedness. The coynte was small, neatly formed, frosted with silky black hair. As the Virgin parted her legs he saw the sex divide. Plump red lips leered moistly at him. Stephanis screwed his eyes shut, horrified by the visual blasphemy.

Behind his eyelids, the vision of the fecund vulva remained. This was damnation, this was ruin. He must fight. He must be strong enough to face the treachery of his flesh. Trembling he rose to his knees. With shaking hands he untied the rope around his waist. As if he was telling a rosary, he played it through his fingers, knotting it at intervals. Raising the habit about his waist, he uncovered the stem of his flesh. Jutting almost straight up, his staff of Adam was flushed a dark red. The two stones between his legs were hard and shrunk up tight against his body. He gave a groan as his turgid organ jerked and throbbed. It was like a live thing, a separate part of his body, with a will of its own.

He must mortify his flesh. It was only through suffering that man rose above his animal-self. Had not the Holy Saints endured tortures and temptations?

Lord. Look down upon this thy servant. Deal mercifully with this miserable sinner.

Leaning back a little so that his staff stood out from his belly, he brought the knotted rope hard down upon it. The pain stole his breath. For a moment, the cleansing rush of agony brought a welcome relief. Tears welled in his eyes. But with the subsidence of pain, there came a heat and a potent stinging which added to his ardour. His staff twitched, standing out ever more strongly, the red flush of it like a beacon. Again and again he whipped his flesh, sobbing aloud at its refusal to release him from the grip of sensual pleasure.

The Virgin's pale mouth seemed to curve in a smile of understanding and forgiveness. She was all-seeing, aware of the frailty of men. She alone amongst women was merciful. 'Holy Mother, help me,' he moaned as the hot, spiked pleasure bunched in his loins. 'Take this burden from me.'

He raised his hand to bring the knotted rope down again, convulsing as a tremor of ecstasy passed through him. His body, surged, crested, and broke. The rope slipped from his hand as the waves of an intense climax swamped him. Throwing back his head, he cried out. Gasping for breath, he squeezed his cock tightly, as if he could contain the semen which spurted upwards in a creamy arc and spattered the marble floor of the altar.

Karolan leaned forward in the saddle, his powerful thigh muscles bunching as he clung to Darkus's heaving sides. Foam clung to the horse's neck. He could smell the soap-tang of its sweat. Horse and rider were near to exhaustion, but Karolan urged Darkus on. Cresting a hill, Darkus checked his stride, launching himself over the boundary hedge and plunging down the bank that led towards the river. Karolan let the horse have his head. Without pausing in his forward momentum, Darkus launched himself into the mainstream of the swirling water and struck out for the opposite shore.

Karolan laughed with delight at the horse's fearlessness. The freezing water made his flesh sing as it lapped against him, raising his skin into goose-flesh. But the cold did not quench the flame of Garnetta from his mind.

All of the searching, organized by Romane, had come to nought. He did not need to hear the whispers to know that there was an undercurrent of suspicion amongst the villagers. Loyalties changed quickly enough when incredulity and fear of the unknown set the smell of brimstone wafting into their crofts. Let them think what they like, he thought viciously, in no mood to care for human-cattle with their little lives.

He had given Garnetta the gift of longevity, raising her high above the mass of struggling humanity, and this is how she repaid him. She ought to have fallen at his feet, sobbed out her gratitude. Instead she had turned her face from him. No one had ever left him before. His anger against her was tempered with disappointment, mellowed by his love and fear for her, but still it burned like a hot coal in his breast. The feeling ate at him, the anguish of it seemed too big to be contained within his flesh. Throwing back his head, he let out a roar.

His cry echoed in the still air. Sheep on the hillside massed together for protection. Clouds of birds rose from the trees in alarm. Darkus swivelled his ears, his eyes rolling back in terror as he kicked out at the swirling icy water. Karolan's shoulders slumped as the rage left him. He spoke softly to the horse, using the voice of power. Darkus, calm now, scrambled up onto the river bank, snorting out water, shaking his head to send drops flying outwards.

Dismounting, Karolan led the palfrey towards a meadow. After scooping much of the water from Darkus's gleaming skin with his cupped hands and rubbing him down with bunches of grass, he tethered him loosely. Wet and shivering as he was, he lay down under the spreading branches of an ash. In the far distance, he could see his peasants at work in their field strips. The burgeoning crops were as green as emeralds. On other manors the pestilence had robbed the land of its caretakers. Farms and crofts were crumbling into ruin, either through neglect or from the attentions of groups of roving brigands.

Garnetta was out there, wandering in a land made foreign by sickness, suffering, and starvation. Had she found shelter, he wondered. She could be many miles away by now, perhaps having joined a band of pilgrims. Sitting straight-backed, he began to breathe deeply, quietening his mind and putting himself into a light trance. He had tried many times to pick up Garnetta's mind-trail. He tried again now. After half an hour he gave up. Readjusting his concentration, he focused on the place between his eyes until he felt the area there grow warm. Normally it was easy to call the Fetch into his presence, but he needed an unusual amount of energy to call up the spirit on this occasion.

His brow furrowed as he conjured up an image of the spirit. Ah, he had it now. Deep within the forest, the ragged shadow-form was hovering around a group of men who were in the process of butchering a stolen pig. The animal had been secured by its forelegs to a branch of a tree. The pig's squeals and efforts to wriggle free were causing great mirth amongst the men who had captured it.

One of the men, called Edwin by the others, took out a knife and thrust it into the side of the pig's neck. A fountain of blood spurted in all directions. While the men captured the outpouring in a number of receptacles, from a battered helm to a wooden pail, the Fetch wove in and out of them, gibbering with pleasure and bathing in their blood-lust. Unaware of the greedy spirit, the men went about their task. One of them, excited by the noisiness of the animal's death throes, drew his knife and sank it again and again into the animal's flank. The others called out encouragement as he carved at the haunch, until the red flesh parted wetly and the hind leg hung free. Shreds of bloody tendon and muscle dangled in the air as the pig contorted. Its uninjured back leg pedalled madly.

Karolan watched with mild disgust as the pig's squeals grew fainter. It gave a final jerk, then hung still, twitching now and then with muscle reaction. Karolan focused solely on the amorphous shadow of the Fetch, drawing it to him with the power of his will. He felt its reluctance to leave the scene. The light within its form was glowing a sickly red. Its attenuated limbs flexed with pleasure as it imbibed the invisible particles of pain and distress. 'Come,' he ordered it.

The air around Karolan thrummed and buzzed as if a thousand bees were about to materialize. He sensed the Fetch's anger at being summoned. Out of the swirling maelstrom stepped a tall, slender youth. His skin was golden, his hair the colour of ripe corn. Golden eyes and moist lips smiled at Karolan.

'I'm impressed,' Karolan said mildly, hiding the shock he felt. The apparition was unexpected. Rarely had the spirit broken through into the world of matter in a solid human shape. It must have fed well indeed.

The Fetch turned to show off the perfection of the form with which it had clothed itself. A well-formed back, deeply indented at the spine, curved down to a pair of taut buttocks. The limbs were muscular, but smooth. The spirit faced him again. Its features were classical. The sculpted lips parted and the tip of a moist tongue appeared.

'Beautiful am I, Master?' the Fetch crooned, sliding one hand down to the slim hips and toying with the light-golden pubic fleece before encircling the heavy phallus.

The cock was thick, ridged with veins. It looked potent, out of proportion with the youth's slender frame. Despite his annoyance with the spirit, Karolan felt a flicker of sexual interest. The Fetch felt it too. It tittered and threw back its head so that the wheaten curls danced. Sunlight gleamed on the gold rings which pierced the youth's nipples. A metal band encircled the pale column of his neck.

'A slave, I am, to your pleasure. Serve you, shall I?' it said, working its hand back and forth along the phallus, smoothing back the tight skin of the glans to reveal the moist tip. At the slitted mouth, a single drop glistened like a pearl or a drop of crystal. 'What is it you relish?' The youth's lips pursed invitingly.

'Stop that,' Karolan ground out. Damn the infernal spirit. It knew his tastes too well. 'I want information.'

The image of the golden youth wavered, the sharp outline of the limbs trembled and the form dissolved on the air, spreading like a spillage of dye into a river. 'Going. Going. Gone,' the Fetch said, its voice sonorous with regret. 'Too, too bad.'

'Where is Garnetta?'

'Oh, that one is lost,' it said airily. 'Shall we make another, Master?'

'What do you mean, "lost"? Explain yourself. Did you find her? Tell me all you know. Remember that you are bound to obey me.'

'I know it, Master,' the spirit said sulkily, its shadow shape drifting on the air as if borne up by the warm currents. The red within its fabric faded and turned to a sullen brown. There was a long pause before it replied. 'Followed her into the forest, as you bade me. Searched well. Found no sign. Then found what remained. Fed well, did I. Wild boar, it was. Messy. Naught left to relish, but pain and fear.'

Karolan sprang to his feet. 'You're lying. You damned fiend! I would sense it if she were dead. Tell me all, or by Hermes I swear I'll never again let you lay hands on me. No matter what disgusting pleasures you offer, I'll resist them. Think of that. No more bargains, no more glimpses into my world!'

The Fetch squawked with rage and fear. 'Too, too cruel. Deny me? You would not!'

'I would. And you know it,' Karolan said flatly.

With a screech the spirit soared up into the branches of the ash. Its shrill, bird-like voice reverberated down through the trunk. Fragments of bark and shredded leaves rained down around him as the Fetch vented its spleen. Karolan sat calmly, his legs crossed at the ankles, waiting for the spirit to calm down. After many minutes, the din ceased and there was silence.

'Well?' Karolan said. 'Do not try my patience further.'

The Fetch materialized, its stringy, shadow-form glowing with a resentful sage-green. 'I will tell, Master,' it said in a subdued voice. 'But a boon I ask.'

'What is it?'

'Find whores. Beg you, Master. Then solace I give. Forgive. Forgive.'

'I'll decide when I've heard you out,' Karolan said. 'No promises. So, speak. Tell me that you lied.'

'Lie, I did. The female went towards the town. When the postern opened at dawn-bell to let out the death-carts, slipped inside did she. Followed her, down the path leading to the river.'

The relief was so great that Karolan felt light-headed. The Fetch's first words had filled him with alarm. Only the fact that he knew it to be an inveterate liar had stopped him from believing it. The river. That made sense. Garnetta would imagine that she could lose herself in the warren of narrow streets and tumbledown dwellings. 'We'll go there,' he said aloud. 'I know the area well.'

'Find whores?' the Fetch said hopefully, its form vibrating with sickly need. Karolan grinned wolfishly. Why not? He felt like indulging the darker side of his nature. It might distract him for a while. Leaping to his feet, he mounted Darkus. With the Fetch twittering exultantly at his shoulder, he steered the palfrey towards Chatesbrook.

As Karolan lifted the leather curtain and walked into the bawdy house, Jack Spicer called out a greeting. Pushing the half-naked girl he was fondling off his lap, he stood up. The girl pouted with disappointment and flounced across the room, making no move to cover her exposed breasts.

'Well, well,' Jack said. 'Thought you were dead of the plague. I've missed your company. I'll wager the girls have too. Can I do you some service?'

Karolan watched the girl, drawn by her fresh-faced looks and strong, young body. Catching his eye, she smiled appreciatively, sweeping him with a measuring glance. 'Give me some of that opiate, I favour,' Karolan said to Jack. 'You have it?'

Jack nodded. 'I've always got what *you* want. For the right price.'

Karolan threw him a coin. Jack whistled through his teeth. 'For that amount, you can have a private show too. Who d'you want? Isabeau or Adeliz? Have both trulls together if you want. Mind if I join you?'

Karolan shrugged. 'Why not?' He glanced at the girl who had not taken her eyes off him since he stepped into the room. Her heart-shaped face was surrounded by a tumble of chestnut curls. 'Bring her too.'

'Sabina? She's new here,' Jack reached for the girl, pulling her close and nuzzling her neck. 'Sabina's special, aren't you, my pretty young one? Costs extra. But she's worth it.'

Sabina giggled, looking from under lowered lids at Karolan. She arched her back, pushing her breasts towards him. They were large and firm, her big brown nipples as well-defined as copper coins. Karolan imagined sucking those teats, polishing them with his spittle, before sinking into her willing body. Despite the ruin he would make, he was tempted to have her. 'And how are you special, Sabina?' he said softly.

She sparkled at him, already dazzled by his beauty as were all the whores. 'I dance, my lord.'

Karolan threw Jack another coin. 'Do you? Then dance for me.'

The back room was as he remembered it. Oily smoke from a rush taper spread a pall in the air. The floor rushes smelt stale and clung stickily to his boots. Lounging amongst the greasy cushions were Adeliz and Isabeau. Both were naked. Sweat glistened on their unwashed skin. They were fondling each other in a bored fashion. Adeliz turned an unfocused gaze on him. 'Ah, the dark lord returns,' she slurred, 'Look but don't touch, eh?'

Karolan emptied the contents of a small glass phial into a cup of ale, amused by Adeliz's barbed comment. Beneath the contempt, he sensed her fear and the hunger for him which she was trying to suppress. He was tempted to reveal a little of himself to her, to shock her just a little, but the opiate, already warm in his belly, clouded his thoughts. He downed another cup of ale, then another. As Sabina moved into the centre of the room, he sank onto the cushions beside the two women. They pawed at him, but he pushed them away, watching only Sabina.

Jack reached for Isabeau, squeezing her fat breasts and pressing kisses to her dirty neck. She pressed against him, fingers scrabbling at the mat of hair on his broad chest. Karolan settled back, as the whores gave their attention to Jack, dimly aware of the Fetch which was visible to him alone as a lighter shape in the shadows in the corner of the room. He sensed the spirit's avid excitement as Sabina began to sway, her heavy young breasts lolling back and forth.

Sliding her hands down to her waist, she unhooked the single button of her skirt. It slid to the rushes, leaving her naked but for a wisp of fabric worn as a halter between her thighs. The dance was crude and without grace, but Sabina's youth lent her an unstudied sensuality. Rotating her hips, she pushed her pubis back and forth. The ribbon of fabric clung to the pouch of her sex, fitting closely to the indentation of the slitted lips.

Reaching between her legs, Sabina gathered up the halter, loosening it so that she could caress herself beneath the fabric. As she swayed and arched her back, she stroked her coynte, spreading the lips of her sex and pushing her fingers inside herself until her moisture seeped out and darkened the fabric. Inflamed by Sabina's antics, Jack threw Isabeau onto her back and mounted her. Squealing, she clutched at him, her big thighs grasping tight around his back as he plunged into her.

Adeliz crawled close to Karolan. Stretching out her hand, she closed it over his velvet-covered thigh. Her hair smelt greasy. A sour smell rose from her armpits. He did not stop her as she trailed her fingers down to his groin and caressed his tumescence. It was more than he had allowed any of the whores to do before. Adeliz held her breath. He could feel her tension as his flesh pulsed beneath her practised touch. Closing his eyes, he imagined that it was Garnetta who stroked him, who whispered obscenities. He had come here to find forgetfulness in the welter of willing flesh, but instead he thought only of Garnetta – of her sweet smell, her clean taste, the silken feel of her cool skin.

Dashing Adeliz's hand away, he lurched across the room. Filling another cup he poured in more of the poppy drug, then drained it in a single swallow. When he looked back towards the cushions, he saw that Jack had pulled Adeliz down to lie beside Isabeau and was taking it in turns to push his cock into them both. The Fetch was hovering over them, its shadow form pulsing and undulating, urging them on to greater excesses.

Karolan watched Sabina, who had thrown back her head, absorbed in a private world of sensation. Her fingers stroked and probed as her hips worked wantonly. The swollen sex pouted around the strip of damp fabric, which she was rubbing against herself. Her mouth opened to emit a soft moan. A stab of lust pierced Karolan's belly. Dizzy now with ale fumes and opiate, he moved forward, fell to his knees before Sabina. Looking down at him, she grinned lewdly. Slowly she removed the halter. Dangling it above his head, she waved it back and forth. The pungent, musky smell drifted down to him. With a soft cry he grabbed her buttocks. Burying his face between her thighs, he delved into her moist red crevice. Sabina shuddered as he pushed his tongue inside her. The girl's juices were rich as butter in his mouth, the strong smell of her fanned his lust.

He was faintly aware of the Fetch, hovering, gibbering with glee as it enjoyed the potent emanations which resonated on the ether. Spreading itself out on the air, it flowed over Sabina as she shook like an aspen, her eyes turned back in her head.

The spirit's form pulsed with turgid colour. Sucking greedily at her energy, it crooned, 'Have her, Master. Drink her death, would I.'

The reedy voice was insistent and the opiate sapped his will to resist it. Karolan was tempted. It took all of his control not to throw the girl onto her back and fuck her mindlessly. Only the fact that she was young and did not deserve to die stopped him. She would be sore for a few days after his attentions, but, this way, would suffer no lasting harm from his caustic saliva.

Sabina gave a series of sharp cries. Her flesh convulsed around his tongue. Karolan dug his fingers into the opulent flesh of her buttocks, one finger sliding into her wet furrow as he absorbed every subtle detail of her climax. He held the girl almost tenderly now, as the after-shocks of her pleasure began to fade. Already her expression was changing to one of consternation as she felt the burning and stinging of all her privy parts.

Swiftly he stood up, led her to the back of the room. He pushed her roughly down onto the stained cushions. 'Spread your legs,' he ordered. She did so warily, her eyes popping with fright. Jack was too busy jabbing himself into Adeliz while Isabeau sat on his face to wonder why Karolan emptied the entire contents of a jug of ale over Sabina's coynte, sluicing her thoroughly both inside and out.

Karolan stood up, swaying. His body still burned for easement. Now that the cold ale had eased her, Sabina reached for him, her painted mouth curving a welcome. Karolan shook his head. The room reeked of sweat and sex. The opiate and ale had combined to make him queasy. He made for the door. A backward glance showed him that Sabina had joined the others on the cushions. Grinning, Jack closed his mouth on her breast. Adeliz surfaced long enough to throw Karolan a glance. In it was longing tinged with disappointment.

'Too good fer the touch of a whore,' she slurred. 'You ever were.'

Outside in the dark alley, he vomited. Hunched over, he waited for the nausea to pass.

'Fed well. Want more,' the Fetch said, close to his ear, its perfumed breath warm on his skin. 'You hunger still. Feel it do I. Desire solace now?'

The ache of frustration surged up within Karolan. Having tasted the singular pleasures of loving Garnetta, his sexual need was more demanding, more difficult to control. Ah, Garnetta. The terror of never finding her again lay against him like a cold sword and brought him to the very verge of hating her.

Reading Karolan's mood, the Fetch chuckled richly. 'Is not this suffering a luxury?' it said huskily in a female voice. *Her voice.*

Trembling Karolan closed his eyes. He had not the will to resist as a soft mouth brushed against his lips. *Her* mouth. Fingers moved to the lacing of his tunic. He smelt Garnetta's perfume, tasted her on his tongue, and did not care that it was an illusion. Fingers brushed gently against his chest, pinching at his nipples until they gathered into hard little peaks.

Sliding down, uncaring of the wet and filth in the alley, he lay flat on his back. Inflamed by the excess of sexual energy it had imbibed, the Fetch was in capricious mood. Soft arms enfolded Karolan, cool firm breasts pressed against his chest. Short hair brushed his cheek. Karolan felt a surge of longing. No – it was not, after all, illusion he craved, but Garnetta herself. And the reality of that was denied him.

'Make me forget her,' he groaned, as the desire within him built to an ache.

'As you wish, Master,' said the Fetch, squirming with its willingness to please. 'No more female.'

Karolan's lips parted to admit entry to an erect phallus. The Fetch chuckled as Karolan began sucking the warm salty tip, welcoming the swollen shaft against the roof of his mouth. He rose up as his hosen were peeled down to his knees. Cleated flesh enclosed his straining organ. With his mouth plundered, his cock buried deeply within hot spirit-flesh, there was nothing but the sensation of spiked pleasure. He felt his legs lifted, folded back until the knees were pressed into his chest. A tongue squirmed inside him, licking around the rim of his anus, teasing, tasting the sweet-bitterness, lubricating him for a harsher entry to come.

The Fetch conjured erotic images to crowd his mind.

Karolan saw himself lying with Harun under the shade of palm trees. The hot sun burned down on their heaving bodies. Within him, Harun's cock laboured towards a climax. The scent of sandalwood and patchouli rose from the dark skin of his Arab lover. Then he was with a woman, as exquisite as she was unique. Her skin was dark also. Her hair fell in skeins of black silk, reaching to her knees. Her soft breasts had a bloom on them like damsons and her coynte was a ripe pouting fig. Ah, he had not thought of her for so long, yet it was she who had led him down the path to ruin.

Nasibia. Harun's sister. How different would his life had been if he had resisted her? Nasibia – the sound of it like a caress. 'No. Not her,' he whispered, freeing his mouth for just long enough to speak.

The memories faded. He grunted as his buttocks were pressed apart. The cock entered his body, stretching him, filling him. Every other sensation became subject to the rhythm of this. His mouth worked on the organ that filled it. Deep within his body, he awoke to a pleasure more urgent yet. Gasping and bucking he spilled his seed.

Then, as he had expected, the Fetch was inside him. The agony of it stitched him to the ground as surely as if iron spikes had been hammered through his limbs. It had never been like this. His eyeballs burned from the inside. His blood, hot and urgent, strained the fabric of his veins. He would not have been surprised to hear them rip. Gritting his teeth, he suffered the onslaught, as the spirit possessed him completely, using him simply as a vessel of containment.

Ripples passed over his skin. Muscles and tendons jerked as if trying to break from their confinement. Every organ ached. It went on and on. Karolan could do nothing but wait it out. In the final seconds before he lost consciousness, he thought how unbearable it would be if the Fetch ever grew strong enough to plunder him without his express permission.

For if that was to happen, it could remain inside him for ever. And there was no telling what mischief it would do in the world of men.

CHAPTER ELEVEN

Garnetta breathed deeply in her sleep as the dream unfolded.

The pictures forming in her mind were at first amorphous, as if shrouded in mist, then the image sharpened. She found herself looking into a garden where bushes blossomed with flowers, fruit trees grew in pots, and a fountain played under the burning sun. Part of Garnetta's conscious mind seemed to be at work. Her heightened senses revealed that this was another of those glimpses into Karolan's past.

'Nasibia,' came his whisper. 'Are you hiding from me?'

Karolan's shoulder-length, fair hair was bright against the folds of his white tunic. He wore loose silk trousers caught in at the ankle. Striding towards the columns of carved stone which held up the roof of a pleasure pavilion, he made a sound of impatience. His hand brushed against a potted palm, setting the leaves rustling in an angry hiss.

He turned, giving Garnetta a full view of his face. It was still a shock to see those well-remembered features. He looked just as beautiful with deep-golden skin and sun-bleached hair. His blue eyes were striking against his darkened skin.

Karolan's voice came again into the dream, urgent, demanding. Garnetta concentrated on observing only, knowing that there was much to learn about the mysterious man whom she hardly knew.

'Nasibia. Show yourself. I tire of these games! I must speak with you.' A clump of tall lilies swayed, the fronds parted, and a woman stepped onto the mosaic tiles.

She was clothed from head to foot in black robes. A kind of leather mask, shaped to fit her face, screened all but her eyes from view. From the eye-slits, glittered a flash of deepest-brown. 'From whence comes this need for haste?' Nasibia said, her accented voice husky, gently teasing. 'Well you know how dangerous it is for us to meet. I had to wait to slip away until Sahain was certain to be gone. The chief eunuch's eyes are sharp. If my brother ever found us out, he would order us both to be stoned to death.'

'I doubt that. Harun loves you too much to hurt you, although I might be another matter,' Karolan said, moving close and reaching for Nasibia's hand.

She extended slim brown wrists on which many gold bracelets gleamed. Karolan brought the small hands to his mouth, kissed each elaborately hennaed knuckle in turn. When he loosed her hands Nasibia raised them and removed her face mask. Dropping it to the tiled floor, she pushed her robe from her shoulders and stepped free of the crumpled folds. Under the dull black she wore full skirts and a breast-length tunic of richly embroidered silk. Tiny mirrors glinted amongst the threads. Her shining raven hair was plaited and twisted with gold cords. A row of gold coins hung low on her dusky forehead.

Karolan cupped Nasibia's face between his palms and kissed her red mouth passionately. Smoothing a hand over her narrow shoulders, he slipped his fingers down to her back, pressing her close against him. 'You are trembling, my heart. What is it?' he said.

'Sometimes the enormity of our crime steals my breath. I have sinned against Allah. Hourly I pray to the Prophet for forgiveness. I ought never to have allowed myself to be bewitched by your golden beauty. You are a creature of fire, one of the *majnun*. But I welcomed the scorching wind of your presence into my life. I cannot regret it now. Oh, Karolan. Would that we could tell Harun of our love.'

'You know that is impossible. There would be great danger for you if it became known that you have been dishonoured.'

She smiled sadly. 'I cannot help but wonder how much time is left to us. Already it is the month of *Sha'ban*. Lord Simon left you here in the month of *Muharram*. Thanks to the skill of my brother, your injured leg is whole. You are eager to ride again, go hunting for wild boar in the reed beds.'

'Nasibia, listen to me. I have received word that Lord Simon's army, camped on the hills overlooking the Holy City, is breaking up. It can be only a matter of hours before he returns this way.'

'So soon? Then he will surely come for you, the brave man who saved his lord's life. And then – we can leave together?' She searched his face for an answer. When he did not reply, she bowed her head, the slender neck looking fragile under the weight of her hair. 'If . . . if you were to stay, you could embrace Islam. The law allows for a Christian to convert. We shall marry. Harun would have no objection. He loves you like a brother . . .'

Karolan laid his fingers against her mouth. 'It cannot be. I have told you. I must go back to England with Lord Simon.'

'Why?' she flashed at him, her head snapping back like a striking cobra. 'Have you some pallid Christian woman to warm your bed there? What can she offer you that I cannot? Oh, I see it now. You have sickened of my infidel flesh. Having taken the jewel of my virginity, you cast it down to be trampled by swine!' Pulling free of his embrace, she spun around, her long glittering skirts swinging out in an arc. As she paced, her sandals made a soft scraping sound on the tiles. The bells around her slender ankles tinkled.

In the monastery, a spasm passed over Garnetta's face. She pushed away the sheet that covered her. One hand brushed against her face as if trying to smear away cobwebs. The scene in the courtyard was almost painfully bright. She could sense Karolan's indecision and the Arab woman's distress.

'You are wrong, Nasibia,' Karolan said, his blue eyes vibrant. 'Calm yourself. Let us talk about this, but pray lower your voice. Someone will hear.'

She placed her hands on her hips. Her beautiful, kohl-lined eyes blazing at him. 'Let them hear! I care not. How easy it is for you to lie. What a fool I have been to be beguiled by your flattery. I am no more use to you. Which did you enjoy the most – taking your pleasure of my body or using me as a tool to gain access to Harun's library?'

Karolan's face hardened. He took hold of Nasibia's shoulders, shaking her so hard that her hair loosened from its pins and streamed down to her waist. She uttered a small cry of alarm and struggled to be free. He kept a grip on her. 'Be silent, I say! Think you that Harun has denied me anything? He and I have been studying his scrolls and manuscripts for many weeks. I have seen the Great and Small books of Khalid ibn Yazid, the Book of Amulets, the many works of Zosimus and Democritus. Together we have conjured up *Shaitin*, leader of the angels, and spoken in ritual with his creatures *Harut* and *Marut*.'

Nasibia blanched. 'But these things are forbidden by the Qu'ran! Is Harun mad? He has never before shared his dark secrets. Once he guarded his knowledge of *al kimiya* from everyone but me. But I am only a woman, after all. Ah, the cursed complicity of men. I thought

Harun loved me best, but he has betrayed me. You have bewitched us, taken everything we held dear. Now you are to carry off this knowledge to your own land.' Seeing something in his eyes, Nasibia gave a sob. Tears sparkled on her sooty lashes. Her sensuous mouth pulled down at the corners. 'By the Prophet, how blind I have been. You and my brother are lovers too.'

Karolan's mouth lifted in a sneer. 'Oh, spare me, I beg of you! Both of you were victims – is that it? You were helpless against my charms? How I pity you and Harun – poor innocents both. But you were more than willing to show this "ignorant unbeliever" the pathways to pleasure according to the poet Abu Sa'id.'

Nasibia's dark eyes narrowed. There was a red flush along each exquisite dusky cheekbone. 'You dare to mock us after we took you to our hearts! Christian dog! How could I ever have thought I loved you. You are more foul than the dung beneath my feet!'

Her hands curled into claws. She leapt for his eyes. Karolan caught her wrists and held her easily. She spat full in his face and opened her mouth ready to scream. Twisting her around so that she was held captive against his body, Karolan pressed one hand to the lower part of her face. 'Stop that, you hell-cat! Listen to reason.'

In the dream the violence and tension was palpable. Garnetta's head tossed from side to side. She wanted the pictures to fade, afraid now of what might happen. Her lips parted and she murmured, 'No. No.'

As Karolan dragged Nasibia towards a clump of ole-ander bushes, the Arab woman fought and thrashed, almost choking with rage. She sank her teeth into his hand, worrying at his flesh until the blood spurted through his fingers. Karolan cursed, but did not remove his hand from her mouth. He tightened his grip, jerking her head around and digging his fingers into her cheeks.

'Christ!' he grated. 'Be still, Nasibia. I have no wish to hurt you!' Nasibia's dark eyes almost popped from their sockets. She seemed to rise up against him, then her whole body went rigid. There was a loud crack and she went limp in his arms. 'Nasibia? Oh my God!'

Karolan removed his hand from her face and placed his ear to her chest. With a groan, he let her go. She fell to the ground, lying in a crumpled heap of embroidered skirts and silky black hair. Looking around quickly to make certain that he was unobserved, Karolan bent down and scooped Nasibia into his arms. Her head lolled back over his bent arm. Her eyes were open and sightless. The lower part of her face was smeared with the blood from his bitten hand. Pausing only long enough to hide the body behind the bushes, Karolan picked up the discarded outer garment and face mask. He put them with the body, arranging the branches and leaves to cover them, then came out of the bushes and stood looking down into the waters of the fountain. The sun reflecting off the water made a moving pattern of shapes across his face.

In the monastery, beads of sweat broke out on Garnetta's forehead. Her short black hair stuck up in damp spikes. Her dream self could clearly see the moment when Karolan's expression changed from one of regret. It did not take long.

Slowly, he began to smile. He inclined his eyes heavenwards, then shrugged before making the sign of the cross on his chest. Placing his hands together, he faced the bush which hid the body, then he executed a shallow, almost insulting bow. 'Is this your vengeance, Heavenly Father, for my doubling the power of Christendom? I would not have chosen this path, but a man must be ready to turn any situation to his advantage.' His voice hardened with bitter irony. 'Come for me then Lord Simon and bear me back home to England. Amen or should I say rather – *Inshallah*.'

Spinning on his heel, he left the garden, his mocking laughter floating on the breeze.

Garnetta awoke abruptly, her heart pounding, the sickly taste of the sleeping draught on her tongue. It seemed to her that she could still feel the heat of the Arab sun, smell the perfume of exotic flowers. It was a moment before her surroundings became clear, resolving themselves into the shadow-printed, stone walls of the infirmary. Turning onto her side, she stared into the darkness. The small oil lamp sent up only a fitful glow, but she found it a comfort. A cold sweat clung to her limbs. She clutched the sheet close. *Karolan had murdered Nasibia.*

Dear God in Heaven. That was terrible in itself, but she sensed that there was a great deal more to discover. She had learned that Karolan had been practising his Black Arts while in the Holy Land. But she still could not imagine what had happened to change him into the creature he had become. *The creature, which he has made me.*

Choking down a sob she pressed her fist against her mouth. She felt drained of all emotion. She began to recite a paternoster, thankful that here at least, in the House of God, she was far beyond Karolan's reach.

It was still dark, although a diffuse grainy quality in the chamber presaged the coming of dawn. The tiny cell was devoid of everything except a pallet bed and a wooden stool. Adorning the wall at the head of the bed was a plain wooden cross.

Stephanis had slept little. He woke with his limbs

chilled and aching. Before the monk came to wake him for the office of Matins he was up and dressed. With the other monks, Stephanis trudged along the corridors to the chapel. This day he paid no attention to the muffled yawns, the coughs, the smells of frowsty robes and stale breath. His thoughts were full of the woman in the infirmary.

Despite his efforts to dispel them, impure thoughts crowded his mind. His loins ached from a recent beating, but his flesh was swollen and rigid. As he sang the first office of the day, Stephanis was beset by doubts. Was Garnetta anything more than a woman who had fallen into sin? Were his motives in wanting to help her pure? He needed guidance. Something of such importance must be relayed to the abbot, but not yet. He would make enquiries. Someone must know something about the woman.

Before Lauds was sung at first light, there was an hour or so to spare. Just time to break his fast with beer from his daily ration and make his rounds. In the infirmary beside Garnetta there were only two monks with the express permission of the abbot to be excused from participating in the regular office. Stephanis called first on Brother Marcus. The old man's face was grey, his skin oily. Stephanis looked into Marcus's eyes, smelt his breath, then laid gentle hands on the stomach which was swollen and as tight as a drum. Marcus grimaced with pain. Stephanis patted the old man's arm. 'Rest you now, brother. I will prepare a purgative. You'll be calling to be helped to the privy in no time.'

After Marcus, Stephanis went to see Brother James. Stephanis unwrapped the binding on the monk's shinbone, steeling himself not to flinch as the smell of the ulcer rose up from the stained bandages. Efficiently he attended to the leg, then applied a pad soaked in wine and bound it with strips of clean linen.

'There, brother,' Stephanis said. 'You may take up your bedclothes and return them to your cell. You must be eager to get back to God's work and participate in the office.'

Brother James murmured his thanks and stood up. Gathering up his bedding, he limped out of the infirmary. Stephanis was now free to devote the larger portion of the day to solving the problem of Garnetta. He felt strangely reluctant to go into the chamber where she lay. Part of him was eager to see her, but he fought against the sinful lust which thoughts of her stirred up in him. Crossing himself and murmuring a *Misere* he went first to the still-house, where he knew that Thomas would be at work.

His assistant sat at the lectern, next to a window, absorbed in reading from an illuminated book which was spread open before him. When Stephanis entered the still-house, Thomas leapt up guiltily. 'I was just going to label these bottles.'

Stephanis smiled mildly. 'Do not fret, lad. I am not going to chastise you. It is never a waste of time to study the writings of St Jerome.'

'You are not angry?' Thomas's eyebrows almost disappeared into his hairline. 'I mean . . . usually you . . . ahem. I'll get to work, shall I?'

'Very well,' Stephanis said, amused. 'But leave those bottles. I have a more pressing task for you. Go you and speak with Brother Amos. I want to know which road he took back to the monastery. Ask him whether the cart stopped anywhere, or paused to navigate a rut in the road. Someone must have seen Garnetta lying hurt and bleeding. She could not have appeared out of the air.'

Thomas crossed himself. 'Like an imp or a witch?'

'Precisely. Get you gone now. Return when you have something to tell me.'

Thomas paused only to set a hooded cape around his shoulders. Stephanis watched him go, then went into the cubicle where Garnetta ought to be just waking from the sleeping draught. She was sitting up, the sheet pulled up to her chin. The livid bruise on the side of her face was turning green around the edges. He could see that the plasters and sheet were free of blood stains. Her wounds had not reopened during the night – somehow he had not expected that they would.

'I have brought you food and here is your shift, newly washed and restored,' he said.

Garnetta took the garment from him. He helped her slip it over her head. Although she moved stiffly, she hardly winced as he drew the folds of linen down over her torso. With the drawstring neck tightened, her arms decently covered, he felt more at ease. 'Are you able to feed yourself? Your bruises must pain you sorely.'

'I am much recovered. Thank you,' she said, as he laid the wooden tray across her knees. 'Is it a feast day? There is no bread trencher to be saved for the poor.'

Stephanis coloured. He had set out the food on his own pewter plate and dish. A pewter cup also held a measure of wine. 'Everyone at Holy Penitence eats off pewter,' he lied. 'And every monk of ill health eats this special food.'

'Then they are fortunate indeed. Roast pigeon, a charlet of milk and eggs, wastel bread. Fruit too. I marvel that everyone at Holy Penitence does not suffer from expansion of the waistline.' Her dark eyes sparkled at him and her red lips curved at the corners.

Stephanis felt the urge to laugh – to throw back his head and give a deep belly laugh. The prospect of losing control in such a way alarmed him mightily. Surely this was immodest speech from a woman who had been close to death? He looked away from the tray where the rosy warden pear nestled next to the other food, looking wanton and lush. He had not been able to resist adding the treat to her tray. Now it mocked him for his foolishness. Under the pretence of checking the level of the sleeping draught in its green glass bottle, he turned his back to Garnetta, giving himself a moment to regain his composure.

It was not going to be easy to look upon her as a case for spiritual charity. There was something – vital about her. Even in the simple shift, with her hair too short for beauty, she had an unsettling glamour. When he turned around, she was eating. The way she ate, like a healthy animal, sucking at her fingers, dipping the bread into the custard-like charlet, sent a pang right through him. Her sole attention was focused on the taste, the textures on her tongue. In the monastery meals were taken in silence and over with as soon as possible. Her simple enjoyment seemed somehow obscene.

He swallowed hard before he spoke. 'You spoke of being confessed?'

It was as if a cloud passed over the sun. She pushed the food away dully. He felt stricken to have been responsible for the change in her, but there was yet within him a gladness to see her looking subdued – even fearful. It was more fitting in the circumstances.

'I am in sore need of being shriven,' she said. 'That ought to have been my first request, but I was hungry. A dream I had confused me . . . oh, how could I have pushed it all out of my mind? I'm as guilty as he is. But I'm not like him. I'm not!' Leaning forward she grasped at his hand. 'Will you hear my confession?'

It took a huge effort of will for him not to recoil from

her. There were only the two of them present. Who else was she addressing? An icy chill crept down his backbone. The passion on her face alarmed him. The grip of her fingers was like iron. His hand began to ache. Covering her fingers with his free hand, he began prising them apart. It took all his strength.

'Calm yourself, madam,' he said, severely, feeling the sweat break out of his pores. 'I'll call for someone to attend to your spiritual welfare.'

'No! It must be you. You have been kind to me. Hear me, I beg you.'

For a moment longer Stephanis wavered. He found himself unable to resist the lure of being taken into her confidence. 'Very well. I shall need a moment to prepare myself,' he said.

Once he had heard the worst, he could begin the work of bringing her back into the fold. He left the cubicle to fetch the things he needed, returning after a few minutes with a vial of holy water, a candle, and a medallion bearing the representation of St Venantius. Garnetta sat with her eyes cast downwards, her lashes casting violet shadows onto her cheek. The flow of her profile and slender neck was an unbroken line, clearcut and pure against the stone wall behind her. It seemed impossible for her to look modest, he thought crossly. But then it was not her fault that her lips were so red and full, her slender white hands so elegantly poised.

Stephanis began to pray. When he had run through the appropriate number of devotions, he crossed himself. Garnetta kissed the medallion when he held it out to her. 'Very well,' Stephanis said. 'You may begin.'

Garnetta bowed her head. The hands in her lap trembled slightly. Stephanis battled with the urge to reach out, to take one of those hands and to run his thumb across the tender white palm. When she began speaking, he found his attention riveted upon her every word.

'Merciful Father forgive me,' she whispered. 'It has been many weeks since my last confession. My sins weigh heavily upon my soul. Heavenly Father – I am sore afraid. My body is not my own. I hear things. See things. Everything is too bright, too loud. I am not like I was. Does this sound strange? I do not understand it myself. I was found by a man when I was near sick unto death with the pestilence. This man, he . . . he brought me back to health. At first he was kind – more than kind. But I discovered that he had done something to me – something terrible. And I became afraid of him. I do not know what he did it nor yet what he has made me.' She ran her tongue over dry lips. 'I know only that I am like *him* now. I fled into the forest, thinking to find help. There I came upon a band of brigands. They were torturing a boy, trying to get him to tell them where his village was. I was so angry at their cruelty and cowardice that I attacked them with a hunk of wood. The boy escaped, but the men overpowered me. They . . . beat me, knocked me to the ground. Two of them forced themselves upon me. Then something happened to the ones who had violated me. They . . . they died screaming in agony, their privy parts destroyed as if by fire. Brother Stephanis, I killed those two men without once touching them . . .' She broke off and began to weep.

Stephanis did not know what to think. He waited until she was calm enough to continue. 'What happened then?' he said faintly.

'The other men were furious that their comrades were dead. They called me a witch. The one called Edwin plunged a knife into my chest and slashed my neck. I fainted from the pain and knew nothing more until the next morning. Somehow I was alive. Although in great pain I walked through the forest until I came to a road. When a cart came past I crawled inside and so found my way here.'

'When did all this happen?' Stephanis asked, certain that she must be raving, but trying desperately to reserve his judgement. When she told him that she had been relating the events of barely two days ago, a cold hand squeezed his heart. His fears about her were confirmed. Either she was lying or it was a miracle. Wounds like those she had sustained ought to have been fatal, not in an advanced state of healing.

As if a dam had burst, the words poured from Garnetta. She spoke about the man who had first helped her. He was dark and powerful, she said, seducing her with his glamour and presence, teaching her bodily pleasures. She had undergone some kind of ritual during which an angel had appeared to her. In the forest, she had been pursued by something invisible, some demon which spoke to her.

Stephanis listened, too awed and frozen by shock to respond. There was no doubt that Garnetta had suffered some kind of abuse, the marks on her proved that fact. As to the rest, he did not feel qualified to advise her. Was she out of her mind or blessed above all women? It was plain that she needed special help, but the thought of giving her up to the examination of the Church Council filled him with dismay. She would be taken from him. That was more unbearable than facing the problem of what to do with her. He must put aside his fear, quell the image of the fiery pit which seemed to lick at the very edges of his sanity. He clutched at the medallion around his neck. St Venantius would help him, intercede with God on his behalf.

There was no need for panic. The devil had played with Garnetta's mind. Who would not be confused and terrified if but half of what she said was true? One thing she said had made a profound impression on him. 'Tell me more about the angel who appeared to you, my child,' he said gently. 'And these voices you hear. What do they say?'

She told him more about the shining being. That part rang with truth. He disregarded what she said about learning that the visitation had been a trick. More Devil's work that. His task was to cut away the fears and doubts which the Tempter visited upon the weak. With the power of prayer he would burn away Lucifer's deceits. 'You are to talk to no one else about this, do you understand?' he said at length. 'I shall help you, but you must trust me.'

She nodded, the glint of tears in her strange dark eyes. 'If you knew how I have longed to throw myself upon God's mercy. I was certain he had forsaken me. He did not answer my prayers for help when those terrible things happened to me.'

'You poor wretched sinner,' he said, the zeal within him deepening its hold. 'The Devil waits to snare those who have lost their way. With my help you shall regain your faith. God is always there. We have only to find our way back to him.'

He placed his hand on her head. Her cropped hair was soft under his palm. He fancied that he could feel the madness rising up from it; sticky, pungent as tar – or was it the veil of sanctity? The thought both thrilled and appalled him. There was a fine line indeed between those who had been touched by God and those who were beguiled by the Tempter. It took an effort of will to leave his hand in place as he said the words of the benediction. '*In nomine Patris et Filii et Spiritus Sancti . . .*'

When he stopped speaking, Garnetta sank back on the bed, her hands over her face, shoulders shaking with silent sobs. Stephanis felt exhausted. He must have time to think. It would not do to act rashly. He must be certain that he was not blinded by pride at having been chosen to take this burden upon himself. It was silent in the cubicle, but for the sound of Garnetta's weeping. Stephanis was absorbed in his own thoughts so it was a moment before he heard someone calling his name.

'Brother Stephanis. Where are you?'

Recognizing the voice of Thomas, Stephanis shook his head to clear it. Recalling that he had sent his assistant on an important errand, he felt a flash of irritation. What was the young fool doing back so soon? As Thomas's footsteps sounded on the stone floor all of Stephanis's pent up emotion erupted into anger. He went swiftly out of the cubicle, his mouth open ready to give his assistant the sharp edge of his tongue.

'Here you are, brother infirmarer,' Thomas said triumphantly, before Stephanis could utter a word. 'I found this scrap at the postern gate, trying to barter his way inside. Says he has information which will interest you. His name is Clem. He saw everything that happened to Garnetta in the forest.'

CHAPTER TWELVE

Karolan picked his way through streets piled high with refuse. The street cleaners had long since ceased their rounds and heaps of human night-soil made walking a hazardous activity. Two men, sitting in a gutter, looked up as the tall, cloaked figure approached. Eyeing him with interest, one nudged the other as he noticed the purse which hung at Karolan's waist. Karolan looked steadily back at them. Neither of them could hold his gaze. When he had moved past, one of them hawked and spat. 'Come to see the sights, 'ave yer? This is a fine garden of roses! The posy you take away will kill you fer sure!'

Karolan walked on, making for the Ship tavern which was frequented by thieves, bandits, and footpads. Naked corpses lay sprawled in the dark, narrow streets. Clouds of flies arose as he passed, then settled again into vacant eye sockets and open mouths. Sleek brown rats darted in and out of white limbs, entwined in the ghastly embrace of death. The stench was penetrating and acidic, burning to the eyes and throat.

His gorge rose as images from long ago crowded his mind – of battlefields where soldiers lay rotting, maggots tumbling out of the eye slits of helms wed to bone by dented metal. It seemed that his ears rang with their screams of agony. Christian and Infidel sounded the same, their blood indistinguishable as it seeped into sun-baked earth. How soon he had learned that war was not glory. War was dying in a froth of blood, trying to shove back your guts inside a split belly. War stank of rotting meat, the sweat of fear and shit. Just like the smell that rose towards him in noxious waves now. 'Blessed saints,' Karolan swore, making the subtle inner adjustment to shield himself from the sensory assault. Once he had saved Garnetta from this, but it seemed that she had come back to seek sanctuary in hell rather than face him.

There was a movement in a dark alley. He projected his extended vision into the gloom where two dogs fought over the corpse of a baby. One of them gave a shake of its head and tore off a piece of flesh, bolting it down in one gulp. The quick beat of canine pulses echoed in his head. He gained a sense of their muddled thoughts – hunger and red-madness; pack law ruling in the tamed gone wild.

Near the docks, the tide was low. Ships leaned drunkenly on exposed mud banks. Leaning out to look over the edge of the harbour he found himself staring down into the white-filmed eyes of a dead woman. She was young and slender, her face a perfect oval. *Garnetta.* For a second his heart almost stopped.

Suddenly the corpse surged up out of the water, waxy limbs dripping a trail of rotting flesh. The apparition hung in the air for a second before landing upright on the quayside. Like a puppet she danced, her head falling back, greenish fluid pouring from her mouth. A salt-rich smell, muddy and rotten, wafted towards him. The dead woman waved her arms, ragged fingers waggling jauntily. The Fetch tittered, the sound bubbling up out of the ruined throat.

Despite his initial disgust, Karolan could not suppress a grin. The spirit loved to make its presence known with such showy gestures. 'I've been expecting you,' he said dryly. 'There's too much misery and death here for even you to gorge on.'

'Never too much, says I,' the spirit said happily.

'Beautiful, am I not, master? Are you not desirous of this form?' The animated corpse shook its head. An eyeball popped free, trailing down the shredded cheek to hang like a glass marble on a thong. 'Strong is your hunger for pleasure of late. Is it strong enough for . . . this?' The corpse lifted its hands to cup its breasts. As the fingers squeezed, pulpy green flesh oozed between them. Shreds of skin flaked off the fingers, exposing the gleam of white bone.

Karolan's lips tightened with disgust. 'Am I to appear shocked by this display?' he said. 'You know me better than that.'

The Fetch gibbered with mirth, sending the corpse into a frantic spin, so that the wet hair was flung out into an arc. Abruptly, it came to a stop, facing Karolan. The facial skin had split. Trickles of sea water and slime dripped from the dead woman's chin. The jaw came loose, dangling from rotten tendons. It lodged on what was left of the woman's chest, hanging there like some ghastly necklace. Jerking and twitching, the corpse flopped a few steps forward, hung motionless for a fraction of a second, then collapsed onto the quayside with a liquid squelching sound.

Invigorated and drunk with pleasure, the Fetch flowed around Karolan, its shadow form glowing with particles of phosphorescence. It exuded a smell of decay, rich and sickly sweet. 'Lovely, lovely,' it crooned. 'Such delicious pain, such layers of suffering.'

'Spare me your vile observations,' Karolan said.

The Fetch chuckled, its excitement and relish almost tangible. Now and then it gave a low-pitched trill. He felt the hot tingle of its passing as it darted through his aura. In a moment it would bargain with him. Having bathed in the pain of others it was always greedy for

208

more sensations. 'Stay with me a while,' he said shortly. 'There will be more entertainment for you.'

'Stay I will,' the spirit said sulkily, forestalled in its demands. 'But first. Is there nothing you require of me?'

'Nothing!' Karolan snapped. 'I am deaf to your pleas at present.'

'Have not asked anything of you,' the Fetch said sullenly. 'Too, too cruel, you are, Master.'

'Oh, stop whining! Have you discovered any trace of Garnetta?'

The fabric of the spirit's body pulsed faintly. 'Not easy to smell the female with so much death. Told about the tavern did I. Men there who know. For more, time I shall need.'

'You have it. All you wish for. Just remember that I *will* find Garnetta. Try not to be too distracted by the feast all around you.'

The Fetch cackled at this irony, expanding into an amorphous smoke-like shape and then closing in to become a thin, black figure with attenuated limbs. It was the spirit's equivalent of a luxurious stretch. As Karolan rounded a corner and stopped before the ramshackle shape of the Ship tavern the Fetch changed form again, fading to became a subtle rippling disturbance on the air.

Karolan ducked under the lintel, went inside. Heads turned in the gloom as he strode across the room and took a seat. Instinctively he withdrew into himself, sending out a veil of energy to mask himself from unwanted curiosity. The men went back to their drinking. Karolan called for ale and looked around. The stub of a candle guttered in the draught from a tiny, unglazed window. Hunched shapes filled the flickering darkness. Now and then a laugh or a curse rose above the general noise. At the back of the tavern, a huddle of men were gathered around an open hearth.

'There, Master,' came the Fetch's voice, close at hand.

Karolan sipped his ale and settled down to wait. After a time one of the men began singing an old campaign song, while the others kept time banging their cups of ale on the wooden table.

'This one's for Barny, God save his soul,' one of them said. 'Aye, and de Peyrac too, even if he was a mean bastard.'

'You is maudlin, Edwin. Must be the ale,' said another.

Karolan focused on the man who had spoken first. He could feel the miasma of suppressed emotion rising from him – grief for a comrade lost . . . something else – guilt? Edwin moved. Karolan saw the garment which lay at his feet. Firelight threw sparks from the jewelled clasp on the red cloak. *Garnetta's cloak.* The man might have stolen the cloak, or bought it from a thief, but he thought not.

A murderous, all consuming rage bloomed within Karolan. He contained it, allowing it to sink and condense, biding his time. It was another hour before Edwin rose unsteadily and reached for the cloak. Weaving his way through the tavern, he went through the back door into the alley outside. After a moment, Karolan followed him. It was dark in the alley, but he easily picked out the shape of Edwin pissing against the wall. Bunching his muscles he sprang. Before the man had time to look up, Karolan was beside him.

'God's lights,' Edwin ground out, starting when the long shadow fell across him. 'Where'd you come from?' His hand flew to his knife hilt, the weapon half drawn before Karolan wrenched it from his hand.

At the touch of the blade Karolan felt a space open

within him. The cold metal burned his skin. He saw images of blood, terror, the knife sinking into flesh. Her flesh. *Garnetta*. For a moment he reeled under the strength of the impressions.

'What d'you want?' Edwin slurred, staggering, his hosen hanging loose at his waist. 'Take my purse. I've nothing worth stealing.'

'Ah, but you have,' Karolan said softly, throwing back the hood of his cloak so that his white skin gleamed in the darkness. 'Your life is forfeit for what you've done. I shall enjoy taking it.'

Edwin blanched as he gazed into pitiless dark grey eyes. 'Eh? Who are you?' he croaked, moistening dry lips. Then a clouded recognition dawned on his face. His mouth sagged open. 'You are like her. The witch-woman . . .'

'Memorable, is she not? Tell me why you killed her,' Karolan said. 'And don't bother lying to me.'

Edwin seemed frozen, then he swallowed audibly. 'She killed my comrade,' he whispered. 'He . . . he were only havin' a bit of fun. He didn't deserve what she did to him. You should have seen the ruin . . .' His throat worked, catching on a sob. 'Me and Barny was closer'n brothers. But I never meant to kill her. I swear, I didn't.'

Karolan placed a hand on either side of Edwin's head. 'Of a surety, you did not,' he said coldly. 'Just like you never meant to watch as your comrades violated and tortured her. Like you never planned to steal her cloak.'

Edwin trembled, held in thrall like a rat before a snake. Captured between Karolan's hands, he could not move his head, was forced to look up into the cold fury of that impenetrable gaze. 'Please . . .' he croaked as Karolan began to lift him.

The pressure on his neck was excruciating as it

supported the weight of his whole body. His spine scraped against the wattle of the building as he scrabbled desperately for a handhold. Then he found himself at eye level with Karolan and saw his death in that implacable face. He writhed helplessly as Karolan's thumbs moved around to gently caress his eye sockets.

'No! Ah, merciful God . . . No!' His scream bubbled up in his throat, but never escaped his lips.

As Karolan exerted an iron pressure with the heels of his hands, Edwin's jaw bone shattered and was driven into the soft flesh of his throat, lacerating and crushing his windpipe. At the same time Karolan's thumbs punctured his eyeballs, penetrating through the sockets and reaching deep into the brain. Edwin, shuddering with the reaction from his straining muscles, was already dead by the time his head collapsed inwards.

Karolan let the corpse drop to the ground. As he bent to wipe the blood and brains from his hands, he felt the hot tingling as the Fetch sped through him, eager to gorge itself. Karolan felt nothing, no anger, just a certain grim satisfaction. The man was dead for his crimes, the sentence no doubt long overdue for murders past. Garnetta was avenged for the attack on her – but not for her murder, as Edwin believed. For no knife stroke could kill her.

The spirit made little sounds of pleasure, like a babe suckling. Karolan left the Fetch feeding off the rapidly dispersing energies and emerged from the alley into a narrow street. He felt the need for company. The bawdy house which Jack frequented was a few minutes' walk away. It had been almost a week since his last visit and the vial of opiate in his purse was empty. As he drew near, he saw that the door of the building hung open.

Inside there was only an old woman, her hair tied up in a dirty cloth. She was on her hands and knees, search-

212

ing for something in the wilted rushes. The room stank of sickness, death, loss of hope. Karolan bent down and laid a hand on the woman's arm. The wrists protruding from her frayed sleeves looked as fragile as glass. 'Know you the whereabouts of Jack Spicer?' he asked gently.

She looked up at him after a long pause. Her thin cheeks were sunken. Her eyes lack-lustre. Deep lines radiated outwards from her mouth. 'I cannot find it, sire,' she said, her voice breaking with sorrow. 'Will you help me?'

'What is it you have lost?' Karolan said gently.

'My babe,' the woman said. ''Twere here when last I looked.'

Karolan patted the old woman's arm. She smelt as if she had been lying in her own filth for days. There was a tidemark of grease around the neck of her gown. The ravaged face staring up at him, suddenly took on a new expression.

'I know thee! Lord Rakka you are, who was ever too good to lay a finger on me!'

'Adeliz?' Karolan said, only now recognizing in the strained features the shadow of the pretty young woman who had been a favourite with Jack. Did she have a child? Lifting her up as easily as if she was weightless, he carried her to the back of the room and set her down onto the wooden settle near the hearth. He found a jug of ale that smelt none too fresh, but suspected there would be nothing better in the building. Pouring a measure he lifted the cup to Adeliz's lips.

'Are you alone?' he asked. 'Where's Isabeau, Sabina, the other women?'

'Gone. Dead. All the world is dying,' she said wearily. 'Did you not know? 'Tis God's punishment.' Her sallow face brightened. 'Jack's upstairs. Come see.' Gripping his hand she pulled him across the room. Where before she had seemed exhausted, now she was possessed of a feverish strength.

She half-turned, flashing him a look over her shoulder. With a practised shrugging movement, she caused the neck of her gown to slip off one shoulder. One of her breasts was revealed, hanging slack and empty against the cage of her ribs. Her collar bones jutted sharply through her skin. He saw the black spots of the pestilence on her neck.

'Why'd you never like me?' she said. 'Mayhap you favour arse over coynte? There's many that's fugoists. I don't mind. Whatever your pleasure, you can have it for free.'

The coquettish gesture was too tragic to repulse him. The smell wafting up from her skirts was like a cesspit in high summer. At the top of the stairs, she led him into a small chamber. There was a shadowed alcove against one wall, filled entirely by a box bed. The bed hangings were drawn.

'He's sleepin'. Wait you there. I'll wake him how he likes it best.' Her grin was confident, suggestive. She hitched up her skirts. Her shift was soiled by her body's wastes. Brown scum caked her thin legs. Pulling the bed curtain aside, she disappeared behind it.

Karolan heard her murmuring affectionately to someone. The bed began to creak, the curtain billowing out with the movements behind it. Karolan moved forward, the sounds of her sighs and groans in his ears. From Jack there was no sound. 'Jack?' he said, grasping the curtain and pulling it open.

Adeliz looked up at him, her face beatific. Humping vigorously up and down, her stringy thighs straddling Jack's hips, she sighed and grunted with pleasure. Karolan did not speak, but stood looking down at Jack's bloated corpse. Jack had been dead for days. Perhaps that was the final thing that had unhinged her mind.

'Loves me, he does,' Adeliz crooned. 'My fine Jack tar.'

Circling her hips, she mashed herself against the discoloured flesh. Her face contorted as she gasped out her pleasure. Feeling sick at heart, Karolan put out a hand to help her off the bed, but she turned on him with a hiss. 'Leave me, you!'

'Come away, Adeliz. You can't help Jack now.'

'Too good fer me still, eh? Didn't want to sully yourself with a whore. Well here's summat for you anyways!' Adeliz's teeth sank into his hand. She shook her head, worrying at him like a dog, her teeth grinding past flesh to grate on bone. Karolan gave a cry of pain, wrenched his hand away. It hurt like hell, but that did not bother him. In a few hours there would be no trace of the injury. His concern was for her. His blood coloured her lips, the false rouge of it enlivening the grey of her haggard face. 'And now you!' she said. 'Meet your Maker. Death's kiss for all!'

For a second he saw her as she had once been, smooth and lovely with bright yellow hair. Then she heaved, clutching at her throat. Her eyes started from her head as her flesh burned and dissolved, the ruined tissue of her throat trickling down into her belly to set up its fire there too. He made no move to help her. She had chosen the manner of her death. It was no worse than that other, which faced her soon enough. Had she begged him for help, he would have given her the same end, and with his blessing. Retching and coughing, Adeliz slumped forward. A rush of blood-stained vomit, bright with shreds of raw tissue, spewed out of her, covering Jack's face and upper body. She gave a sigh, stopped breathing. Karolan took hold of the bed curtain, yanking it from its pole. Covering both bodies, he turned to leave the room.

A disturbance in the air heralded the Fetch. Its shadow form was rounded, gleaming and sleek from its previous encounter. He did not need to look to know that the spirit had slipped under the cover and was rapturously imbibing its favoured humours. 'Blessed pain,' it crooned. 'Generous you are, Master. Ah, it is too, too sweet.' Karolan ignored the rustlings and the wet slobbering noises of the spirit's enjoyment.

Downstairs, he sat beside the hearth, staring into the cold ashes. The manner of Adeliz's dying seemed to him to encapsulate the suffering of the many. It became easier with passing time, as others aged and he did not, to feel contempt for lesser beings with their little lives and petty quarrels. Perhaps he also despised them because he could never possess what the meanest of them took as God-given – a woman to love and children of his own.

All that had changed with Garnetta. His world had been a sweeter place when she inhabited it. He stroked his chin pensively and poured himself a cup of stale beer. It tasted flat and sour, but he drained the jug anyway. Crossing the room, he leaned against the frame of the door leading into the street and he gazed out at the thickening light of evening. The surface of the river, rippling with the current of the incoming tide, ought by rights to have been flecked with the glow of ships' lanterns, but all was dark. A stillness hung over the docks.

He wondered where Garnetta could be. It might take weeks, months, to find her. The one thing which gave him comfort was the fact that she could come to no physical harm. Had she discovered that fact yet? He smiled thinly, remembering the exultation he had felt on finding out that his body mended faster than other men's. Then too, he had discovered that no wound, however mortal, was fatal to him. He felt pain like any man; he could be cut and would bleed, but something about his transmuted flesh was enduring. Only prolonged burning or beheading might destroy him, but that he had not put to the test.

Upstairs, the Fetch emerged from the frowsty bed curtains, gleaming with the surfeit of pleasure. Golden lights danced within its shadow-form. It felt warm all the way through, ready for new sensation. *Want to be inside skin. Want to breathe. Want to look out of human eyes.* Its need was all encompassing, driving out all else from its devious and half-formed mind. The shifting matter of it changed shape as it considered in which form to appear before Karolan.

Would his master prefer a woman or a young man? It hesitated, partially transformed. Pale excrescences bulged from the grey shadow-shape of it, flowing into breasts and buttocks, then withdrawing and re-forming into sleek and elegant curves. It remembered the female. How sweet it had been to tease her, to awaken the fright within her and drink deeply of fear's essence. It thought of exploring more of the female – even of being allowed to enter her skin, run up the insides of her veins, seep into the warm, wet cavities within her. *Yes. Oh, yes. Want to. Want to. Want to.* Karolan would not know. And if the time came when its master found out that the spirit had betrayed him, the female would have sunk too far into the syrupy web of pleasure to emerge easily.

The Fetch began to glow and lengthen. In a few moments it was transformed into an elegant winged creature, with the face of a handsome young man. The limbs were long and clean, muscled and shimmering with motes of silver and pearl. The shoulders were broad, the waist slender. 'Behold,' it said, its voice rippling with sibilant notes of pride. 'The angel of the Lord is nigh and brings a message to the chosen one.' With an animal yelp of eagerness, it launched itself out of the physical world and into the realm of the Astral which it used as a vehicle to travel in time or distance.

CHAPTER THIRTEEN

'Now boy, I want the truth,' Brother Stephanis said. 'No need to be afraid. No harm will come to you, if you answer me straight.'

Clem looked up at the infirmarer, who had the face and build of a soldier, and wished that he had gone straight back to his village. Until the monk told him that no harm would come to him, the idea of being harmed had not entered his head. Trying not to show his uneasiness, he pushed his shoulders back. He opened his mouth to speak, but it seemed that his tongue was cleaved to his mouth.

'Come now,' Stephanis prompted. 'You told Thomas that you saw what happened to Garnetta. Is that true?'

Clem had not known the woman's name. Garnetta was it? He nodded warily. 'She saved me. The brigands, soldiers on the loose, they was hurtin' me. Wanted to know where my village was. But I wouldn't tell.'

'You are a brave lad,' Stephanis said. 'Garnetta saved you, you say? How?'

Clem swallowed. Now that he thought back on it, the whole thing seemed very unlikely. Miracles were not acted out before lowly folk like himself. He screwed up his face, rubbing at his dirty cheek as he sifted through the events, trying to decide how much to tell. 'She mun 'ave bin watchin' what they did to me. She ran at them, hitting out with a club. Bashed one in the arm and broke another's nose.'

The infirmarer raised his eyebrows, a look of suspicion on his broad face. Clem quaked and dug his bare toes into the rushes. 'A woman alone? She beat off the brigands with a club?' Stephanis said. 'A little unlikely wouldn't you say, Thomas? And very foolish of her. What happened then?'

'The . . . the soldiers was too shocked to do anythin' at first. Then they grabbed her. Took the club away. Hit her, all of them. She fell down. Two of them – one was the man whose face she spoiled – they pulled off her shift. They . . . it was sinful. I canna speak of it.'

'They forced her into carnal sin?' Stephanis prompted.

Clem nodded miserably. 'Screamed and screamed she did. She was bleeding from between her legs. They finished with her . . . then it was the men who was screamin', rolling on the floor, holding to their privy parts. The two men died. Then the others started cursin', callin' her names. They cut the woman with knives. I thought she was dead for sure.'

'Where were you when all this was happening?' Stephanis said.

Clem hung his head. 'Hidin' in some brambles. I couldn't help. I was hurt too.'

'Of course you were. No one is accusing you, boy,' Stephanis said gently.

'After the soldiers left, I stayed hidden 'til morn. When I woke and went to look, the dead soldiers were there still. The woman had gone.'

'So you saw the soldiers' wounds? You saw them clearly?'

Clem nodded. 'They was mortal bad. Privy parts raw, all burnt away. I was glad,' he said with passion. 'It was judgement on them fer what they did to the woman. She belonged to God.'

'What do you mean, "belonged to God"?'

'One of the soldiers said that Garnetta was fleeing from a nunnery.' He coloured as he recalled what else Gille had said.

Stephanis seized on his words. 'And? What else did he say?'

'She had mayhap been found swyving a priest,' Clem said reluctantly.

There was a burst of laughter, quickly muffled, from Thomas. Stephanis glared at the young assistant. 'Bawdy foolery,' he said. 'What did you do next, boy?'

'I tracked Garnetta. She was bad hurt. Ought to 'ave bin dead. All that blood. Bruises everywhere too. She was talkin' to herself. Mutterin', like her wits had fled.'

'What did she say?' Stephanis asked, reaching out to grab at Clem's ragged sleeve. 'Tell me, boy. Who was she addressing? Did she use a name?'

Clem shrank away, unable to meet the penetrating gaze of the infirmarer. The monk had a strange look on his face. Clem was reminded of how the soldiers had looked just before they violated the woman. He felt a ripple of fear. Surely they both were safe here? 'I dunna know,' he said warily. 'Could not hear too well. She walked fer hours. Then she found the track. When cart came past, she climbed into it. I knew 'twas Brother Amos at the reins. So I followed Garnetta here.'

When he finished there was silence. The infirmarer took Thomas aside. They conversed briefly. Clem fiddled with the frayed hem of his tunic, feeling very small and insignificant. Thomas gave him an encouraging smile, then left the chamber.

'I have sent Thomas to fetch food and drink for you,' Stephanis said, patting Clem's head. Clem resisted the urge to duck away. 'Bread, cheese, and ale. You'd like that, lad? Good. While we are waiting we shall have another talk. Sit now.'

Clem pressed his skinny buttocks to the very edge of a wooden settle. This monk made him uneasy. His voice was gentle, his manner kind enough, but there seemed something leashed within the big, muscular frame.

'I suspect that there are things you have not told me,' Stephanis said, pleasantly. 'Now, I shall have the truth. It would be better to tell me all unless you favour a birching at the least. Liars can have their tongues cut out.'

Clem nodded, his knees starting to shake. 'I thought you would not believe me.'

'My child,' Stephanis said. 'Let me be the judge of the truth. I am guided by God and am well equipped to deal with these matters. I shall ask you some questions. You need only nod or shake your head. That way there will be no mistaking your meaning.'

Clem nodded glumly, feeling that there was a flaw in this reasoning, but unable to find words to express his doubts. 'If I tell you all, you will let me go?' he said.

The infirmarer smiled, but there was no warmth in his face. 'Of a surety.'

Clem gulped. When Stephanis asked about the 'voices' that Garnetta had heard in the forest, he nodded, hardly listening to what he was asked. Stephanis spread writing tools onto the table. 'Now, lad. I shall go through all that again. You shall make your mark at the end of the testament. You think that you saw something beside Garnetta? A pillar of light – yes? A voice came out of this?'

Clem nodded miserably, no longer caring what he was agreeing to. All he need do was tell the monk what he wanted to hear, then he could be on his way.

'Garnetta called upon this light for help? Did you hear her call out to the Holy Virgin when the men were violating her? Ah, you did.' Stephanis's quill scratched across the parchment, now and then squeaking when the ink ran dry.

The sound set Clem's teeth on edge. He fought down

his rising panic, acutely aware of the smell of the monk's robe, his unwashed body. Brother Stephanis's breath smelt like sour milk. He watched a flea settle onto the back of the monk's hand and begin to bite. Stephanis was too engrossed to brush it away.

'A few more questions,' Stephanis said. 'Then you will have earned your food. You are certain that the soldiers were stricken with a morbus to their privy parts after they had violated Garnetta?' And so it went on.

Clem agreed to everything, not even raising an eyebrow when Stephanis supplied details of his own. His head was reeling by the time Stephanis finished writing. After sprinkling the parchment with sand, the monk shook it, then smoothed it flat once more. Handing the quill to Clem, he said, 'Here boy, make your mark. I'll steady your hand.'

'I can do it alone,' Clem said stiffly, proud that his father had taught him to shape the C and L that signified his name.

'Good,' Stephanis said, rolling up the parchment and sliding it into a drawer. 'Come with me. Let us go and see where Thomas has got to with your food.'

Clem could hardly contain his relief. He felt the oppressive fear lifting. Perhaps it was being inside the monastery that frightened him. Most of his life was spent in the open air. Only during the hardest weather did he sleep in the family croft which was made of wood, wattle, and straw. Clem distrusted stone, tiled floors, ceilings so high that shadows got trapped in the dusty corners where rafters met the walls.

Following Stephanis, it occured to him that the kitchen seemed a very long way from the infirmary. They walked for a long time, descending ever more deeply into a maze of narrow stone passages. Suddenly he felt himself grasped by the upper arms and thrust into an open doorway. He fell forward, sprawling onto a cold stone floor. A heavy wooden door slammed shut behind him. Scrambling to his feet, he banged on the door. His heart thudded in his chest. The silent blackness of the cell terrified him. A scream rose up in his throat and emerged as a thin wail, the echoing sound of it in the dark turning his bowels to water. Then a grille in the door slid open. He felt the blast of Stephanis's sour-milk breath.

'Save your voice, lad. No one can hear you. You can stay there until I decide what to do with you,' the infirmarer said. 'I'm not convinced by your story. That notched ear of yours is likely the mark of a thief. You came here looking for gain, not to do your simple Christian duty.'

'But Gille cut my ear!' Clem sobbed. 'They burned my leg with hot iron!'

'If that's the truth, then you have nothing to fear,' Stephanis said. 'A stay in that cell will not harm you.'

'I did what you wanted. Now I want to go home,' Clem whimpered. 'I'm hungry. You said . . . I would have . . . food.'

'I am a man of my word,' Stephanis said stoutly. 'You will find the food to one side of the door.'

The grille slid shut. Clem heard the sound of sandals retreating along the passageway. He slid down the door, until he was sitting on cold stone with his back resting against the wood. Slowly he stretched out both hands, feeling around until he discovered the loaf, cheese, and a jug of ale. Grabbing the bread, he hugged it to his chest, picking off chunks and stuffing them into his mouth. Tears poured down his cheeks and dripped off his chin. His mouth was so dry he could not swallow. Spitting out the mess of half-chewed bread into the palm of one hand he sat staring into the darkness.

His fingers tightened on the loaf, the only evidence he had that Brother Stephanis intended to keep him alive. His sobs began to subside.

'Oh, Mam,' he sniffled. 'Oh, 'elp me, Mam.'

'But I do not need to lie in bed. I feel so much better,' Garnetta said to Stephanis.

He smiled. There was something almost paternal in his manner. 'The healing power of God is remarkable, when channelled through prayer. But you must allow me to be the judge of your state of health. You need to become stronger. The seyney, while it has many merits, is apt to weaken a person somewhat.'

Garnetta leaned back contentedly against the pillows which Stephanis had piled behind her to cushion her against the cold stone. She felt no surprise that he planned to submit her to a series of blood-lettings. The practice was considered efficacious even for the healthy. Monks attending for regular seyneys looked forward to a period of rest and change of diet.

'You deem it necessary for me to be bled?' she asked.

Stephanis looked surprised at the question. 'Indeed. You have cleansed your mind with your confession and made your peace with God. Now we must cleanse your flesh. Galen recommends this sovereign method for balancing the humours.'

Garnetta recalled a conversation with Karolan. He, it seemed, was no great advocate of blood-letting. She remembered that he spoke of Arab doctors. Her cheeks grew warm as she saw again the dream images of Karolan with the handsome man called Harun. Mixed emotions rose up in her when she thought of Karolan kissing that man, lying in his arms, sharing caresses with him. It was Harun who had tended Karolan's wounds whilst in the Holy Land and taught him about medicaments. Karolan's healing skills came from a dubious source indeed. That was reason enough for allowing Stephanis to bleed her.

'Very well. I agree to the seyney,' she said and saw by the look on his face that he had expected her simply to submit to his greater knowledge and status. She pressed her lips together, cursing her loose tongue. It was difficult for her to remember to show the modesty and forbearance demanded of women. 'Who was that boy you were speaking to yester morn?' she said to divert his attention.

Stephanis's reaction was odd. He looked at her sharply. 'Boy?'

'I heard you speaking with a lad . . .' she began, realizing only then that Stephanis might think it strange that she could have heard his conversation through the thickness of several stone walls.

But Stephanis did not seem to notice anything odd about her question. 'Oh, just a beggar lad. Thomas brought the boy in. I sent the lad away after a good meal.'

She knew that he was lying, but could find no reason for it. The thread of his thoughts was not easy to catch, submerged as they were beneath the layers, stacked up like bolts of cloth, from his years of training in self control. Her newly honed instincts told her not to trust him completely, but he was her only hope of salvation now. She decided to allow him his secrets.

'When shall you bleed me?' she said.

'On the morrow, after Vespers, when you will have eaten your supper.'

Garnetta accepted the tray of food which Thomas brought into the cubicle. Her mouth watered as the smell of roast meat filled the chamber. This day there was roast pigeon, a dish of umbles seethed with leeks, a custard-like dowcet of cream, eggs, and currants, and more of the delicious wastel bread. Two quinces, a blush on their firm, yellow skins, lay next to the pewter jug of wine.

Stephanis beamed at her pleasure. 'Today is the feast of St Isidore,' he explained. 'We drink wine instead of ale. Enjoy your meal. I have much to do.'

Left alone, Garnetta began eating with relish, concentrating on the sensual pleasures of taste, texture, and smell. She pushed her doubts about the infirmarer to the back of her mind. Why must she ever look for complications? *Because you are wiser now in the ways of men. Every one of them wants something from you. Karolan, the brigands, Brother Stephanis too.* She refused to listen. Since her confession, she felt lighter of heart. The power of prayer was all encompassing. The mercy of God immeasurable. She felt a sense of peace so sweet that it lay like a veil upon her senses. *Whatever I am, I am still God's child,* she thought.

With a sigh, she sipped a cup of wine, feeling relaxed after her meal. Placing the tray on the side table, she sank back onto the pallet, allowing a feeling of drowsiness to sweep over her. She was aware that Thomas came quietly into the cubicle and took away the tray. In the space left behind by his passing, she felt a silence descend. It was more than the usual peace of the monastery, broken only by the soft tolling of a bell in the distance. This silence was absolute – like a pall of thick grey wool. In its depths was the sense of something poised – waiting.

A shiver passed down Garnetta's spine. She tried to open her eyes, but they felt heavy, so heavy. All she could do was look through the net of her lashes as the cell began to flood with light. Was she dreaming? The air shimmered and pleated, dancing with motes of silver. Where there had been nothing, there was now a shimmering curtain. A black slit appeared in the fabric. The line grew fat about the middle and she saw that fingers, slender and white, were pulling it apart, stretching open the rupture to form a doorway.

Garnetta's heart rose up into her mouth as shafts of light streamed in through the widening gap. Then a body appeared and a slender, glowing form stepped into the room. A young man, long of limb, with the face of a saint and skin that glowed softly like a pearl, approached the pallet and knelt beside it. The warm smell of licorice and almonds filled the room. Something about the scent was familiar, but Garnetta was too much in awe of the angelic being to be able to think. The smile on the young man's face was beatific. She absorbed every detail about him. The broad shoulders, slender waist and hips were well-muscled under the poreless skin. At his shoulders was the faint suggestion of wings. And there, at the base of his belly, were his privy parts, beautiful in their proportions.

It did not occur to her to wonder why he was naked. His perfection was explanation enough for anything. Finally, she found her voice. 'Who . . . who are you?' she whispered.

'You know me not? I am yours,' he said in a voice like honey. 'Yours to lead or to guide you. Yours to command or destroy. Protect you shall I, cherish and keep you. One of the chosen you are. Only give me the word and we shall be one.'

She had seen this vision before. The words, the cadence of the voice were achingly familiar. This was *her* angel. The one who had come to her in the tower, during the ritual. What did this mean?

Suddenly there was no need of answers. A feeling

began to gather pace within her. It was as if a great drum was beating, somewhere far off. As it moved towards her the rhythm of it changed, deepened, and gathered pace. Light flickered around the kneeling figure, pricking outwards like the halo of a saint in a painting, making the daylight look dull by comparison. Locks of silver hair brushed against the broad shoulders. Slowly Garnetta raised her hand, her eyes fully open now. She stretched out her arm towards the apparition. When her fingers touched it she felt skin; warm, smooth, solid. A tingle passed through her fingers, rippling up her arm, spreading downwards over chest, breast, and waist to centre in her lower belly.

A shudder passed over the young man. She saw the tremors flicker across his chest. Did she imagine it or was there a deeper glow in the place where his heart was? She smiled at him and was touched by the expression of anguish which flickered across the pearly face. The eyes were golden, deep-set. The sculpted lips, as if drawn all around with gold ink, parted on a sigh.

'Beautiful you are,' said the young man, his voice harsh with passion. 'Precious to me. Give me leave to serve you. Bless you shall I, above all women. And I too shall be blessed by your regard.'

Garnetta's limbs felt heavy. The desire rippled and bloomed throughout her body. She stretched languidly. The scent of her own body, clean and sweet, rose around her. Oh, yes, she was sore in need of being blessed. Karolan had awakened her body to pleasure. Only now did she remember what a potent drug that was. 'Yes,' she murmured. 'Oh, yes, my angel, serve me.'

Instantly she was embraced by sensation. Her back arched as she strained towards the man who enfolded her. The glowing face was close to her own, those sculpted lips pressed firmly to hers. It seemed that all the surface of her skin was being stroked. Little spears of delight spread upwards from her toes. She tasted the moist salt of the angel's mouth as the lips parted. His firm tongue explored her own.

She moaned softly, held tight against the gleaming body, the muscles moving warmly against her skin. Then she felt her thighs being spread apart and experienced a moment of resistance. It was too soon. The taste of fear, the recent recollection of harsh hands on her, the tearing pain and feeling of her blood running down her legs, swamped her. 'Wait, I beg you,' she breathed, her breath shallow, the pulse beating at her neck.

Was she cursed always to remember the pain of violation at the moment of pleasure? The angel did not heed her, but her panic faded. His touch was clean, welcome. This was not an assault. There was something of violence in the hands that caressed her, it was true, but this was a force bent only on serving her needs. This was a concentration of great strength, tempered to her will. She cried out and surged against the body that held her to the pallet with a silken strength. Her thighs were opened wide beneath him, her hips tipped up to admit the entry of his hard flesh. Fingers stroked her buttocks, her moist cleft, opening and softening her in readiness. She felt the slickness of her swollen coynte as the gentle stroking brought her towards the edge of pleasure. Karolan had awoken her to this need and now the tension within her throbbed and pulsed.

'Now. Enter me,' she gasped, her mouth sliding across the firm lips and moving down to kiss his chin.

Gripping her waist with both hands the angel lifted her onto his cock. The thick phallus filled her, forging into her, pushing aside the clinging walls of her flesh until it lodged against her womb. Garnetta felt a hand press against her mouth and pushed her tongue between the fingers, lapping at the musk tasting skin. As the cock thrust into her, she lifted her legs and wrapped them around the taut buttocks. Digging her heels into his back, she gripped him, lifting herself up and pumping her hips shamelessly in the pursuit of her pleasure. She felt loose-limbed, succulent.

The shining being gave a low chuckle. She moaned throatily as he bit at her nipples, holding one breast tightly so that he could suckle her while ploughing her inner recesses. It seemed impossible, but she felt his mouth all over her – between her buttocks, her toes, in her ears, at the hollow of her throat. She was drowning in sensation, borne along on the tide of the most exquisite feelings. Then she felt him swelling within her. Surely she would tear, but she did not.

He was hot and hard. She enclosed him completely, loving the way her flesh was dragged as he moved within her. Drawing out he rimmed her entrance, using just the big swollen glans to tease her towards the ultimate release. Every muscle in her body tightened as she strained against him. Her arms and legs were thrown wide. The sound of their joining filled the cell – harsh breaths, the kiss of flesh against flesh, the subtle wet noises of their joined sexes. She could smell them both. Musk, salt, the spice of sweat – and overlaying all was the faint odour of licorice. The angel was silent, concentrating only on serving her.

'God. My God,' she whimpered, beside herself with the glory of it. Her fingers clawed at the sheets as she caught the thread of her climax. The angel shuddered against her as she sobbed and threshed. He seemed hot. Too bright. The feeling of his slim body between her legs was like a benediction.

Afterwards, she could not remember what had

happened next. All became confusion. Where the pleasure had been outside, now it was *inside*. Her skin was suddenly cool, as if the angel had withdrawn himself from her all at once. There was a dreadful pressure in her head, as if her skull was filled to capacity and the bones were trying to expand. The roots of her hair ached and stung. Her ears rang and her eyes swelled. Tears ran down her cheeks. Somehow the pleasure had become pain, but even then the boundaries of sensation were confused.

Her womb burned and spasmed. She felt every orifice invaded, stretched and then filled with a hot, throbbing fullness. Her belly grew taut, her lungs swelled, and she felt a creeping horror at the itching *inside* her skin. She could not see. Blackness crowded her vision. She imagined that fingernails were raking at the back of her eyeballs. A ball of terror knotted in her belly. Opening her mouth wide, she let out a silent scream.

This fear was an invasion, robbing her of the sweetness of pleasure, sending ice racing through her tortured veins. She could not even cry. It was as if bonds of metal pinned her to the pallet. Suddenly she felt a loosening, was able to speak. 'No more,' she grunted, her tongue as thick as a mutton collop in her mouth.

Abruptly the sensation stopped. The shining form was back, whispering, soothing her with words and touch. She lay against the warm chest and felt the dread ebbing away. Had she imagined the last few seconds? She did not know, but sleep was beckoning and would not be gainsaid. Her head rolled back onto the pallet. She was unconscious the moment her cheek touched the sheet and did not see the moment when the angel stepped back through the 'door' into the silver curtain of the air.

Nor did she see Stephanis's face, sweating and bleached of all colour, as he let fall the worsted curtain and hurried out of the infirmary.

CHAPTER FOURTEEN

In the chamber above the warehouse the only sound was of wheezing as each painful breath was squeezed into the lungs of the man who lay on the bed.

Karolan looked down at the old man, wondering how long he had lain there in his own filth, too weak even to reach the cup of water at his bedside. Judging by the state of the woman's corpse on the stairs, this man had been alone for many days.

Filling a cup from the flask of clean water that hung at his belt, he poured in a few drops of herbal tincture and slid a hand behind the man's head. 'Drink. I'll aid you.'

The hands that clutched at him were surprisingly strong. 'Bless . . . you,' he managed to say, his voice merely a whisper. 'My . . . my wife?'

'I'm sorry,' Karolan said. 'She is at peace. Rest now whilst I make you clean.'

The man turned his face to the wall. Before the sickness took him, he must have been tall, well-fleshed, but the skin had shrunk tight to the big frame. Karolan glanced around the chamber. The furniture was solid, well-made. The rushes close to the bed were stained with vomit and excrement, but the rest were clean. A clothes press stood against one wall. Inside he found clean sheets and nightshirts. He was lifting out a pile of clean linen when there were heavy footsteps on the stairs. He heard a cry of rage and anguish, then it seemed that a whirlwind entered the bedchamber. Karolan had a brief impression of an enormous, fair-haired man who smelt of salted leather and sweat before he was seized about the throat.

'Ach! Christ's bones, you bastard!' the man grunted, his voice heavily accented. 'They're hardly cold and you're robbing them! I'll cut out your cursed looter's heart.'

Karolan used the sides of both hands to chop hard into his attacker's waist. For a moment the blond man loosened his grip, but he hardly seemed to feel the blow. Despite the man's aggression, Karolan held back. The giant might tower above him, but he was no match for Karolan's preternatural strength. Then as the thick fingers squeezed tighter and tighter, Karolan's vision darkened. Pressing his thumbs into the man's kidneys Karolan jabbed – hard. When the giant let go of his neck, he brought his knee up into the man's groin and gave him a hard shove backwards.

There was a sound like a pig's bladder deflating. The big man collapsed groaning onto the rushes. Clutching his privy parts, he rolled onto his side. It took some time for him to recover. Wiping away blood from a cut lip, he made no attempt to rise, but sat looking up at Karolan, blue eyes vivid against his weathered skin.

'I ought to kill you for that. No man has ever laid me out. Ach. What does it matter? Take what you want and go. I have not the will to slit your thieving throat. Leave me, so that I may bury my mother and father.' His shoulders sagged, but there was no suggestion of weakness in the broad, handsome face, only a weary acceptance.

Karolan opened his mouth to explain. Before he could speak there was a movement from the bed. 'Gunter?' came the dry croak. 'Is . . . is that you, son?'

The big man leapt to his feet. In a trice he was leaning over the old man. Careless of the stench he picked him up into an embrace like a bear's hug. 'Father? Praise be to God. I saw poor mother on the stairs and thought the worst!' Karolan watched in silence as Gunter laid his father onto the bed, his face tender and full of joy. Gunter turned to face Karolan, his expression hardening. 'You here still? Strange behaviour for a thief.'

'Aye, if thief I was. I heard a call for help when I was passing. Come, man, let's not waste time. There's a chance of saving your father.'

Gunter gaped at him, taking in details of Karolan's costly black garments. He struck the centre of his own forehead with the heel of his palm. 'Ach! A fool I am to think you nothing but a looter!' He grinned, showing strong, gappy teeth. 'Forgive my lack of manners. I always did act first and think later.' He extended a hand.

Karolan found his own hand enveloped by a muscled paw and pumped energetically. He grinned, liking this blond giant whose tender feelings belied his outward appearance.

'Tell me what I must do,' Gunter said.

'Have you means of making a fire? Good. Set some water to heat.'

Gunter went off to do as he was asked. By unspoken agreement, they left the corpse of Gunter's mother to be dealt with later. The needs of the living took preference over the dead. Once the water was warm, they stripped and washed the old man. Karolan measured out more of the herbal draught.

'What's that you're giving him?' Gunter asked suspiciously. 'The apothecary who tended me when I had an ague gave me a concoction of bird shit, snail shells, and henbane.'

'And what did you do with him?' Karolan asked.

'I told him to take his own poison. When he refused, I kicked his skinny arse out of here, that's what!' Gunter said.

'I'd have done the same,' Karolan said, laughing. 'You

have nothing to fear from this draught. It's just willow bark to lower a fever, thymus to fight infection, and something to make him sleep.'

'And a few simples will banish the pestilence?' Gunter looked doubtful.

'The draught will help his suffering, but the blaine must be lanced and drained.' So saying, Karolan took out the rolled packet which contained his medical instruments.

Gunter blanched when he saw the razor-sharp lancet and other cutting tools. 'Must this be done? Father is so weak. The agony of it may kill him.'

'He'll die for certain if we do nothing,' Karolan said, putting a fresh candle into the holder. 'The draught will help. Besides, he's a strong man – like his son.'

When the candle flame burned bright and clear, he drew the lancet back and forth through the flame to cleanse it, then approached the bed. Folding back the sheet, he laid open the nightshirt to reveal the ugly black tumour in the old man's armpit. Gunter watched closely as Karolan held a piece of clean linen around the blaine. As he raised the knife, Karolan said, 'Hold him down. If he twists as I cut him, I may do him serious injury.'

'For heaven's sake be swift,' said Gunter, his face pale.

As Karolan stabbed the lancet into the tumour, Gunter leaned his weight on his father's shoulders. The old man shrieked and thrashed. Bloody pus spurted onto the linen. Karolan squeezed the pad of fabric around the blaine until it stopped leaking. The stink that rose from the pus surpassed all previous stenches. Even Karolan's stomach heaved in protest.

'Jesu. God and all His saints!' Retching, Gunter staggered across the room.

While Gunter's back was turned Karolan spat into his

palm and smeared his caustic spittle onto the wound, then he wiped and cleaned the lancet before packing his instruments away. 'He'll live. Your father's one of the lucky few.'

'Amen to that,' Gunter said, having recovered. 'All thanks be to you, friend. You are leaving at once? Nay, wait. Have a sup to eat. Father's sleeping now and needs no watching. Come into the back room.' A shadow passed over his face. 'I have but one task more to do, then I'll be glad to join you.'

Karolan knew that Gunter meant to deal with his mother's body. He did not offer to help, sensing that the man wished to pay his final respects in private. He went out of the bedchamber into a small room overlooking the river. The window shutters were open. A cool breeze blew into the room, bringing with it smells of tar, fish, the underlying taint of rot. There was a fire burning, which made the little room almost cheerful. An iron spit held a cauldron.

Through the open doorway Karolan could see a store-room. Barrels and bales were stacked almost to the ceiling. There was a truckle bed against one wall. He guessed that Gunter used this room. Stretching out on a settle, he propped his booted feet on the hearthstone. He rubbed gritty eyes, unable to remember the last time he had slept the night through.

Since Garnetta's desertion, he had slipped easily into his old habit of frequenting the taverns and bawdy houses. He roamed the dark streets and malodorous alleys, searching for diversions, always accompanied by the Fetch. The squalor, the depths to which humanity could sink, fascinated and amused him. He had felt a flicker of emotion at Jack's passing, but his prime emotion was annoyance. Now he would have to find a new supplier of drugs. The deaths of the three whores,

Adeliz, Isabeau, and Sabina, had not affected him unduly. Whores lived short dreary lives, the pox as likely to carry them off as a drunken pimp or the pestilence.

On the morrow, when he had slept, he would bind the Fetch into his service and send it out again on the quest to find Garnetta. It was time he set the capricious spirit to work. By now, it must be glutted with pleasure. Not since his days as a soldier of fortune, when the Fetch had been at his side on various battle-fields, had it fed so well. Now that he had time to think about it, he realized that he had not sensed the spirit's presence for some hours. Which was unusual. It liked nothing better than to gloat over its doubtful pleasures. He imagined it bathing in bitter emanations, the murky colours within its shadow-shape, shifting and flowing like dark ribbons in muddy water.

He closed his eyes and instantly saw the image of Garnetta's face. He began thinking about how good it had been to lie with her – to hold her and look into her face, to lay his cheek against her hair, savour the clean scent of it. Simple enough pleasures, pleasures which had started him dreaming. And then to have had the promise of happiness snatched from him. It was not to be borne. Suddenly he felt his anger at her dissolving. She had fled from him in fear of her life. That saddened and depressed him. Ah, but he was getting maudlin, his mood brought on, no doubt, by lack of sleep. Even his remarkable body needed a measure of rest. He allowed his head to fall back against the high back of the settle.

Garnetta. Come back to me. I want to tell you about everything. What made me as I am. Why I am guilty of so many crimes.

When Gunter returned, Karolan looked up wearily. Gunter flashed him a bleak smile, recognizing a fellow sufferer. 'You look like you need more than ale to give you fortitude, my friend. I have just the thing.' He dragged a heavy sea chest into the room and raised the lid. He passed Karolan a blue-glass bottle. 'The best rum. See here, lemon fruits, cinnamon wood, nutmeg. I'll make you a brew to warm your heart and wring tears from your soul.'

Karolan laughed. 'It sounds wonderful.' It was what they both needed, to drink themselves into oblivion and then sleep for long, dreamless hours.

When Karolan woke, the morning sun was pushing its way in through the cracks in the shutters. It was pleasant to lie still in comfort. For a moment he did not move, recalling the conversation of the previous evening. The more Gunter had drunk, the more talkative he became. It appeared that his mother had been German. She had come to England as a stowaway, after escaping from her vicious domineering father. She had got no further than the port, where she met Abel Woolmonger. Captivated by the German girl's fair hair, blue eyes, and fiery personality, Abel had asked her to marry him within a week. Their first child had been named for her maternal grandfather, Gunter.

'Hence my name,' Gunter said, grinning. 'Always causes comment on first hearing – Gunter Woolmonger.' He was now owner-captain of a cargo ship, the *Helga*, his family having grown wealthy from trading in English wool. Abel had planned to build a house in the countryside to please Gunter's mother, whose childhood had been spent on a sheep farm. 'Ach. So much for that now,' Gunter said, pouring himself more rum. After many weeks away, the *Helga* had returned to port, only to find that there were no dockers to unload her. After a brief investigation, Gunter ordered the unmarried men amongst the ship's crew to stay aboard and guard the cargo. 'Only too pleased to stay, they were,' Gunter slurred, grinning broadly. 'Seen what the Death can do to a community. Spreads like a blaze. Whoosh. Jus' like putting a match to straw. Naught to do but flee before it. 'S bad. Very bad. Poor mother. She was a good woman. My little Mutti. What a temper – but gentle? She taught me the German tongue, y'know? 'Twas her who advised father about wool.' He gave a muffled sob that ended on a hiccough. 'Ah, well. The Lord keep her, eh? Have another drink. We could all be dead on the morrow. Here's to the pest . . . the Death – curse his hollow eyes and bared teeth!'

Karolan held out his goblet. Gunter filled it to the brim. 'There are methods that offer protection. I can tell you about them,' he said. But Gunter was staring in a maudlin haze into his goblet, tears trickling unchecked down his weathered cheeks. Karolan concentrated on drinking enough rum so that he too would be too numbed for coherent thought. Soon they slumped onto the settles and slept.

Now Karolan yawned, sat up, and stretched. The sugary smell of rum still perfumed the air. Despite having drunk a whole bottle of the dark brew, he felt no ill-effects. On the settle opposite, Gunter stirred. The sea captain looked as if he felt the effects of every drop. Opening bleary eyes, Gunter grimaced and shut them quickly. His thick fair hair stood up in unruly spikes. Smacking his lips at the rank taste of his mouth, he swung his feet onto the floor and sat up.

Scratching at his groin, Gunter reached for a nearby chamber pot. Unlacing the front of his hosen, he held the pot close to his body and let out a long sigh as the sound of piss hitting pottery filled the room. The smell of his urine was strong and healthy. 'I should take this

241

to market,' he said, grinning. 'Must be almost pure spirit!'

Karolan chuckled. 'Wit so early in the morn is an admirable thing.'

Having finished, Gunter passed the pot to Karolan. Karolan used it, then crossed the room to empty it into the river below. Gunter went to see how his father fared. Karolan heard the two of them speaking. Abel's voice was stronger, although tinged with grief. He was certain the old man would recover.

Stripping to the waist, he poured warm water into a dish and added a few drops of oil. The pungent, earthy scent of patchouli rose into the air. Plunging his hands into the perfumed water he washed his face, arms, and body. Gunter returned in a few minutes, subdued but full of admiration for Karolan's skills with a knife.

'Father'll need watching, but he's on the mend. Once he's on his feet, he'll find enough to do with the business to run. Servants have all run away. We'll need to find others if we're not to founder. Mother worked hard to help build up the business. Aye, well . . . I shall always be grateful for what you've done. But for you I would have lost both my parents. Name any service, my friend, and it is done.'

'I did little enough,' Karolan said dismissively, embarrassed by the fulsome thanks. It was a new experience to have someone place themselves willingly in his debt. He dried himself on his linen under-shirt, then smoothed back his wet hair, shaking the drops from it like a dog. While he took a clean shirt out of his pack and slipped it on, Gunter filled a cup with water and scrubbed vigorously at his front teeth with a grubby finger. After swilling out his mouth, he spat into the bowl which Karolan had used for washing.

'There's water left in the cauldron. Plenty for your needs and your father's.'

'Ain't healthy to wash too much,' Gunter said, dragging his fingers through his blond hair in a combing motion. 'Though I'm not averse to being clean. I take a bath at Christ Mass and Easter like everyone else. Priest says a man's natural oils protect him from the sickness. Sweet smells only tempt the Devil to linger.'

'Perhaps so, but there are smells enough in the streets to clog my nose, without the smell of my own sweat to add to them,' Karolan said. 'Besides, I learned the habit of taking baths and perfuming the body whilst in the Holy Land. It is something I have become accustomed to.'

'Ach! A crusader. I knew that was a knight's trick you bested me with earlier,' Gunter said without rancour, rummaging in the open sea chest. 'So – what's a man like you doing in this region? Ah, here's what I'm looking for.' He gave a sound of satisfaction as he withdrew a piece of bacon, a bag of onions, and a loaf of hard black bread.

'I'm looking for someone,' Karolan said, settling down to watch as Gunter cut two thick slices of bread, then piled them with slabs of fat bacon and rounds of raw onion. 'I'd thought I'd find her easily, but this area is in turmoil with the Death rife.'

'Mayhap I can help you. Whom do you seek?'

Karolan bit into the bread. The saltiness of the bacon and the pungent flavour of the onion was wonderful. 'A woman,' he said, chewing. 'My ward. She left my house, late one night, unseen by anyone. She's afflicted with a fever of the mind. Garnetta was afraid that someone in my house would hurt her. There was no reason for this. I value her highly and have only her welfare at heart.'

Gunter blew out his lips on an onion-scented whistle. 'Women get strange fancies, right enough. She's alone in town? You must be sore afraid for her.'

'I would be more afraid if Garnetta were not a re-markable young woman. She is more capable than most of taking care of herself.'

'Say you so? How is this?'

'I taught her some warrior skills,' Karolan lied smoothly. 'And it will be clear from her manner and clothing that she is a gentlewoman. Any thief would weigh the chance of a ransom against the pleasure of doing her harm.'

'True enough, regarding robbery. But the pestilence is no respecter of rank,' Gunter said, cutting more slices of bread. 'Is not your biggest fear is that she is lying in some hovel, sick unto death?'

'Aye,' Karolan said, accepting another of the huge slabs of bread. 'Corpses aplenty, I've seen, but none that bear her face.'

'Well thank the Lord for that,' Gunter said, crossing himself. 'I'll do all I can to help. For now, at least, I'll pray for her safety.'

Karolan thanked Gunter and stood up. 'In the event that you have anything to tell me, I'm staying at the inn at the end of the street.'

Gunter looked askance. 'I won't hear of it! You'll stay here and welcome. I can bed down in father's room. You can have use of the truckle in the storeroom.'

Karolan opened his mouth to protest, but Gunter would have none of it. He clapped a brawny arm around Karolan's shoulders. 'No man shall say that Gunter Woolmonger does not pay his debts. Besides, what if father was to need more of that herbal medicament?' Defeated, Karolan grinned. And the matter was settled.

Thomas hesitated before tapping on the door of Brother Stephanis's cell. The infirmarer had been short-tempered and preoccupied of late. Suspecting that

Stephanis had a touch of fever, he had come to ask whether the infirmarer wished him to brew a cup of soothing chamomile tea.

When there was no answer from within, Thomas pushed open the cell door. He saw Brother Stephanis kneeling on the stone floor and heard him reciting prayers. Thomas would have backed out silently and left Stephanis to his devotions, except that he was rooted to the spot by the fact that Stephanis was stark naked. With his big shoulders and muscled back, he looked more like a soldier than ever. Below the weathered neck, there were weals on the pale skin, some of them crusted with dried blood. Thomas gasped at this evidence of self-punishment. What sins could Stephanis harbour that merited such harsh measures? Alerted by the sound, Stephanis twisted round and turned haunted eyes on Thomas. Thomas's eyes widened as he saw Stephanis's prodigious erection – and what Stephanis had done to himself.

A thin cord was knotted around the base of the engorged phallus, which jutted upright, the veins almost bursting through the skin from the pressure of the rope. Stephanis's scrotal sac was cruelly compressed by more of the cord. The hard stones bulging around the loops seemed to thrust the dreadful swollen organ into greater prominence. 'Forgive me . . . I . . .' Thomas stammered, unable to look away from the imprisoned cock. In the midst of his disgust, he felt an unwilling fascination.

'Don't leave!' Stephanis said hoarsely. 'I am beset by temptations. Whatever I do my staff of Adam will not subside. Images crowd my mind. Ah, God deliver me! I am bewitched!' Raising his hands he banged clenched fists against his forehead.

Thomas hesitated, then he closed the door behind him. Walking carefully past Stephanis, he perched on the edge of the narrow bed. Despite himself he was impressed by Stephanis's fortitude. His member must pain him greatly, for Stephanis seemed not to realize that he was fumbling with the cord around his ballocks, scrabbling at the twine which was pressed tight into deep grooves of flesh.

'Try as I might, I cannot banish the obscene images from my mind,' Stephanis said. Groaning, he hunched into a bow-shape as if seeking to embrace with his body the sin within him. 'A succubus besets me with dream images.'

Thomas trembled with awe, feeling his own body awake as Stephanis spoke. He knew instinctively that the infirmarer was speaking about Garnetta.

'I saw her lying on her pallet, her limbs spread in abandonment, all the secrets of her body in plain view,' Stephanis said. 'I cannot forget how she writhed, working her hips, lifting herself as if for some invisible caress. Her thighs wide-spread, the haired lips of her coynte pressed apart to show the moist folds. The shadowed orifice so exposed and pulsing – actually opening and closing – like the wet, red mouth of some infernal sea-creature.' Stephanis moaned loudly and pressed his hands to the rigid flesh at his loins.

Thomas saw how the turgid shaft leapt and twitched as if the cock had a life of its own. A silken droplet gathered at the slitted mouth, leaked down the purple glans. Stephanis's belly was sheened with sweat. The cell stank of unwashed flesh, the salt-sour odour of repression. Stephanis's voice was a tormented drone. Thomas had never heard anyone speak such obscenities. Despite his discomfiture, he was afire with lust. He shifted on the bed, pressing his hands into the lap of his robe.

'Her face was bound by such pleasure,' Stephanis said, wonderment making his voice soft. 'Her skin glowed from within. Ah, her breasts were a tempting fruit for a sinner's mouth. I could have borne it better by candle-light, or under cover of darkness, when colours are smeared as when a hand trails over a wet canvas, but it was daylight, I was spared nothing. Her limbs as white as wax; her face pure, her exquisite skull black-smudged, as if touched by the artistry of a scribe's ink-brush. The only colours in the world – white, black, and red. Oh, God – was ever a red so bright, so beguiling, as graphic as shame itself.'

Stephanis convulsed, covered his face with his hands. Thomas hardly dared to breathe. Stephanis must indeed be bewitched to speak in such colourful language. Thomas could almost see Garnetta lying with her demon lover.

'She lifted her legs, opening her knees wide, so that her buttocks opened. I saw the channel leading deep inside her. Thomas, the coynte is a fount to trap the unwary. Foul and sinful it is. But, God forgive me, it is beautiful in its way. So delicate the contours. Garnetta's hips thrust back and forth as she took her pleasure, moaning the while and threshing her head back and forth. There was perfume too, salt and musk – something like blood. It made me want to weep.'

Recalling the scent, a tremor passed over Stephanis's face. His eyes searched Thomas's face, seeking for understanding or disgust – and for something else. Thomas could not move, caught and held by the tortured passion in the infirmarer's eyes. A sense of the inevitable settled over him. His own excitement and tension sent tingling sparks all over his body. Slowly he stood up. Turning around he lay belly down over the edge of the bed. If Stephanis should speak he would lose his nerve. There was silence in the cell but for the sound of harsh breathing as Thomas raised the hem of his robe and bared himself. The forbidden act stung him to his soul.

He felt a shaking hand settle on each of his buttocks. As Stephanis caressed his rump, he groaned softly, arching his back and opening his thighs wide. His cock and balls were pressed beneath his belly. As Stephanis handled him more intimately he pressed his aching phallus to the rough woollen blanket. There was a pause, then one thick finger worked into his anus. He smelt tallow as Stephanis worked the oily substance into him, loosening and softening the tight orifice. He gathered himself for the penetration to come, dreading and relishing it in equal measure.

Stephanis gave a muffled sob as he knelt between Thomas's thighs, the bulbous tip of his phallus nudging between the parted cheeks. Thomas held his breath as he felt himself opened. As the bound cock entered him, the ridges of twine scraping deliciously against the tight ring of muscle, he sank down towards Stephanis's belly. Stephanis bent over, muffling his agonized cries against the woollen folds of Thomas's habit as he bucked and jerked within the boy's body. They toiled together, both consumed by the wet heat of their joint pleasure. Finally Thomas spent himself in shuddering spurts. Stephanis drove into his now quiescent form, shaking the boy's body with the force of his thrust until the semen jetted from him.

Thomas did not move for a time after Stephanis pulled out of him. When he rose finally, he kept his face averted until he had covered himself. Wiping himself clean of the oily slickness on a fold of his robe, he glanced at Stephanis who was looking down at his dangling flesh in revulsion. A viscous thread hung from the tip of his cock. He dashed it away in a fury.

'See what that woman has brought us to?' he said tearfully. 'Oh, Thomas forgive me. How low I have fallen. Kneel with me and pray.'

'But I wanted it. The sin is mine too,' Thomas said in a low voice.

'Oh, God. How great is her power to corrupt! We must pray harder.' For a while they knelt together, then Stephanis said gently. 'Leave me now. Go about your work. This was not your fault. The flesh is weak when women cast their spells.'

Thomas left the cell. His body felt replete with pleasure, but he was afraid too. Garnetta's spells must be powerful indeed if they could urge Stephanis and himself to carnal acts. Surely no monk was safe. Thomas felt the hair on the back of his neck rise. The enormity of what had taken place impressed itself upon him. He must seek help. Plainly, Stephanis was near breaking point. Thomas was reluctant to speak of his sin, but he knew that it was his duty to report it.

As Stephanis donned the crudely made hair shirt he could not suppress a gasp. The fibres sticking out of the weave scraped his abraded skin, prickling and burning like all the fires of Hell. He belted the shirt with the length of twine. It might as well have been a rope of brambles around his waist, the effect was the same. Gingerly he covered the hair shirt with his habit of bleached wool.

A tear of self-pity glistened on his cheek. God's ways were His own, but why was it so often lay people who were graced by visits from angels or heard heavenly messages? He had spent a large part of his life at Holy Penitence, atoning daily for the sins of the world. Never had there been the hint of a vision, the slightest echo of a heavenly voice. It ought to be me, he thought, allowing himself the luxury of a gorgeous flush of envy. *It ought to be me*. He wanted to shout the words aloud, to let them ring out from the top of the ruby tower.

Chapter Fifteen

John de Mandeville, Abbot of Holy Penitence, looked calmly at the man who stood before him. Although he kept his face impassive, the irritation welled up within him. On the table in front of him were spread the accounts on which he had been working before Brother Amos sought an audience. The abbot's precise hand was apparent in the columns of figures placed beside him. John took pride in the way he managed the finances. He had been busy juggling with the money likely to be saved by selling off the entire clip of wool – a gift of thirty woollen habits from a local lord, to mark the glorious victory of the English at Crécy, meant that they would not need their own wool to clothe their backs this winter. He made a note to send word to Gunter Woolmonger that he had more wool than usual to sell.

It was most pleasant trying to decide where the saving could best be put to use, but Brother Amos had intruded on this reverie. Looking at the dour, heavy face of the kitchener, John's spirits sank. What would it be this time? Another petty grievance – someone taking apples from the store, or eating more than the single conventual loaf stipulated daily for each monk. 'Well, Amos. What brings you to me at this hour of the day?' John was pleased to note that his voice did not betray his inner feelings.

The kitchener's skin looked greasy. A pungent smell of onions, lard, and sweat rose from his habit; the cuffs, John saw with distaste, were stiff with food stains.

'It concerns the infirmarer,' Amos said.

Ah, thought John, it is a matter of health. By the sour

look of the man's face, the tightness around his thin lips, John guessed the morbus to be of the bowels. 'You may speak freely,' he said.

'It is known to you,' Amos said, 'that there is a woman in the infirmary?'

John nodded, his fine white brow creasing. 'Brother Stephanis sent word of her. A gentlewoman, a poor benighted soul, I believe. Her family have not yet come forth to claim her. Was she not attacked by brigands and left for dead? I am told that her progress has been rapid. I am to speak with Stephanis later on this matter.'

A smirk twisted Amos's mouth. John felt a surge of dislike. God forgive him, but it was not easy to feel charitable to all His creatures. Well he knew that pettiness and paucity of spirit were rife within any company cloistered together for good or ill. But it was his task, before God, to ensure that the monks rose above such things. 'I have no time to waste listening to kitchen gossip,' he said more sharply than he intended. 'Say your piece and be done.'

Amos flushed darkly, looking affronted. 'I came here to do my Christian duty,' he said with laboured piety. 'You should be made aware of what the brothers are saying. They think that this woman has been touched by the hand of God. A short time ago she was near dead of her wounds. Now she is unmarked. It is not natural. Only God or the Virgin can bring about such a miracle. And . . . this woman says that an angel guides her. Stephanis has a testament to the fact . . .' Amos's voice tailed off, his eyes sliding sideways as he realized that, in his eagerness to ingratiate himself, he had said too much.

John felt a stirring of alarm. Such talk could lead to an outbreak of unwarranted zeal. For long moments he was silent, tapping the pads of his tapered fingers against his lips. What if it *was* true? He allowed himself to imagine what it could mean. Their own saint who would bless the sick at appointed times – Pentecost for example. Vendors, beggars, pilgrims, all manner of suffering and infirm souls would set up camp outside the gate. Holy Penitence would become a desirable place for the sons of rich men, a repository for monies from sinners great and small. John sighed. It was all too easy to let oneself become embroiled in showiness and vainglory. The reality of doing God's will was the daily drudgery of servitude.

'I mean not to speak against a fellow brother,' Amos said, breaking into the abbot's thoughts. 'But Stephanis is obssessed with this woman. Others too speak of dreams they have had. She is . . . ah, very winsome.'

'Indeed,' John murmured, looking over the head of the kitchener to where the first stars of the evening glimmered through an open window. 'Temptation ever comes in pleasing guise. Give me a moment to think.'

He knew Stephanis to be a man who found it difficult to school his desires and channel them into prayer. John, himself, had heard Stephanis's confession on the eve of Stephanis's consecration and been discomfited by the passion he glimpsed in the ex-soldier's face. For such a man, the pathway to grace was paved with sharp stones. It did not surprise him that Stephanis should fall prey to this Jezebel. He turned his attention back to Amos, his expression hardening. 'How know *you* about all of this?'

'It is the talk of all the monastery. Thomas, the layman, told it to Brother Luke and he told it to –'

'Yes, yes. I know how these things come about. I am concerned with the truth, not the rambling of idle tongues. You brought this woman to Holy Penitence, did you not?'

Amos gulped. 'It was none of my doing. The woman climbed into my cart. I only found her when the barrels of fish were unloaded. Her eyes were wild. Her lips flecked with foam. There was not a place on her body that was not broken and bruised. She bore the marks of a knife and had been sore abused in . . . in the privy parts. Even so, there was something . . . compelling about her . . .' He paused, then said stoutly. 'I told Stephanis not to admit her. Others heard me and will bear witness. I thought that the woman would bring the sickness amongst us, but she has brought something far worse.'

'And what, in your opinion, is that?' John said, with what he thought was admirable restraint in the circumstances.

'Temptation,' Amos said loftily. 'Stephanis is besotted by the idea that this woman is protected by the Holy Virgin. But he speaks with such passion . . . I would say that the woman has cast a spell over him. The other monks compare her to the blessed St Bertrina –'

'Enough!' John rose to his feet. 'You may leave this matter with me.'

'Yes. Well, as I said. It was my duty . . .' Amos said, tight-lipped.

John watched the kitchener turn on his heel and walk to the door. Not until the door had closed behind him did he move. Then he ran a hand over his lean jaw, feeling the roughness of the grey bristles against his skin. Why had Stephanis not come to him at once? This sort of thing could have far-reaching effects. He decided not to wait until the appointed time to speak to Stephanis, but to go directly to the infirmary.

Garnetta rolled up the sleeve of her shift and rested her elbow on the side table. As Stephanis bade her to, she flexed her fingers a few times until the veins on her inner arm stood out clearly.

Stephanis bent over her, a lancet in one hand, a cupping device in the other. Thomas stood by, holding a bowl and a blood-band. Garnetta felt calm. There would be pain, but pain soon faded. That was a lesson she had learned well. Besides, she felt armed by the memory of what had happened a few hours ago. The angel, *her* angel had appeared, walking right out of the air and into the daylight. The memory left her with a glowing feeling of pleasure. It was as if all of her, outside and in, had been touched by something invigorating, calming, and cleansing. She and the angel were linked. They would always have each other.

As once I thought I would have Karolan. He had told her that they belonged together. For ever. Another lie. But that was a hurt too raw to contemplate. She dragged her thoughts back to the angel. How intimate was his touch, how bright his regard. The memory was too precious a thing to share. She might have spoken of it to Stephanis, but for the knowledge that it was improper to have lain with the shining being. Physical pleasure was of the flesh, not the spirit. Reason imposed its own logic. But if God's messenger had lain hands upon her – how could it be wrong?

She looked up at Stephanis. His broad face was pale. He was sweating. His hands were steady, however, the incision he made swift and sure. It looked as if he drew a red mark across her skin with the tip of the razor-sharp instrument. There was a second of discomfort, but no more than that of a sharp scratch. The blood welled onto the level of her arm. It looked purple against her white skin.

'Keep your arm flat, so that the blood does not run off,' Stephanis said, attaching the cup skilfully to her vein, then binding it into place. 'There. Spilt not a drop. Thomas, position the bowl under the cup.'

The infirmarer's skill was admirable. His strong square hands were unmarked by a single smear of her blood. 'Is all completed?' she said, looking down at her arm, now bound chastely with a piece of spotless linen. 'I expected more pain and a lot more mess.'

Even as she said the words she caught the edge of Stephanis's thoughts and knew that he had chosen the method of cupping over the other choices of scarification or radical venesection. She sensed an unease in him. For some reason he would have found it unbearable to watch if her blood had escaped in a hot-red, spurting fount. This sluggish, blue-tinted trickle was somehow more manageable – more decent. She noticed too that the smell of his body was stronger than usual. Under his chalky, sour smell, she could detect the flatter smell of dried semen. She found the knowledge reassuring. It made Stephanis more fallible and her own experience with the angel more earthly.

'Rest now,' Stephanis said. 'I'll return later to remove the cup.'

Garnetta closed her eyes. It would take some time for the bowl to fill. She need do nothing but relax. Thomas and Stephanis went out of the cubicle and into the still-room. She heard footsteps as someone else followed them. The visitor spoke with the well-modulated, cultured voice of authority. With her extended senses she gained an impression of a keen intellect combined with a developed sense of purpose. An older man. The abbot.

She could hear the abbot speaking with Stephanis through the stone walls. Mention was made of sending men into the forest to find the bodies of the men she had killed. 'I will have the truth of this,' the abbot said stiffly.

'These are serious claims to make. Where is the evidence that this woman is not simply deluded? If, as you say, there was a witness to these miraculous happenings, where is he?'

'I know not,' Stephanis said, and Garnetta knew that he lied. 'The boy slipped from my grasp. He has likely returned to his village. But I have his testament here, in this drawer.'

'It was witnessed?'

'Ah, no. The boy was half-starved and near fainting. I questioned him swiftly. I sent Thomas to fetch food. That is why I was alone with the lad.'

Garnetta heard the young assistant mumble something in assent. The abbot sighed. 'This is a fine mess indeed. You should have sought counsel with me at once, Stephanis. You have acted above your station. Let us wait until a search of the forest has been made. I will pray for guidance and suggest you do the same.'

'I have done nothing else since Garnetta arrived,' Stephanis said.

'Indeed? And have you received enlightenment?' The abbot's voice rang with thinly veiled sarcasm.

'Of a kind. I think perhaps Garnetta was sent to give us inspiration and focus for our faith.'

The abbot drew the breath in through his teeth. A sound of exasperation and annoyance. 'From what I have heard this woman is not as innocent as you would have her. Come to me after Compline. I like this not. Do you realize what a nest of hornets you have stirred up with your rash talk of this woman's saintliness?'

'I believe that she speaks truly,' Stephanis said. 'I heard her confession –'

'*You* heard her confession?' the abbot thundered.

'Well, yes. She begged me to listen. Said that she trusted only me . . .'

'Speak no more of this until we are alone. Now. Take me to the cubicle where she lies. I will see this . . . this creature for myself.'

'But . . .' began Stephanis.

'Now. If you please,' said the abbot, in a voice that brooked no argument.

The sound of footsteps drew close. Garnetta looked up without surprise as the two men entered her cubicle. She smiled warily, knowing that her fate was in the hands of the tall, rather austere looking man whose piercing grey eyes were fastened on her face. His white hair framed a face that was ascetic and beautiful in its way. His lips were thin, his nose patrician. He had deep eyelids, fretted with purple veins. He smelt of dusty skin, overlaid with the faintest smell of lavender.

'So this is your – saint, Stephanis? She is but a slender thing and looks too frail to bear the weight which you would heap upon her.'

'God give you good day, sire,' Garnetta said evenly.

'And you, madam,' The abbot said frostily, looking her over with a measuring glance. 'As you are being bled, I will leave you to rest. Later, I shall wish to speak with you.' Without saying more, the abbot left the cubicle. Stephanis threw her a reassuring smile and went with him. She heard the abbot say dryly, 'You would not take this woman's part so ardently if she were crook-backed, had sagging skin, and was disfigured by warts.'

The sound of sandals on the rushes faded into the distance. Garnetta was troubled. The abbot's hostility had flowed towards her in waves. A fair man, he might be, and a seeker of the truth, but if he was to decide that she was a dangerous influence, he would not shirk from doing whatever was necessary for the good of those under his charge.

In the narrow streets, fires burned brightly, sending pungent smoke billowing into the night sky. The oily river reflected a patchwork of yellow, red, and black. Flames licked greedily at piled corpses, crackling and spitting as they crisped blackened skin. Men with vinegar-soaked cloths tied around their mouths swept up piles of refuse with besoms. Others shovelled up mounds of nightsoil.

Karolan leaned out of an upstairs window, watching the activity. Beside him was Gunter's father, pale and wan looking still, but on the way to full health.

' 'Tis near a miracle to see men cleaning the streets,' Abel said. 'Some of us shall survive after all, praise God. Come into the back. There's food aplenty. Gunter's sea chest seems bottomless.'

Karolan accepted a bowl of stew containing oats, onions, and chunks of bacon. He had grown to respect Gunter's father. Abel was quietly dignified in his grief and doing his best to salvage what he could of his business. 'Where's Gunter, this day?' Karolan said, beginning to eat.

'At a meeting of the guild of Merchant Staplers, discussing the heavy duties on raw wool. Gunter has an idea to export cloth ready woven.'

'The merchant guild will give their permission for this?'

Abel laughed shortly. 'I think not, but you can tell Gunter nothing. Our warehouse is stacked high with raw goods, fells and skins, then there's the Holy Penitence clip to bid for. Gunter sails for Flanders at the end of the month.'

Karolan nodded. As his friend moved around the

town on business, he made enquiries about Garnetta. So far there had been no news. He sensed that the Fetch knew more than it appeared to. The spirit was more than usually capricious. Perhaps it was simply distracted by the abundance and potency of the pleasures to be had all around. The very air was boiling with fetid fumes, teeming with the sickly, invisible trails which were irresistible to the Fetch. It was time he used a little trickery against his recalcitrant familiar.

After Abel had gone down into the warehouse, Karolan went into the storeroom. Closing the door behind him, he stripped off his boots and hosen. Emptying a vial of oil into a vessel, he anointed his face, hands, and genitals, then lay on the truckle bed. For a few minutes he lay still, emptying his mind and putting himself into a light trance. Then, slowly, his fingers tingling with the concentration of power, he ran his hand down over his body, stroking the firm muscles of his chest, working his way to his groin. Breathing deeply, Karolan stroked his hardening flesh, concentrating on the sexual energy trail which was building in the ether. He conjured an impression of Garnetta, using the strength of his will to bring the details into focus. It seemed that he could feel her lips against his skin, the subtle sensation of the pulse at her throat as it throbbed and bounded beneath his fingertips. Her taste, her smell, the feel of her skin – all of these things enfolded him, serving to create a deeper tension within him. He stroked his rigid shaft more firmly, smoothing the soft skin over the engorged centre. The air thickened, vibrating with a core of sexual intensity.

'I hear your call, Master. You hunger deeply. Solace you, shall I?' said the Fetch, its sibilant voice close to his ear. Its cloying scent flowed over him.

Opening his eyes, Karolan saw that the spirit had

materialized as a nun. The blasphemy made him smile. The nun's face was a pure, sweet oval. Underlying the expression he glimpsed the reality of the spirit's cunning nature. It could never entirely disguise the unearthliness of its form. 'Your shape is pleasing,' Karolan said, his voice husky as if he was anxious for satisfaction. 'Show me more.'

The Fetch laughed softly, the sound like rustling wet leaves. The 'nun' pushed back the hood of her cape to reveal black, close-cropped hair, a neat, shapely skull. Ah, clever, mused Karolan. She was not really like Garnetta, but the resemblance was close. Lifting the bottom of the cape, the nun discarded it, then slipped her robe over her head. Clad only in a thin under-shift, she bowed her head modestly, exposing the tender nape of her neck.

Despite himself, Karolan found his eyes drawn to the graceful form. He saw a young woman, hardly out of girlhood, with slender limbs and narrow hips. By contrast her breasts were large, thrusting out proudly from a delicate ribcage. The shift clung to her body, outlining the neat pink nipples, the slight swell of her belly, cleaving to the lightly frosted mound at the junction of her thighs.

'Please you, do I?' the Fetch purred. The nun undulated closer, managing to look both chaste and wanton at the same time. 'Quench your hunger I shall, Master. What do you pledge in return?'

The nun glowed faintly in the region where her heart would be. The form before him wavered, as the spirit fed on the tendrils of sexual energy emanating from its master. Despite its languorous voice, Karolan knew that it longed for him to give it the word, then all pretence at servitude would disappear. It would dart joyfully into him, its rapacious form squeezing inside the tight envelope of his skin, invading every organ, tasting and savouring his blood, breath, semen.

'You please me well enough,' Karolan said, bringing himself closer to a peak of release.

The dark energy thrummed and whirled around him, specks of light glinting in the ether. The nun's eyes followed the movement of his hand. As his flesh burgeoned, a bead of moisture gathered at the tip of the glans. The nun licked her lips, took a step towards him, her sweet face compliant. The disguise was too convincing. Karolan felt a flutter of warning. The spirit appeared to have enormous reserves of strength. Karolan was suddenly alert. Trickery and evasion were the Fetch's natural emotions – if emotions it truly had, beyond greed and need.

'Wait,' he said. 'Answer me a question before we proceed.'

'Want no questions,' the Fetch said sulkily, its reedy voice emerging through the nun's pale lips. 'Called me to serve you, did you not? Let me do so, Master.'

'Have you more news of Garnetta?' Karolan ignored the petulance in the spirit's voice.

The 'nun' gave an eloquent shrug, causing her breasts to jiggle invitingly. 'That one is gone,' she trilled. 'No matter. Make another.'

'Where have you looked for her?'

'Amongst the dead that clog the streets and alleys. Fine is their perfume. Amongst the living too, but found her not.' The Fetch chuckled. The little nun who clothed its form brought her hand up to her mouth in an artless gesture of seduction. 'Oh, how I have bathed, Master. Such delight is there in sorrow and pain.'

Karolan hid his astonishment. The Fetch ought, by now, to be desperate, begging to please him, not flaunting like this. He sensed too that it was withholding information. It was more assured, and invigorated in a peculiar way. He could not think why that was. Unless . . . 'You have made yourself known to Garnetta,' he stated.

The Fetch squawked with dismay. The nun's form shimmered and trembled.

'Answer me! Curse you. Have you pleasured her and lulled her with your fiendish caresses, tricking her into giving you permission to invade her flesh?' Karolan's voice vibrated with fury as he realized that this was exactly what the Fetch had done. Hermes, how could he have been so blind? With the infusion of Garnetta's female essence, the spirit had gained power over her. Power enough to defy him too – and what else?

'Damn you! I ordered you to let her be!' Karolan flung a hand in the air. The build-up of energy formed into a gaseous bubble. Sparks crackled in the air, showered around the Fetch.

The nun recoiled as if Karolan had struck her, she gave a terrified shriek, tears starting from her eyes. She began to fade, her limbs as dusty as if they were made of flour which was being blown by the wind. Faintly now, he saw how her tears soaked into her shift, the fabric forming little peaks around her erect nipples. Her hands smoothed down her sides, the fingers angled towards her groin in a desperate gesture of wantonness. The pale, rosebud mouth moved in a last tremulous smile. There was a frightened sob which ended on a sad little chirrup. And the Fetch was gone.

'Come back here!' Karolan thundered, his voice ringing with power. 'Upstart sprite! You are bound to me for eternity and will obey me.'

The ritual was ruined. Swiftly he said the words of ending and pushed himself upright. Yanking his shirt down to cover himself, he swung his legs over the side of the bed. The energy in the room subsided. Motes of sparkling dust drifted to the floor. The air rippled and pleated. Then the Fetch appeared in its usual guise. Within its shadow-shape were red-brown streaks of consternation. The glow at its chest area was a sickly green. 'Forgive. Forgive,' it bleated. 'Appeared to the female in the forest, did I. Wanted to taste. Wanted to feel. Mistress to me, is she, as you are my master. Something of her, moves within me. Not harm. Never harm. Only give pleasure, do I. As pleasure I give you.'

Karolan stared at the spirit in amazement. It actually seemed to have a sort of fondness for Garnetta. This was something entirely new. He was not sure what to think about that. One thing of which he *was* certain. The Fetch knew where Garnetta was.

'Tell me where she is,' he said, his voice cold. 'I should punish you for playing me false. But I'll be merciful if you are truthful now.'

The Fetch chittered and spun in circles, alarm radiating off it in waves. Under its terror, Karolan perceived something else – a willingness to challenge his authority. As the spirit stopped spinning, the fabric of its body began to thin and spread out until it resembled a graceful, loose-limbed creature surrounded by a watery green haze. The fading spread inwards to the pulsing centre of its being as it disassembled. Karolan recognized what was happening, but was amazed by the audacity of the spirit's defiance. The Fetch was retreating for protection to the hinter-world of the elementals whence he had called it all those long years ago. Once there it would take on its original undine form. As a water sprite, under the protetion of a Diva, it was beyond his reach. It would take a powerful ritual and a great deal of concentrated will to force it to emerge at will.

'Where is Garnetta?' Karolan said, exerting every

measure of his will to keep the Fetch from fading clean away. 'Speak! I command you!'

For a second longer it hovered. There was only a thickening on the air now, a greenish haze, glistening with threads of silver. At the final moment, before the spirit blinked out, it spoke, its voice hollow and far away. 'Captive . . . but safe.'

And though Karolan raged at the spirit's capriciousness and trickery, he had to be content with that for the time being. When he emerged from the storeroom it was to find Gunter in the adjoining room. Gunter threw him a puzzled look.

'You alone? I heard you speaking to someone. Ach, had it been a plump wench with you, I'd say swyve her and hail met! Just tell me if you want to bring a lass back. I'll make certain to steer clear.' Karolan laughed dismissively, reaching for a cup of wine. 'D'you never feel the need?' Gunter said, in his blunt, hearty manner. 'There's plenty who'd be willing. A man with your looks and bearing. Unless you came back from the Holy Land with an unnatural vice! The Infidels take pretty boys as lovers. No offence, mind, though fugoism's not to my taste.'

'None taken,' Karolan said, thinking briefly of Harun and the delightful hours they had spent in each other's arms. He had taken many lovers, both men and women over the years, his desires and emotions always burned white hot. But he saw no reason to say as much to his new friend. He shrugged. 'I was wounded in the privy parts. Now I no longer crave a woman's touch.'

'By all the saints! You were gelded? I have heard that this is done to prisoners of war. Forgive my loose tongue, my friend. I shall never disclose your secret. One day I might learn think before I speak.'

Karolan gave a dismissive gesture. 'Think no more

on't. Sit with me. I'd relish some company.' They sat in companionable silence for a time, then Gunter said casually, 'That lancet you wield is surer than any sword. Where did you come by this learning?'

Karolan sipped his wine. 'I read the writings of learned Arabs and learned much from Henri de Mercery at the university of Montpellier. He had some odd views about the treatment of wounds, but no one under his care lost a limb or suffered a mortification after surgery. I first saw a corpse cut open there for the purposes of study. Can you imagine that? I was so excited by what I saw.' He grinned. 'Do you know that surgeons hereabouts swear that the stomach is a cooking pot in which food is kept on the bubble by the heat of the liver!'

Gunter blanched at the mention of dissection of corpses, trying not to look shocked. 'And this is not so?'

'Indeed not. I have seen the lie of the organs within a man. Wonderful and passing strange is their form. But medicine will not progress while the church forbids all free-thinking and keeps surgeons from doing their work. The writings of Galen of Pergamos are considered sacred works, yet his knowledge is based on cutting up pigs and apes. I tell you, my friend, God did not exhaust all his creative power in making Galen!'

'Indeed?' Gunter looked troubled. 'Such views smack strongly of heresy.'

Karolan looked at him sharply. 'Why do I have the feeling that it is no accident that we are speaking of such things? Now that I think of it. Why are you here at this hour of the day? It is early for you to seek night comforts.'

'I came to bring you a warning,' Gunter said. 'It matters not to me, whether you are heretic, de-frocked priest, or in the pay of the king of France himself. You saved my father's life and I am in your debt for that. But

265

your views are not popular and, forgive me, you express them a little too freely. In this climate of terror it is not wise to draw attention to yourself. It is but a small jump from to suspicion to condemnation. The church is a jealous mistress. Tread softly, my friend.'

CHAPTER SIXTEEN

In the vaulted main room of the infirmary sunlight poured in through an open window. The scent of herbs wafted in on a warm breeze. The abbot, the prior, Stephanis, and a number of other church notables were gathered together to watch the proceedings. With them was an old woman, a midwife.

'Why is it necessary for me to submit to this . . . examination?' Garnetta said, eyeing the woman's greasy hair and unwashed skin. Her gown was stiff with dried blood stains. There was a rank smell of wine on her breath.

'For evidence,' Stephanis said, obliquely. 'You may not refuse.'

Evidence of what? Garnetta's throat closed with dread. Somehow there had been a shift in Stephanis's and the other monks' attitudes. She did not know what caused them to look at her with that mixture of suspicion, fear, and awe; she felt threatened and very alone.

That morning, John de Mandeville had questioned her at length, listening in silence while a scribe recorded everything. Then he asked her to lay her hand on the Bible and swear that everything she said was true. When they all knelt in prayer, Garnetta spoke the prayers aloud as she was bid. Then, as now, they watched her closely. What had they expected her to do, cough up a toad? After the long questioning, she went meekly back to the infirmary. Now she was expected to let this disgusting old woman lay hands on her. Lifting her chin, she looked the abbot in the eye. 'This is to be a public examination?' she said.

The abbot nodded. 'You said you suffered a violation

– where now is the evidence? The bodies found in the forest were too damaged by wolves to be able to verify the cause of death, but you admitted you killed these men. What are we to believe? Stephanis swears you were aided by the Holy Virgin, but he is misled by your youth and beauty. Certain of his actions make his judgement questionable.' He paused, his grey eyes cold and impartial. 'I, however, suspect that there are devilish forces at work here. This act of verification must be witnessed.'

'Very well, if submit I must. But I am a gentlewoman. I object to being handled like an animal at market. Cannot my modesty be preserved?'

The abbot raised an eyebrow. 'Pride, madam, is a sin. You belong body and spirit to God. This is God's work we are doing. There is nothing shameful in His sight.' He gestured to the crone. 'Matilda. You may begin.'

Garnetta tried not to flinch as Matilda approached. The woman was as brown and wrinkled as last year's oak apples. The hand she extended was almost fleshless, the joints swollen and misshapen. Beneath each ragged fingernail there was a rim of dirt. 'Now then, lovedy. Be you not afeard. Mother Matilda knows her craft, yes she does. Loosen the neckline of your shift now.'

'My . . . my neckline?' Garnetta said. She expected the horrible old woman to simply slide her hands beneath the hem of the shift and fumble between her thighs.

'Oh, aye. I must look at the bubs, dearie. That's the only way to tell fer sure if a woman's given suck to a babe.'

'But I have not had a child. What's that to do with anything?' Garnetta threw an anguished glance at the seated men. There was no help to be had from that quarter. Each of the monks wore a similar look of guarded impartiality.

'You object?' asked the abbot coldly. 'Have you something to hide?'

'No,' Garnetta said. 'I was just taken by surprise.' Her fingers shook slightly as she untied the drawstring at her neck. Slowly she pulled the neckline wide, allowed it to slip down to her waist. Although she knew that in a few moments' time she would have no modesty left to protect, she gathered the folds of the shift close.

As Matilda reached for her breasts she shuddered, trying to distance herself from the feel of the dirty, papery skin against her flesh. The midwife leaned forward, pinching hard to make the nipples stand out, then squeezing them as if she was milking a goat. She thrust her head forward, sniffing. 'No sign of milk from paps,' she said. 'I can allus tell by the smell. This wench's no mother. Leastways, she's suckled no babe. Don't mean that a man hasn't been at 'er though. I'll need to look closer to see if any man has breached her below.'

The abbot's mouth thinned with distaste. 'Proceed.'

Garnetta closed her hands into fists, tried to focus her mind on something, anything to distract herself from what must follow. She thought of Karolan and was surprised when her eyes misted with tears. If he had been here, he would have protected her. He would never have allowed her to be humiliated in this way. She felt a surge of longing for him, so intense that her heart hurt. She missed him, whatever he was, whatever he had done, she could not shake him free of her mind.

'Off with that shift and up on the table with you,' Matilda said. 'My ole eyes ain't as keen as they were.'

Garnetta forced herself to open her stiff fingers and let the shift fall. No one spoke. She could feel the tension in the room and did not need her extended senses to tell her that every man was indulging himself with feelings of sexual arousal. What beasts were most men. At least

269

Karolan did not hide what he was. These men, with their shield of the ruby cross, armed against criticism by the robes of their calling, were hypocrites all. It was her helplessness and passivity that inflamed them. They despised her, not themselves, because her flesh had the power to move them. Careful to keep her eyes downcast, lest they should see the contempt there and condemn her for that too, she sat on the edge of the table and swung herself aloft.

'Lie back and let your knees fall apart,' Matilda said. Garnetta did so, feeling the tendons at her groin pull as the backs of her thighs pressed onto the rough wood. Her anger made her feel better. Let them see, let them all see, she thought. I have nothing to be ashamed of. The sin is theirs.

Matilda peered close. Garnetta felt her breath against her skin. Remembering the sour smell of it, her stomach roiled. As Matilda probed between her thighs she tried to relax, knowing that the examination would be less unpleasant. Matilda jabbed at Garnetta, the rough edges of her nails scraping the membranes hard enough to draw blood. Garnetta felt a finger enter her and almost gagged at the thought of the filthy hands on her.

'Wench's a maid still. See the blood?' Matilda said, withdrawing her finger and wiping it on her skirt. Her eyebrows drew together as she continued to rub at the finger. The skin reddened, began to crack and weep blood. 'What's this? Some trickery's afoot.' Holding her finger in the air Matilda stalked towards the abbot, her face screwed-up with pain. 'My finger's burning up! The woman's put a hex on me! You never told me she was a witch!'

The abbot rose to his feet. There was a shuffling and muttering as the other monks stood up. Garnetta stood facing them, her shift clutched in front of her.

'I did nothing,' she said. 'You saw what happened. The crone scratched me.'

'Silence!' the abbot ordered. 'We'll hear no more of your lies and trickery. I know what you are. You'll spread your foul sexual corruption amongst us no further! Constrain her. Bring in the testing device!'

Garnetta found herself held fast. There came the noise of wood against stone, as a curtain was drawn back and a wheeled contraption pulled into the centre of the room. The chair of carved wood had a high back and armrests. In the centre of the wooden seat was a large circular hole – just like a birthing chair, Garnetta thought, except that this chair had iron rings at strategic points. She realized that the abbot had been fully prepared for the turn of events. Her first impressions of him had been accurate. This man was her enemy.

'Secure her to the chair,' said the abbot, his voice strident. 'This woman shall be made to reveal herself.'

Garnetta looked to Stephanis, expecting him to speak in her defence, but he only looked at her with an expression of wariness. Matilda called down curses upon Garnetta, the burned finger thrust into the folds of her filthy skirt. Garnetta struggled as her shift was torn from her, the anger like a hot coal in her belly. It took six of them to drag her across the room. As her back slammed against the unyielding wood, she cried out. 'Let me go! Stephanis! Help me!'

The abbot threw Stephanis a sharp look. 'See how this Jezebel calls to you!'

Stephanis blanched. 'I've been misguided,' he said in a voice of abject horror. 'I was weak to give in to her wiles. May God forgive me.'

The abbot's voice softened. 'You shall do penance for your weakness. Now – bring forth the things we need for the testing.' His eyes downcast, Stephanis did as he was bid.

Garnetta's wrists were secured to the armrests, her ankles confined with leather straps. Held fast against the wooden chair, her buttocks protruding through the hole in the seat, she stared straight ahead. Her widely spread thighs were all that prevented her from slipping through the hole. Already her muscles protested at the strain. The carved wood bit into her back. She was forced to sit up very straight, her breasts thrust into prominence by her position.

The churchmen watching all wore expressions of piety which barely masked their lust. She hated them all. Stephanis stepped forward and placed a wooden tray on the table provided. Garnetta caught the glint of metal, saw a pile of wooden objects. Her flesh recoiled with horror at the thought of what they would do.

She must think past this crippling fear, for that was what unmade her. But she could not be brave in the midst of so many enemies. Was there no one she could trust? *You can trust Karolan. Call on him.* The thought came unbidden. She thrust it away. No. She was not yet ready to do that. His was perhaps the worst violation of all. *Ah, but you cannot forget him, can you? Your body still burns for him. All you have to do is reach out with your mind. He is waiting. He will not fail you.* She clenched her fists, unwilling to listen to her inner voice.

'We shall begin,' the abbot said. 'This woman's licentious nature will be revealed. She is a trickster and a liar, bent on seducing holy men. Did she not appear to you in a dream Stephanis? Place images in your mind? The lewd nature of these things forcing you into an unnatural act with Thomas?'

Stephanis nodded miserably. The others watching whispered amongst themselves. The abbot's patrician face was flushed across the cheekbones. He beckoned to Stephanis. 'You shall assist me. And you, scribe, record every detail. The bishop must be notified of these events.'

Under the pretext of testing Garnetta's bonds, Stephanis leaned close to her and whispered. 'Do not fear. There is freedom in suffering, glory in mortification.'

She glared at him, unable to find the words to express her loathing. Stephanis seemed to crumple beneath her gaze. Blanching, he stood back. When the abbot gave an order, Stephanis reached below the chair and took hold of a winding mechanism. The sound of metal grating on metal filled the room as the chair was cranked up until the seat was raised.

'Observe how I shall reveal the demon lust within this body. She is ripe with evil and salacious humours.' So saying, the abbot took an object from the tray, grasped Garnetta's left breast and attached a sprung wooden peg to the nipple. Garnetta winced at the sharp pinching pain. Her entire breast began to throb. The abbot attached a peg to her other breast, then in quick succession added two more pegs to each nipple. Garnetta screwed her eyes shut as the soreness vibrated through her chest.

'See how the demon within her resists us!' the abbot said. 'Give me the paddle. The unclean spirit will beg for mercy when I beat it from her flesh!'

There was a loud crack, as the wooden paddle met Garnetta's exposed buttocks. She convulsed at the shock of it. The sound of the blow was almost more terrifying than the smarting pain it bestowed. The abbot laid to with a will, placing the blows so that the underside of her thighs received a share of the punishment. Garnetta writhed, trying to escape the torment, but the wood wedged her tight, forcing her buttocks to gape. As the abbot spanked her, the edge of the paddle flicked against her anus until it too was a hot well of suffering.

Sweating and gasping, she surged against her bonds, hardly able to draw breath between each new assault. The pegs on her nipples swayed, pulling at her abused flesh. The paddle slapped against her buttocks again and again. All her senses became condensed into one sizzling, throbbing ache. She was certain that the skin must split and the blood spray the infirmary floor, but the abbot knew just how far to go before inflicting real damage. Just when she thought she must faint, the spanking stopped.

Garnetta allowed her chin to drop onto her chest, drawing great painful breaths into lungs constricted by her efforts not to weaken and utter pleas for mercy.

'A virtuous woman would be weeping for shame,' the abbot cried. 'This creature revels in her sin! Her fortitude is indeed unnatural.' He bent close to Garnetta and hissed, 'I *shall* drive the demons from your lustful flesh. Do not doubt that you will be compelled to void them!'

She raised her head, blinking away the sweat that dripped into her eyes, and glared her defiance. Picking up a handful of the wooden pegs, the abbot put his hand between her widely spread thighs and grasped her coynte. Pinching one of the labia tight, he attached a row of wooden pegs. Already sore from the paddle which had, now and then, struck her pudenda, Garnetta gave a low moan. The abbot attached another row of pegs.

She rose up against her bonds, feeling the leather cut into her wrists and ankles. From the neck down her flesh was a riot of pain. Her thighs and buttocks boiled and simmered, her coynte felt swollen with agony, but far worse were the avid expressions of the watchers. If only she could rob them of their unclean pleasure. Somehow she distanced herself for long enough to turn her will inwards. It was all she needed. The stillness within opened up, swallowing the pain. Instead of a black maw of suffering, she found a place of security, of warmth and sweetness. Her fear drained away, for she knew now that they could not hurt her if she did not allow it. The pain receded, seemed to come from a great distance. Raising her head, she managed a tremulous smile.

The abbot gaped, his mouth working furiously. 'Foul creature!' he spat. 'Steeped in the sin of Eve! You dare to mock the Holy Church!' Incensed he slapped her face, but still she would not weep. 'The clyster, Stephanis,' the abbot said. 'Let us purge this abomination!'

With shaking hands, Stephanis picked up a jug containing a mixture of wine, powdered root of rhubarb, pepper, and turpeth – a powerful cathartic. After stirring the mixture well, he poured it into a clyster bag.

Garnetta fell silent, tensing at the new assault as the metal nozzle of the clyster was pushed into her anus. As Stephanis squeezed the pig's bladder, the liquid was forced into her bowels. She clenched her stomach muscles, fighting the urge to bear down. The mixture felt heavy and oppressive within her. Almost at once it began to burn as the turpeth scoured her bowels. As the clyster was withdrawn, her anus convulsed. Droplets of sweat stood out on her forehead. She trembled as her body gave in to the impetus to empty itself. With a rush of shame, she bore down and voided her body's wastes onto the stone floor. The pungent smell rose up around her, animal, primeval. With it came a catharsis. They could do nothing more humiliating to her. Raising her head, she saw that the abbot's white robe had been splashed by the filth. A chuckle vibrated in her throat.

The abbot's face turned puce, bound by anger and revulsion. 'Take her away. This creature is beyond redemption! The bishop shall decide what is to be done. But I shall recommend that she burns!'

CHAPTER SEVENTEEN

Hiding the scourge in the folds of his robe, Stephanis unlocked the door to Garnetta's cell and slipped inside. As his eyes became accustomed to the dimness, he saw her sitting on a pile of straw, a stillness about her that spoke of deliberation. Her bare feet protruded from the bottom of her shift. How narrow and fine those feet were. For a moment he wavered in his purpose. She looked more glorious in the creased and grubby shift, than many a woman would look in cloth of gold.

'What do you want?' she said calmly, her metallic grey eyes alight as if they contained some arcane knowledge to which he would never be privy.

'I am found guilty of lustful feelings, unclean actions,' he said. 'For this I have done penance, but it is not enough. I come to beg for your help. The hex you have put upon me is strong and enduring.'

Her self-possession was almost unearthly. 'Whatever it is that I am, I am no witch, Stephanis. You are deluded. This suffering of yours is your own doing.'

The lie stole his breath. Oh, the trickery of this temptress. Was there nothing that could prompt her to admit her foulness? Before he lost the courage he pulled his habit over his head, then fumbled with the twine around the hair shirt. In a moment he was naked, save for the rope around his genitals. Garnetta watched in silence, the chains at her wrists and ankles clanking together as she changed position on the straw. It seemed to Stephanis that he could feel the weight of her regard. The dread of it was delicious. Hands shaking slightly, he placed the scourge on the stone floor. Slowly he turned his back, crouching down, so that his chest brushed the cold floor and his bare rump was held up in the air.

Clenching his teeth upon a blissful rush of shame, he advanced backwards, towards her. He imagined her looking at his mortified flesh, feeling respect for his noble suffering. How could she not be impressed by the rope which compressed his stones and staff of Adam? The ache in his belly from the constriction was present night and day. The badges he wore on his skin were many. The hair shirt, compressed by twine, had scraped a raw trough around his waist. The rough fibres in the cloth had abraded the weals on his shoulders and back, irritating the flea-bites which peppered his torso. Many of the wounds were suppurating, but he had resisted putting any salve on them.

When Garnetta still did not speak – no doubt out of awe – he waggled his rump helpfully. 'As you were once a child of God, I beg you to do me this service,' he said, his voice hoarse with need. 'Because of you I have fallen. I have been beguiled, tempted, bewitched. Cleanse me with the scourge. I beg you.'

'Oh, do get up,' she said. 'If you could but see yourself. You look . . . ridiculous.'

A deep flush crept up Stephanis's face. She *must* agree to beat him. His balls contracted against the rope with mortification. 'Please,' he murmured, his belly cramping with a rush of pain.

'Enough! You sad, pathetic creature. Master your own lusts. Do not rebuke me for your failings!'

Her words fell on him like blows. Slowly Stephanis rose to his feet. He felt stripped to his bones, exposed in a way that no man ought to have to endure, especially before a woman; that creature inherently flawed by her sex. An abiding anger curdled in his stomach. Trembling with emotion, he pulled his habit back on. It was as if scales had fallen from his eyes. He flashed Garnetta a look in which there was hatred now instead of longing.

Her face was implacable, a slender oval in the gloom. 'You look at me with the face of honesty at last. I never was saint nor demon. What I am is something set apart from you and perhaps all others. A man finer than ever you'll know is my maker. He saved me from death by ceding me a dark gift. And God help me, I am proud of that at last! For my lord is an honest rogue. He hides not behind lies, repressed desires, and false piety – as do you!'

Stephanis's skin shrank against his skull. 'Blasphemy!' he hissed. 'God made the world and all in it, madam! Speak you not of this Other, whoever he may be.' Only now, did he see her clearly. Her beauty had always been something otherworldly. Garnetta had no need of a grimoire, a toad-familiar, or wax manikins. Like Eve she had embraced the serpent. 'So, you are beyond help,' he said evenly. 'Your own words condemn you. When you are put to the fire, I shall be there to watch.' At the cell door he fitted the key in the lock, then glanced over his shoulder. 'It is still possible to repent. God's mercy is great. Shall I kneel with you now and pray?'

She turned her face to the wall and would not look at him. He heard her say softly, 'It is passing strange that every act in this world, both good and bad – merciful or evil, is done with the blessing of the Lord.'

'What you plan to do holds much danger,' Gunter said to Karolan. 'You do know that you'll be arrested, your house and lands confiscated, the proceeds going to swell the church coffers? No one can wrest a heretic from the clutches of the church and escape censure! Then again, you being a lord – there'll have to be a hearing . . .'

Karolan looked up from the book which was spread

open on the table, his eyes flashing wickedly. 'Did you know that there are seven kinds of fever, Gunter? Putrid, hectic, tertian, quotian, quartan, ephemeral, and sinochus?'

Gunter slapped his forehead with the heel of his hand. 'This is no jesting matter! You are not listening to me!'

'Mistake me not, Gunter. I am. It is just that you are such good fodder for bait! To be serious. Directly I leave your house I'm away to my manor. I must give instruction to my steward, Romane. There are . . . well, many things I have no wish for the watch to see, should they decide to search for fugitives.'

Gunter looked at Karolan sharply. 'Incriminating things? Ach, a charge of witchcraft against you would indeed put your vassals at risk.'

'You amaze me, Gunter. You suspect me of being an adept of the black arts, yet still you wish to help me?'

'Of a surety I bloody do!' Gunter growled. 'I don't care if you sup with Old Nick himself – 'twould not surprise me too much if you did! A man does not come easily by skills such as yours. You know a great deal about the world and its secret ways. More than I, and I've travelled more extensively than most. You speak with authority of science and forbidden things. Then there's the fact that you've seen more of the sickness than is wise or even foolish, but you've taken not a moment's illness.' He paused, his blue eyes intense with emotion. 'All that, I care nought for. You saved my father's life. For that, I call you friend. There's passage abroad the *Helga* for you. You'll need it, if you truly are set on the course of a madman.'

Karolan slapped Gunter on the back. 'That's the most I've heard you say at one time! But thank you. I shall need your help to escape once I have Garnetta.'

Gunter groaned. 'I ought never to have told you about

the woman they're holding over at Holy Penitence. I had only a garbled story from a half-crazed lad who I found begging by the side of the road. This lad, Clem, told me such a story of brigands and virgins, truth and betrayal, spilt blood and spirits and errant monks, that it ought to be written into a mummers' play!'

'He told the truth, my friend. Don't ask me how I know that Garnetta's being held at Holy Penitence. I just know. I have to go and fetch her.'

Gunter scratched his head. 'Well, if you must, you must. Should you need some extra muscle when you go to face the abbot, I'm your man.'

Karolan nodded shortly, 'Good man,' he said, closing his book. 'I'll let you know. Now, I must take my leave. As you have seen fit to remind me, my time is suddenly grown short.'

Romane watched calmly as Karolan put a leather bag of coins onto the table in front of him. 'Must you leave England and become a fugitive?' he said. 'You could petition the king for help. You have served him well in the field.'

'That would take time. Something Garnetta does not have.'

Romane looked at him gravely. 'This woman has brought you much trouble, but you value her highly indeed if you are willing to endanger yourself. I never did believe your tale about Garnetta being a runaway wife. Whatever she is, she is something fine and rare. As you are, my friend. I hope you will be happy together.'

Karolan grinned. 'Oh, I intend to make certain of that. But time is of the essence. I regret that this final visit must be brief. This money is for you. Here are signed documents, freeing all those under my protection. It is the best I can do for you all.'

Romane smiled sadly, the lines cutting deeply into his face. His silver hair looked thinner, his stoop more pronounced. In just a few weeks Romane seemed to have aged, but his loyalty was as steadfast as it had always been.

'There seems little to discuss,' Romane said. 'What can I add but my regrets? As for myself, I have made provision. I shall do as you ask for your vassals, but they will fare well enough. Whoever comes to take your house and lands will need workers. The machinations of lords and churchmen affect those who till the land less than you might think.'

Karolan smiled at the old man with affection, knowing that he was right. Romane's wisdom, his knack of doing the right thing without stopping to question or condemn, had served him well over the years. He could still remember the skinny, lame boy who had been so eager to please, the light of intelligence bright in his narrow face. He was tempted to confide fully in the steward, but thought better of it. Romane had his suspicions, let them suffice. He knew nothing that would incriminate himself were he to be questioned by the church council.

'Where will you go?' Romane said.

'To Flanders. A friend has offered Garnetta and myself ship's passage.'

Romane's faded blue eyes were blurred with emotion. 'Then I wish you God speed. I do not expect we'll meet again in this world. It has been a singular experience to serve you, Karolan.' The two men embraced.

At the door which led to his tower, Karolan turned and waved. 'Fare you well, dear old friend,' he said under his breath.

Even as he took the stairs two at a time, his thoughts were moving forward a few hours to when he must return to the town. Every instinct screamed for him to hurry to Garnetta's side, but first he must destroy everything in the laboratorium. Romane was only partly correct. The new owners of his lands would need his peasants to labour for them, but if it became common knowledge that their lord had been a heretic and necromancer, then the lives of everyone who had ever known him would be endangered.

After stoking the furnace, he moved around the laboratorium, gathering together all the things which must be destroyed. The flames licked greedily at the parchment, vellum, and other written materials which he heaped upon them. It took a long time to rip apart the great tomes with their covers of leather decorated with silver wire and gems. All must be destroyed; the drawings, rich with symbolic imagery; the ledgers with their countless columns of figures and computations; the complex scientific diagrams. The rare and ancient works, which he had brought from the Holy Land, must also be burnt. He could not suppress a pang of sorrow as he unrolled a scroll covered with beautiful flowing Arabic script. He had killed Nasibia and Harun to obtain those works, unwittingly setting in motion the string of events which led ultimately to his transmutation.

Well it could not be helped. Any one of the tracts was enough to incriminate him, lay suspicion upon Romane and others of his household. Once alerted, the church was ruthless in its efforts to root out those it regarded as enemies of Christendom. Yet for all of his feelings of regret, he felt little grief. This work could be begun again. He had done it before. He was sweating by the time he began breaking apart the wooden racks which held alchemic instruments. He consigned them to the flames, then emptied the glass bottles which held the preserved babes – some so ancient that only a revolting soupy sludge emerged. The sad little relics, mementoes of his abortive attempts to get normal women with child, sizzled and melted in the furnace. He hardly dared allow himself to think about the possibility of having a child with Garnetta. That was something for the future – for when they were far from this place. Finally the laboratorium was empty of anything incriminating. He gathered together the few items he had set aside. There was one final ritual he must perform before he left this place for ever.

Stripping off his garments he poured water into a vessel and added a combination of pungent oils. After washing himself all over, he went to the four corners of the laboratorium and said an invocation. In the centre of the chamber, he drew a circle on the floor and within that a five-pointed star. After final preparations, he sat cross-legged in the centre of the star. On the floor in front of him he placed an uncut emerald, as big as the palm of his hand. Emptying his mind, he put himself into a trance. For almost an hour he sat as if frozen, a faint sheen of sweat pearling his limbs.

Gradually the walls of the chamber darkened and drew inwards. In the near distance a faint glow appeared, which grew brighter and took on the form of a window. A greenish light, pale and murky, flowed out of the window. Karolan watched as the window grew bigger. Now he found himself looking through the opening onto a seashore, where sluggish grey waves crashed upon a beach of black sand. At the horizon a diseased, purple sky met the water, spreading a violet glimmer on the monsters that churned and boiled in the seething waves. The wind shrieked and howled, gusting sickly, yellowish sea-spray against spikes of rocks.

Now he could see the sheer side of a cliff face, the dark

openings of many caves. Nothing moved upon the shore. Piles of weed, black and slimy-looking gave out a faint phosphorescent glow. There was a fetid smell of salt and rotting things. The very air was dank and oppressive. He sensed that there was a powerful presence in one of the caves. Emanations of great age and a stolid, deep intelligence impressed themselves upon him. 'I bid you come forth,' he said, his voice commanding but respectful.

There was a movement from deep within the cave. He heard a sound as of wet coils unwrapping, then a heavy body dragged itself over the sand towards the cave entrance. 'Who calls upon me?' The voice was low-pitched, rasping, painful to his ears. 'Are you one who comes to gaze upon my beauty?'

Karolan did not answer, but waited patiently. In a few moments a huge shadow emerged from the mouth of the cave. It was so dark and dense that it seemed as if the night itself had emerged and was seeping like ink up the cliff face. Karolan fought down his terror, gazing at the diva with awe. This was the first time he had dared to converse directly with such a being. All his previous rituals had concentrated on calling upon lesser elementals. It was only his desperate need to bind the Fetch into his service that gave him courage to ask a diva for help.

The window was almost blocked by the huge form that reared up before him. Now he could see details of the being's form. In the violet tinted light of the shore, the scales covering the lower body of the woman glistened wetly. There was a clashing sound as the iron-hard scales rubbed together. As the diva swayed back and forth, Karolan could see the gaping sexual aperture at the underside of her tail, where her belly melded into the greyish scales. The thick, leathery sex-lips opened and closed, making greedy sucking sounds. A noxious, grey-brown slime trickled from the aperture. Karolan's gorge rose. He fought against his revulsion, concentrating on holding himself in the trance. As long as he stayed within the pentagram he was safe.

Slimy green strands, in which were threaded shells and human bones encrusted with limpets, framed the woman's face. Hanging from a hook in one of her ears was the rotting corpse of a drowned man. Thousands of tiny crabs and shrimps moved over the woman's face and body, their claws busily grooming her. She lifted pincer-like hands to push the green strands back from her face and turned her sharp beak nose and gaping fish eyes upon him. The dark power rolled off her, spreading towards him like the waves breaking on the fetid shore behind her.

'Who calls upon me?' she said again.

'One who asks for your assistance,' Karolan answered.

'Give me your name,' said the diva, her lipless, facial orifice opening to show a fringe of waving, crab-like mouth parts.

Karolan was not so foolish as to name himself. 'I am a traveller come seeking one of your kin. I seek an undine – a water sprite.'

'Ah, a son of the higher realms, you are. By what right do you come seeking one from my domain?'

'By the right of blood and flesh. The sprite is bound to me,' Karolan said. 'I wish to command it to come forth into my realm. But it has hidden from me.'

The diva grinned, her waving mouth parts clicking together with a sound like the chittering of a monkey. As she tossed her huge head, the bones in her hair clacked together. Crabs and shrimps were sent flying in all directions. 'If I give you this sprite, what shall you give me in return?'

Karolan picked up the emerald and held it out,

reaching through the window. His hand looked very small against her monstrous shape. He was careful not to over-balance. 'I offer you this bauble which is the colour of the sun on water.'

'Come closer, son of the upper reaches. I cannot see you clearly.'

'But I can see you, great one. Your beauty holds me in thrall,' Karolan said, holding his position although his muscles ached with the strain. The arm which was extended through the window was growing numb with cold. The diva hissed her displeasure. He thought he had failed and made to withdraw his hand, when she slithered across the sand towards him, her tail humping in muscular spasms. The stench of her grew stronger. He almost gagged at the penetrating miasma of rotting fish and decay. Reaching out one of her pincers in a surprisingly delicate movement, she took the emerald. Karolan steeled himself not to recoil or show any sign of weakness.

The diva's lidless eyes studied him for a moment. They were filmed and milky. He heard the wet rasping of her breath, felt the chill emanating from her cold-blooded flesh. 'Seeker of my lesser kin, you are passing ugly,' she said with a rich chuckle that set her mouth parts waving and threshing. Giving a satisfied nod, she slipped the gem beneath one of the scales in her tail. 'The one you seek is in a place far from here. Watch and behold.' Turning her back she dropped down onto the sand and began slithering and humping her way back to the cave.

Karolan withdrew his arm and allowed himself a sigh of relief as the huge shadow faded into the distance. Inside the window, the seascape faded. The sky grew lighter. He found himself looking down onto a scene of rolling green hills. Strange trees, tall fern-like plants bordered a waterfall, which foamed and boiled over great slabs of limestone rock. Within the flow of water, he saw pale elongated forms. Some of them resembled young men and women with sharp features and long hair, while others were four-legged and had the appearance of delicate hares and fawns.

All of the sprites were laughing and dancing in the water. He saw how they changed form, the hares becoming women and the fawns becoming men. So rapidly did they change shape that the whole mass of them seemed to glisten and pulse. Glimmers of silver light speckled the sprites and their tinkling laughter rang out on the water-scented air. Karolan waited for them to notice him. It did not take long before one or two became curious and edged towards the window. Colours of pale blue, grey-green, and a delicate hue like the inside of a mussel shell, glowed softly within their forms. Others followed the first curious beings. Soon he found himself being observed by many of the slender creatures. Their faces were vague and misty with the mere suggestion of eyes above noses which were no more than indentations. In the region where the heart might be there was a certain pulsing, glowing denseness in their fabric.

Karolan recognized the sprites as the Fetch's kin, but he could not tell which of them was his familiar. Then he noticed that one of them had held back and was sheltering within the waterfall. He hid a smile. 'You were never so chary of drawing near to me when you dwelt in my world,' he said. 'Come forth now and return with me. Your master has need of you.'

There was consternation amongst the other sprites. They began to chirrup in high voices. He caught the odd phrase amongst the rustles and cheeping.

'It speaks, says I . . .'

'What is it?'

'Like it not . . .'

'Nor I. Beware . . .'

The sprite, which had been sheltering within the torrent of water, flowed with the stream down over the rocks and emerged onto a moss covered mound. Stepping free of the water, it resolved into a shape Karolan recognized. Now he saw that the Fetch looked markedly different from its kin. In this, its home dimension, it was made of ethereal, spirit material – yet its form was denser than that of its kin, the outline of skull and limbs more pronounced. The Fetch's eyes were dark, greenish pools, wide and tilted at the corners. The nose was a small bump and there was an impression of nostrils and a mouth. Its limbs were slender, but where those of its kin ended in an amorphous smudge, the Fetch had faint fingers and toes.

Karolan noticed that the Fetch wore an expression of sadness. Within its form the colours were tainted, the blue and green muddy and dull. He understood. The sprite had been changed by its association with himself. Having experienced the doubtful pleasures of the upper realms, it had been tainted as well as enriched. It had tried to return to its own world, but it no longer truly belonged. Just like it did not really belong in Karolan's world. For the first time Karolan realized that he and the Fetch had something in common. They were both set apart from their own kind.

'How now, upstart sprite,' he said not unkindly. 'You must return with me.'

The Fetch gave a bleat of alarm, capering back and forth across the rocks. The other sprites made way for it, keeping their distance, glancing suspiciously at the window. 'Be calm. I am not angry with you any more,' Karolan said. 'I know where Garnetta is. I need your help to release her.'

'Not angry, with I?' the Fetch whimpered. 'The female you have?'

Karolan nodded. 'I know you lied and played me false, but that does not matter now. I forgive you. Come with me. There's much to be done.'

The Fetch took a final look around. The other sprites kept well back from it. For a moment an expression of anguish passed over the Fetch's face, then the faint glow in the region where its heart might be began to pulse. 'Forgive I? Then come with you I will, Master,' it said. 'My place, it is, to be beside you. Serve you well shall I.'

'That you will,' Karolan said sternly. 'There will be no more fleeing back here. I've wasted valuable time coming in search of you. If you ever do this again, I swear I'll ask the diva who lives by the sea to collect you – personally!'

The Fetch gave a squawk of alarm. 'Will not come back – ever! No pleasure here for me. Not pain and suffering enough to bathe in. Too, too bad.'

Karolan suppressed a grin. 'Good. Then draw near. Enter the upper world.' The Fetch moved close to the window. 'Hurry now,' Karolan said, feeling exhaustion creeping over him. In a trice the Fetch had jumped through the window. Karolan was aware of it as a ragged shadow hovering around the edge of the chalk circle. The sweat ran down his face as he began backtracking through the ritual. He had been dangerously weakened by his encounter with the Diva, but his concentration did not lessen for even a moment. His muscles jerked with tension as the bright square of the window shrank and grew dark. The vista beyond faded, then there was nothing but darkness.

Karolan continued to sit upright only by a supreme effort. He clasped his hands to his solar plexus, holding the energy within his body. The walls of the laboratorium came into view. Karolan said the words of ending, then slumped forward, his face grey with exhaustion. The Fetch darted back and forth, crooning softly at the edge of the circle as Karolan retched and gasped. It was some time before he felt strong enough to crawl across the floor until he was outside the circle. Immediately cool fingers stroked his skin and ruffled his hair. He smelt the faint odour of licorice and almonds. 'Tired are you from travail. Rest you must.'

Karolan had not the strength to resist as hands began massaging his shoulders. He groaned with pleasure as his tired muscles relaxed. The spirit flowed back and forth over his skin, its touch warm and soothing. He found himself wondering at these caring actions. Had the Fetch learned to be unselfish at last? He closed his eyes as fingers massaged his calves and feet, absorbing the tension and exhaustion. Gradually the bone weariness faded. He had begun to think that the Fetch had indeed learned a lesson in chastisement, when its touch underwent a subtle change.

The caresses grew languorous, more intimate. He sensed the Fetch's growing hunger. After its self-enforced exile, it simmered with the need for its preferred sustenance. He suppressed a grin, as his familiar began acting true to type.

'Stop that. We must go to find Garnetta. There'll be fuel enough at Holy Penitence for you to enjoy your doubtful pleasures!' The spirit's hands were withdrawn, reluctantly. He sensed that the Fetch was sulking and laughed aloud. 'Well, upstart sprite. At last you do my bidding,' he said, rubbing the sweat from his body with his shirt. 'If you had done so earlier, much suffering might have been avoided.'

'Never too much suffering,' murmured the Fetch.

Karolan ignored it. 'Still, it was perhaps time for us to

move on. Romane has grown old. I need to seek out someone else I can trust. We shall start again, in a new country, this time with Garnetta.'

'Ah, the female. Much pain has she suffered. Gorgeous is her distress. Passing sweet her pleasure,' the Fetch crooned, lost in erotic imaginings.

'Don't tell me what you know of that now or I'll lose my newfound patience with you!' Karolan rapped. 'All I care about is finding her again. You shall help me.'

'Find her. Help you. Yes, Master.' The spirit subsided into silence, subdued colours of purple and indigo flickering within its shadow form.

Dressing quickly Karolan buckled on his sword. 'Stay close to me,' he said to the Fetch as he secured a hooded cloak around his shoulders and knotted a leather purse at his waist.

At the stable, Darkus pushed his nose into Karolan's hand in welcome. Karolan stroked the palfrey's velvet cheek, before mounting and riding out of the yard. He was conscious that the Fetch had taken him at his word. It was a faint, reassuring presence next to his right shoulder. Bound now by a single purpose, he urged Darkus into a gallop and headed for the road leading towards Chatesbrook. He did not think to look over his shoulder for a final glimpse of the manor where he had spent the past thirty-five years.

Gunter waited for Karolan on a stretch of common land outside the town's postern gate. For some time he had been watching the trickle of people coming to the St John fair. Jugglers and tumblers rubbed shoulders with pilgrims coming to kiss the reliquary which held the fragment of Our Lady's fingernail. Drovers came with sheep and farmers with crates of chickens and poles strung with conies.

Gunter wished he felt more cheered by the sight of so many visitors. But he knew that it was not simply that the pestilence's strength was abating or that tradition was stronger than fear. It was something far more base. He did not relish telling Karolan the news that the crier had given out yestermorn.

Still, it was a plain fact that with so many travellers arriving, it would make it far easier for Karolan to enter and leave without attracting undue attention. Shading his eyes as he caught sight of a horse in the distance, Gunter scrambled to his feet. He waved and stood by as Karolan pulled Darkus to a halt. 'Well met, my friend,' Karolan said, slipping out of the saddle. 'You look troubled. What's amiss? Have you had second thoughts about letting an erstwhile felon on board your ship?'

Gunter laughed shortly. 'Never, but I bring bad news. There's to be a hanging on the morrow on the eve of St John's fair.'

'I suspected something of the sort,' Karolan said, glancing at the postern gate which was blocked by two women arguing about the ownership of a goose. 'The promise of such entertainment is what draws a crowd. But that could aid our purpose. We'll not be noticed amongst so many. Who's to be kicking air? Looters?'

'Aye, but that's not the whole of it. It's Garnetta. She's been found guilty of heresy and moral corruption. They are going to burn her after the hanging.' Karolan was quiet for so long that Gunter did not think he could have heard him aright. 'I doubt the Devil himself could get to her now,' he said gently. 'There's such a huddle of church dignitaries in the monastery guesthouse. The whisper of heresy brings them scuttling like rats round a sewer.'

Karolan only nodded, his face blank and unreadable. Gunter was alarmed by Karolan's lack of response. He had always seemed in control of any given situation. Now his self possession seemed to have deserted him. It pained Gunter to see his friend staring fixedly at the brightly painted cart holding mummers' costumes, whilst the actors walked by its side.

'You cannot set foot inside Holy Penitence and demand her release now,' Gunter said. 'It's too late for that. I hesitate to suggest this, but I thought . . . that you or I might be allowed into her presence. We could make it a quick and painless end for her. Leave her as if sleeping . . .'

Karolan turned to him then. Gunter felt a flicker of alarm. For a moment he thought his friend truly mad, for his eyes were wild with excitement, his mouth was curved in a grim smile. 'Come, Gunter. There's work to do if I am to cheat death again,' Karolan said. 'Oh, we'll give them a spectacle to remember and no mistake! What was that you just said?'

'Ach. Nothing at all,' Gunter said, dazedly. Had he heard aright? Karolan spoke of cheating death, 'again'?

CHAPTER EIGHTEEN

For most of the night Garnetta had watched the construction of the platform in the market place. No doubt the sound of hammering, the growing pile of kindling, was supposed to help her decide to make her confession. It mattered not now. They would burn her shriven or unshriven.

She ought to be in abject terror of losing her immortal soul, but she felt only sick at heart, afraid and very alone. It would not end like this. She would recover from her wounds, as she had done before – many times, for finally she realized what Karolan had given her. The dark gift had made her body and soul inviolate. Whatever pain or injury she suffered, her flesh endured. Ah, but she feared the agony of the fire. Could even *she* survive a wholesale burning? The agony would send her mad. And if she survived the destruction of her flesh, how dreadful would be the healing? She trembled with horror at the thought of it. Fire, all consuming, seared the flesh from the bones and melted vital organs. Her teeth clamped down on a rush of nausea as she imagined her eyeballs melting, her body-fat boiling and sizzling, running in acid trails down her limbs.

No. Oh, dear God. No. I cannot bear it. I must escape. There has to be something I can do. Someone who will help me. The answer came gently, soothingly into her disordered thoughts. *Karolan.* She wanted to open her mind to him, but still she resisted. Because of him, she had fled from the tower. He was the demon who terrified and appalled her, but now she knew that the world had worse to offer. Karolan had shown her kindness and been gentle. She knew that he would have told her the truth in his own time. Her own fear and doubt were her enemies.

From the glimpses into his past experiences she knew that he too had suffered. She saw him now as sinned against, as well as having wronged others. But dare she trust him? It would be an act of faith to remove the shield with which she had closed him out of her thoughts. For a moment she experienced doubt. Would he be waiting? Did he still care? Taking a deep breath, she reached into herself, her extended senses vibrating like the deep note of a harp. There came the sensation of a curtain twitching and then – there he was. She had forgotten how it felt to touch his mind. It was almost impossible to describe the feeling. It might be compared to seeing in colour for the first time, or tasting fine wine after a lifetime of drinking only water. He filled her completely, the beat of his existence in every breath she took, the silk shadow of his intellect surrounding her like a cloak of cold fire. The vaporous mind trail of Karolan's persona was all powerful. She knew at once that no one else had ever mattered to her the way he did. She no longer cared what he was or what she had become. It was enough that like called to like. Her place was beside him.

Opening her heart, she called out to him. *Karolan. Help me.* There was no hesitation. His answering voice was strong and steady in her mind. *Be not afraid. I am coming for you. Have patience.* She felt his joy and relief. The evidence of his regard became something tangible, a soft benison that soothed and quietened her, chasing away terror and doubt. Did he truly care so much then? She had not misread him. He had been waiting all this time. A calm settled over her. She was no longer alone. If anyone in all the world could set her free, it was Karolan.

And then, despite the hammering beyond the window, the sounds of laughter and merrymaking as the crowds gathered to watch the spectacle, she curled up on the frowsty straw and slept.

Hours later, she woke abruptly, shielding her eyes as the gloomy cell was flooded with light. The oily smell of burning rushes filled the air. It took only seconds before her eyesight adjusted. Four monks had entered the room. Three of them she did not recognize, but the fourth was familiar. 'Well then, Stephanis,' she said coolly, standing up and stretching her limbs. 'Is it time?'

Stephanis gulped audibly and nodded, motioning for the other men to stand back. He looked miserable and dejected. The skin hung slackly at his jaw. She had heard that he had asked to be transferred to another monastery, but the abbot had refused his request. Stephanis's punishment was to accompany her to the place of execution. 'Will you kneel with me now and renounce Satan and all his works?' he said.

Garnetta laughed in his face, pleased to be able to deprive him of her fear. 'Will that stop you from burning me? I thought not. Save your entreaties for those who welcome them.'

'I shall not give you up,' he said ardently. 'You may call out to me at any time throughout your ordeal.' His voice wavered. She thought he might burst into tears, but he collected himself. 'The task of bringing you back into a state of grace is a burden I bear willingly.'

'I do not doubt it,' Garnetta said acidly. 'I have seen what pleasure you derive from affliction, be it your own or that of others!'

One of the watching monks tittered. Stephanis winced, his face so bleak that she felt a moment's pity for him. 'Even now, you persist in wickedness. The hold of

296

the Tempter is strong. But no one can withstand God's cleansing flames. Bring her outside brothers. All is ready.'

Garnetta did not struggle as they bundled her to her feet. Even had she thought of trying to break free, there was nowhere to run to within Holy Penitence. The dull roar of the crowd echoed through the corridors as the monks bore her along between them. Without Karolan's presence within her she would have been sore afraid, but there was a sense of unreality to the proceedings. Her heart beat fast, her pulses pounded in her ears, but the feeling was more of excitement than terror.

Everything had happened so fast since John de Mandeville had taken charge; the ordeal in the infirmary, the convening of a council, the hours of questions. She was branded a heretic, but she no longer knew what was meant by that. Just by being herself, it seemed that she sinned against the Church. How ironic that, just when she was beginning to accept herself as something rare and fine, she should find herself under sentence of death. Lost in her thoughts, she felt removed from the journey through the monastery. It was as if this was all some bad dream that was happening to someone else.

Then the outer door leading to the street was flung open. A wall of sound and light crashed in upon her. The noise was deafening, the smell of sweat and sour bodies churned her stomach. Despite her faith in Karolan's powers to help her, she cringed away from the hostile faces, the mouths stretched wide to yell obscenities.

'That's her! The wanton!'

'The cursed heretic! Don't look in the witch's eyes!'

'Devil spawn! May you rot in hell!'

A seething mass of onlookers pressed towards her. Raised fists shook overhead. Other hands were raised to pelt her with rotting food. She felt a blow and looked down in surprise to see that a gnawed bone had struck her on the breast. A hail of filth and offal fell around her, some of it hitting the monks who held her. The hate which came off the crowd in great hot clouds alarmed and confused her. Why were these people howling for her blood? None of them knew her. But she sensed that the great gathering acted like a single beast, the individual subsumed beneath excitement and blood lust. They did not see her as a person, but as an object for their entertainment. All the hate, the confusion, and fear engendered by the pestilence had been distilled into righteous outrage and all of that was directed towards her.

At her side Stephanis wore a look of terror. No doubt he wanted this dreadful thing over and done with. With her gone he would no longer be torn by self disgust. Others would forget his transgressions. He could resume a normal life. His face was red and sweating. She could smell the acrid odour of his body. 'Bind her to the hurdle! Swiftly now!' he ordered. 'The abbot and the church fathers are in place.'

One of the monks led a mule towards her. A low wooden cart, like a sled, was attached to the animal. Rough hands took hold of her, forcing her to sit on the hurdle. Although still chained hand and foot, they wrapped coarse rope around her, binding it tightly below her breasts. One of the monks slapped the mule's rump and the animal lurched forward. As the hurdle jerked and bumped over the cobbles, Garnetta fought to stay upright, her bones jarring painfully.

Crowds of people pressed up close to Holy Penitence as she was dragged towards the waiting procession. She had a jumbled impression of brightly coloured robes, trimmed with gold braid. At the head of the procession was a monk, robed in red, carrying the banner depicting the ruby heart surmounted by a cross. Ranks of cowled monks stood ready to march, every one in four of them swinging a censer, the others carrying candles. The sweet, peppery smell of incense was heavy on the air. Last of all came the churchmen of note, all of them dressed in their finest robes. Since the sumptuary laws allowed the clergy to wear finery, they wore fur-trimmed hats and perfumed gloves. Most carried jewelled breviaries or crosses.

John de Mandeville, wearing a jewelled cross on his breast and clothed in a robe of white, cowled with red, lifted up his arm and the procession moved forward. The mule gave a jerk and the hurdle, bearing Garnetta, scraped over the cobbles. The vibrations numbed her bones and made her teeth rattle. She pressed her lips tight against the rubbing of the coarse rope which chafed viciously at her skin. Soon her shift was smeared with blood. *It does not matter. None of it can harm me. Karolan is coming for me.* The noise of the crowd beat at her ears. She closed her eyes momentarily, weary of the bestial expressions, the foam-flecked lips spitting curses. Soldiers of the watch beat back the crowd with the flat of their swords when the spectators came too close for safety. Stephanis walked ahead of her. She could see his broad stocky form, his tonsure gleaming in the light of many flambeaux and candles. On each side of the hurdle walked more monks, chanting prayers.

'Here, witch! Something fer you!'

An object sailed through the air and landed on the cobbles beside her. Garnetta bowed her head under the onslaught of rotten vegetables and dung that rained down upon her. She almost gagged as something smelling vile exploded against her mouth. Excrement clotted her hair, stuck to her skin. Unable to wipe her face, she shook her head to clear away the filth. *Karolan. Where are you? How much more of this must I endure?* She could sense no answer and for a moment felt faint as terror washed over her. Faces loomed out of the crowd. Each of them contorted by hate, their mouths twisted, their eyes glazed with collective madness. Surely this was a vision from hell. It seemed impossible that she could escape. *He could not have forsaken me. He could not.*

The mule stopped, the hurdle coming to a halt so abruptly that Garnetta was thrown onto her side. Her cheek struck the cobbles. She bit back a cry of pain as hands reached out to right her, then felt her shift torn from her shoulders, lewd fingers seeking to paw her breasts. She screamed in terror of being crushed as the hurdle was jostled. Those nearest surged towards her, grabbing for her hair, pulling out chunks as keepsakes. Suddenly Stephanis was at her side, his face alight with outrage as he grabbed a flambeau from the nearest soldier. Brandishing it in the faces of those who had a hold on her, he yelled, 'Get back! God shall judge this woman, not you!'

There were cries of pain and more curses as the crowd was forced back. Soldiers of the watch crossed their pikes to form a barrier, preventing other spectators from breaking free. Under cover of the commotion, Garnetta felt the rope untied. Jerked to her feet, she was hustled forward, stumbling as eager hands helped her climb a set of wooden steps. Dazed by the fall, her injured cheek and scalp stinging painfully, she did not at first realize that she had stepped out onto a wide platform, at one end of which was a gallows. The monks who held her, pulled her upright. She saw the huge pyre topped by a stout wooden stake.

Despite her resolve not to show any fear, she faltered

at the sight of the pyre. The crowd jeered loudly as she stepped forward. The noise was deafening. She felt blinded, made dumb by the sea of people. Jagged shadows were thrown by the fire brands held aloft by soldiers ringing the platform. Orange light flickered on sweaty faces, made hostile expressions into demonic masks. The miasma of raw emotion was crushing, suffocating. *Are you there Karolan? I cannot feel you in the midst of all this.* Her composure wavered. How could he possibly help her now? How could anyone? *Karolan can. He is master of the impossible. He will come.*

Another roar went up from the crowd as three men were led towards the gallows. Two of them were weeping. The third was pleading for mercy. A priest stood by, reading from the Holy Scriptures as the hangman slipped nooses over the condemned looters' necks. The crowd hissed and spat, jeering when one of the men lost control and wet himself.

'Mercy! Have mercy!' he screamed, his face contorted by sobs. The second man wept quietly. The third seemed to have fainted.

Garnetta looked away, feeling sick as the men were hoisted into the air. From the crowd's reaction she knew that the bodies were jerking and threshing in the air. The looters were probably murderers too, but she felt compassion for them. It was hard to die well in public.

'Burn the heretic!'

'Aye, toast the wench's toes!'

To the sound of more laughter and jeers, Garnetta was taken to the back of the platform and half-carried, half-dragged onto the pyre. The breath was forced out of her lungs as she slammed against the wooden stake. A wave of dizziness overcame her. She sagged at the knees, hardly aware of the hands that secured her to the pole. Stephanis ascended the steps and walked towards the pyre. He stood by as the other monks walked away and took up their positions at a distance. Garnetta refused to look at Stephanis, even though he called out to her to repent. In his hands he held a long pole, topped by a wooden cross. Her lips curled with derision as Stephanis fell to his knees and began to pray.

Glancing towards the gallows she saw that the three bodies were swaying gently, turning round in graceful circles. They, at least, were at peace.

John de Mandeville, climbed the steps, stood facing the crowd. The great cross on his breast blazed with rubies. As he pushed back the red cowl, rush-light glimmered on his silver hair. The abbot held up his hands for silence, his patrician face serene. A hush settled over the crowd, the silence heavy with expectation. Part of the enjoyment of the spectacle was the prepared speech, which would warn all of the dangers of heresy.

In the ensuing quiet, Garnetta looked out over the great mass of people. She had never seen so many gathered together at any one time. The market place and streets leading into it were crammed to capacity. The lull was unearthly. She felt held in some strange hinterland where nothing was real. The taint of blood-lust in abeyance cast a veil over her senses. With a sort of weird clarity, she saw the vendors selling food and drink weaving in and out of the crowd. Pedlars held trays of ribbons and beads, which people could buy to mark the occasion. Parents held their children aloft, so that they could get a better look. A fight had broken out between two opposing groups of apprentices.

Then the silence was split asunder by the ringing tones of the abbot's voice. 'This night we are to consign a heretic to the flames. Let God be the judge of this woman's sins! Wretch that she is, she is unrepentant!

302

Despite being given every opportunity to turn away from Satan, she persists in her sin!' He paused for the expected outcry. A howl of rage went up from the crowd. Garnetta could not help flinching from the renewed screams of hate and the curses of those nearest to the platform. Gobs of spittle flecked the boards. If she had been within their grasp she had no doubt that they would have torn her limb from limb. Again the abbot held up his hand for silence. The crowd responded. 'There is no salvation, but for those who embrace the Lord! This woman sought to bedevil and beguile men of the cloth, to lure them into ways of wickedness with her lies and falsehoods!'

'For shame!'

'Burn the wench!'

'Aye,' rang out the abbot's voice. 'Burn she shall. So that she will be cleansed by God's Holy fire. But there is still time for her to repent, that she may be shriven and admitted to Heaven in a state of grace.'

'Repent! Repent!'

Stephanis held up the pole, topped with a wooden cross, and brought it close to Garnetta's face. She had but to lean forward to kiss the cross and the crowd would be weeping at the prospect of a sinner saved, instead of baying for her blood. She looked Stephanis full in the face and was not surprised to see that he was weeping freely. Great tears rolled down his face. His voice shook as he shouted above the din. 'Admit your sins. I beg you. You will spend eternity in purgatory if you do not. In the name of God the Father! I implore you to kiss the cross!'

Garnetta turned her face away and heard the crowd's collective groan. All this held no reality for her. Karolan would come soon. He must. Oh, but it was difficult to keep faith with him and not waver.

Stephanis began to shriek, 'There is no more time!

The faggots are being lit. Why are you so stubborn? Garnetta! Repent! Repent!'

'She'll repent, when her toes are burning!' someone yelled.

Even as the abbot began speaking again, his measured tones absorbed by the growing excitement of the crowd, two monks moved forward and put a taper to the pyre. Threads of smoke rose into the night sky. The acrid smell of it caught at the back of Garnetta's throat. She felt the first stirrings of real panic. This was too close. Why was Karolan leaving it so late? She sent a silent, desperate message to him.

No. It cannot end like this! Karolan! Flames began licking at the edges of the wood. The abbot's voice rang out clear and strong, warning everyone to guard against straying from the path of righteousness. Stephanis fell to his knees, sobbing openly. Garnetta gave a hollow laugh. So it had all been for nothing? Karolan was no more than a trickster after all. All his promises were but illusions. He was not coming for her.

Strangely she felt less fearful than detached. After all she had suffered, all that she had lost, perhaps this was a fitting end. She did not even go in terror of her lost faith. If all that awaited her was a pit of blackness, then that was better than the half-life she would have without Karolan.

'Repent,' sobbed Stephanis, as tongues of flame pushed up through the faggots. 'Acknowledge Christ as your Lord, so that you may enter the Kingdom of Heaven in a state of grace!'

'God and all His saints have forsaken me!' Garnetta cried, finding her voice at last in her anger and despair. She lifted her chin and stared through the rising smoke at the abbot. 'And I curse you churchmen all! With your cant and your hypocrisy. Your fear of women and of your own flawed natures. I only regret that the master I serve has forsaken me also!' Her voice cracked on a sob.

She looked away from Stephanis's shocked and deathly face. Aye, let those be the words he carried with him for ever! And if he thought she spoke of the devil – well perhaps she did. The smoke grew thicker. She knew that the wood had been dampened to prolong the spectacle. Though her heart felt fit to burst with terror, she resolved to breathe deeply of the smoke, so that the end might be quick. *Karolan. I did not think you would fail me.*

Suddenly she became aware that the mood of the crowd had changed. There were cries of alarm and fear mixed with the screams for her death. For a moment she could see nothing for the smoke, then the wind blew it clear and she saw with amazement that the three hanged men were – dancing? In a grotesque parody of life, the arms and legs were jerking and flailing as if they were being worked by a diabolical puppet master. The dead heads lolled back and forth, the jaws moved up and down in soundless laughter.

Then, into her mind, she heard Karolan's voice say clearly. *Have no fear. Join with me. None of this can harm you. You and I are invincible.* She felt faint with relief. Tears welled in her eyes, spilled down her cheeks. *Join with me.* She pushed away the terror, opened her mind fully. And was flooded by the unbreakable chain of Karolan's steadying presence. As her extended senses melded with his something was conjured between them. A sensation akin to warmth flooded her limbs. But it was something less tangible, like liquid light. She felt it coursing through her body and recalled feeling something similar when she had run into the forest clearing to save the boy from the brigands. But that had been nothing like this – this was so . . . exhilarating. It was energizing too, a force that could be focused into a point of bright clarity. There was a roaring in her ears. *That's it, my love. Concentrate all the power of your mind and push it downwards. I'll help you.*

She felt powerful, unafraid. If Karolan said nothing could hurt her, then she believed him. The damp wood crackled as the smoke dispersed. Flames sprang up all around her. She cringed away, expecting at any moment to feel the agony as her skin began to burn. But there was no heat. The fire around her grew dull. She thought at first that she must be putting the flames out by the strength of her will. Then she heard shouts of horror from the crowd, saw Stephanis's face frozen into a rictus of mortal terror, his lips moving in a silent prayer as he looked from the scaffold where the hanged men laboured in a grotesque death-dance, then back to the burning pyre.

Turning her head to one side she saw that her arm was actually glowing. The fire was not growing dull. *She* was getting brighter. It seemed that she saw her surroundings through a haze. Somehow her flesh had taken on a new form. Flashes of colour obscured her vision. With a brittle sound, the chains fell free of her limbs. She held out her arms, fascinated by the terrifying prismatic radiance of her skin.

'An angel! Is it sent by God?'

'Nay! She is Lucifer's bride!'

Garnetta looked around with wonder. Those at the front of the crowd fell to their knees, sobbing for mercy, tearing their clothes. Others scrambled to escape, trampling anyone who stood in their way. The air rang with screams of pain and abject fear. Scraps of prayers were torn and scattered on the air. Soldiers and churchmen alike fled. She saw a bishop trip over his furred robe. People surged over him in their panic to escape the market place. John de Mandeville stood grey-faced and open-mouthed on the platform. Stephanis threw the hem of his habit over his head, rocking back and forth, gibbering with fear. And through it all, the three hanged men danced jauntily, while a reedy, mirth-ful voice rang on the air.

She distinctly heard one of the hanged men say, 'Too, too delicious!'

This was impossible. Ridiculous. Garnetta threw back her head and laughed for sheer joy. Turning around she spread her arms wide and bathed in the cool flames of the fire. Then she stepped out through the burning brands and alighted onto the platform. 'You!' she said sternly, pointing to John de Mandeville.

And the worthy abbot picked up his white robe to reveal a pair of scrawny ankles, leapt off the platform and took to his heels. She turned to Stephanis who was hunched into a ball and pushed at him with her toe. He gave a kind of yelp and straightened up. She saw that his hair had gone white and the corner of his mouth was drawn downwards. One of his eyes was half-closed and drooping. Holding one hand to his chest he limped pain-fully down the steps and disappeared into the remnants of the crowd.

Then, across the partly cleared market place, came a dark shadow. *Karolan.* She felt a surge of pride as Darkus galloped towards her at full speed and leapt up onto the platform. Rearing above her, hooves thrashing the air, he let out a triumphant whinny. The cloaked figure on his back, threw back its hood to reveal a death's head. Vacant eye sockets mocked the crowd. It was a mummer's mask, but those who dared to look back over their shoulders, swore that the devil had come for His own.

Darkus scattered the burning brands with his hooves, nostrils flaring as he stamped and snorted. Garnetta reached up with both arms as Karolan leaned over in the saddle and scooped her up. He settled her on the saddle before him. She leaned back against him, feeling the welcome hardness of his chest. As he held her to him, the unearthly light around her faded, bleached and absorbed by some alchemy of their touching bodies.

Karolan's eyes flashed through the slits in the mask as he urged Darkus to launch himself from the platform. The crowd fell away in renewed terror as the palfrey forged a path through them. Removing the death's head mask, Karolan grinned down at her, his eyes savage and mocking in the moonlight. 'Well, my errant beloved. Whom do you prefer as your saviour? God or the devil?'

Garnetta swayed against him, a feeling of fatalism so strong within her that she could taste it. The scent of him was intoxicating. She had forgotten his smell of spikenard and musk. Now she felt the immediate quickening of her body's responses. Her desire was dark, bitter-sweet at the centre, the forbidden nature of it all the more compelling. The feel of him was all around her, inside her head, pounding in her blood. In his presence she saw the reflection of herself and with that, finally, came acceptance. Her soul seemed to turn over.

'I'll take the devil, my dark lord,' she said ardently, seeing his beauty through a sheen of tears. 'As long as he wears your face!'

Karolan bent his head to kiss her passionately. 'Ah, Garnetta. I'll never let you be harmed again. Can you ever forgive me for what I've done to you?'

She smiled proudly up at him, the salt taste of his tears on her lips. She felt a sense of completion that was bone-deep. The question as to whether she was cursed or gifted had been resolved completely in her mind.

'Rather I should fall at your feet and thank you for choosing me. We belong with each other. You once told me that in the tower. Now I understand why. Whatever is to come, I want to share it with you.'

'Then hold tight to me. We're bound for Flanders. There we'll make a new life. My only and rarest love. The time we've lost together is nothing. The endless years stretch ahead of us, each one like a jewel.'

As she relaxed into his embrace, Garnetta knew that the coming years would be difficult and perilous. There was still so much unanswered between them. But she did not care, as long as they were together.

On the gallows the three hanged men gave a final twitch and were still. The air beside them shimmered, pleated. A ragged shadow-shape that pulsed with lambent colours of red, purple, and gold blinked into view. The Fetch's stretchy form bulged happily, replete, sated with rich, fear-tainted emanations.

As it sped after the diminishing figure of Darkus, it gave a high, trilling note of self-satisfied laughter. In its part-formed mind, it recalled other journeys, new beginnings. But where before they had always been two, now they were three.

'Male and female. Master and mistress. What possibilities for I? Oh, too, too delectable!'